TODAY'S MASTERS OF SUSPENSE PRAISE GUY DURHAM AND HIS ELECTRIFYING NEW THRILLER, *EXTREME PREJUDICE* . . .

"In an age of the highest-tech warfare and espionage, Guy Durham proves again that he has mastered that vital, arcane world of intrigue."
—Martin L. Gross, author of *The Red President*

Durham presents "the dark corners of espionage. So vivid, you'll be looking over your shoulder for weeks."
—W.E.B. Griffin, author of *The Corps* and *Brotherhood of War*

"*Extreme Prejudice* is especially good. You won't learn more about spies without a security clearance."
—Marc Olden, author of *Gaijin* and *Oni*

"*Extreme Prejudice* is a thinking person's thriller. What it has to say about the economic and political context in which the book's action takes place is even scarier than the plot."
—Dan Greenburg, author of *Exes*

Durham's writing "moves faster than a B-2 bomber."
—Richard Herman, Jr., author of *The Warbirds*

"A master thriller-writer who keeps you on the edge of your seat."
—Noel Behn, author of *Seven Silent Men*

Also by Guy Durham

STEALTH

EXTREME PREJUDICE

GUY DURHAM

BERKLEY BOOKS, NEW YORK

The author gratefully acknowledges permission from the following source to reprint material in its control: For lines from "Down in the Depths (on the 90th Floor)" by Cole Porter, copyright 1936 Chappell & Company (renewed). All rights reserved. Used by permission.

This Berkley book contains the complete text of the original hardcover edition. It has been completely reset in a typeface designed for easy reading and was printed from new film.

EXTREME PREJUDICE

A Berkley Book/published by arrangement with the author

PRINTING HISTORY
G. P. Putnam's Sons edition/May 1991
Published simultaneously in Canada
Berkley edition/January 1993

ISBN: 0-425-13574-8

A BERKLEY BOOK® TM 757,375
Berkley Books are published by The Berkley Publishing Group, 200 Madison Avenue, New York, New York 10016.
The name "BERKLEY" and the "B" logo are trademarks belonging to Berkley Publishing Corporation.

PRINTED IN THE UNITED STATES OF AMERICA

10 9 8 7 6 5 4 3 2 1

To my own Susannah

In Appreciation.

To Sterling Lord, George Coleman, Miranda Cowley, and Jim Morris for their inspiration and guidance.

To Emanuel Kapelsohn, Gertrud Ruhr, Laryssa Lauret, Kazuko Hirota, and Dr. Elizabeth Beautyman for their professional, technical, and translation assistance.

And, most of all, to my family—Melinda, Sarah, Nathan, and Thelma Durham—for their love, patience, and support.

You all know what you did, and no one ever needed it more than I.

And sooner may a gulling weather Spie
By drawing forth heavens Scheme tell certainly
Then thou, when thou depart'st from mee, canst show
Whither, why, when, or with whom thou wouldst go.
But how shall I be pardon'd my offence
That thus have sinn'd against my conscience?

—John Donne
1572–1631

Vienna.

He sat precariously, and very still, on the edge of the ledge overlooking the *Stephansplatz*. His arms were clasped around his legs, below his knees. Six floors below, a small girl stared up.

As if alerted to the rhythm of some precise internal metronome, he began rocking back and forth. The girl pointed and called to her mother. A small knot of people gathered.

The man on the ledge increased the momentum of his rocking. His eyes, staring over the gray rooftops of Vienna, saw nothing. Once the eyes had been a clear, almost startling blue. Now they were vacant, the irises hazy and glazed, like the glaucous covering of the scales of fish, or the surface of egg yolk.

Somewhere in the distance a siren began its wailing plaint. The knot of people became a crowd, and the crowd became the animal all crowds become in the entertainment of torment. A group of young men began whistling and yelling, catcalls and curses rising to the target above.

If the man on the window ledge noted any of this, he gave no sign. His rocking accelerated.

Inside the darkened room, beyond the man in the window, a radio crackled. The dial was set to 540 kHz, Magyar Radio. The announcer's voice competed with the static of too much distance. The language was Hungarian, the syllables lilting, almost musical. Softly, almost unheard over the radio's sound, a door clicked shut.

In the square, *Polizei* spilled out of their vehicles and began cordoning off the area, pushing the spectators back. The crowd moved grudgingly, keeping their eyes on the man above, afraid to be cheated of the spectacle. A woman fell and was helped to her feet by the man with her. Both kept their eyes on the rocking man all the time.

The great bells of the *Stephansdom* began tolling in hollow, droning tones. The sound startled a squadron of pigeons which exploded and rose, a confusion of gray and white, from the great cathedral roof Allied bombers had once converted to rubble.

The rocking man's rhythm seemed to increase. And then, as suddenly as it had started, stopped.

Somewhere within the maze of sensory receptors and nerve cells of the man's brain, a connection was completed.

And as the crowd watched, Phillip Odell Mathieson, forty-three, commercial officer of the United States Consulate in Vienna and senior operations officer of the Central Intelligence Agency, tumbled forward. Even as he gathered momentum, he remained in a sitting position, like a practiced athlete beginning a comedy dive into a pool.

Mathieson's skull struck the concrete paving of the square with 33,400 foot-pounds of energy. In a space of milliseconds, damage to the upper portions of the cranium first terminated the brain's higher functions. Then, as the damage extended to the lower brain, more primitive functions ceased as well.

The brain stem and the spinal cord were driven deep into the cranial cavity, compressing the brain itself. Spaces within the cavity filled with blood. Five vertebrae immediately behind the brain stem suffered compression fractures and lateral displacement.

At the same moment, trauma to the windpipe shut off Mathieson's breathing. The pupil of Mathieson's left eye dilated, although the other pupil remained as it was at the instant of impact. The body went into seizure, limbs thrashing spasmodically, heels thrumming on the pavement. For a moment the convulsions decreased, then became violent once again. Finally, mercifully, Mathieson's body grew still.

In the electric silence, the crowd around the body became uncomfortable. Now, translating themselves once more into individuals, they eyed each other nervously. One by one they began walking away, picking up the pace, distancing themselves in a parody of dignity.

A young policeman raced toward the mass of tissue, bone,

and fluids that had been Phillip Mathieson, and threw a black plastic tarpaulin over it.

Across the square a young Japanese frowned at his watch, then began striding toward the Kärntnerstrasse.

BOOK ONE

Spy in the Sky.

Whirling through the cosmos, the eye blinked, and saw all. A moonless night enshrouded and secreted this section of earth. Even so, the eye penetrated the darkness, piercing the soil of the earth itself to discover what lay beneath.

The eye was codenamed LACROSSE. It was, at the moment, moving at 17,000 miles an hour, peering at the Moscow Beltway 300 miles below.

It saw by side-looking, synthetic aperture radar. It saw through clouds, fog, snow, and rain. Day or night made no difference; everything lay exposed to the eye's infinite curiosity.

Years before, an earlier version of the eye surprised everyone by penetrating sixteen feet of dry sand in the Sahara, revealing beds of vanished rivers that had once carved out valleys as vast and wide as the Nile. Since then the eye had been treated with great reverence, funded generously, and given preference over other, less gifted satellites of the National Reconnaissance Office.

The center of the eye itself was no larger than a match head. It was created to do one thing well: collect particles of radiated energy to be translated into images. Fifty thousand pounds of surrounding equipment, including a small nuclear reactor, existed to serve the eye, to give it every advantage for its task.

Fired into space in 1989 as part of the secret payload of Atlantis, the eye produced daylight-bright, stereoscopic images of all it surveyed.

As it raced through the darkness over Russia, the eye was controlled from a building in Sunnyvale, California, called the Big Blue Cube. Inside the Cube, the Satellite Control Facility streamed commands upward to the spy satellite, hurling it with accuracy over vast tracts of denied territory.

Before the night was over, the eye would scan the launch facilities at Pletsetsk and Tyuratam, the nuclear test sites at Semipalatinsk, the laser beam facilities at Sary Shagan and Nurek, the radar arrays at Abalakova and Krasnoyarsk, the tank factory at Kharkov, and other installations of the Soviet Army, Navy, Air, and Rocket Forces.

Even as the eye soared over its prey, its images were being converted into digital information, encrypted, and shot in an electronic stream to a radiation-hardened tracking and data relay satellite.

From there, they were downlinked on a frequency of 21 GHz to a ground station in White Sands, New Mexico. Then they were distributed to the Defense Intelligence Agency's Analysis Center at Bolling Air Force Base; the Navy's facility in Suitland, Maryland; the Office of Imagery Analysis in Washington; and the new supersecret CIA processing facility in Reston, Virginia.

Finally, the images from LACROSSE would be sent to Federal Building 213 on the corner of First and M in Washington, D.C., where interpreters from both CIA and DIA would run them through their big Cray supercomputers.

The eye was working well this night.

Unlike other spies, it never slept, always behaved in an exemplary fashion, and seldom aroused the ire of people in Accounts. The engineers who served it respected its predictability. The analysts who interpreted its product admired its resolution. And the intelligence officers and politicians who owned it positively gloated over it.

But on this night, the eye had seen something the engineers would miss, and the analysts would discover, and the owners would find disquieting in the extreme.

The pathologist from Langley was exhausted. He'd been roused out of a sound sleep in his Chevy Chase home and ordered to Vienna immediately.

It seemed an Agency man had fallen, jumped, or been pushed from a sixth-story window in Vienna. The *Bundespolizei*'s capital crimes bureau had taken charge of the investigation, but it was discovered the man carried a diplomatic passport. Authority was then transferred to the *Sicherheits-buro,* which telexed Langley.

Now, twenty-eight hours later, the pathologist was going over the autopsy report for the last time. Dental charts flown in from D.C. made the ID positive. There had been considerable trauma to the body, which exhibited as much ectopia as the pathologist had ever seen outside a battlefield. But the Austrian dental tech rearranged the teeth in approximately the same order they'd have had before Mathieson's leap, and they matched neatly.

The hypodermic tracks were consistent with those of a high-intake addict. A few were wide of the mark, as if the addict had been too disoriented even to find the vein. Around the tracks the skin was jaundiced. The amount of heroin present in the blood samples was considerable, but not enough in itself to cause death. There was also one needle mark with unusual enlargement, similar to IV trauma, suggesting the man had recently been hospitalized.

Quite obviously the man had been sitting on the window sill in a narcotic haze, and had simply nodded out. Unfortunate that the window had been so high, and the pavement so hard. The pathologist stretched and yawned.

He wondered what was so important about this particular spook. But then he'd learned over the years to keep his curiosity within limits. His job was far more interesting than his previous one in the New York City ME's office. The pay was certainly better, the travel pleasant, the problems more intriguing.

He was looking forward to getting back to the hotel, and catching a quick nap before going to the *Staatsoper.* Beethoven's *Fidelio* was playing, a bit of the real Vienna, part of the old Austro-Hungarian Empire which lingered on, ghostlike, at every turn in this city.

Yet something nagged at him. Something tiny, probably insignificant. *What was it? Something about the body?* He put it down to exhaustion. Yes. Christ, he was tired. He knew he'd feel better later, once he'd rested, once he'd had something to eat.

Perhaps after the opera he'd stop by one of the *Beisel*s near the hotel for some good local cuisine. He hadn't been

in Vienna since right after the war. He ought to be feeling
relaxed and happy. Ought to.

"*Vielen Dank,*" he said to the hovering attendant, noting
the man's curious gaze. He took off the rubber apron and
left to scrub up.

Act Two of *Fidelio,* and still he couldn't concentrate.

> *So eile, ihm sein Grab zu graben*
> *hier will ich stille Ruhe haben*
> *Schliess' die Gefang'nen wieder ein,*
> *mögst du nie mehr verwegen sein!*
> *nie, nie mehr verwegen sein!*

The pathologist from Langley fidgeted in his seat, struggling to keep up with the German libretto, knowing full well
he should be enjoying himself. But wasn't.

Damn the job, he thought. *Can't I ever learn to turn it off?*

Several times in the past, he'd had this same tingling annoyance, this same vague discomfort. And every time, it
ultimately produced a turning point in his analysis. *So there
was something anomalous,* he realized. *Something there that
shouldn't be there. Or something missing, something too small
to notice easily, but which the subconscious nevertheless registered.*

He returned his attention to the stage.

The baritone was gesturing grandly, warming to his role,
spreading his arms with authority, his voice filling the great
Staatsoperhaus, enrapturing the audience.

> *O unglückselig harte Pflicht—*

There was something about this one, something that simply didn't—

And then the pathologist realized:

The arms. The arms. The thought ran through his consciousness like a sudden electric current. *The track marks on
the arms—they were all new!*

He almost stood up at that instant.

If all the needle marks were new—and he'd counted more
than thirty of them—and the amount of heroin present as

low as it was, then someone had made those marks to simu-
late an addict's tracks. The body was not that of an addict.
The death, then, could easily be a murder. Not a suicide.

The pathologist bit his lip, his eyes following the singers
on stage, his mind ranging far afield. He'd have to get back
on the horn to Langley, correct his report before it went up
to Hartman. *Damn!* He should have caught it at once.
Would they get the Austrian *Bundespolizei* involved? Or
would it be strictly an Agency IG[1] job?

The fleshy baritone was taking his bows, the well-dressed
audience thundering its approval, much as it had in the time
of the Hapsburgs.

As one by one the operagoers rose to their feet, the pathologist inched his way out of the great theater.

─────────────────────────────── 2

Pretorius.

They sat in the morning light at the top of the garden,
Michael Pretorius perched on the edge of the ancient trestle
table, David Lloyd George slouched less ceremoniously on
the ground.

At the lower end, not bothering to conceal itself among
the cabbages, a large, well-nourished rabbit glared up
malevolently.

Pretorius and Lloyd George ignored him. Garden warfare
had progressed to the point where proprietor and predator
had reached a certain accommodation.

After a series of unsuccessful strategies (including one
involving cayenne pepper, a nightly chorus of sneezing rabbits, and a final fiery harvest of inedible vegetables) Pretorius
yielded. In the end, he simply planted three times as much as
needed, and let the furry felons plunder unhindered.

Pretorius sipped at his coffee and looked across the valley

[1] Inspector General's Office of the Central Intelligence Agency.

at the patchwork-quilt fields. In the distance, cattle and sheep stood motionless against flawless green grass. Great slow shadows of clouds swept across the fields, dipping and rising along the bosomy landscape.

Devon, Pretorius was thinking, *has more sky than other places on the planet. Walking or driving along the top of a Devonshire ridge (if unobstructed by hedgerows), you've got a half-sphere of the heavens all to yourself.*

Pretorius' life was good here. The ancient stone cottage and barns of dark Devon slate laid edge-on, mortar at a minimum, gave him a sense of peace and stability he'd never known. A feeling that not very long ago would have been unthinkable. Even dangerous.

Tranquil as his life now was, it had its ripples. And one of these was, at the moment, engaging his attention.

"Susannah's been complaining again," he addressed David Lloyd George in his most diplomatic tone. "About your sleeping on the couch."

David Lloyd George regarded Pretorius with a sidelong glance.

"You've got to stop it, you know. It's driving her crazy."

Silence. DLG lowered his head to the ground. Bored or contemptuous or both.

Pretorius pressed on. "We've told you before, time and again." DLG closed his eyes, extinguishing the image of his critic, and expelled his breath audibly.

"You've got a decent bed. Cedar chips. Flannel cover. Everything you could want, right?"

Granite silence.

"Lots of dogs would do *anything* to have a bed like that. Would travel miles. Hundreds of miles. Just read Herriot."

An infinity of silence, a silence that spoke libraries.

"Look," Pretorius pressed on, "you're every bit the wonderful and deserving beast we all know you to be. But Susannah hates collecting fur every time she sits down wearing anything dark. So from now on it's your own bed. *Arrivederci,* couch. Right?"

Despite the logic of Pretorius' argument, David Lloyd George fixed his master with a look that registered the Betrayal of Accumulated Centuries of Canine Trust.

Like all bull terriers, his eyes seemed sadly misplaced, far too high on the head than any decent dog's eyes ought to be. But in The Dreaded DLG, the misplacement seemed to underscore an expression of deep and perpetual inquiry.

This expression served David Lloyd George well. People thought twice when dealing with him; looking directly into DLG's eyes was uncomfortably like looking into the eyes of an old man trapped within a dog's body.

Even Pretorius was sometimes intimidated by the dog's accusing stare. But he knew the effect was illusory, and that David Lloyd George wanted no more in life than to be Pretorius' companion and confidant. Susannah often chided Pretorius for talking more with DLG than with her, citing their long walks as an excuse for the two of them, man and dog, to converse beyond her earshot.

Pretorius loved the rambles with DLG, feeling a closeness to the Devonshire countryside as if he'd lived here in another life. Nearly ten years earlier he'd taken a medical discharge from the DIA (Defense Intelligence Agency) after having nearly been blown into oblivion on the East German border.

Somehow he'd been drawn to this, the most lyrical portion of England's West Country, and in his first week met Susannah Kenney. For the first time in his life, Pretorius found himself in love.

Love presupposes a largely uncritical trust. And trust, up to that point, had been alien to Pretorius. Whether it was an inherent device by which the body and mind sought to heal itself, or simply a weakening of long-learned defenses, Pretorius began first to trust, and then to love, with a strength that dismissed all risk.

Like a child opening presents, afraid of opening them too quickly and ending the delight, he started unsealing his emotions. To help the healing, Susannah had found David Lloyd George and placed the dog in the startled Pretorius' care.

Since then, except for once being coerced to return to his former life for a nearly suicidal mission, Pretorius lived contentedly in the eighteenth-century stone cottage near Dartmouth.

Susannah, beginning to make a success of her small restaurant over in Somerset, lived with him in the cottage several days a week, entrusting him to David Lloyd George's care the rest. To David Lloyd George, Pretorius soon became not only Lord and Master, but World and Universe.

Whether it was The Dreaded DLG, or Susannah, or even Devon itself that accomplished the transformation, nobody would ever know. Michael Pretorius was changed. For the first time he began living a life that for years had been denied him.

Most afternoons in the warm weather, Pretorius took Susannah and David Lloyd George out sailing on the River Dart. He owned a wooden sixteen-foot lug-rigged surf dory topped with a single canvas sail. He preferred the centuries-old design and materials to newer, more efficient models involving Dacron and Terylene and Fiberglas and other such synthetics.

Pretorius grew lean and tanned. His muscles responded to the play of line and sail. His skin felt the tingle of good salt seawater drying under a West Country sun. Ever by his side, the Dreaded DLG became a regular sea dog, stumpy legs adjusting automatically to the boat's moods.

Pretorius felt at peace. He hadn't experienced the sweat-soaked, sitting-bolt-upright nightmares in more than a year. He was as good as new, except for the scar tissue that ran in a puckered diagonal ribbon across his back. In damp weather the scar would ache, and echo things best forgotten.

He looked down at David Lloyd George. "You're a stubborn, calculating son of a bitch," he observed, scowling unconvincingly at the dog. Then he smiled and stood. "Come on. Let's go make ourselves some breakfast."

They entered through the kitchen doorway, under a trellis heavy with hybrid climbing tea roses. Inside the cottage was cool, the Aga cooker a circle of warmth this chill April morning.

Under the practiced eye of Susannah, Pretorius had developed a deft touch for traditional English cooking, especially the game dishes leading the resurgence of eighteenth-century English *haute cuisine*. As a result, David Lloyd George became overly fond of his master's cooking, deigning to touch the hated Pup-E-Kibble only as a last resort, and then only after a great display of distaste.

Swinging back a hinged lid on the Aga's top, Pretorius placed a cast-iron skillet on the hot stone. He preferred iron skillets for their heat-spreading ability, but more for memories of his grandmother cooking with similar skillets and saucepans on her wood-burning stove.

Into the center of the skillet he plopped a dollop of good Devon butter, which instantly sizzled and spread. Pretorius now had David Lloyd George's undivided attention. The dog pressed his oversized head against Pretorius' leg, staring up with an expression of adoration. Pretorius smiled at the dog's instantly interchangeable attitudes.

What a politician you'd have made, he thought. *A dissembler to the teeth.*

Pretorius poured a light batter onto the sizzling surface. As this thickened, he placed six thinly sliced apple circles on the left half of the batter, their edges touching. The mixture bubbled merrily and began to brown. He brushed the circles with butter, then sprinkled them with confectioner's sugar.

With a surgeon's skill, Pretorius inserted the spatula under one side and lifted it reverently, folding it back over the apple slices. He hefted out the result and laid it on a waiting plate of cheesecloth, letting the butter drain away. David Lloyd George was now thumping his stump of a tail on the wooden floor in a *ratatatat* staccato.

This dish, Apple Fraize, was a West Country succulence dating back to the late eighteenth century, a dish Susannah's grandmother had taught her as a girl. Curiously enough, it was very like a dessert Pretorius' own grandmother had made for him as a boy in North Carolina, called half-moon pie. And so, for a variety of reasons, Pretorius was looking forward to sitting down with his breakfast and the coffee he'd made earlier.

The front doorbell jangled.

The Dreaded David Lloyd George padded swiftly to the front, taking up his station lest an intruder intend trifling with the household.

Pretorius opened the oaken door, revealing the postmistress waiting in her smock coat, her hair seemingly sculpted from bits of Brillo. In her hand was a slim blue envelope.

"Letter just come all the way over from America, Mr. Pretorius," she announced with what she imagined to be her most beguiling smile. "Knew ye'd want it the minute it came in."

"Mrs. McCallum, that's very thoughtful of you," he replied, disengaging the envelope from between the postmistress' reluctant fingers. "You really needn't have brought it all the way down here."

He suspected the wily postmistress had been staring at the envelope all morning, finally bringing it to him in hopes he might open it in her presence. She'd have given anything to know its contents. For Mrs. McCallum was insatiably, incurably curious, possessing a magpie's zeal for collecting tidbits of information about the village inhabitants.

Pretorius, had he wished, could have given her chapter and verse on the clandestine opening of envelopes. For example, a split sliver of bamboo, inserted from one side just under an envelope flap, could be rotated to roll up the letter around it, then withdrawn, removing the letter for reading. Later, the letter could be easily rewound around the bamboo, reinserted, and the sliver withdrawn. All without physical or chemical disturbance to the flap.

Such knowledge, of course, would have made Mrs. McCallum's day; possibly even her decade.

In fact, knowing McCallum read every line of every postcard, Pretorius encouraged friends to write him outrageous messages to enliven her surreptitious readings. The friends responded enthusiastically, and Pretorius marveled at their inventions. It was, in fact, a wonder the old girl didn't have cardiac arrest, considering the prurient nature of their more inspired efforts.

Thanking Mrs. McCallum, who was still craning her neck to get a better view of the parlor beyond Pretorius, he gently closed the door. He looked closer at the envelope. The return address was Mathieson, 852 Park Avenue, New York.

Mathieson, Mathieson, he mused. *What's Phil Mathieson writing me about?*

Phillip Mathieson had been a classmate of his at New Haven. A brilliant student and, like Pretorius, a member of Scroll and Key, Mathieson had been scooped up by CIA recruiters in his junior year. He'd surfaced occasionally in Pretorius' life, usually with consular cover. The last Pretorius had heard from him, Mathieson was a commercial officer with the U.S. Department of Commerce, at the American Consulate in Shanghai, in the dark and brooding Victorian mansion in the Huai Hai Middle Road.

But that was years ago. Ten, maybe twelve years in all. Since then, Pretorius suspected, Phil Mathieson must have done some fast climbing in the Agency, what with all the purges and resignations in recent years.

Pretorius walked over to his desk and took up the oversized Randall Bowie knife he used as a letter opener.

As he began opening the letter, he realized it couldn't be from Phil Mathieson. It was written in a fine Spencerian hand that hadn't been taught in half a century.

Dear Michael, the letter began.

> *Phillip always admired you and felt you were rather special, one of his few genuine friends. As you were both in the same occupation you obviously know something of his life, and of the stress under which he lived. By now you may have heard of his death in Vienna two weeks ago, and although his work was by its very nature depressing and difficult, I'm sure you'll agree Phillip was not the sort to contemplate suicide, let alone commit it.*
>
> *I was asked by one of his superiors who visited me not to make anything more of it as it might "embarrass the Agency" as he put it. I frankly know of nowhere else to turn other than to you, and so I write this letter.*
>
> *I am unfortunately unable to travel, being confined to my home these last few years. Could you possibly visit me? Please telephone and let me know of your decision.*
>
> *Yours very truly,*
> *Mrs. Miranda Mathieson.*

He stood near the window with the letter in his hand, unable to believe it: *Phil Mathieson? A suicide? Christ, it's a rotten business. When a man like Phil decides to cancel his own ticket, it's got to be worse than ever.*

Pretorius looked out the window at the road leading up to the village, and remembered. He'd met Mrs. Mathieson once at school, when she and her husband had come to pick up Phil for a weekend up at Newport. A tall and willowy woman in a wide floppy straw hat and a summer print dress, elegant and romantic. *A music made visible* was the phrase that came to mind.

Pretorius remembered her well. He'd just lost his own

mother the previous month; she'd been driving up to visit him at New Haven. A tractor-trailer driver hit his brakes hard coming into a toll plaza, jack-knifing the gargantuan vehicle on the ice, twenty tons of steel snapping back like a maddened alligator's tail.

Her car had been in its path.

In the weeks following, Phil's parents had been not merely solicitous, but unusually thoughtful. For several weekends they'd had him to their home in Tuxedo Park, and somehow the loss of Pretorius' mother was borne if not more easily, then more understandably.

He wondered how Miranda Mathieson felt, knowing her own son would never come home. Like all parents of suicides, she likely wouldn't be able to accept it. Couldn't accept that someone born of her own body could reject life itself, could throw away the gift she'd given him within her womb. Pretorius realized he'd been holding in his breath, and expelled a sigh.

It wouldn't be hard to visit her, he thought. He'd been putting off a trip to the U.S. for some months: The lawyers had been after him to wrap up his grandfather's farm in North Carolina, empty since the old man's death. He could stop by New York before going down to Greensboro, and make the appropriate sounds to Mathieson's mother.

Maybe he could help her accept her son's suicide, and stop seeing assassins under the bed. Or maybe he could just help her feel better about Phil's death, no matter how it happened.

Susannah would be back from London later tonight, and he'd discuss it with her then or in the morning. Pretorius looked down at the waiting David Lloyd George, who made an impatient wurfling noise.

3

Nagata.

Timothy Nagata was a dangerous man.

Some said the most dangerous in Washington. Not because of what Nagata could do, but because of what he *knew*.

Timothy Winslow Nagata, Ph.D., thirty-six, was a career scientist with the Defense Intelligence Agency. He'd previously been assigned to SDIO's[1] Red Team for two years, where his job was to poke holes in the system before the opposition could poke more disastrous holes in it themselves.

Tim Nagata knew the weaknesses of the entire space-shield program better than any espionage agent ever could. And now, he was a DIA analyst assigned to NPIC[2] (En-Pick to its intimates), where he interpreted the product of America's reconnaissance satellites. Which kept him up to date on approximately 90% of all U.S. knowledge of Soviet defenses. He had SI/KH—Special Intelligence/Talent-Keyhole—clearances, giving him access to spy plane and reconnaissance satellite product.

Although NPIC was a CIA facility, both DIA[3] and CIA analysts toiled in this warehouselike structure, sharing the fruit of the reconnaissance satellites' labors.

When Nagata first started at NPIC, he'd considered imagery interpretation drudge work. Nothing to challenge the imagination, and nowhere near as important as his work on the Red Team. Until today, he resented coming to work in this seedy section of D.C., at the drab beige building that looked more like a Levitz furniture warehouse than a slick CIA facility.

But today Tim Nagata was changing his mind. Fast.

[1]Space Defense Initiative Organization.
[2]National Photographic Interpretation Center.
[3]Defense Intelligence Agency.

Glaring at the screen, he tapped his pencil against his teeth. He leaned forward on the console and gentled the shuttle/jog knob counterclockwise. The high-definition image slowly scrolled, revealing an enormous moundlike bulge on the ground. A blister of earth, covered with grass, rising hundreds of feet high. It was one of seventy-five structures ringing the Moscow Beltway.

There was nothing new about the mounds themselves. They'd been reported as early as 1971. Each was about the size of two or three NFL-scale football stadiums. Previous satellite reconnaissance as well as the improved imagery of LACROSSE's radar revealed each to be topped with 800 feet of earth, over a 100-foot-thick reinforced concrete roof. The sideways-looking radar, receiving images from several different angles, enabled mathematically precise measurements to be made later by computer.

The structures had been identified as underground command posts. But discounted by CIA as strategically unimportant. Still, the sheer massiveness and expense of these structures worried many of the interpreters.

And worried Timothy Nagata especially.

He leaned forward over the console and, his eyes constantly on the screen, began to manipulate the image. Composed of thousands of individual pixels, the image could be altered easily through digital means. Calling up pictures previously stored in the huge computers at NPIC, Nagata began superimposing images on the new material from LA-CROSSE.

On several multispectral photographs, he compensated for cloud cover to bring up more ground detail. He applied different colors to different images. He dialed up the contrast to define certain shapes on the roadway leading into the bunker.

Adjusting for differences in camera angle and lens distortion, he developed six perfect matches. They ranged over a period of twelve months.

Then he began a tedious process of electro-optical subtraction, going back through the images, deleting everything on the screen except the progressive activities of the last few months.

What he saw finally in the high resolution image made him

expel a long, low, wondering whistle. Tim Nagata leaned back in his padded console chair and stared.

There, at the mouth of the gargantuan bunker, great activity was taking place: trucks unloading food, blankets, containers of drinking water, small arms and ammunition, and medical supplies.

All being done within the last two months, only at night, and then only when cloud cover would have normally prevented satellite observation.

But the Soviets had discounted LACROSSE's radar-imaging powers, and with their bias, didn't appreciate that spies like Timothy Nagata, controlling and interpreting their satellites, could see more and understand more than a hundred HUMINT[4] resources on the ground.

Timothy Nagata hooked his thumbs into his red suspenders, and studied the screen. Then, to confirm his hunch, he ran the same process on twelve other command bunkers, and finally, six hours later, he had his answer: Each bunker revealed the same unusual activity over the same period of time. Periodic restocking? Maybe. But maybe something else.

Although the first viewing had been in real time and deserving of special attention, the DIA analysts at Bolling had missed the string of vehicles.

At the CIA's Office of Imagery Analysis, they'd noted the vehicles, but considered anything to do with the bunkers to be of zero intelligence value. As a former DCI once put it, "Under a MAD (Mutual Assured Destruction) exchange no one would survive anyway."

But Timothy Nagata believed anything lurking under 800 feet of earth and 100 feet of concrete had a damn good chance of surviving just about anything. And that possibly, just possibly, all the weapons reductions talks were meaningless if the West had zero survival facilities and the Soviets had the enormous number he knew existed.

What it came down to was this:

In a nuclear exchange Moscow's leadership would survive.

---

[4]Human Intelligence, as opposed to ELINT, Electronic Intelligence; SIGINT, Signals Intelligence; or COMINT, Communications Intelligence.

Their counterparts in Paris, Bonn, London, and Washington would not.

Besides the bunkers for the Kremlin, the Rodina[5] had provided—at unimaginable expense—similar command bunkers for every military district in the Soviet Union.

Every Soviet factory also had its own huge survival bunker. So had every apartment building built after 1955. And every public structure of consequence near a probably targeted area, whether city, port facility, factory, or military district headquarters.

The incredible thing was, even with the Soviet Union facing an economic cataclysm, Kremlin leadership still felt such shelters were worth draining the Treasury.

And every major underground bunker in the Soviet Union was being stocked up. *But for what? And when?*

With a shock, Nagata realized the Soviets had the best bargaining chip of all. They could bluster, and posture, and trade away most, indeed, almost all of their strategic arsenal and conventional troops—and still possess the one essential strategic advantage:

Survivability.

This element had eluded the considerations of the Western arms negotiators. Indeed, had utterly escaped the thoughts of their masters in the Western capitals.

After all, bomb shelters were a relic of the paranoid fifties. As out of date and dead as Crazy Joe McCarthy, or an Edsel with a "Win With Stevenson" sticker.

Timothy Nagata reflected.

If he reported his conclusions, he would likely be singled out as yet another bunkerphobe, another armchair alarmist. He would be watched carefully for a while, a notation made in his file, and the matter ultimately forgotten. The report would be buried deep in the bowels of the NRO.[6]

But if he passed it over, if he didn't report his conclusions, then—

[5]Motherland.

[6]National Reconnaissance Office, operating under the cover name "Office of Space Systems." Located in Pentagon area 4C-956, and responsible for all aspects of U.S. satellite reconnaissance. Has the largest budget of any intelligence organization on earth: $6 billion.

He sat and stared at the image on the screen.

Finally, Tim Nagata made his decision. He picked up the secure in-house phone, a STU-IIIR/SecTel 1500 Motorola, and punched at the number pad.

The phone chirruped. He continued staring at the screen, where the largest of the Moscow bunkers was freeze-framed. He hummed to himself as his brown eyes raced over the image. Finally a laconic voice answered. Nagata asked for Colonel Zeller, identifying himself. A click, and then:

"Zeller speaking."

"Colonel, this is Dr. Nagata downstairs. I've got an anomalous situation I've worked up for analysis. Think it's important enough for you to take a look at."

"How long will it take?" the voice snapped. "I've got a car outside waiting to go to a presentation."

"Five minutes. Six, seven at the most."

"I'll be down. Set it up."

Nagata looked at the handset. *Well,* he thought, *now I've really put the cat among the pigeons.*

Zeller was about two levels above Nagata's NPIC immediate superior. He was CIA, on more or less permanent TDY (Temporary Assignment to Duty) from the Air Force. But he had a reputation for not sticking to the party line. Nagata figured his one chance for getting an audience was Zeller. The other Agency people would only play it the company way.

The downside was simple: If Zeller thought he was out of line, the people Nagata had bypassed would promptly barbecue him. ("Tempura *à la* Nagata, please. For one.")

Still staring at the screen, he felt, rather than heard, the monitoring room's door open. Spinning around in his padded chair, he saw a tall man—tanned, spare, ascetic—and two buttoned-down junior staff types.

"Let's see what you've got, Dr. Nagata," the colonel said in a professional, matter-of-fact rasp. Nagata imagined Zeller would order the bombing of a city in about the same tone.

Nagata rolled his tape, halting the image from time to time to point out specific details, or to underscore his conclusions. He was economic in his presentation style, something he'd perfected during his stint with SDIO.

Zeller interrupted now and then, quickly rapping out his questions, always to the point, but nothing Nagata hadn't anticipated.

And when Nagata finished his minipresentation, Zeller simply stood very still for a few moments, then said "Nagata. Don't discuss this outside this room. Don't discuss it *at all* unless and until I get back to you. Clear?"

"Clear."

"And you are, as usual, to make no assumptions about what you've pointed out to us. It may have many interpretations, not all of them terribly important."

"Yes, Colonel," Nagata returned.

The colonel nodded his satisfaction, spun on his heel in a military way, and left the room with the two assistants following like pull-toys.

Drawing a deep sigh, Tim Nagata logged himself out on the keyboard. The screen went blank. Yet he continued looking at it, thinking.

Finally he stood up, straightened his tie, and shrugged his tall, angular body into a much-beloved, moth-holed Harris tweed jacket. He walked out of the monitor room and down the corridor. He nodded now and then to other people whose faces he was only now, after his first two weeks, beginning to recognize. On the women's room door some joker had taped a carefully lettered sign: DENIED TERRITORY.

He checked out through security, handing in his ID badge on its beaded chain, and left the building. He leveraged his lanky frame into his undersized Honda Civic, and was waved through the gate by the Federal Protection Agency's civilian guard.

It was Friday, and he'd been looking forward to the weekend, to spending some time with Kazuko.

Now all he could think of was the satellite racing high overhead, and what it had seen, and what it meant.

4

Susannah.

"Trouble with morning," concluded Susannah after her first sip of coffee, "is it comes at such an awful time of day."

"Mmm," returned Pretorius, in acknowledgment but not agreement.

Pretorius was, in fact, happiest in the mornings. Each morning around six, when the sun traced its way across his pillow, Pretorius would be awake in a matter of seconds. For this unique and unnerving ability, Susannah was never quite able to forgive him.

"Coffee's drinkable," she announced.

"Should be. It's Mocha Java."

"Ah." Another sip, deeper, more reflective. "Thought it was the Blue Mountain stuff."

"Overrated, Blue Mountain."

Susannah wrinkled her nose, amused. Pretorius took his coffee as seriously as Robert Oppenheimer took the Manhattan Project. He roasted his own coffee beans, and brewed their grounds in a Swiss plunger pot, a chromium-and-glass contrivance like a scale model of something out of Fritz Lang's *Metropolis*.

Susannah continued to sip from her cup, languorous heavy-lidded eyes at last beginning to open and inspect the room and its contents.

"T'riffic morning," she finally decided. "Looks to be decent out."

"Mmm."

"Michael, old thing, how's about we take the beast out for a drive. Tear up the roads."

"What a good idea. We haven't had a good ride around the country for weeks. Be good for the car, to say nothing of us." He smiled at her. Her lazy blue-green eyes were accented by her high, almost Tartar-like cheekbones. Pretorius called them upside-down eyes.

Susannah was likely a throwback to the days of invading

Danes, before pillaging had been replaced by less productive sports such as soccer, before Britain settled down to the job of being a respectable sceptered isle.

"There's a brilliant spot for a picnic I found," said Susannah, warming to the task. "Down near Start Point. I'll make Scotch eggs."

"And we'll bring along some of that good sharp cheddar," added Pretorius. "You know, the really vicious stuff in the back of the fridge."

"Yum." Susannah wriggled to a more upright position in bed, finished her cup, and placed it on the small and tottering tripod table next to her. "You've been wanting to give the old Jag a good blowing-out. We could even go for an overnight, you know, up to Tarr Steps, to Dulverton. Get some fishing in. Stay at that spiffy little place by the clapper bridge. You know, the one with the nice owner in the blazer, and all the fishing poles and Wellies in the hall."

Pretorius really had been wanting to take the car out for a run. A mirror-bright black Mark VII Jaguar sedan restored by Pretorius, the car strained at the leash at normal speeds. Pretorius would often take it out on the M5 Motorway and let it all the way out to 130 miles an hour, without any noticeable shake or shudder. The Jaguar was one of his favorite toys, and Susannah loved the way it gave him pleasure.

Looking at him now, his tall and tawny body outlined by the sunlight streaming in through the window, she frowned slightly. "Michael," she ventured, "do you think we shall always be this happy?"

"No question."

"But I mean, will we ever take this—and each other—for granted? You know, when we're both frightfully old? I should hate it if we turned out to be a pair of quarreling old curmudgeons."

He went over and sat on her side of the bed. She squirmed slightly to give him more room. The sheet slipped down from one delicious breast. He considered it with a great show of dignity, then kissed her warmly on the lips. "No chance. Consider your fate sealed. All hope abandon, ye who mess with Pretorius."

"But I do worry at times. Seems so good now."

"You worry too much, you know. Doesn't do to worry. Takes away valuable time from far more important things. Things, for example, like—"

"Oh, Michael," she breathed, slipping her arms around his neck and drawing him down. "You're a great horrible brute. Girl has no chance. Just none. But I do love you so."

He drew aside the sheet between them with difficulty and began nuzzling her cheek. Outside the window, newly issued leaves rustled lightly. Crows cawed their whiskey-tenor chorus, while other birds warbled and whistled and chirruped. And Susannah and Pretorius made love in the warmth of the morning, feeling lucky to be alive in such a place, at such a time.

They drowsed as the sun flooded the bedroom on the cottage's upper floor. Afterward, as they were sitting up having another cup, Pretorius raised the idea of going to America.

Susannah frowned, lower lip pouting. "Darling, you know I can't *possibly* go now. Restaurant's just beginning to get the holiday people. And Sheila's not nearly ready to cope on her own. She's manic enough now. She'd go right round the twist."

"Well," proposed Pretorius, "maybe I just go over and get all my stuff done with the lawyers, take care of one or two other things, then come right home." He leaned over her and began tracing one finger around a nipple, which was becoming slowly but pronouncedly erect. "It's only two or three days. Got to get the damn farm settled sometime."

He had begun working on the second nipple when she happily, sleepily drew him down to her again.

5

Kazuko.

Tim Nagata sat watching Kazuko as she filled the cedar tub with scalding hot water. She wore a short cotton *yukata*, loosely sashed. Her rich and glossy hair fell well below her waist, and the swell of her ivory breasts was visible as she leaned forward to kiss him on the forehead. He closed his eyes in pleasure.

He was fascinated by her. She came from one of Japan's most respected families, one of several behind the big *gurupu.*[1]

In contrast, Tim's own family had emigrated from Japan just before World War II, settling in California. After their release from an internment camp for Japanese-Americans, the Nagatas moved to Baltimore, where Tim was born.

He was raised not as a *nisei*[2] aware of Japanese traditions, but as an American whose parents happened to be Japanese. Despite the humiliation of the internment camp, the Nagatas were determined to be as American as they could be. No Japanese was spoken in the Nagata home, nor was any element of Japanese culture dominant in their lives.

Tim had few Japanese or Japanese-American friends. He had gone out with only one Japanese girl in his life.

And now Kazuko Fukuda was opening a new world to him, a world both exotic and exhilarating.

It was obvious her family was wealthy. Although an exchange student in government studies at Georgetown University, she lived well, even lavishly. In contrast to Tim's beat-up little Honda, Kazuko drove a gleaming white Acura Legend.

But it was not wealth that intrigued Tim Nagata. It was Kazuko's being the key to discovering, for the first time in his life, his heritage.

She owned a condominium on Connecticut Avenue, a luxurious apartment furnished with Western furniture in the living room only. The rest was in the traditional Japanese manner, including a large cedar tub in the bathroom with a white-tiled cold plunge bath next to it.

Kazuko turned off the water and looked around at him, brown eyes questioning. "Well, you might as well get in. Don't be a baby."

[1]The giant industrial/financial oligopolies which, in concert with the government, control Japan's economy.
[2]Second-generation American of Japanese descent.

Embarrassed, Tim stood up and loosened his *yukata,* shrugging out of it. He saw her eyes take in his tall and muscular body, eyes that were evaluating, curious, intelligent. He'd never been naked before her.

Stepping over to the *ofuro* and slowly lowering himself in, Tim gritted his teeth at the heat. Kazuko hid her smile with her tiny hand.

"God! " he managed to say. "I've seen lobsters boiled in colder water than this!"

Kazuko rocked with laughter. *She was,* he thought, *the most wonderful woman he'd ever known. Correction: the most wonderful woman he'd ever* know.

She was standing up now, slipping out of the short robe, revealing her perfection without a hint of self-consciousness. Her breasts, large for a Japanese, were slightly uplifted, almost offering themselves of their own volition.

"Please don't stare so!" she teased. "Surely you've seen a naked woman before?"

Tim, now feeling the combined effects of the hot water and the *sake,* smiled dreamily. "But never *such* a naked woman."

She placed her arms tenderly around his neck and drew him to her. "You are such a child, such a boy, in so many ways," she said wonderingly. He kissed her eager lips, drinking her in as if she were a heady and all-intoxicating wine, wishing to drown in her, to lose himself utterly in her.

Their lovemaking was slow and exquisite, and for the first time Timothy knew the intertwining of romantic and sexual love. Sometime near dawn, as the light began to gather color, they fell asleep.

Over the next three weeks, Tim courted Kazuko with a schoolboy's wondering dedication. She was out often in the evenings, seeing school chums, attending courses, and dating. Tim would call her around ten, hoping she would be in, and if she was, she would invite him over for the night. On several nights the phone rang without answering, until finally Tim would fall asleep, worrying who she was with, what she was doing.

On her free evenings, they'd go to one of the small restaurants she knew in Georgetown and talk endlessly. Kazuko would laugh and accuse the usually shy Tim of being a chatterbox. And, indeed, he couldn't remember when he'd ever talked so long or so enthusiastically. Everything she said was so interesting; everything seemed to spark new areas of inquiry.

He loved her stories of how she grew up in a wealthy Tokyo suburb, raised by a wealthy uncle who showered presents on her, and who ultimately became one of the most powerful men in the ruling Liberal Democratic Party. Her family had a long tradition of government participation, dating back to the early years of the Meiji Restoration when a Fukuda had been the emperor's closest adviser. This had created the basis for the family's fortunes, and even a succession of wars had not stayed the steady escalation of their wealth.

She told him much about her family and began to speak of the two of them someday going to Japan. She couldn't believe he'd never gone, or that his family had passed along so little of their heritage.

On two occasions she asked him about his work, and both times he dismissed it with descriptions of technical research on weather satellites. This seemed to satisfy her. She wanted to know more and more about his youth, and what it had been like to grow up Japanese in America.

Timothy Nagata had never been happier. But in his brief life with Kazuko, the only thing permanent would be change.

When he woke he knew he was alone. Next to him the futon was empty except for her perfume.

The light was streaming in, luminous and warm, and it looked as if it would be a wonderful Sunday. Maybe they'd drive down to Little Washington and have lunch at the inn. Or maybe drive over to Annapolis, take a boat out on the Chesapeake. The wind would be good.

But where was she?

Gone to Brennan's for some rolls? Gone after the Sunday *Times?* He raised himself up on one elbow and scowled at the clock. Ten seventeen. He hadn't slept this late in years. Which wasn't surprising, considering last night's intake of alcohol.

They'd been invited to a party in Georgetown at the home

of a friend of her family. Most of the guests were Japanese, and he'd been treated like royalty. Everything he said seemed to be either outrageously witty or terribly important, and the people at the party were so very *nice*.

These are your people, Kazuko had said. *Everything about you is Japanese: your eyes, your hair, your skin, your sensitivity.* She was in love with him, he realized. He had already been in love with her one month, two weeks, and one day.

In the first few weeks, he found himself jealous of her dating anyone else. She'd been seeing a handsome young cultural attaché at the Japanese Embassy, and it drove him crazy.

When he finally asked her to see just him, only him, she teased him about it, accusing him of being proprietary, of being old-fashioned, stopping only when she realized it was causing him so much hurt. That evening he moved in with her.

On the few nights he'd returned to his own apartment, he missed not only Kazuko, but the Japanese surroundings, the futon, the decor. *Genetic imprinting strikes again,* he thought. *Thank God I wasn't descended from Attila the Hun; mud huts and yaks are in short supply in D.C.*

He was lying there thinking randomly when he heard the front door lock turn. He closed his eyes and waited.

A few minutes passed without a sound. Then the smell of hot black coffee, with something indefinable added, began floating into the bedroom. And he felt the long soft curtain of her hair fall across him, and the butterfly delicacy of her lips brush against his cheek once, twice, three times.

"Time to wake up, you inscrutable slant-eyed devil," she whispered. "Mama-san's got some goodies."

He reached up and embraced her, and they rolled over and over, off onto the tatami mats, giggling and kissing.

She was amazingly strong, and it was only with difficulty that he managed to pull her silk gown away, freeing her breasts, kissing them, kissing her tummy, tickling her into spasms of laughter. "Ooooh God, you *are* a devil!" she managed to wheeze, catching her breath. "But I do love you, Tim. I love you *takusan, daijobu?*"

"*Daijobu,*" Tim whispered. "Oh, yes. Very *daijobu.*"

An hour or more later, when they were having their coffee

in the living room and attempting to penetrate the bulk of the Sunday *New York Times,* Kazuko looked over to him and said, "You were talking in your sleep again last night."

Tim frowned. "Really?"

"Yes, really. You worried about something, darling?"

Tim looked deep into his coffee. *Christ, was the LA-CROSSE stuff getting to him that much?* "Not really, nothing I can't handle. Just work stuff. You know."

"But I *don't* know, darling. You're so damned uptight about your precious weather satellites. Everybody sees it all on network TV, anyway, so what's the big deal? You and Willard Scott having a thing?"

Tim laughed. Her Japanese accent, combined with a fluent command of slang, was the most charming sound he'd ever heard. He found himself thinking strongly about taking her back to bed.

"I said, it shouldn't be a big deal, a bunch of little weather satellites. Nothing to lose sleep over, unless you're a turnip farmer or some damn thing."

"It's not just that, Kazuko. I—well, I can't go into it." Tim had explained he was working on an experimental project involving some new weather satellites launched earlier that year. But not who his employer was. Nor the real nature of the job.

He also hadn't told her the FBI often ran checks on CIA and DIA employees, and if he'd been spending a lot of time with foreign nationals, and if he'd told them just what his job was, the job would dematerialize in about five seconds flat.

She sniffed. He looked sharply at Kazuko, but her brown eyes were staring stormily out the window, her lower lip projecting in a magnificently kissable pout.

"Honey, I do work for the government, not very glamorous stuff, but it's sensitive. It has to do with some new weather radar systems, and I had to sign a standard secrecy agreement. That's all."

"Humpf." She remained silent and aloof. The lower lip projected a fraction of a millimeter more.

"Would you like another cup of coffee?" A peace offering.

"Go get your own damn coffee," she blurted. "I've got all the coffee I want from you."

"Look," he said, "even if I told you what I was doing, you

haven't got the engineering background to understand it. It's technical, it's—"

She threw a huge pillow from the couch at him. "Now you think I'm stupid too! You really take the cookie, Mister Hot-Shot Doctor Timothy Fucking Nagata!"

He started laughing as he dodged the pillow, which only succeeded in making her more angry. *"You think you're really hot shit, don't you?"* she screamed, a five-foot-one tower of fury. "Well, you can just get to hell out of here and go over to your *own* damn apartment, and see if I give a fuck! You're always in my way around here, anyway!"

She raced into the bedroom and began throwing out his clothes. He was lying helpless on the couch, laughing until the tears ran.

It was only when all his clothes were in a muddled heap on the living room floor and she slammed and locked the bedroom door, did he realize: *Christ, she's serious!*

No amount of talking through the door did any good. Not a sound came back, not a syllable, certainly not an encouraging word.

Finally, reasoning she'd get over it if she were left alone, he went into the kitchen, got a Hefty bag from beneath the sink, and filled it with his clothes.

He closed the door after him and went down the corridor to the elevator. He didn't press the button right away, hoping her door would open, and she'd come tearing down the hall in her kimono, crying to be forgiven and be kissed.

But no. The corridor was quiet as a tomb. He reluctantly pressed the black button and the soundless elevator came up to carry him away.

In the next few days, calls to her apartment produced only a cryptic, caustic answering machine message. Flowers brought forth nothing. Letters vanished into the void.

Timothy Winslow Nagata was inconsolable. He had few friends, and even they told him he was behaving badly.

"Damn, man," said George Candoli. "She's only human. Women in D.C. outnumber men by a long shot. Get *real.* You're living in the biggest happy hunting ground of all time, and you can't do anything except feel sorry for yourself? Man, you don't need your girl back, you need a *shrink!*"

A week, two weeks, an eternity dragged by, and nothing.

He knew only lonely mornings and lonelier nights. And then, one night when Tim decided to wait for her in front of her apartment, she came home giggling on the arm of the cultural attaché from the Japanese Embassy.

She was dressed in a white, full-length cocktail gown, a Mary McFadden neo-Grecian design with wide gold ribbon separating her breasts in a shimmering X. She looked dazzling. The cultural attaché was nuzzling her.

Tim tried to sink down in the seat of his car, to make his six-foot-three form invisible. As Kazuko was about to enter the lobby on the arm of the young man, she saw the car, saw Tim, and whispered something to her date. The young man looked in the direction of the car, then took Kazuko in his arms and kissed her with passion, which she returned in equal measure.

They were the longest eight and a half seconds Tim Nagata ever had to endure.

Kazuko and the cultural attaché parted company at the entrance lobby, and she slipped inside. The attaché sauntered away, walking down the street whistling. Tim gradually sat up in his car, tortured, tormented, alone. He stared down the fashionable Georgetown street, seeing people coming home with each other, people about to go to bed with each other, people about to live wonderful warm lives with each other, and—

A tap on his passenger-side window startled him.

And there was the impish face of Kazuko, the most beautiful, most desirable face he'd ever known. Grinning. And beckoning to him with one finger.

The District of Columbia Police towed the car at ten the next morning. Timothy Winslow Nagata, asleep upstairs, wrapped in the arms and the legs of Kazuko Fukuda, couldn't have cared less.

6

Manhattan.

It was a relentless rain, penetrating raincoats, creeping beneath collars, evading even the most expertly wielded umbrellas, finally soaking knees and sloshing socks until anyone and anything caught in it felt like a subspecies of marine mammal.

The New York Telephone Company van slammed to a stop and slid open its doors, spewing out three men in slickers and hard hats. In the pelting rain they trotted, heads tucked down, to the service entrance of 852 Park Avenue. There they were admitted by the super, one Arthur James McConnell. They shrugged out of their slickers, grinning, shaking off the wet like dogs.

McConnell and the men exchanged comments about the downpour. They told him about the problem afflicting the three blocks between 75th and 78th, all along this side of Park. Hell of a day for the phones to go out, they said. Hell of a day, McConnell agreed. A power surge had sabotaged service in some apartments, not affecting others at all. They'd have to check which was which, but it looked like the damage was going to cost the phone company lots of bucks.

"Well, they can afford it," said McConnell. The men grinned again.

After checking the terminal boxes in the basement, the repairmen disconnected service to apartment 8D, the Mathieson apartment, and explained they'd need access to the apartment to check the instruments, meaning the phones. The power surge had damaged some instruments in the building just next door, they said. Some of the newer phones couldn't take the sudden extra voltage.

Arthur McConnell was relieved they'd located the problem so quickly. Mrs. Mathieson seldom left the apartment and was known to be hell on wheels whenever there was any failure of building service. He took two of the three up on the service elevator, and explained to the housekeeper that the men needed to examine each of the telephone instruments and the wiring to see if anything needed repair.

Persuaded only by the officialdom of The New York Telephone Company, the housekeeper agreed. But, she pointed out, Mrs. Mathieson was having her mid-afternoon nap in the master bedroom. They'd have to come back if they needed to check that one too. The men said No, they could probably isolate the problem without disturbing Mrs. Mathieson.

The housekeeper glared at the men's wet shoes until they removed them before entering the apartment. Leaving the repairmen in care of the ever-vigilant housekeeper, Arthur McConnell took the elevator back down to the basement, where the third man was doing some work, and where McConnell's current bottle was cached.

In the apartment the two men worked quickly, professionally. Two of the telephones needed minor repairs, but fortunately they'd brought all the necessary parts with them. One junction box was also replaced.

After ten minutes' work, the repairmen pronounced the problem solved. The housekeeper was pleased. If Mrs. Mathieson had awakened to find strange repairmen in the apartment, she would have been extremely irritable. As it was, the housekeeper decided not to mention the visit to Mrs. Mathieson. She was not sure she'd done the right thing in admitting them in the first place.

Across the street, in a hospital room especially commandeered by a court order, one of the men from the van put his headphones on and adjusted the level, watching the voice-activated tape recorder's VU meter.

All three transmitters were functioning. The lithium batteries were good for at least three months, maybe more. Every syllable spoken in the apartment of Miranda Mathieson would be recorded automatically.

With the lights out, the man could see into the Mathieson apartment quite clearly. He also had a clear view of everyone entering or leaving 852 Park Avenue.

Mitsubishi. Fuji. Subaru. Suntory. Sony. Toshiba. Yamaha. Kirin. As the taxi slewed its way through the rain, Pretorius read the billboards on the Grand Central Parkway.

Isuzu. Panasonic. Onkyo. Sapporo. Honda. Akai. Things had changed. Even in England, the Japanese weren't nearly so omnipresent. Suddenly, a sleek red sports car swerved in front of them, then shot ahead like a jellybean from a pea-shooter. He noted the logo in chrome, above the New York State license plate: Nissan.

The rain hadn't slowed up a bit. He'd forgotten how intense the rain could be here. MGM rain, Susannah called it. He wished she were here with him now; tonight they could go to the Cafe Carlyle, listen to Bobby Short. Tomorrow morning, breakfast at the Plaza's Edwardian Room. Eggs Benedict. Champagne and orange juice. He frowned, looking out at the driving rain. Too bad. The last time—the only time—she'd been here, they'd been so wrung out they couldn't wait to get back to Devon.

The taxi inched its way through the toll plaza on the Triboro Bridge, the last barrier into Manhattan. *Next time,* Pretorius thought. *It's always too long, too lonely until the next time.*

He was to be proved only too right.

The *kyastah* (newscaster) laughed and turned back to the camera. "Coming up now on *Morning Nippon,* some pretty funny American tricks—let's have a look."

The screen cut to a videotape of a group of middle-aged American men engaged in a bizarre contest. Each took turns reaching into a barrel filled with rattlesnakes, and yanking them out one at a time. The *kyastah*'s voice over the footage explained that the winner would be whoever got the most snakes out without getting bitten. The screen cut back to the *kyastah,* a young man now laughing along with the studio audience, and his female colleague, giggling prettily behind one hand.

The show showed two other videotapes of Americans engaged in unlikely, even weird activities: a man in Louisiana who'd converted one bedroom into a shrine to a roll of toilet paper he'd stolen from Graceland, the Elvis Presley Museum; a couple who'd walked in frogman flippers from Cottonwood, Arizona, to Los Angeles. Traffic, sports, and weather interrupted the fun, as did the news—which featured as much news about the United States as about Japan.

The U.S. news featured a recent shoot-out in Miami between rival drug dealers, involving automatic weapons.

Cutting back to the still-smiling *kyastah* and his assistant, the show closed with credits and titles, and the show's theme music, "That's Entertainment."

_____ 7

Miranda.

She had been beautiful, and beautiful she was still, although the years were beginning to display small victories.

Her neck had a Nefertiti curve, lifting the elegant head as if on a pedestal. The cheekbones were high, accenting crystalline blue eyes. The fullness of the lips seemed oddly sensual in a woman of her years. The smile was curious, almost mocking.

The light of dusk filtered in through the tall curtained windows behind her. From time to time, a breathlike breeze lifted the curtains. She'd positioned herself where the light would be most flattering, and where she would be able to examine her visitor most directly.

Miranda Mathieson welcomed Pretorius without rising from her settee, offering him a soft and astonishingly smooth hand.

Her skin was the white of fine cool marble. She had not, she confided, been out of the apartment for months. She did not elaborate why, nor did Pretorius ask. She held him in thrall.

It had been that way, too, when he was twenty and at New Haven, the weekend she and her husband had come to collect Phil. Even now, in her late sixties, she was capable of effortlessly spinning a spell.

A maid materialized, and Pretorius was offered sherry and a linen napkin from a small silver tray.

As he drank his sherry, Pretorius listened to Miranda

Mathieson's carefully modulated voice as she detailed the events immediately after her son's death.

The telegram of clichéd condolences from an assistant under secretary of state. The pitying, patronizing telephone calls from friends. The arrangements for flying her son's remains back from Austria for burial in their family plot in Tuxedo Park. And finally, the inevitable "closing-the-loop" visit from the Wonderful World of Spooks.

Pretorius interrupted. "You said somebody from the Agency visited you after Phil's death?"

A fleeting frown, as if the memory should not have been triggered. Then she said, "A tall, almost *too* well-groomed man named Tate. Very well-spoken." She cleared her throat, one hand touching her neck in a fluid, graceful motion.

"And what did he say, Mrs. Mathieson?"

"Oh, he mostly asked questions about Phillip, and about his friends. Tate did say Phillip had been engaged in some sort of highly confidential negotiations at the diplomatic level. He'd risen quite high in the CIA, you know. He also said somehow Phillip had become involved with a rather fast set in Vienna. They found hypodermic marks—I think the man Tate called them tracks—on both arms. I frankly find it ludicrous to believe Phillip would have done such a thing, either thing. Suicide, I mean. Or drugs of any kind."

She took a sip from her glass, held it up to the light as if to inspect the sherry's strawlike color, and continued. "Why, Phillip almost never even took a drink. His father and I often teased him about it. And everyone knew how very much he hated drugs, the whole idea of it.

"He'd lost a girlfriend years ago, a perfectly *beautiful* girl who'd become an addict, gone through all sorts of treatment centers, and then vanished.

"The girl's parents got a phone call one day, and found her dying in Bellevue in one of the public wards. She'd become a prostitute and had contracted AIDS, one of the first people we'd ever heard of with it. By the time they found her parents, she'd become little more than a cadaver. Phillip was shattered. He even took a furlough, or whatever they call it, and went away by himself. To the Yucatan, I think it was."

Pretorius leaned forward in his chair. "And the questions

the Agency man asked. Can you remember precisely what they were?"

"Well, they were the kind of questions people ask when they want to downplay their importance." She looked at him thoughtfully, blue eyes alight with intelligence. "I think—I think he wanted to know if anyone had—got at him, either here or in Austria."

"Got at him? What do you mean?"

"Well, I think they suspect Phillip of—Tate didn't come right out and say it, but the way he talked—it was as if they were conducting a very awkward investigation. Almost as if Phillip were suspected of being, well, a *traitor,* or something."

She turned to look out the window, blinking back the moisture welling up in those remarkable eyes. Pretorius remembered Phillip Mathieson's own eyes, so like hers. He thought of offering his handkerchief, then thought better of it. A woman too proud, he realized, to be recognized as crying. He asked her again: "And do you remember any of his *specific* questions?"

She stared down at her hands clasped in tension, knuckles knotted. "He asked if Phillip had gotten any letters here since his death. And if anyone had called asking for him—or if Phillip himself had telephoned me around the time of his death. I told him no, that I hadn't heard from Phillip or any of his friends for some time. Phillip, of course, had very few friends at all, which I suppose had to do with his work. He was very insular, you know. He wasn't always that way, just the last few years or so."

Pretorius nodded, knowing too well the enshrouded personality you take on when you're in too deep to take chances on trusting, or committing to things like friendship or love. "Mrs. Mathieson, did Tate ask about anybody in particular?"

"No. No one by name."

Pretorius paused, then: "And did he explicitly tell you Phillip had . . . taken his own life?"

"No, not in so many words. But that was the implication; that was clearly the implication. Especially when he talked about the hypodermic marks." She was agitated now, reliving the discomfort, the indignity of the interview with the Agency man.

Pretorius leaned forward, and placed his hand on hers. "Mrs. Mathieson, I don't for a minute think Phillip was ever a user, let alone an addict. And I can't imagine him ever taking his own life. He was brilliant, one of the best. People had marked him for very high things."

He watched her carefully, hoping to gentle her distress. She was high-strung at the best of times, Pretorius realized, like a thoroughbred. And like dealing with a thoroughbred, you had to first establish your own calmness and strength before you could begin to handle her.

She lifted her eyes to his. "He thought the world of you, Michael. Did he ever tell you that? No, I suppose not. He rarely paid compliments. It would have been like—well, like showing emotion when you shouldn't. But he liked you. And he told me you were in the same sort of work, but for another part of the government. I suppose you know that's why I wrote to you." The eyes were cautious, taking in everything in their clear and crystalline watchfulness.

Something tingled at the back of Pretorius' consciousness; his senses were alerted. "And just what did he say about me, Mrs. Mathieson?"

She stared down at her interlaced fingers. "Only that you had been in—that sort of work in the Navy, and later for another part of the government. He didn't say which. He wouldn't. But he said that if ever anything unusual happened to him, anything unexplained, I should get in touch with you. And not talk with anyone else."

There was an interminable minute of silence. The sounds of the big Park Avenue apartment were suddenly sensed: someone vacuuming in a distant room, a tallcase clock ticking.

Pretorius ventured, "May I—did the man called Tate happen to ask about me? Or did you mention my friendship with Phil?"

She looked at him witheringly. "Michael Pretorius, I may be old, but I'm not cracked."

Pretorius laughed and so did she, breaking the tension. Her laughter was like a schoolgirl's. Had he only heard and not seen her, he would have guessed her to be a woman in her twenties. Pretorius guessed that within Miranda Mathieson, beneath the increasingly fragile exterior, she was as fresh and vibrant as a schoolgirl.

"Did the man Tate say anything else? Anything small, almost insignificant that might have struck you as odd?"

"You *do* sound just like a policeman." Smiling, waiting for the effect of the smile.

He waited her out.

The lips, almost pouting. Then: "There was—there was this one funny habit of his."

"Yes?"

"Well, it was as if he were waiting for a phone call. He never looked at his watch, but he was definitely waiting for the phone to ring."

"This phone? How do you mean, waiting for it to ring?"

"He kept looking at it, now and then. Almost furtively. You know, the way some people try to sneak a look at their watch when they're trying to think of a polite way to excuse themselves?"

"And you thought that odd?"

"Yes," she said. "Struck me as a singularly nervous thing to do, when in all other respects he seemed, well, quite composed."

Pretorius eased himself out of his chair and walked over to the telephone, carefully turning it over, looking at the markings underneath. Pressing his thumb on one of the two receiver rest buttons, he unscrewed the mouthpiece and tipped out the microphone disc onto his palm.

"What are you doing, Michael? What's the matter?"

He shook his head and raised one finger to his lips. Then he replaced the instrument and began writing a note, which he handed to Miranda Mathieson together with his pen.

She read his note as Pretorius made conversation about his memories of Michael when they were at college together. Mrs. Mathieson wrote her reply on his note. The note and the pen passed between them several times.

As he finally said goodbye to Miranda Mathieson, he struck a match to the note and placed it in an ashtray. Before the blackened edges curled inward on themselves and the words disappeared, they read:

Has anyone been in the apartment? Repairman? Electrician? Don't speak. Write on this paper.

No one.

This phone has a transmitter in it, the kind that works whether the phone is in use or not. Keep your conversation natural until I contact you some other way and tell you how we can talk further. I'll find out what this is about.

"Well, I just wanted to say how very sorry I am about Phil," Pretorius said, looking at the now-omnipresent telephone. "Everybody who knew him loved him, and we'll all miss him."

Miranda Mathieson simply stared at him, eyes now red-rimmed, widened with alarm. The telephone suddenly seemed an evil thing, squat and black and menacing, as if a tarantula had sprung into the sumptuous elegance of the living room.

She didn't get up as he left. After a few moments, she rose haltingly and stumbled to the window, looking down, holding back the racking sobs threatening to destroy her façade.

In the building across the street, the technician lifted off his headset and rubbed his ears. He reached for the Motorola UHF portable on the table by the window.

Below, on Park Avenue, a man got out of the passenger side of a dark gray Ford and positioned himself. The driver of the car started the engine and waited.

Going down in the elevator in Miranda Mathieson's apartment building, Pretorius realized the front door would have to be under visual surveillance. Anybody who'd had the phones wired in this way would be keeping careful track of visitors. He looked at his watch. 8:20 P.M.

He punched the button marked B, and as the door opened in the basement found himself facing a man with the aspect of a choleric leprechaun. The man was wearing an ancient cardigan and carrying a large box of white gloves, most likely for the doormen and hall porters.

"Can I help you, sir?" the leprechaun asked with a rising Irish inflection.

Pretorius smiled. "Yes, I think you can. Is there a side exit to the building?"

The man looked at Pretorius doubtfully. "Sorry, sir. Visitors aren't allowed in the basement area."

Pretorius frowned. "Perhaps you could just escort me to the side exit. There's someone out front I'd rather not see just now." And he produced a ten-dollar bill.

The currency disappeared as if part of a conjurer's act. "No problem, sir. If you'll just follow me?"

Pretorius emerged from the building, looked up and down the street, and then vanished.

Along 78th Street, yet another Mercedes was being broken into by yet another radio thief, and the car alarm obligingly began its emulation of a mastiff being disemboweled. No one paid attention. It was the twelfth car alarm that had gone off in the block that day.

After waiting at least ten minutes, the man on the street pressed the PTT button on the cord snaking down his sleeve into his palm. Tucking down his chin, he spoke quietly into the microphone concealed behind his necktie.

The driver of the car listened, then flipped the frequency switch, and spoke into the radio's microphone. He put it back on its cradle and waited for the other man to return to the car.

The people on the other end had not been pleased. It would now be expensive and time-consuming to locate the visitor to the Mathieson woman's apartment.

But they would find him. They would find him.

_____ 8

New Beginnings.

Kazuko rolled over. "Know what this is?" she asked, placing his hand on the lazy swell of her abdomen.

It was nine in the evening. They'd been making slow, delicious love since six-thirty, when Tim had gotten home from NPIC. "The most beautiful tummy in the world?" he ventured, eyes wide in mock perplexity.

"No, you *gaijin* dummy. That's your son, or your daughter. It's Timothy Junior. Might even be a little Kazuko. Mean and bitchy like me." She watched for his reaction.

"Sure," he grinned. "Someday, maybe, if your diaphragm slips."

"I mean it," Kazuko murmured, nuzzling her cheek against his. "We're going to have a baby."

He sat up suddenly, staring into the sable eyes. "You're not kidding? We're really going to? You mean, you and I? I'm going to be a *father?*"

"Yes, idiot, and I'm going to be a mother," she laughed, enveloping him in the silkiness, the warmth of her arms. "Incredible, the logic of it all, *ne?*"

"No. I mean yes, but when? When did you find out? When?" Tim's mind was racing. *His Kazuko*—

She was looking out the window. In an almost distracted tone she said, "I saw the doctor today, at lunch. Looks like we're going to have our baby in September. She said sometime around the fifteenth."

"My God," he laughed. "We'll have to get a bassinet. I'll have to learn how to change diapers. It's going to be wonderful!"

Kazuko turned to him and made a face. "Dunno how wonderful cleaning up a kid's poo is going to be." Eyeing him carefully, she said, "Sure we want to have the baby in the first place?"

"What do you mean? Of *course* we're going to have our baby! We're going to be *parents.*"

"You're forgetting one little thing." She held up a hand, wiggling the ring finger.

"What? We'll have everything ready. We'll get a larger apartment, we'll—"

"We're not *married,* kiddo," she prodded.

"We'll *get* married. Right now. Today. Well, soon as we can get a license, a blood test—"

She drew him close, tears streaming. His pounding heart beat against her rounded breast. Their lips brushed, touched, held. They began to make love once more.

In the next apartment, the voice-activated tape recorders were functioning well.

Twice a day a technician came to change the big 10½-inch reels and remove the completed ones from the premises. The technicians were the same two men, and the building management understood they were executives of a large Tokyo-headquartered consulting firm.

They were temporarily assigned to Washington, working on something to do with the U.S.-Japan trade imbalance. Both men were very pleasant, according to the building manager. Typically polite.

No one from the building was permitted in the apartment. Special locks were installed on both doors. In the event of unauthorized entry, mechanisms were in place to shut down all equipment and trigger a prerecorded telephone call to an office in Alexandria, Virginia.

They'd chosen Molokai because of its position almost midway between the U.S. mainland and the Japanese home islands, and because the resort was used to handling almost as many Japanese as Americans.

The room was named The Leilani Ballroom, after an Academy Award–winning song of the 1930s. It was the only room large enough to accommodate both trade legations as well as the press. Four ceiling fans lazily stirred the air over an enormous mahogany table. Video cameras, tape recorders, and bored reporters crowded the table's perimeter.

The outcome of the talks was predictable. Not much would change, but both sides would have a chance to state their cases for political effect. The president's speech writers had already finished the first draft of the U.S. Trade Representative's remarks on the talks' results, and had handed them to him just before departure for Hawaii and the talks themselves.

They'd dubbed the negotiations "The Molokai Accords," which seemed to have a nicely historic yet cooperative ring to it. The president, in fact, had already given his press secretary, the oleaginous Marvin Pertweiler, a "well-done" based on that phrase alone.

It was, at least up to this point, business as usual.

The two negotiators faced each other across the huge

table, microphones bristling before them. Each came with his own battalion of staff members, replete with computers and briefcases for instantly providing supporting data.

The U.S. Trade Representative, DeWitt Howell, was tall and lanky, with a hawklike face. A thatch of thickish iron-gray hair gave him a striking similarity to the economist John Kenneth Galbraith.

Jimmu Yohae, his Japanese counterpart, was a youngish man with a receding hairline and longish sideburns, the author of several books on Japanese management theory and global trading. Intelligent eyes glittered behind tortoise-rimmed spectacles. His hands were clasped in front of him on the table, fingers loosely interlaced.

He smiled and nodded pleasantly as the American explained the U.S. government's position. "You see, Mr. Yohae, the practice of deliberately undercutting free-market prices—and underwriting the loss with government subsidies—is not in the best interests of free trade."

Yohae smiled, thinking privately: *They do not yet understand the difference between free trade and strategic trade. All these years, and they still expect us to play by their childish rules, and bow to their childish complaints. Do they never read their own history? Surely the Rockefellers, the Vanderbilts, the other rich Americans of the turn of the century would find their behavior most puzzling.*

Howell continued calmly, producing charts which showed Japan's rapacious progress in the microprocessor market. "—and, until that time, your chip makers were selling their products at very competitive prices. Then, the very same week U.S. Memories was disbanded, your chip makers—NEC, Toshiba, Mitsui, Fujitsu, Mitsubishi, and Matsushita—all raised their prices. That, Mr. Yohae, is hardly playing on a level playing field."

Yohae, still smiling, wondered at this man's naïveté. *Well, of course we'd raise our prices. That's the whole point of gaining a dominant position; only a fool would continue to offer products at a low price when there's no need to.*

"We are also concerned," Howell went on, "at your behavior in forcing those American manufacturers who have become dependent on your microprocessor chips to concede seats on their boards as well as shares of ownership to Japanese interests. It smacks, quite frankly, of blackmail."

This language was unusually forthright for a U.S. Trade Representative. The prior holder of that office had merely rubber-stamped the administration's wish to praise free trade and avoid anything that might aggravate their Japanese "trading partners." *But this Howell seemed different,* thought Yohae. *Something lies just beneath the surface. This one might bear watching.*

Shuffling his documents, Yohae stole a glance at his watch, thinking how very cooling it would be to dive into the pool just outside this room. But it seemed as if the American was determined to rehash the same old arguments, to voice the same petulant, childish complaints of unfairness, of Japanese protectionism, of dumping. He could almost write the *gaijin's* script himself.

"—in every case you have used government subsidies to support absurdly low prices, increasing your share of market, driving American manufacturers out of business—manufacturers who have no subsidies—and then raising your prices to their real level, and occasionally beyond."

Yohae smiled. "It seems, Mr. Howell, that you find it unfair that we now charge market-driven prices, where before you found it unfair that we didn't. But we should not dwell on the past. We should look forward to the future." He beamed becomingly at the video cameras now focused on him.

"The essence of free trade is the individual, and it is the individual that is creating a world without borders, a world opposed to the nineteenth-century mercantilist model in which country is opposed against country," he continued smoothly. "Surely we are not forcing the consumer to choose our goods. The consumer, whether Japanese or American, is perfectly free to do so. We are both democracies, are we not?"

Howell inwardly fumed: The president had given him strict instructions not to antagonize the Japanese, but he was chafing at Yohae's deft deflection of market-rigging responsibility.

"We're obviously not here to challenge the consumer's right to free choice," Howell interrupted. "We're here to settle differences which include your country's insistence on 'dumping' goods in our country at cost or below cost—purely to drive our own manufacturers out of the market or out of business altogether." He was thinking of how GE and other U.S. manufactuerers had hurriedly retreated from nearly every area in which the Japanese had employed these tactics. "And when it comes to country opposing country, Japan has more protectionist barriers—through both legislation and more devious means—against U.S.-made goods than most people can possibly imagine. In the instance of Allied-Signal's 'metglas' technology—"

"Mr. Howell, if I may differ—" Yohae held up his hand in polite protest. "Your manufacturers are as free as ours are to lower prices to whatever level they can sustain. But your CEOs are now driven by short-term profit instead of long-term market share. And your administration refuses to even *consider* a national industrial plan. Perhaps *that* is why," he said, spreading his hands widely for emphasis, "our products inevitably prosper in free trade." He smiled winningly at the cameras, which then panned to the U.S. side of the table, to reveal a lineup of uniformly grim-visaged Americans.

Howell seethed. He gritted his teeth and wished to God his president had given him the latitude he needed. He wished he'd never been hornswoggled into taking the goddamn job in the first place. *No matter,* he thought. *I'll be out of it in another three months, then I'll write the book. I've already got the title:* Pearl Harbor Two: Japan's Global Economic Attack.

Howell stretched to relieve the tensions coiled up within him. His mind raced, and then he made his decision. *Oh well, what the hell. Sometimes you're just in the right place at the right time, and things have got to be said, despite orders, despite diplomacy, despite the president's goddamn free-trade mythology.*

He took a drink of water and, taking a deep breath, smiled broadly at the beaming Japanese across from him. "Mr. Yohae, you know as well as I that your country is *not,* truthfully speaking, engaging in free trade. What you are engaging in is economic warfare, plain and simple. Conquest, not cooperation. You just haven't had the decency to declare it openly." *There.* He'd said it. *Wonder how many minutes before the president's man gets on the phone and tries to yank me the hell out of Hawaii.* The thought oddly pleased him.

Yohae's smile froze in place. The sudden silence in the room was something you could almost touch.

Then, after a beat, all hell broke loose.

Reporters began shouting questions, interrupting the proceedings. Others ran for the telephones. Yohae was seen murmuring hurriedly to his ruffled staff.

Howell simply grinned and stretched in his chair once again. He calculated the White House would be on the horn in about five minutes flat, asking him to retract, to apologize, to kowtow to the bastards as all his predecessors had done. *To hell with them all,* he thought to himself. *They can stick the goddamn job. I've only said what everybody's been dying to say who isn't an elected politician, or some other kind of goddamn total wimp.*

Jimmu Yohae, no longer smiling, leaned into his microphones, hunching his shoulders. "It is unfortunate that the American trade representative seems unalterably opposed to the international spirit of cooperation that is embodied in free trade." He paused dramatically, with what he hoped was an expression of Utmost Concern on his now unsmiling face. "In the light of this, I don't see what is to be gained by continuing this discussion. We must therefore respectfully withdraw at this time. Thank you."

With that, Yohae got up from the table, shuffled together his papers, and led his stumbling herd of assistants from the room.

The American delegation stared at Howell in shocked, bewildered silence, as if he were a cowboy who'd suddenly blundered, six-guns blazing, into a Junior League tea party. Each had the identical thought on his or her mind: *Jesus o Jesus o Jesus, don't let me get fired for being in this place at this time with this fucking rabid lunatic of a son of a bitch bastard.*

But DeWitt Howell, at this moment, had no such misgivings. He felt as if a great burden had been lifted from his shoulders. He felt happier than he'd been in years.

He leaned back in his chair, smiling at the waggling cameras, the gabbling reporters.

"Now, ladies and gentlemen," he began, "if you have any questions?"

_____ 9

Reflections in a Glass.

After he left Miranda's apartment, staying on the street was out of the question. Whoever the watchers were, they were sophisticated. They'd have vehicles. They'd also have two-way radios.

Pretorius checked the block behind him, then quickly turned the corner and slipped into the Hotel Carlyle's Bemelmans Bar.

He chose a seat enveloped in velvety darkness, and gave the white-jacketed waiter his order. Pernod on the rocks seemed to go with Ludwig Bemelmans' murals and the music of Cole Porter.

It was good to be here again, he thought. *Although it would be better, far better, with Susannah. She'd love the romance of this place. She'd love the music.* The pianist was singing one of Pretorius' favorite Cole Porter lyrics:

> *With a million neon rainbows burning below me*
> *And a million blazing taxis raising a roar*
> *Here I sit while deep despair*
> *Haunts my castle in the air*
> *Down in the depths on the ninetieth floor*
>
> *While the crowds at El Morocco punish the parquet*
> *And at '21' the couples clamor for more*
> *I'm deserted and depressed*
> *In my regal eagle nest*
> *Down in the depths on the ninetieth floor*

Pretorius began thinking again of Phillip Mathieson, and of the way he'd been terminated. "Termination with extreme prejudice" was one of the phrases used by Agency people. Anything to avoid the words "killed" or "murdered."

CIA guys, he recalled, *love the ellipticalness, the weirdness of Agency nomenclature. It was part of the lore.* Pretorius looked into the swirl of cloudy liquid in his glass.

The incident had started in a bar not too different from this, he remembered. *Dark, like this one. But the music hadn't been Cole Porter's, and the city hadn't been New York, and the street had been a far cry from Madison Avenue.*

Pretorius had been assigned to a Frankfurt unit by DIA as a kind of test, after they'd brought him over from the Office of Naval Intelligence. He'd been the fair-haired boy all through recruiting and training. They'd respected his facility with German, with firearms, with physics and electronics.

But once in the field, he was a questionable quantity until proven otherwise. And he'd come close, oh so close, to not merely being tossed back to the Navy, but to being a corpse in a Frankfurt alley. *The only thing that had saved me that bitter winter night,* he reminded himself, *had been Mathieson. The late Phillip Mathieson.*

On that night the fat man had sat on the bar stool slowly turning the pages of the comic book. No laughter, no smile altered the impassive blubber of his face. It was as if the fat man were studying a technical manual, committing it to memory, savoring, devouring each detail.

From his vantage point in the darkened bar Pretorius could see the cover of the fat man's comic: Mickey Mouse, printed in German. *Funny,* he'd thought at the time. *Over two hundred years of the United States, and our most popular export turns out to be a celluloid mouse.*

Pretorius looked away. He didn't want to be seen staring. To attract notice, any kind of notice, would mean an easier ID later in case of trouble. He checked his watch.

The contact was now a half hour late. Too late for comfort. Sometimes agents liked to string out their control to see what would happen if they didn't show or were late. And sometimes an inexperienced officer would betray a second man covering the meet, or dial a number he shouldn't, or go someplace he shouldn't, or do something else equally dumb.

The man Pretorius was waiting for was an East German. Pretorius' bosses said he had the scoop on some new Soviet gallium arsenide chips that could radically upgrade mission and flight control systems on military aircraft. Said the chips resembled ones developed ten months previously at BFEC[1] in Columbia, Maryland.

Although security at BFEC itself was tight as hell, Pretorius' bosses suggested maybe the Soviets had somebody in place in the Pentagon itself. Everybody in DIA always got nervous about agents-in-place inside the DoD, like imagining burglars under the bed.

In any case, this could be a high-yield operation. Pretorius' superior officer, a former Marine colonel named Kreindler, said he should be flattered to get a plum like this. It could mean a letter of commendation.

All Pretorius had was a sketchy description of the German, the time and place of the meet, and authority to spend up to 5,000 DM initially. If, that is, the contact seemed right and the chips seemed real.

But it was getting too late. Pretorius decided it was either a feint, or the guy had gotten shook, or somebody had screwed up the time or place for the meet. Finally, looking once more at his watch, Pretorius put a 10 DM note on the counter for the bartender, and left.

The weather outside had deteriorated. What had been a light snowfall was now a blizzard, the snow driving horizontally, sharp and stinging.

Pretorius bent his head forward against the blast. The snow was coming so thick and fast it stung his face. He winced as the wind knifed through his thin coat. He decided against going back to the hotel. If he was being followed—and he estimated the chances at about three to one—revealing his bolt hole would be less than brilliant. Instead he made his way back to a rathskeller he'd passed earlier, up in the Rittergasse.

He couldn't remember a more punishing snowstorm. As

[1]BFEC (pronounced Beef-ek) = Bendix Field Engineering Company. One of the top U.S. military defense suppliers, involved in many top security projects and widely respected.

he slogged up the narrow, twisting streets of the Old Town, he had to lean almost at a twenty-degree angle into the wind to keep moving. No one was on the streets now, which made checking for a tag much easier. Still, the snow had cut visibility down to thirty feet or so. A tag would have to be too near for comfort to see or be seen.

After about fifteen minutes he got to the rathskeller, chilled to the bone. The front window's small, old-fashioned panes were frosted over, smearing the interior into an abstraction of colors. *Good,* thought Pretorius. *Tougher for somebody to check out who's inside.*

He shouldered his way through the ancient door and managed to push it shut against an insistent wind. An old couple at a table near the door glanced up briefly, then returned to their huddled muttering. Pretorius chose a small table near the fireplace and shrugged out of his snow-frosted overcoat, glad to escape from the storm howling outside.

The restaurant smelled of good German beer and *Wurst.* The walk-in fireplace was piled with thick sections of tree trunks, blazing in defiance of the storm howling outside. The fire, too, contributed its own scent; Pretorius wondered if the logs were applewood. A blonde waitress, in a blouse that left little of her bosom to speculation, took his order with a smile.

Too bad I'm on the job, Pretorius mused. *Would be nice to see what's she's doing after the storm.*

The dinner was simple, but perfect for a night like this: *Schnitzel à la Holstein,* with potato dumplings and red cabbage. The beer was one he'd never heard of before, a dark rich local brew with a nutlike flavor.

Pretorius was feeling content and even beginning to relax a little. Then the door opened and the fat man waddled in, small piggy eyes taking in the room at a glance, finally locking onto Pretorius. A small, wizened ferret of a man came in behind him, shoving the door shut with difficulty. Both were covered with snow, and looking distinctly displeased. The fat man motioned toward Pretorius with a nod of his big porcine head, and the two came over and sat down beside him.

Pretorius felt something on his knee as the fat man said, without expression, "What you're feeling is a large-caliber pistol, *mein Freund,* with a suppressor. We will gladly disintegrate your knees unless you accompany us, and no one will hear a thing. We've already wasted far too much time on you as is, and we have only limited patience. *Komm. Mach schnell!"*

Pretorius rose and pulled on his coat. The small man led the way, the fat one keeping close behind Pretorius.

Once outside, the blast of wind seemed to be stronger than ever, and Pretorius, struggling to stay upright in the storm, felt a sudden shove as the fat man prodded him with the pistol in one of his kidneys.

The three stumbled through the labyrinth of narrow streets, leaning into the wind. Pretorius wondered how he could get through his coat to the .45 Lightweight Commander without getting himself shot in the process.

And then, as they rounded a corner onto one of the main streets, a lone figure—huddled in an oversized British-style duffel coat against the blast of the storm—blundered into them. At first, Pretorius thought it was a drunk. Then he recognized the face just as a weapon, a Sterling Patchett L2A3 submachine gun, swept up from beneath the coat and opened up on the fat man. The rapid-fire stuttering of the shots were muffled by the storm, but they brought the ferret-like man swiveling around with a small automatic. Pretorius chopped it out of his hand and followed up with a forward stroke directly to the ferret's throat, immobilizing him instantly.

Gut-shot, the fat man sagged slowly to the snow-covered sidewalk, clutching his abdomen, wondering eyes beginning to glaze over. Still, the man in the duffel coat kept him covered with the subgun and glanced just once at Pretorius, who now had the smaller man's pistol. "You sure pick strange people to go on strolls with, Pretorius," said Phillip Mathieson.

Later, when the *Bundespolizei* had removed the body of the fat man and handcuffed and led away his companion, the two Americans walked back to Pretorius' hotel. Mathieson explained that CIA had been watching the fat man, who had been implicated in a number of killings of Western agents throughout Germany.

The fat man and the ferret, free-lancers cashiered from the

Sicherheitsdienst,[2] had set up a system whereby they baited a trap with a particularly juicy bit of intelligence, then waited to see who'd fall for it. The victim would be tortured for names, which the two would then sell to the East German intelligence *Apparat.*

Once it was obvious nothing further could be extracted, Mathieson explained, the agent would be killed in a particularly gruesome manner—to obliterate the marks of torture—and left to be found in an alley.

Pretorius' bosses had fallen for the story of the stolen chips, and as a result he'd almost been history. If it hadn't been for Mathieson.

Now, a lifetime away, Pretorius remembered and reflected.

All right, he decided, finishing his drink. *I've owed you one a long time, Mathieson. Time for you to collect.*

10

Kazuko & Company.

Timothy Nagata was, in many respects, on top of the world. Kazuko and Tim were married in a Shinto ceremony arranged by her friends, and the baby was expected in September.

She was starting to show with a gentle swelling of her belly. Her breasts were significantly larger, and Tim thought she'd never looked sexier. "You're just like all the *gaijin,"* she teased. "You want to keep your women pregnant and barefoot."

In contrast to his personal life, Tim's professional life was charged with tension. The Joint Chiefs kept asking for more and more updates, more presentations from the CIA's Talking Dogs. At Tim's level, he had no idea how seriously the NSC and the president were taking the product from LA-

[2] West German Security Service.

CROSSE. But the generals and admirals obviously considered it prime-time viewing.

He started to share some of his concerns about the Soviet buildup with Kazuko. He realized their relationship was based on trust, as she pointed out, and two people who were having a child should have no secrets. Even so, at first he felt uneasy talking about NPIC. And especially LACROSSE.

She'd looked surprised when he said the radar satellites he was involved with were military, and not weather birds. But then she'd been fascinated, and as he explained how they worked—and their extraordinary capabilities—she couldn't believe he was involved in something that important, that, well, *exciting*.

As the JCS kept up the pressure, Tim kept longer and longer hours. He felt worn out, and knew he was overdue for a physical. But he couldn't take the time off. Not now. Not with all this.

Then on a Tuesday afternoon, after bolting down a microwaved hamburger and coffee in the NPIC canteen, Tim felt waves of nausea and the beginnings of a severe tension headache. The muscles at the base of his skull were knotted. Massaging them didn't help, nor did the usual three Tylenols.

He signed himself out, inched himself into his tiny Honda, and drove through D.C.'s purgatorial afternoon traffic to Georgetown. Kazuko would be at school, he knew, and it was just as well. He didn't want her worrying about him. The important thing was to keep Kazuko calm and happy in her pregnancy, and Tim was getting to be an expert at that.

He parked in the apartment building's underground garage and took the elevator up to six. Walking down the corridor, he got out his key and slipped it into the lock.

Even before the door was fully open he became aware of a sound in one of the rooms, a sound unlike any he'd heard.

His first thought: *My God, we're being burgled. Should I slip out and call the cops? Or confront them here and now?*

Deciding his Wyatt Earp side was distinctly less strong, he began to quietly leave when he heard Kazuko's voice, high, keening.

And then he heard the man.

He froze at the door and slowly, carefully closed it. He

advanced from their foyer to just inside the living room, looking for a weapon, anything. His eyes found the antique Meiji samurai sword resting on its cradle on the big camphorwood chest, and he moved to it soundlessly, lifting it from the mounts.

"Now! Now! Now!" he heard his wife shouting. The man started moaning loudly.

Tim slid silently into the bedroom. The couple on the bed wouldn't have cared even if they had seen him, so devoured were they by their passion.

The man was thrusting himself into Kazuko again and again. She urged him on, heavy breasts shaking with every thrust, nipples erect, hands clenching at the man's biceps, red nails biting into the flesh.

With a sickening lurch, Tim recognized the man: *It was the cultural attaché from the Japanese Embassy.*

Suddenly Tim heard Kazuko scream—and realized that beneath her still-thrusting lover she was staring straight at him.

The man leaped off the bed, immediately springing into what Tim recognized as a martial arts position. Kazuko edged off backward, eyes wide, sidestepping to get away from the bed, distancing herself from what was to come.

Tim held the sword low, weighing it, realizing he had no training whatever in this kind of thing. A fine sheen of sweat broke out on his skin. He moved slightly to one side, giving himself some room. His head was throbbing.

The man advanced silently, profiled three-quarters, hands circling, knees bent.

With the peculiar ability of the threatened to see with exacting clarity, Tim saw the edges of the man's palms were heavily calloused. He was young, too, perhaps no more than twenty-five, twenty-six. The smooth face held no expression. The eyes were steady, empty, concentrating only on what now had to be done: the termination, silently and quickly, of the opponent. Tim thought, *If this guy's a cultural attaché, then I'm Mr. Rogers.*

Kazuko moved nearer the window, unconscious of her nakedness, pendulous breasts swaying.

The man advanced to within eight feet of Tim Nagata before the blade flicked out in a sudden sweeping arc. The man jumped back, keeping his eyes on Tim's eyes all the time.

The man tried another attack as Tim let the blade drop too low, but quickly darted back as the damascened edge swung up within range. Tim was now enraged, and moved toward the man, raising the sword up for a swift downward blow—and the man saw his chance.

With a speed measurable only in microseconds, his feet seemed to fly into the air by themselves. Tim, with a swiftness he'd never known, hit the floor, but not before taking the hardened side of a foot directly on his chest, knocking him back, forcing him to drop the blade.

The man rolled past as Tim scrambled to get the shining weapon now just out of reach.

Kazuko now made her move. As her lover rose again to his attacking position, one foot lashing out to strike Tim Nagata's chin, she grabbed one of the chromium dumbbells Tim kept in the bedroom for his morning exercises and hurled it directly at Tim's head. But the naked man's foot had already connected with its target, kicking Tim's jaw to the right, and the ten-pound object struck the man's foot instead, knocking him off balance.

As his attacker hit the floor on his hip, Tim rolled to the sword, grasped it by the sharkskin-covered hilt, and swung it hard in a sweeping arc, slicing well into the man's calf, half-way into the femur, nearly severing the lower leg. Blood began spurting and the hacked and splintered femur, unable to sustain the weight, snapped and the man collapsed—but not before his calloused palm struck Tim hard in the kidney.

The pain was searing, unimaginable. Still Tim held on to the sword and managed to stand up, raising the damascened blade high above his head in a two-handed grip.

The explosion seemed to rock the room. Kazuko was standing now by the bureau, and she was holding a pistol. Tim was suddenly conscious he'd been shot. Blood trickled from a wound in his side, just above his hip. There was no pain. She raised the pistol again, aiming for center of mass, Tim's chest. He realized with a shock: *Christ, it's not just him. It's Kazuko. She's trying to kill me too.*

The naked man, writhing on the floor in a widening, darkening pool of blood, was screaming something in Japanese to Kazuko.

Her eyes flicked to him for an instant. Tim used that split-second of distraction and threw the sword. Instinctively she threw up her arms although the blade fell clattering to one side. Tim rushed her. He grabbed the gun hand and another explosion filled the room.

They fell to the floor, rolling, her long black hair loose. She held on to the gun fiercely, trying to angle her wrist for a close-quarters shot at Tim. Her strength was terrifying, like that of someone twice her size. Her eyes were bloodshot, bulging with hatred as she summoned all her effort for one killing shot.

The muzzle of the pistol edged little by little toward Tim's face. He saw the hole change from an ellipse, as viewed from slightly to one side, to a progressively rounder and rounder orifice.

Tim was trying with all his strength to keep the weapon from turning toward him. But her leverage was greater and the hole was now directly facing him. Her face was twisted in its intensity, in its fevered desire to fire the shot that would destroy him. Her finger tightened on the trigger, the fleshy pad of the forefinger beginning to flatten, to whiten with the pressure.

Then—as if he knew it was the only thing that could save him—Tim suddenly relaxed and rolled to one side as the weapon fired and the bullet ripped past his head to lodge in the plaster wall eighteen inches above floor level.

He slammed his fist toward her head, but as he did she brought the weapon up, trying for yet another shot. His fist slammed into her knuckles and the weapon went flying. She scrambled to her feet, now trying to escape, stumbling into the living room as Tim pursued her.

Later, when he was being questioned, he would often try and recall precisely what was going through his thoughts in those last few minutes. *What he was actually trying to do: kill her, stop her, save her—what?*

He caught up with her at the door as she was clawing at its Segal lock. Thinking the door was locked when it was not, she'd turned the latch, locking it.

As he came at her, her eyes widened and she ran across the

room toward the door leading to the terrace. She crashed through its glass, spilling out onto the terrace itself, before her weight carried her to the waist-high railing and over it. As she fell, tumbling over and over, to be finally frozen for all time in Tim Nagata's memory as he looked down twelve stories and saw his wife's body, naked and from this distance still beautiful, on the roof of a parked car, the metal indented six inches beneath her body by the force of its impact.

The Japanese Ambassador had been summoned to the State Department suddenly. There had been no explanation. According to his aide the summons had been curt, almost rude.

A quick consultation with his staff soon revealed the probable subject: the death of the young *Nibetsu*[1] officer whose cover had been cultural attaché. *Had the man left any damaging evidence? Was he involved in anything embarrassing to Dai Nippon?*

Ikeda wished these intelligence people weren't forever masquerading as embassy or consular staff. It didn't help to know most of Japan's intelligence officers were legitimate employees of trade organizations and commercial firms. Having them on your staff was like living in a house and knowing the cellar was packed with gelignite.

Ikeda was a small man, wearing his ambassadorial formality like a great cloak, as if to compensate for his size. He'd been appointed after an undistinguished twenty-one-year career as a civil servant solely in the home islands. He was predictable, and far from precipitous. He was ideally suited to his position.

Ikeda usually looked forward to his visits to the Americans' Department of State. The rooms housed one of the world's great collections of eighteenth-century furniture, and his sense of formality was always stimulated and pleased.

But he wasn't looking forward to this particular visit. No, he sensed it would be among the most difficult of his career.

[1]Agency responsible for collection and analyzing military intelligence, generally operating in conjunction with Japanese embassies around the world.

Still, this was why he was here. This was why he was ambassador.

He was ushered into the Under Secretary Thomas Knowles' office after being kept waiting for ten minutes. He realized then they were trying to unnerve him by an intentional lapse of protocol.

Games, he thought. *There were always games, and the nature of the games often told you the nature of the real contest.*

Knowles was standing there, and at his side was a man whose face Ikeda immediately recognized. Richard Coldwell, Director of Central Intelligence. *It was the young spy's death, then.*

Knowles merely said, "Ambassador?" and gestured toward a single Chippendale armchair facing his desk. The two Americans remained standing until Ikeda had arranged himself in the chair, then seated themselves.

Neither of the Americans was smiling. Ikeda crossed his legs in the silence before the under secretary spoke. "Ambassador, as you and your countrymen have repeatedly reminded us, you are partners in democracy with the United States. Certainly the Japanese people feel a kinship with ours, especially now that Japan has entered a new and prosperous era."

"That is true," interjected Ikeda, smiling. "Few nations have so strong a commitment to similar goals as do yours and ours."

This was met with a few seconds' silence, which Knowles used for effect before speaking. "Then why is it, Ambassador, that you have deliberately planted a nest of spies in our nation's capital? Why have you tried to steal our defense secrets? And why, Ambassador Ikeda, have you nearly caused the death of one of our most valuable federal scientists, working in an area of extreme sensitivity?"

Ikeda leaned forward. "Secretary Knowles, you bewilder me. I hardly think—"

"I know," retorted Knowles. "It does appear that you hardly think. If you *thought,* Ambassador Ikeda, you'd have realized your espionage hoodlums don't belong in the capital of the United States, and that by planting them here—and commissioning them to corrupt one of our most sensitive installations—you have recklessly endangered relations between our two countries."

Coldwell then stood up and withdrew a number of eight-by-ten glossy photographs from a folder, placing them face up on the under secretary's desk.

"These are two of your spies, Ambassador. As you doubtless know, both these people are dead following an unfortunate incident yesterday afternoon in which a senior Defense Department scientist was himself nearly killed. He's been hospitalized for psychiatric treatment. It develops that one of your spies, who entered this country late last summer, had managed to get this young man to marry her. The other, posing as a cultural attaché in your embassy, was actually her lover.

"And this—" the director said as he showed the ashen ambassador a further set of photographs—"is the secret communications room your people set up next door to the residence of your Miss Fukuda and Dr. Nagata. Further investigations led us to arrest a number of people in Alexandria who were found in possession of materials which can only be described as highly classified."

Coldwell then resumed his seat as Ambassador Ikeda sorted through the photographs one by one, his face impassive. When he got to the photograph of Kazuko Fukuda's corpse, face buried in the metal of the car's roof onto which she had fallen, Ikeda's facial muscles contorted briefly. There was a stillness in the room, broken yet emphasized by the ticking of the Hoadley tallcase clock in the corner.

The ambassador leaned forward to place the photographs on Knowles' desk. He made a sweeping gesture with his hand, as if he hardly knew how to react. But there could be only reaction, given the situation. "Secretary Knowles, Director Coldwell—this is most distressing. If, indeed, these individuals have violated the privilege accorded them by either diplomatic status or, in the case of the young woman, a United States visa, then you are indeed due our deepest and most profound apologies." Ikeda was aware that every word was being taped, so he was careful to admit nothing, and to keep the incident only within the realm of remote possibility.

Knowles stared hard at Ikeda throughout this statement, then cleared his throat and spoke in a low, intense tone:

"Ambassador, make no mistake. The evidence is in our hands. Each of these two Japanese nationals have known intelligence backgrounds. The man Uchikawa, was no more a cultural attaché than I am. He was *Nibetsu,* through and through, and his accomplice, the Fukuda woman, had been a JETRO[2] employee for several years before applying for a student visa to the United States."

Ikeda looked at both Knowles and Coldwell expectantly, his fingers steepled. He could imagine the consequences if the Americans decided to make an incident of this. His career would, without question, be forfeit. Not because of any involvement in placing the operation here, but because of failure to contain its consequences.

"If what you say is so, Secretary Knowles, we shall order an immediate and complete investigation." He paused and spread his hands expansively. "Nothing is farther from our wishes than to jeopardize what both our nations have labored so conscientiously to build over nearly five decades. I shall speak immediately with the prime minister."

Director Coldwell now took the initiative. "I'm afraid you still fail to understand, Ambassador. The investigation is complete: we've known about these two for some time, and we're fully prepared to prosecute the remaining members of their team. Given the current state of U.S. public opinion, the arrest, trial, and subsequent imprisonment of Japanese spies in the United States could hardly fail to damage— perhaps irreversibly—relations."

Knowles knew what was going through Ikeda's head at that moment: *relations* was being translated as *trade.*

Imports of Japanese cars and electronics were beginning to slump as people finally realized millions of American jobs had been effectively eradicated. U.S. politicians had been mouthing platitudes about "free" trade, while the Japanese practiced not free trade at all, but trade warfare—involving complex, cleverly masked subsidizing of cost of goods, enabling them to drop prices and slowly drive American brands out of the market, in the case of electronics, and close

[2]Japanese External Trade Organization.

up factories, in the case of America's faltering and ill-managed auto industry. At the same time, price-fixing, or *dango,* effectively prevented many American goods from entering the Japanese home market.

Knowles remembered a film of a few years ago, *Roger and Me,* in which the baseball-capped director/protagonist spent most of the film lumbering after General Motors Chairman Roger Smith to finally ask him why GM had done this terrible thing, closing the plants in Flint, Michigan.

The neo-proletarian director, Knowles thought, *should've been pursuing all the people who bought Hondas and Nissans and Mitsubishis in preference to American cars. Buttonholing them and asking, "Do you realize my hometown went bust because you, and hundreds of thousands of other Americans, voted Japanese with your check for $12,000?"*

It would have been closer to the truth. But it wouldn't have made nearly as funny a movie. And, he realized, *some of the interviewees would've likely decked the director.*

Ikeda interrupted Knowles' thoughts. "Please be assured, Mr. Secretary, that Japan will do anything to prevent a disruption of relations between our two democracies. What would you suggest in this case?"

It was what Knowles and Coldwell were waiting for, the message they'd summoned Ikeda here to give him.

Knowles leaned forward, arms folded on the desk, deepened furrows in his brow. "We will put a quiet end to this unfortunate matter if the following conditions are met:

"One, the individuals we have apprehended in the Alexandria operation are to leave this country within five days and are not to return.

"Two, certain other individuals who work directly or indirectly for JETRO to MITI (Ministry of International Trade and Industry) will leave with them.

"In particular," Knowles continued, "several people who are part of MITI's Bureau of Heavy Industry, in the Special Survey Group of the Information Room, are to cease and desist their efforts in penetrating the American computer industry. They are to leave this country within the next five days as well. Director Coldwell—" and here he nodded in the intelligence chief's direction—"has prepared a list, which

he will give you along with the photographs you've just
seen."

"Our government will be pleased to consider your request.
You must understand, though—" began Ikeda. But Coldwell interrupted.

"It's not a request, Mr. Ambassador. It's simply what will
happen unless you withdraw those people immediately.
You'll read about it in the papers, and you'll see it on television. And so will millions of the residents of your most
important market."

The Ambassador of Japan to the United States swallowed
hard, and nodded his head once, sharply. He rose to leave.

Knowles and Coldwell were on their feet in an instant.
Knowles offered his hand to the Japanese as a matter of
courtesy. Ikeda looked at the American's proffered hand for
a moment, then shook it and the hand of Coldwell too.

"I shall contact you soon, after I've had a chance to
discuss this with my government. It may take a few days."
Ikeda looked anxious.

Knowles inclined his head. "Use them wisely, Mr. Ambassador. Use them wisely."

The door closed behind Ikeda, and the assistant escorted
him down the corridor toward the elevator.

11

Spy in the Box.

Neon spattered on rain-slicked streets as he ran, scattering
quicksilver images of pachinko parlors, noodle shops, record stores, coffee shops, electronics dealers. All the pulsing
colors of the Tokyo district called Electric City rippled and
slid beneath his feet.

The runner's adrenaline was high, his nerves tingling.
From time to time he paused to look in shop windows,
choosing those with an angled position to check the area
behind him. No one seemed to be following on foot or by

vehicle. Still, to be sure, he ran through a vegetable market, followed by a volley of curses into an alley choked with cardboard and garbage.

He picked up speed. In ten minutes he found the street named Kondo Jimbocho, and slowed to a walk.

He paused at the building numbered 53-23. According to all public records and appearances, the building was owned by a small independent marketer of electronics. The fact that a few of their products happened to be sold to the military explained the more visible security measures to both employees and visitors.

The runner looked at the glass front doors as if seeing them for the first time. From a side pocket of his corduroy jacket he produced a wrinkled piece of paper. He looked from it to the building's front, apparently checking the address.

The paper was blank. He had been here at least a dozen times in the past year, wearing different clothing, affecting different appearances. This time he wore a nondescript black baseball-type jacket, faded jeans, a khaki shirt with its tail out, and black-framed eyeglasses. An unruly comma of black hair spilled over a pale forehead. He was young, possibly twenty-six or twenty-seven. To passersby he appeared to be a person of no consequence, likely a messenger.

This was not too far off the mark, for he was in fact a messenger. But the message he carried was from one of the most respected names in the American intelligence community. A message which, if intercepted, would likely result in a closed trial of the American, and probable conviction on charges of espionage and treason.

He walked to the service entrance ten meters down the street. After pressing a button, he was admitted by a surly-looking security guard who gave no sign of recognition. He walked past a second guard seated at a metal table and entered a service elevator.

The elevator rose two floors and its doors opened slowly onto a small, brightly lit room. There, a man in a business suit patted him down for weapons and recording devices. The runner's wallet was examined briefly. It contained nothing interesting. A driver's license, several telephone cards, a few business cards, a laundry ticket, a girl's photograph, a few worn receipts.

The security man recognized the runner. He did not know his identity, nor did he wish to. It was enough that he was expected, and that his driver's license had the one small red mark along the left border.

The runner was escorted down a corridor and into a dressing room where he found a package on the bench. It contained a disposable paper kimono and paper slippers into which he changed quickly, placing his street clothes and shoes in the empty package.

He opened the door and handed out the package to the security man. He closed the door once more and waited for the metal detectors and other monitors to complete their tasks. After a twenty-second interval, a buzzer sounded and the door clicked open onto the now-empty corridor.

The young man walked to the corridor's end to a gray metal door, and pushed the aluminum bar which ran across it at belt level.

The room he entered was white and brightly lit. It seemed to have no shadows. Within the room was a second chamber with walls, floor, and ceiling of transparent acrylic plastic.

The chamber was like many found in consulates and embassies around the world, made especially for sensitive conversations and briefings. A small Lucite door fitted with a flexible vinyl gasket allowed entry to the inner chamber. The door was one meter wide, but only one and a one half meters tall. Entry was possible only by kneeling.

The chamber's "floating" floor was dampened with mechanical vibration absorbers. Electronic devices constantly monitored the chamber for hidden transmitters.

Within the chamber a man who appeared to be in his sixties sat on a thin *zabuton,* heels tucked under buttocks.

His hair was a shock of white, his skin heavily lined. He could be taken for the head of a large corporation, even a senior officer of one of the great *gurupu.*

The name he had chosen for this occasion was one of many reserved for various functions. The name with which he was born was terminated in late August of 1962, when he was catalogued as having died in the crash of a private aircraft off the Hokkaido coast. To a handful of government officials, to a few within Japan's intelligence community, and to certain other people interested in his movements, he was known by a single name: *Dragonfly.*

Thick white hair was combed straight back from a high forehead. His eyes, large and direct, examined the other man through thick lenses held within thin gold frames.

"You are late once more," he observed as the younger man entered the chamber and sat opposite.

"It was necessary to ensure I was not followed." The runner had a cocky air which irritated Dragonfly.

"Kindly leave yourself enough time to honor your commitments as well as practice your tradecraft," the older man returned dryly.

The runner's unspoken acceptance of this criticism was a quick bow of the head.

Dragonfly regarded the young man without expression. *This one will have a only a limited future,* he thought. *Useful to a degree, but lacking in judgment.*

"Your report, then," he reminded.

Again, another quick motion of the head. Then an almost mechanical recital. The report had been carefully memorized, for one did not want to waste the older man's time. Dragonfly's patience was legendarily short.

As he listened to the report, delivered in a carefully modulated but somewhat sing-song voice, his brow furrowed. The entire report indicated anomalous behavior of a most alarming sort.

Both the CIA and the DIA had clear evidence of clandestine but vigorous Soviet preparations for a generated thermonuclear attack. The new radar-imaging satellite had retrieved pictures of high activity, not of a war-games variety, among their submarine fleet, their rocket forces, and several of their bomber commands.

The Soviet military had gone beyond mere maneuvers, beyond war games.

Why, thought Dragonfly, *in this state of Soviet-American relations, when both nations had come so far in the cause of world peace, would the USSR be preparing for imminent war? None of the activities fitted the profiles of the current leadership. Except perhaps, for Lev Zaikov, First Deputy Chairman of the Soviet Defense Council. Zaikov was an unrelenting hawk, and he was now in charge of the Soviet's main economic and military/industrial organ. Zaikov had always been a worry. Still, that wouldn't explain this—this madness.*

It made no sense. No sense whatever.

He interrupted the young man several times, questioning several points, seeking to find flaws in the intelligence or in the analysis of it. The little extra the man could tell him still supported the original conclusion.

Dragonfly, of course, had other sources. They too confirmed the report. At Misawa Air Base, just 400 miles south of Sakhalin, the AN/FLR-9 "Elephant Ear" antenna had intercepted two communications which were chilling in their implications.

Naichò, Japan's premier intelligence agency, had several highly placed people within the KGB itself, Russians amassing small fortunes in Swiss and Liechtensteiner banks for their services.

Yet even these agents-in-place were unaware of any offensive plans. Despite goading by their Japanese case officers (living under commercial covers in Moscow), the agents reported no KGB participation in these actions. Although *Ulitsa Dzerzhinskogo 2*[1] was alive with meetings for the last two days, no fresh product seemed to be surfacing. Nothing was known.

At last, the younger man finished his report. Dragonfly considered the implications in silence. There were no questions. After several minutes, he dismissed the other with a curt nod.

The man bowed his head sharply, and left the box in silence. The last sound in the room was the click of the automatic lock as the door closed. Dragonfly closed his eyes and concentrated.

Even when all is not known, patterns may be detected, he reminded himself. *What is the pattern here? If no pattern is immediately visible, then what represents the negative space around the pattern, so we may begin to interpret what the pattern may be?*

Still concentrating, he removed the heavy-lensed glasses, and began peeling off the white combed-back hair, revealing

[1]Address of the KGB in Moscow.

a shaved head. His fingers probed inside his cheeks and extracted, after a moment, two wax plugs which had plumped out his face.

Finally, with a dampened towel he removed the makeup. Lines of age disappeared, as well as the smooth and even tan.

Dragonfly was now unrecognizable from the individual to whom the young man had presented the report.

He pursued his thoughts. *Anomalies, what are the anomalies? Those are the hints of the shapes of patterns, the shadows which sometimes reveal the substance. We have,* he noted, *two anomalies. The larger, of course, is war preparations in time of an unparalleled prospect for peace. And the second is the utter lack—or seeming lack—of KGB participation in or knowledge of these preparations. Unthinkable, given traditional Soviet power structure.*

Never, in the history of the USSR, has a major military commitment ever been made without the full involvement and knowledge of the Chekists—the intelligence apparat.

But wait, he realized. *The KGB aren't the only Chekists these days. No. What is the GRU involvement in all this?*

Dragonfly rose to his feet in one fluid motion. *The GRU is so inextricably a part of the military, it would be impossible to compartmentalize anything of this scale from them! We shall have to see,* he concluded, *what we can learn of this. For that may reveal the pattern. That, indeed, may be the parting of the mists.* He left the box, and went to what appeared to be a conventional executive's office on the same floor.

Anyone watching the front of the building would never see him leave.

But within a half hour, a Mercedes limousine would pull up in front of a new office building several doors down on Kondo Jimbocho, and receive a smartly dressed, shaven-headed executive into its velvety depths.

DeWitt Howell, recently relieved of his post as U.S. Trade Representative, spent much of his time now on the lecture circuit, making occasional TV and radio talk show appearances.

More and more he called attention to the Japanese assault on the economy, and to the far greater threat—America's own lethargic disinterest in saving itself. U.S. capital investments were still being sacrificed to meet Wall Street's un-slakeable thirst for the short-term bottom line. Forty percent of the cash flow of American corporations was being siphoned off to pay debt service to banks, and healthy R&D budgets were now only a memory. Yet people wondered why so many Japanese products seemed superior to our own, with more and better features, and lower prices.

Meanwhile Japan let a few more token U.S. goods into its domestic market, pursuing protectionist policies at home while praising the virtues of free trade overseas. Howell had the lack of tact to point this out on a network television interview, and stations around the country received a tidal wave of telephone calls, faxes, and telegrams congratulating him. Many suggested he run for the presidency in the next election.

The president, to whom the words "free trade" were ever sacred, brooded darkly over this. In the end, he decided to chastise Howell further by having him dropped from the shortlist of those being considered for ambassadorial appointments.

Howell, he thought, was a good man. But obviously a troublemaker.

12

Arthur Hornbill.

Arthur Devies Hornbill loathed the World Trade Center.

Specifically, he hated his quarters at Six World Trade Center, where DIA leased a series of glaringly fluorescent offices for its New York–based activities.

Hornbill regarded such places as a plague visited upon the land, and the carriers of it modern architects. Such persons, he contended, were mere jumped-up engineers, no more architects than housepainters were artists. What flimsy inspiration they possessed was, in Hornbill's opinion, filched from B. F. Skinner, architect of the Skinner Box. No self-respecting human nor self-respecting rodent would ever willingly live or work in such a container, he maintained.

Which was why Arthur Hornbill was seldom seen at his own office. And why, when Pretorius called him for a meeting, Hornbill suggested the University Club.

Looming like a lost Florentine palace amid the mercantile glitz of Fifth Avenue, Hornbill's club echoed the era of J. P. Morgan, August Belmont, Diamond Jim Brady, Cornelius Vanderbilt, John D. Rockefeller, and Andrew Carnegie.

It stood in disapproving contrast to the glitter of Trump Tower, Museum Tower, and Olympic Tower and all the other elevated boxes that styled themselves towers, as anomalous as a coach-and-four in a 7-Eleven parking lot.

The University Club suited Hornbill admirably, for Hornbill was an anomaly as well.

Hornbill had been blooded in the U.S. Counter Intelligence Corps during World War II, then progressed through CIG[1] and CIA before finally being installed in McNamara's Defense Intelligence Agency. All along, he'd avoided being tagged with titles. He considered it an unnecessary conceit, an encumbrance to one in his line of work.

Despite having once served under Hornbill in an extremely dangerous mission, Pretorius was never able to determine Hornbill's exact rank within the DIA. Nor, in fact, were many of the people working directly or indirectly for the man himself.

The fact was, Hornbill had no title in the accepted sense. He was highly salaried, reported to no one but the director, and served as a roving senior officer without brief.

But it was rumored that Arthur Hornbill was one of the three or four most powerful men in the intelligence community, and bureaucrats were known to tread lightly around him. More than any other individual, Hornbill might know some of the missing pieces in the mystery surrounding Mathieson's death.

Hurrying along Fifth Avenue toward Hornbill's club, Pretorius was amazed at the number of men wearing trenchcoats. It resembled the main route to the Battle of the

---

[1]Central Intelligence Group, immediate precedecessor of the Central Intelligence Agency.

Marne, or a street filled with foreign correspondents. He passed several "Going Out of Business, Everything Must Go" signs on overlit electronics stores, darkly saturnine, salesmen lurking sharklike within.

Finally he reached the club and turned right on Fifty-fourth Street to enter the foyer.

"Michael, old thing," Hornbill boomed at Pretorius, shaking his hand with enthusiasm. "God's trousers, but you look fit. Things going well? Getting in some sailing, are you?"

Pretorius shook Hornbill's hand vigorously. "Couldn't be better, Arthur. It's good to see you." He stood back, eyeing the corpulent Hornbill. "Diet going well, I see."

Hornbill glanced down at his girth. "I'm just a man who can't say no. Must go back to some genetic survival instinct, I suppose. Keeping fully fueled at all times, that sort of thing. But tell me, how's the fair Susannah? Still keeping you in game pies and rice puddings?"

"She's keeping me well fed; *too* well fed. But I can't complain," returned Pretorius.

"Well, can't say you don't deserve the good life. Especially after what you've been through. Come in, come in."

Giving Pretorius a quick tour, Hornbill conducted him into the two-story-tall Reading Room. The capacious room could accommodate over five hundred men, as it often had in the past—including the tumultuous day in the late eighties on which its members voted to accept members of the opposite sex. ("After all, we're not living in the nineteenth century," one advocate said. "Oh?" retorted an opposing member, "And if we're not, whose fault is it?")

At the moment, no more than a dozen or so members were ensconced in sagging library chairs arranged artlessly around the great room, reading their newspapers, or having their noonday snoozes.

"Every so often," confided Hornbill, "a porter comes by and checks the dates on the papers, to see if they're really only sleeping."

"Pretty amazing," Pretorius remarked. "This place looks more like something in London in the nineteenth century, instead of New York in the twentieth."

Hornbill laughed. "Well, once upon a time, New York

had a bit more style than it does now. The clubhouse goes back to 1898, to McKim, Mead, and White. Mostly McKim." The two men entered the gleaming glass and mahogany cab of one of the club's elevators. Hornbill punched seven.

"Stanford White was the more colorful of the partners," he continued, "so now just about any New York building designed by the firm is invariably accused of being single-handedly created by White, with the exception of our edifice, which staunchly attributes itself to McKim. Although White did stain those big foyer columns with tobacco juice, to harmonize with the marble walls."

"White, Stanford White," mused Pretorius as they stepped out at the seventh floor. "Didn't he get shot by somebody's husband?"

Hornbill beamed as if at a prize student. "Yes, absolutely. Evelyn Nesbitt, her name was. White had done a sculpture of her as a sort of nude weathervane, which he then placed atop the old Madison Square Garden. Ticked off the girl's husband no end. Caught up with White at a dinner there— singularly appropriate venue—and shot him dead. Two please, Mr. K. Smoking."

The club's dining-room manager, a sartorially resplendent Israeli in his early sixties, saw to their seating with a flourish, and placed Hornbill's own jar of Colman's mustard at the table. Hornbill was obviously a fixture at the club, and many of the members nodded to him as they made their way over to a small table by a window.

Pretorius looked around the enormous room, three stories tall, paneled in oak with detailed carving. "Fairly dramatic days, they seem to have been," he observed.

"Indeed they were," agreed Hornbill. "People simply seem to have no sense of drama these days. But tell me, Michael, what brings you to our fair shores this time?"

"Some personal things, settling some business. It's one of those I wanted to talk with you about."

"Really?" Hornbill's tufted eyebrows arched quizzically as he attempted to ignite the much-charred bowl of his pipe, a churchwardenlike briar that gave him an eighteenth-century appearance. After several Vesuvian eruptions, Hornbill finally got the thing started, and leaned back to listen.

"Well," said Hornbill, pausing, making small *pock* sounds with his pipe. "If there's anything I can do to help, just sing out. We owe you one or two, especially after that last bit."

Pretorius shifted uncomfortably in his chair. "That's kind of you to offer, Arthur. By the way, how goes the Job?"

"Passing fair, passing fair. Nothing really changes, you know. Even after we cleaned all the jetsam out, we've still got politics. Endemic to the trade, you know. At least, thank God, we seemed to have plugged up all our little holes." *Pock pock pock.* A wreath of smoke floated lazily upward to join the ceiling's cloud mural as Hornbill watched its progress.

Pretorius remembered all too well the operation that had purged the CIA of penetration agents, and almost cost him his own life. Hornbill had drawn him into what had proved to be the U.S.'s most ambitious disinformation program: a successful attempt to make the Soviets believe a new form of Stealth bomber would be the new lynchpin of American strategy.

The Soviets, to counter this supposed threat, diverted even more of their inflated military budget to radically upgrade their radar defenses. A decision that, in the end, cost the Soviets billions and helped shatter an already fragile economy.

Pretorius had been used as a sort of Trojan horse, programmed with spurious engineering data. He'd been delivered into the Soviets' hands, and was interrogated at a supersecret KGB facility within the United States, narrowly escaping with his life.

He'd learned a lot about himself then. And he'd found an inner strength he'd not known before, even in his days running agents across the DDR² border.

"Coldwell still running the show?" asked Pretorius, his attention returning to the moment.

"Ah, yes. Coldwell," smiled Hornbill. "I'm pleased to say he's the best DCI we've had since Helms. And the president actually *listens* to him. Can you imagine? His Holiness listening to a mere *mortal?*"

The dining-room captain placed menus before them, and

²Deutsche Demokratische Republik, or East Germany.

Pretorius smiled. The incumbent president was known to Washington insiders as a supreme egotist. One congressman had even suggested a bill to cement over the Potomac, in case the Chief would someday attempt to walk on it and drown in the process.

"Sounds as if things are ticking over pretty well, then," observed Pretorius.

Hornbill nodded. "Best thing is, now we've gotten things pretty well coordinated. Coldwell's a real DCI, taken all the intelligence services in hand, much like John McCone. Now we're really making some progress. Lots less back-biting. Still think we should have just one service, though. Make things simpler still. But Michael," said Hornbill, interrupting himself, "you haven't come here to discuss the fine points of my employment, have you?"

"No, Arthur. I've got a couple of pieces of a puzzle. And if it doesn't open up something you'd rather keep contained, I'd like some answers."

"Fire away, old friend, fire away."

"You knew Phil Mathieson."

A frown. Then a blank, unrevealing façade. "I knew young Mathieson, yes. Lots of promise. Great pity. You went to school together, as I recall."

"We did. We kept in touch a little over the years, but the business keeps you from, well, you know—"

"I know. No friends, no problems."

"Arthur, was he iced?" A pause. Pretorius tried to read the older officer's face. Unfathomable.

Hornbill regarded Pretorius with an unflinching stare. "You don't have a need to know," he finally offered.

"Then he was."

"You're assuming. Never assume."

"You're thinking, Arthur. You're thinking, Does he have the *right* to know. Not just the need."

"You're a pain in the ass, Michael. Anyone ever mention that before, in your young and tactless life?"

"Only you, and as I recall, you regarded it as a cardinal virtue."

"Um." Hornbill drew deeply on the pipe. He shifted in his chair, and pulled down the vest of his tweed suit, always a sign of discomfort. Forces were warring within Hornbill's brain; he was evidently making up his mind about something. Pretorius waited him out.

"Well." *Pock pock pock.* "I suppose you've got the right. But don't get involved, Michael. Stick to your own good life in Devon, with the fair Susannah. It's our affair. And not your own." Hornbill's glance flicked down to the street outside, where the crowds were hurrying, it seemed, in a perpetual state of lateness.

Pretorius waited for the big man to begin. After staring out the window a minute or so as he marshaled his thoughts, Hornbill spoke.

"Lots of unanswered questions here. Lots of worrisome details. Such as—why does a man with so promising a future suddenly decide to square the circle? Why does a man who abhorred even alcohol suddenly decide to take up heroin? You know there wasn't a track on his arm over a week old."

Pretorius watched Hornbill carefully.

"And why does a man do himself in, in that particular way. Mathieson had access to any number of things to make it easy, less painful, less—messy. Why do a nosedive into a Vienna sidewalk?"

Hornbill seemed lost in thought, working his way through questions that seemed on the surface to have no answers. Worse, that seemed to have no edges he could pry up to get some kind of intellectual leverage. Pretorius felt the older officer's frustration, almost a palpable thing.

"What's behind it, Arthur? You've got to have *some* idea, some suspicions."

Hornbill looked at him oddly, as if suddenly discovering him there. "That's just it, old friend. Not an earthly. Not a clue. Not a particle."

"Was he involved in anything big, anything that would've made him—inconvenient?"

"No, nothing. Things were all quiet on the Eastern front. Oh, the usual business, of course. Bits and pieces of Warsaw Pact stuff. One of our own embassy staff being caught with a fairly sticky lady. But nothing out of the ordinary, nothing he hadn't handled a hundred times before. And in most of it, he was pretty far removed. He'd gotten to be very senior, you know. In line for a rather large plum back home, once he'd finished this tour."

"Like what?" Pretorius, seizing on the one piece of unusual information.

"Can't really say," returned Hornbill. "Irrelevant now, anyway."

"But could it have anything to do with his death?"

"Again, can't say." Hornbill was stonewalling Pretorius. Pretorius glowered.

"Well, don't look like that, old friend," Hornbill grumbled. "Isn't as if you were on the Job, you know."

"Arthur, somebody's got his mother's apartment bugged. First-class job. Can you look into it? If it's a legitimate Agency investigation, I'll back off. But something's up. Something that stinks."

Hornbill regarded Pretorius with his owlish, incurious stare, a look that with less experienced recipients would be enough to unnerve. But Pretorius merely stared back.

Hornbill, after an eternity of puffing on the pipe, finally spoke. "You know, of course, that even if I had some real answers, I certainly wouldn't be at liberty to tell you."

"I know."

"What is it you really want, then?"

"The obvious. If it's not kosher, I want to know."

"And precisely *why* should you know?"

"Because he was my friend." A level, steady stare.

Hornbill put down the pipe and spread his fingers. "But, my dear Michael, surely you know that's no reason."

"Arthur, look," Pretorius said in exasperation. "I've got a personal interest in this. I've got to *know,* because—well, because I owe both Mathieson and his mother that. I'll cooperate and keep quiet if the Agency just puts me in the picture, whichever way it falls. That's all I want."

"Certain that's all you want?"

Pretorius smiled deprecatingly. "I'm not looking to get back in the business, if that's what you mean."

"That's part of it, and I'm glad to hear it. But the trade doesn't take kindly to former spooks intruding on our sacred turf. Especially when it concerns the rather sensitive death of a senior officer."

"So what are you telling me, Arthur?"

"I'm telling you there's a rumor around that the IG's people are following up on."

Pretorius looked up sharply. "Rumor? About what?"

Hornbill leaned closer. "You didn't hear it here. But the story goes that your friend Phillip had a few too many close dealings with the folks from Dzerzhinski Square."

"Don't be ridiculous. I mean, everybody in the business has had talks at one time or another with the KGB. It's part of doing business in Europe. They tell us a few things, we tell them, we move things along. But if you're telling me they had their hooks into Phil Mathieson, well, that's—"

Hornbill tapped Pretorius' arm softly. "I'm not *saying* that, dear chap. But there are people, some normally reliable people, who *are* saying that. And the IG's bloodhounds have to check it out. That's all."

"What's the source?"

"Not our people."

Pretorius looked thunderstruck. "The *Russians?* They're hearing it from the Russians?"

Hornbill simply stared at Pretorius impassively.

Pretorius slumped back in his chair. "Jesus," he said. "I can't believe it. Not Phil Mathieson. He was—"

"Lots of people thought the world of Kim Philby, Michael. Including Jim Angleton, when he and Philby were in D.C."

"Sorry, Arthur." Pretorius shook his head. "This one just won't wash. No way. There's something else going on here. Something that Phil was into, something he never finished. Something that finished him instead."

Hornbill watched Pretorius carefully. "You're starting to get too involved, Michael. Back off. You don't *need* this in your life, you know. Leave it to the pros."

Pretorius made a face. "Leave it to the IG's office? Come *on*, Arthur. You know what they are. Leave it to them and they'll have everybody thinking Phil Mathieson was Beria's bastard son."

"Look here, Michael. Nobody's out to blacken Phillip Mathieson's memory. I'll see just what they've got, and if it's anything serious, well, I'll expect you to call it quits. If it's unfounded, or just somebody's idea of a witch hunt, then I'll get Coldwell to put a damper on things. Fair enough?"

Pretorius nodded. "Fair enough, Arthur."

"But," continued Hornbill, leveling a finger at Pretorius,

"You'd best hand over whatever you pick up, if it's anything relevant to Mathieson. Don't think about bargaining. The people looking into this play rough. Even with friends. I might even say *especially* with friends."

A silence. Pretorius looked out the great window onto West 54th Street. "All right. I'll call you later to see what you turn up."

"Don't get drawn into this, Michael. You're well out of things now. And you ought to keep it that way. Now let's order some food," suggested Hornbill pointedly, signaling an end to the discussion.

The man attempting to follow Pretorius into the University Club had been politely but firmly rebuffed by the alert porter, who had a sixth sense for identifying Those Who Belonged and Those Who Did Not.

The would-be intruder, reluctant to show his identification, instead waited on the sidewalk across and down the street until Pretorius finally emerged.

As the man began following his quarry, he failed to observe a brooding, corpulent figure watching them both from the Club's draperied windows.

13

Acceleration.

In soundless space, the eye raced in its arc. Two hundred miles below, humanity pulsed, worked, deceived, unaware of the eye noting its activities.

Three days earlier, COMIREX[1] voted to probe certain facilities which, according to the eye's previous observations, were unusually active only at night, and then only when cloud cover was present.

[1]Committee on Imagery Requirements and Exploitation, responsible directly to the U.S. National Foreign Intelligence Board.

War games were out of the question. The activity indicated either a treaty violation or worse: clandestine preparation for a nuclear exchange.

COMIREX needed evidence to present to the National Foreign Intelligence Board. The NFIB would then make its recommendation to the National Security Council and the president. On several other occasions, with intelligence product less sensitive than this, we let the Soviets know of our surveillance and evidence, and the Soviets either backed down or reduced the level of their activities.

But this was different. And so different measures were in order.

The eye was directed to orbit lower and concentrate on certain areas. This was no easy task, for a great deal of programming was necessary to alter LACROSSE's path. In the end, considering the urgency, only minor adjustments were made to the original program, in the hope that sideways-looking radar, although far from the targets, would be able to pick up enough to determine if other forms of reconnaissance would be needed.

It appeared the Soviet RVS (*Raketnyye Voyska Strategicheskovo Naznacheniya,* Strategic Rocket Forces) was setting up for something big. Something short of a full alert. More than 300 of the RVS's 1,398 missile silos were showing activity above the norm. In those installations, the newer SS-25s were replacing the SS-11s and SS-13s at an accelerating pace.

The V-VS (*Voyyoenno-Vozdushnyye Sily,* Soviet Air Force) was also busy. Virtually all reconnaissance aircraft—including 170 MiG-25 Foxbats, 50 MiG-21 Fishbed Hs, 130 Yak-28 Brewer Ds, 170 Sukhoi-17 Fitter Hs and Ks, and 20 of the sleek Sukhoi-24 Fencer Ds—were either on standby or active patrol. The balance seemed delicate. Just enough to monitor intrusions of air space on a large scale. But not enough to signal intention of active aggression to U.S. observers.

The Soviet aircraft carrier *Tbilisi,* largest warship built by any nation since World War II, was observed in the Black Sea with a full complement of sixty aircraft. A complement of Su-25 UT Frogfoot light attack aircraft was noted on her deck, as were a number of MiG-27s and Su-27s.

At Aleksandrovsk-Sakhalinskiy on Sakhalin, more sub-marines than ever were docked. Night loading crews were swarming over the bloated black boats. Only the smallest of working lights were used.

Deep within the bowels of one of these, unseen by the spy satellite soaring overhead, Lieutenant Vyacheslav Aleksandrovich Gostev nursed his coffee. Both hands gratefully cradled the thick ceramic mug, absorbing the warmth. Gostev's bloodshot eyes glared at the bulkhead of the officer's mess as the sounds of the loading reverberated achingly through the boat.

Gostev was not happy. Gostev was, at the moment, attempting to survive a hangover of epic, soul-staggering proportions.

Something weird about the whole damn thing, he managed to observe to himself. *Whole fucking base busy as beetles in a potato bin. But only at night, and only in bad weather, under cloud cover.* They had not been placed on alert status, yet the emphasis on speed was undeniable.

His Delta III–class SSBN had come in from the Sea of Okhotsk five days earlier. And every day, the officers and crews had liberty, at least such liberty as the port of Aleksandrovsk could offer. At six o'clock, drunk or not, everybody had to be back, primed with thick black *Turetskoye* coffee, to bear a hand with the missiles.

The big SS-18 MIRV-capable missiles had all been removed so heavier retaining gear could be installed. Tests had recently revealed too much play in the cradles of the lethal cylinders. Welders spewed rooster-tails of sparks throughout the boat. The sour hollow clang of metal against metal rang again and again, and now and then a dull *whump* was heard as each of the missiles was restored to its rightful place. All these served only to underscore the torment of Lieutenant Gostev.

The shipyard workmen had also been installing various quieting devices in his boat, part of a program that began at the same time as the 11th Five-Year Plan. A program made possible through spies in the dazzlingly trusting American Navy: Whitworth and the father and son team of the Walkers.

In the next berth, one of the three new Delta IV boats was

snugged in its slip with its lethal cargo of 16 SS-N-23 SLBNs. Enough to incinerate the West Coast of the United States.

Next to that, an Akula-class torpedo attack submarine was being fitted out with the new Type 65 wake-following torpedoes. Over twenty-eight feet long, these behemoths could knife through the water at over thirty knots. And they could suddenly appear, slicing directly toward your hull, from well over fifty kilometers away.

On the base itself, behind the large windows of the administrative offices, a small, almost frail figure peered out at the activity in the yards below. The eyes squinted in pleasure behind the bottle-bottom–thick lenses which were his trademark, and which caused his staff to call him, when well out of earshot, The Owl.

No vestige of a smile was ever known to distort the razor-straight seam of the lips. But his subordinates knew a certain glint in the eyes indicated The Owl was pleased.

As with all subordinates, they also knew which events were most likely to produce that effect. When operations were functioning in flawless order. When someone was being particularly humiliated. Or when someone was showing him the cringing deference The Owl felt was due his rank and position.

All these things pleased The Owl, whose true name was Vsevolod Mikhailovich Petrosyants, and whose rank was that of a Colonel-general in the GRU. And tonight, General Petrosyants was particularly pleased, for the preparations were nearing completion. If the weather held one more night, he and his staff would be able to return to the Aquarium, to GRU headquarters.

Far overhead and many hundreds of miles off-axis, the eye controlled from the Big Blue Cube in California continued in its arc. Sakhalin Island, being too far off its original orbit, had not presented an optimal imaging target. Still, even with this disadvantage, it was enough to indicate the Aleksandrovsk-Sakhalinskiy sub pens were far more active than they'd ever been.

But what was the nature of the activity? Which types of missiles, and which classes of submarines were involved? To the eye's controllers in the Blue Cube, it was clear that other, more vulnerable means of reconnaissance might have to be used.

The eye, having done its best over Siberia, continued with its labors. In less than thirty minutes, it would be furnishing White Sands with images of Cuban airfields.

General S. Symington Felker of the National Security Council felt for where the phone should be but wasn't, knocked over the chilled remnants of a cup of Sleepytime tea, finally found the lamp cord and the switch located on it, and flicked on the retina-scorching light.

The phone revealed itself on the floor where he'd placed it before going to bed. By the fourth ring, the general had the receiver grasped in his stubby fingers and was struggling to sit upright.

"Felker," he managed to growl.

The voice at the other end was terse, respectful, exacting in its description. Felker, listening hard, arranged the pillows behind his back for maximum comfort. As the voice continued, the general felt a flush slowly rise from his lower back to his forehead.

He asked two questions. The voice at the other end answered these accurately, professionally. Felker blinked at the bedside clock, estimating how long it would take to get showered, shaved, and into uniform.

"Have the car downstairs at 0400 hours." Felker spoke in the monotone of those accustomed to command. "Tell Avilez, Pera, and Price to meet me there. Hold all information until everyone—repeat, *everyone* on the team—is there. I want zero speculation. And I want a phone patch into Signorovich at NSA,[2] ready and waiting. Got it?"

The general replaced the receiver and stood up, stretching. *Well,* he thought. *This is what they pay you for, soldier. This is why they hand out the little brass stars.*

Still, it was at least five minutes under the shower before the fear began to subside and Felker once again was fully in command of his thoughts.

---

[2]National Security Agency at Fort George G. Meade, Maryland. Responsible for signals intelligence collection and analysis. Known to its intimates as SIGINT (Signals Intelligence) City.

14

Kernersville.

You've got to try it, just once, the spectral figure beside him urged. *But it's so far down,* he heard his own voice say in strangled tones.

Nonsense, the other scoffed. *It's really very easy. And safe. You just have to know how to do it.*

As he said this, Phillip Mathieson smiled, his head a rotted skull, patches of skin and matted brown hair clinging to splintered brownish bone. And with a wave of his hand, the specter leaped from the tower.

Mathieson seemed to float downward, downward forever, gently, gracefully spiraling before coming to rest, standing upright at the base of the tower.

Do you see? Do you see now, how easy it is? You can do it, the figure shouted up. *You can do it.*

No, I can't—I can't—and Pretorius suddenly felt a cold hand on his shoulder, pushing, pushing.

He was on the edge of screaming when a gently insistent voice said, "Would you put your seat in the full upright position, sir? We're getting ready to land."

Pretorius rubbed his hand over his face. "Sir?" insisted the stewardess, her blonde hair cut in a short Dutch-boy style, red lips perfect in a catlike amused smile, teeth impossibly white.

"Right," an embarrassed Pretorius finally said, pressing the button that brought the seat forward.

The landing gear ground down with the sound that, to Pretorius, always seemed to signal the aircraft's underside being shredded. He leaned forward uneasily, looking out the window, down to the rich red Piedmont earth and the green fields of tobacco the earth yielded to those who worked it.

Somewhere down there, close to the airport, was his grandfather's farm. Unlike Pretorius' parents' place in up-state New York, his grandfather's had been a year-round working farm.

It was a place for family gatherings, and for teaching young Pretoriuses values that would last forever.

His grandfather had been a Quaker. In apparent contradiction, he enjoyed good homemade whiskey, used tobacco, swore fluently when provoked, and furnished four sons for the army's sole and exclusive use in World War II, and a fifth son, Michael's father, to the OSS.[1]

The patriarchal Joseph Arlindo Pretorius had been against legally sanctioned violence and killing since the day when, as a boy in the 1880s, he'd witnessed a hanging on the hill in Greensboro. Yet he could see the necessity of defending country and family against evil, even if it took violence to counter violence.

Joe Pretorius had been a friend to everyone. He was even known to heal burns, a not inconsiderable talent in an age of wood fires and kerosene lanterns. Known by locals as "wishing out fire," this involved reading a certain passage of scripture in the presence of the afflicted person, after which the pain would immediately stop, and the skin begin to heal.

For nearly a century, the farm had been the center from which the Pretoriuses came, and to which they would inevitably return.

But those years and those days were now over. They'd been over, in truth, for the ten years since Joseph Pretorius had died.

Over the years, pieces of the farm had been sold off or given to sons and daughters. Now only ninety-seven acres were left. Pretorius inherited these and the old house from his father, but he'd been reluctant to sell. The memories were long and deep, as much a part of him as the shape of his hands, or the sound of his own voice.

Pretorius entered the terminal and found the Avis counter. After signing and initialing the usual forms, he picked up a big Chevy and swerved out of the airport onto the new four-lane county highway.

The drive into Greensboro took about twenty-five minutes. Only the pine trees seemed familiar; all else was changed, formatted into the easily replicated landscape that

[1]Office of Strategic Services; in some ways, the forerunner of the CIA's covert action section.

was now most of America. The Burger Kings, Mobils, Kentucky Frieds, Radio Shacks, Pizza Huts, and J C Penneys.

The firm of lawyers inhabited a building resembling a greenhouse with a glandular dysfunction. An inner atrium, balconies spilling over with the tendrils of every conceivable jungle plant, framed a three-story waterfall. The noise of the water masked the clacking of people quick-marching across the marble floor, scurrying for the eight elevators that served the tower.

The lawyers, three middle-aged men and a young woman described as a paralegal, greeted him enthusiastically. *It must be an exceptionally slow day,* thought Pretorius, *for it to take four legals, para or otherwise, to accomplish a thing so simple as this.*

They were pleased Pretorius had finally decided to settle the business about the farm. Said they could get a good price. Said developers were working up the land up next door for an industrial park, cementing over the soil with parking lots and office buildings. No time like the present, they said. The time of farms like his grandfather's was long over, and in some ways it was good he'd held on to it this long. Prices are up, they said, but you never know. You never know.

Pretorius felt torn about putting the final strokes to the power of attorney, to letting them sell the farm. He knew he'd never live there, of course. Nobody in his family had anything to do with farming tobacco now. But going back a hundred, a hundred fifty years, all his people had been tobacco people. And that, he supposed, was what tugged at the corners of his conscience.

He finished the flurry of papers, shook hands with the still-smiling attorneys, and let himself be displayed in the glass elevator as it plummeted soundlessly down twelve stories.

Back in the car, driving north, his thoughts kept drifting more and more to the old farm. He hadn't seen the old place in—what was it?—in nearly eleven years. A year before his grandfather died.

His fingers flexed on the steering wheel. He looked in the rearview mirror, scanning for nothing in particular. He adjusted his seat, switched from one radio station to another. Checked the fuel gauge. The oil. The water temperature.

Finally, unable to do anything but what his subconscious was telling him, Pretorius took the next exit off the interstate and, tracing his way over the old back roads partly by instinct, partly by memories, let himself find the sign marked Pleasant Ridge Road.

Turning onto it, he suddenly found himself looking down a broad four-lane concrete highway, clean and shining in the sun.

Jesus, he thought. *This used to be a clay road, beer cans and weeds marking the shoulders.* He could remember the time there'd been more tractor and mule tracks than car tracks.

The highway passed a new shopping center, two gas stations, a 7-Eleven, and finally Pretorius recognized what had once been Lee Huffine's dairy farm, now looking vaguely self-conscious in its new *persona* as the Rolling Meadows Golf and Tennis Club, Members Only.

He made a right turn onto another new road, a road he had once known well. This one had always been red dust in the summer, and red ruts rimmed with ice in winter, and now it was black asphalt, the rich red earth at last unmoving, unchanging, resting just beneath. He looked along the left for the familiar profile of the old house. And then, finally recognizing it, slowed.

He found the entrance, now screened with waving weeds, and turned into the old driveway.

At first the house seemed unchanged. But as he got closer, he saw the infection of neglect. Decay was evident, even omnipresent. Aging gray clapboard revealed itself beneath flayed strips of once-white paint.

He parked the car in the tall grass. To the left of the house towered the big pecan tree where he and his grandfather held counsel throughout his childhood. On the other side, just outside the kitchen window, his grandmother's damson plum tree prospered still, bearing fruit for the birds, mice, and squirrels who were now sole protectors of the house.

As he walked up the steps, he saw two chains fixed to the slat-board ceiling to the right, chains that once resisted a small boy's most determined porch-swing trajectories. In front, the ravaged screen door sagged from a single rusted hinge. The door beyond yawned open, its top panel dagger-shards of shattered glass. The darkened hall beyond stretched to a rectangle of light, the doorway to the back porch.

Floorboards missing. Scraps of paper, beer cans, smashed and rusted kerosene lamp lying on its side. The wind, fluttering a reprint of a minister's radio message spoken Christmas Eve, 1937, on the Mutual Network.

To the left, his grandparents' room. The sheet-metal stove of cozying warmth in the winters. The bare springs of his grandfather's big bed, set at right angles to the frame of his grandmother's tiny one. His grandfather had stood six feet two inches; his grandmother, just under five feet. Curvature of the spine had bowed her even more than the farm work, and the scale of her tiny bed seemed like a child's.

The parlor on the right. A severe Victorian room with a fireplace that had never known a stove, and the brown horsehair sofa that prickled the neck of a ten-year-old Michael Pretorius.

Here, when they died, the Pretoriuses were presented in their caskets to silent shuffling files of friends and family. All except his grandfather, who outlasted most of them and quit the club gently in a Greensboro nursing home at the age of 105.

The closet under the stairs was empty. Here had hung all the hunting jackets with their big flap pockets filled with shotshells, their fabric filled with the fine warm smell of tobacco and good hunting dogs. And here his grandfather had kept the little .22 single-shot rifle, a top-loader, with the bolt you pulled back and swung up to discover the chamber into which you would carefully edge the cartridge.

He remembered the way the brilliant little brass shell felt when he inserted it, before he swung the housing back down again to snap shut with a satisfying *snick*. He could smell the gun oil still, and the polish he used to rub into the scarred walnut stock to make it shine.

Pretorius learned to shoot with the .22 out back of the barn, plinking at rusted cans. When his grandfather judged him ready, he'd gone hunting with his dad and his uncles Jabe, Woody, Max, and Charlie, bringing back squirrel and rabbit which his grandmother would transform into supper.

Spending so much of his childhood on the farm, Pretorius thought of guns as tools, nothing more mysterious than a hammer, or a tractor. He wondered at city people's fascination with guns, and their horror of them. But the way guns were used in a big city, where they were only associated with criminals or police, could explain the cold unreasoning fear, the shamanism attached to them there.

On the farm in those days, you were either a good shot or you were a vegetarian. His uncles had been good shots. And Pretorius discovered he owned a natural eye for it, one of the things that made him attractive to the people at ONI (Office of Naval Intelligence) and DIA.

Down the hall to the right he came to the door to the dining room. Like the rest of the house, the dining room had horizontal slat wood walls, pale green. A fly-specked reproduction painting of a square-rigger under full sail hung above a massive dark sideboard. The big dining table was gone now, auctioned off by lawyers or carted off by thieves.

A doorway led into the tiny kitchen where his grandmother cooked for twelve or more on the green and white Kenmore wood-burning stove. He closed his eyes and could smell the wood smoke, the crisp bacon frying, the half-moon fruit pies stacked and cooling on speckled blue tin plates.

As Michael Pretorius stood alone in the shattered house, the ghosts of faraway time began to gather, and their sights and sounds and smells focused and became reality.

In the stillness of the summer noon, the old man and the boy sat beneath the pecan tree. The old man wore much-laundered coveralls over a white shirt buttoned up to the neck. A rakishly tilted, battered fedora belied the dignity of his years.

He and the boy cracked and ate the dusky-flavored pecans dotting the grass around them, and discussed matters of great import: squirrel hunting, their upcoming trip to Mattie Williams' General Store, the old gray Ford-Ferguson tractor, the delicate health of the mule named MacArthur, the ineffable flavor of half-moon pies.

Talking with the old man, the boy first experienced the feeling he would always know as ethereal, and mystical, yet somehow more sharply real than anything touchable. It would support him through his darkest, most tormented times. It would give him strength when no other source seemed near.

From time to time, catbirds' cries pierced the near silence, shrilling up from the thickets near the road. On the road itself, an occasional plume of red dust betrayed the passing of a pickup truck or car.

The boy's grandmother had gotten him up early to help pluck eggs from beneath the protesting guinea hens, pour grain into the mules' troughs in the hay-scented mustiness of the barn, and slosh swill into the galvanized tub out by the hog pen.

Even at seven in the morning, the steaming Carolina sun sent trickles of sweat running down his narrow boy's back, and he felt light-headed lugging along the grain bucket, two-handed, behind his grandmother's tiny scurrying form.

It was good, now, to finally sit in the dry coolness of the shade with his grandfather, and reflect on the morning, and think about the rest of the day to come.

Tonight he and his cousin Donald would sit under the tin roof of the tobacco barn, keeping vigil on the burner curing the big leaves strung from sticks, crisscrossing the breath-snuffing hot interior. If it rained, as they hoped it might, the drops pelting the tin would produce a fine feeling of shelter and sanctuary.

To stave off hunger pangs (even after a dinner of Brunswick stew, fried country ham with red-eye gravy, black-eyed peas, cornbread, and half-moon pies all around), the boys would roll apples back in the flue pipe with a stick, roasting them to a succulent crumpled brown.

In the chill light of dawn, they'd wriggle out of their dew-dampened sleeping bags, and steal back to their beds in the warm and welcoming house where, in an hour or so, their grandmother would waken them once again.

Pretorius now stood still, very still in the little kitchen, looking out the window to the disintegrating tobacco barn. The tin roof had discolored to rust. A large piece had been whipped up by the wind, and was dangling, hanging like an aircraft's mangled rudder at a crash scene. Even a hundred yards away, he could see the tall weeds growing under the lean-to roof in front of the little barn, where he and his cousin Donald had spent their nightly vigils.

Well, hell, he thought. *All things die, even places, even homes like this one. The only things permanent are memories.* He walked back through the old house, avoiding holes in the rotted floor boards, and closed the ruined door.

The watchers were good. They also knew the subject was trained, and the surveillance important, and that if they gave him any indication of a tag, they'd be given the reading-out of their lives and an extremely nasty notation made in their records.

The subject had been in the abandoned house almost a half hour before they finally saw him leave and get in the rental car.

He didn't seem to be carrying anything into the place when he went in, and appeared to be carrying nothing when he came out. Still, if it had been a drop, whatever was picked up or left would likely be small.

One of the two men made a note to check out the ownership of the place through the county courthouse. They put the field glasses away.

As the subject passed them, they were wrestling a beat-up fifty gallon drum out of the back of their pickup truck, and laughing and wiping their hands on their overalls as if they were about to begin a long afternoon's work.

The Carolina sun was getting hotter as Pretorius drove north to Middleburg, Virginia, and to one Luther C. Beeson, Lieutenant General, United States Army, retired.

———————————————————————— 15

Broadlands.

Middleburg, Virginia, is blessed with rolling countryside, considerate weather, a modest portion of crime, and two uncommon groups of inhabitants:

Middleburg is home to some of the world's most valuable thoroughbred horses. It's also home to a small but tightly knit group of retired intelligence officers.

They're there because, quite frankly, spooks find it easier to be with other spooks. They know people who've never been in the trade have no idea what it and they are about.

Conversations between spooks are easy, almost intimate. Conversations between spooks and nonspooks tend to be less fluent, occasionally opaque. Even among friends.

For example, there are some stories you just don't tell to outsiders because either you can't for security reasons or you don't want to suddenly find people staring at you as if you had recently zoomed in from Mars.

Which is why spooks tend to congregate with spooks, even in retirement. And why Middleburg was the perfect spot for the September years of Luther Calhoun Beeson, Lieutenant General, U.S.A. (Ret.).

As a young light colonel at Langley years ago, Beeson spent his off-duty weekends hunting in the woods and fields around a small town named Tyson's Corner. At the time, it was ideal hunting territory. In the chill breath of fall, fields of frozen stubble yielded pheasants, grouse, rabbits, and deer. And it was close. A ten-minute drive from the Agency, and there you were, out in the fields with your Browning over-and-under.

But then one year the Washington Beltway slashed through the fields and woods of Tyson's Corner, gouging out the land in great chunks, replacing it with asphalt and concrete and a ceaseless stream of automobiles and trucks.

Because of this new-found convenience, many high-tech companies and consultants serving defense and intelligence found it tempting. Real-estate developers bought parcel after parcel from astonished farmers. Beeson, realizing the potential, bought a sizeable parcel of farmland early, selling when prices peaked.

He took his profits and bought Broadlands. It had been a plantation in its halcyon days, back before Union troops swept like a scythe through northern Virginia. Reduced by both Grant's and the decades' depredations to a moldering, tottering shell, Broadlands took nearly sixteen years of vacations and weekends before Beeson restored it to habitability.

The result was worthy of a general's retirement residence.
The drive was lined with age-old oaks standing sentinel,
leading to a circular driveway in front of a crisp white,
black-shuttered Greek Revival mansion. Rocking chairs
painted glossy black were positioned strategically along the
veranda. A man in starched civilian khakis sat motionless in
one of these, glaring at the car which had just boiled up his
driveway.

Beeson's eyes were steel gray, his crewcut machined from
the same metal. Walking across the gravel to the porch,
Pretorius was aware of the eyes' gun-barrel intensity.

"You're Pretorius," a parade-ground voice accused.
"Hornbill said you'd be coming whether I liked it or not."

Pretorius winced, then smiled. He'd not told Hornbill of
his intention of visiting Mathieson's former superior. *Arthur
still stays a step ahead,* he thought.

"Sorry to intrude, General," he said. "It's about Phil
Mathieson."

Beeson stood up from his seat, rising to his full six feet
four inches, and offered an oversized hand. "Glad to meet
you, Pretorius," he said in a friendly tone. "Arthur said you
helped him out a year or so back. Said you're not a typical
intel weenie."

"I didn't really help him out, General," returned
Pretorius, noting the strength of the other's grip. "It was a
little more complicated than that."

He noted the spit-and-polish condition of everything on
the porch. The paint, the planters brimming over with ivy,
the brass brightwork on the huge front door. Pretorius
looked hard into the gun-metal eyes. "I hoped you might
have the answers to a few questions about Phil. This isn't
official, as I guess you know. I was a close friend; we went
to school together."

Beeson looked at Pretorius curiously. "Happy to tell you
whatever I can, but it's not much. I was, well, sorry to hear
about Mathieson. Don't suppose you've heard the official
version, or even the real one. Or have you?"

"No, that's why I'm here. To put together some pieces,
and maybe figure out what really went on in his last few
weeks. Too many things don't add up."

Pacing back and forth agitatedly, Beeson rubbed his big

hand over the back of his neck and stared at the glistening paint on the porch floor. "You're right on the money there. Mathieson sure as hell wasn't the kind of guy to do what he did. Or do what they *say* he did."

"You knew Phil pretty well, then."

An intent look, then: "Well enough to consider him one of the best."

"Funny thing, he said the same about you."

Beeson smiled. "Phil Mathieson was, as usual, full of shit. Well, we might as well get comfortable before we get into this. I swear I get pestered more often now than when I was working. Let's go get us a drink."

"Sounds good to me," said Pretorius. "It's been a long drive." They went through the cool front hall of the house and turned into a splendid Adam-style dining room. There, on a mahogany sideboard, was a full bar. "Name it, odds are I've got it," the general said pleasantly.

"A good single malt would go down just right, General."

"Laphroiag, Glenmorangie, or Lagavulin?" inquired his host.

"Damn," said Pretorius, laughing. "Never thought I'd find Lagavulin in the wilds of Northern Virginia."

"It's been my experience that you find the very best things in the wilds of Northern Virginia," said Beeson, pouring with a rock-steady hand. "That's one of the reasons I decided to live here."

General Beeson poured himself a bourbon and branch-water, and the two men toasted each other. Each took the measure of the other across the top of his glass.

"Let's go sit out back, out by the granary," invited the general, leading the way. "More private."

Pretorius detected no other signs of life in the big house. Yet the place was well cared for, every wood surface either crisply painted or polished, all the furniture selected with the eye of an expert.

The granary had been, at one time, precisely that. But it had been converted into a pool house for one of the most imaginative swimming pools Pretorius had ever seen: a fifty-meter double swimming lane with irregular sides leading to a free-form pool, all edged with smoothed boulders, gentled with moss and ferns. The bottom of the pool was painted dark green, possibly even black. The effect was like something deep in the woods.

"Army must pay better than the navy," observed Pretorius dryly.

Beeson smiled, shaking his head. "Army doesn't pay shit, any more than the navy does. I got this through a little judicious off-duty swindling of real estate developers, and God, don't they deserve it."

He paused and looked sidelong at Pretorius. "But you're not here to talk about real estate. You want to know if your buddy decided on his own to try a half-gainer into a cement sidewalk."

Pretorius nodded, taking another sip.

The general leaned back and stretched. "Well, you know I haven't been with the Agency for some time. Retired a few years back, when the new guys took over the candy store. Different place. Different game. Hell, I'd had my innings.

"Some of the best times and some of the worst were in Nam. And Phil Mathieson got dropped right in the middle of it, right in my lap. I was a bird colonel then, running half the stuff out of Sixty Pasteur Street,[1] Cholon. He hadn't seen any action, just been sent to Fort Bragg, to Fayetteville for psyops, then out to Fort Huachuca for CI. He looked about twelve years old.

"I thought, 'Well, shit, here's another nice Yalie wants to play cowboy and will get gotten by the getters in about five seconds flat.' But he had this thing about him, this kind of tough thing inside, past the baby fat, past the rich-boy good looks.

"Now in Saigon we had all *kinds* of cowboys. Some of the guys, you know, figured they were out there to see just how bulletproof they really were. I mean, hell, it beat the marines or regular army. And the kind of deal we had going was pretty irresistible to some. You had your own hours, your own hootch, all the women you can screw, and the pay was *way* over anything they could've got in straight service.

"We got some pretty good people then, in those days. So I was kind of pissed off when they sent out this, this *kid.* You needed one extra baby-sitting job like you needed more

[1] Address of CIA headquarters in Saigon during Viet Nam War.

paperwork. His 201 looked good, though. Top marks from Huachuca. Colonel Dorfman put a heavy recommendation in.

"So I decided to throw him to the wolves, see what kind of shit he had going for him. If any. Those days, you had to find out fast who you could count, who you couldn't, and you had to do it fast. No second chances.

"We ran a drop into Laos, dropped Mathieson, two other people of ours, and four Nungs, a long-range patrol to go after this ammo dump on the Ho Chi Minh trails. He had to link up with some irregulars, go into NVA[2] turf.

"Now the NVA were really good in the jungle. The best. They could fucking *smell* where we were, and track us for days, waiting, just waiting, for you to doze off. Waiting for just one mistake. Just one." He held up a single stubby finger for emphasis and took another deep swallow of his bourbon.

"Mathieson, though, he had balls. Balls and stamina. Kept going right from the time they hit the LZ, second the slick set down, didn't sleep for fifty-six hours. Got to the depot, blew the *shit* out of it, greased maybe a dozen NVA, made his way back to the pickup point with both our people in one piece, and then, when he got back to Saigon, well that boy ripped up the *town.*"

Beeson leaned back in his chair and took a deep breath of the cool, clean Virginia air. "Then, about two days later, Mathieson's going down the stairs at Pasteur Street, and this gook throws this bundle of rags into the door just as Mathieson's hitting the last step.

"Gook's on a bicycle, Mathieson grabs the bundle, picks it up and lobs it like Doc Blanchard right at the gook's back, and the fucking thing detonates. Splatters Charlie all over the street. Mathieson doesn't break his stride, keeps walking right across the street, to that bar we used to hit, sits down and orders himself a nice cold San Miguel, cool as you please. Doesn't tell anybody about it. We found out from some French journalist, saw the whole damn thing.

"So you could kind of say Mathieson bought his ticket in with that one. Something had changed in him, too. He got that kind of light in his eyes, the kind you see people get in

[2]North Vietnamese Army.

the field. Like they find out something private about themselves, something central and individual, something they have to keep under wraps.

"I'd seen it happen before. I think each of us in our genes has got this *imprint,* this pattern of violent, fighting behavior that allowed our ancestors to survive, no matter what. So we can go up against saber-toothed tigers, Medes, Persians, Nazis, gooks, whatever. It just needs the right trigger, the right stimulus, to tap into it, and then *Bingo!*—you got yourself a top-rated, first-class, Sunday-go-to-meeting killer.

"Mathieson, I think, had his shit *exceptionally* close to the surface. It wasn't like having a short fuse, or being hotheaded. Nothing like that.

"It was just there, ready to be pushed. Like the button on a switchblade. Out it comes, cool and quick and sharp. And then back in. *Zzzzzzt.*

"So I knew I had an A-1 candidate there. Had the brains, had the control, had the instinct. I needed him. The Agency was leaning on me in lots of ways. I was stretched thin on men, and the politics going down were unbelievable. Every two or three weeks I'd get a tickler from the embassy. Langley was getting all kinds of shit from Senator Church and his pull-toys, all the bean counters on his staff, and we had to have some successes, something *visible,* for Christ's sake.

"We were also having a bitch of a time keeping ourselves funded. Like I told you, I was stretched thin, real thin. If it hadn't been for Air America and all the dope they were hauling, we might as well have folded up our tents. But we didn't. We didn't."

Beeson looked off toward the hills, over to right of the big barn, to where a rider was taking a fence with an enormous albino hunter, like a big white bird. His gun-barrel eyes snapped shut momentarily, then opened wide, as if fighting off sleep.

He looked at Pretorius as if discovering him there for the first time, closed his eyes again, and leaned back once more in the big chair, crossing his ankles.

The voice, when it began again, was a steady monotone, more deliberate. "We sent more poor bastards out on ops that didn't have a chance in hell of succeeding, just because some State Department prick would be visiting, or some congressman, and if the op went well, we'd pull in the politico, throw a party with the team, and make the visiting fireman feel he'd been part of it all.

"Charlie had these tunnels all around the northwest of Saigon, the Cu Chi tunnels. Two hundred fucking *miles* of tunnels, can you believe it? Used to piss us off something fierce. They had hospitals, they had ordnance workshops, kitchens, dormitories, the entire enchilada down there.

"They even stole a whole fucking ARVN[3] *tank* back in sixty-six, buried the fucker, tunneled around it and used it and its radio as a kind of command center. Perfect. Just beautiful. Got to admit Charlie had some kind of style, right?

"Well, Mathieson kind of took it as his personal mission to fuck up Charlie in those tunnels. He thought up all *kinds* of things, like he once got five or six old trucks, requisitioned them from the ARVN, ran vacuum-cleaner hosing from the exhausts down into the tunnels, poured carbon monoxide down there five, maybe six hours, until the trucks ran out of gas. Used to go down there alone, sometimes, with grenades and a sawed-off shotgun and a real good set of earplugs. Like a terrier going down after rats.

"What with all this, Mathieson got good, very good. And word got back to Langley. So every time we had a visiting VIP, they had us trot him out. They loved him. Good-looking kid, well-spoken, Groton, Yale, what could be bad?" Beeson rubbed a big hand over his grizzled crewcut and grinned, reflecting.

"Couple of times we scared shit out of the visitors, though. Mathieson thought it might be good to send this one senator up close to the Cambodian border, give him a real taste. Knew the senator had it in for us, was a buddy of old Frank Church's.

"Now you know it was one of our SR-71s that found out Charlie was using Cambodia for his hide-and-seek games. We got photos that practically let you read the serial numbers on their AKs. Still, Church and a lot of other people thought it was naughty to go in after the bastards. They'd

[3] Army of the Republic of Viet Nam.

rather we just wait around until they came back over the border in the middle of the fucking night to waste us.

"Well, on this run the team got in one hell of a firefight, rounds flying every which a way, and this senator was crapping himself. Then they found one of the ARVN colonels was running with Charlie, right there, in black pajamas, a guy they'd had drinks with in Saigon just two nights before. Senator couldn't fucking *believe* it. Shut him right up. Didn't make him a convert, but it shut him up real well."

Pretorius smiled at the gray-haired general. "So how did Mathieson come out of Nam? I only saw him a couple times after that, not for long either time."

Beeson took another pull on his bourbon and branch, and looked at Pretorius reflectively. "I guess you could say Phil Mathieson came out of Nam a whole lot tougher than he went in. It gave him steel. He was a real fighting machine by the end of his tour. Outstanding. Wish I'd had a dozen like him, before Nam and after."

Pretorius pressed the older man. "And after Nam? What was his next assignment?"

Beeson carefully placed his empty glass down on the patio stones. "Next he drew Salvador. Never been to Salvador, myself. But I knew guys there, same time as Mathieson.

"The Agency got him positioned as an instructor at the University, got him all kinds of refs, nobody on staff knew. He took over a network of about a dozen agents, though. The guy before him had been a little sloppy, and it turns out one of them was a double. Set him up real good, once, out at the airport.

"Mathieson, they say, had gone to pick up a girlfriend at the airport, some fashion designer from New York. He was waiting in the second-floor bar there, looking out at the runway and having himself a nice cold *Cerveza Pilsener*, when these two FMNLF[4] *pistoleros* come in. Mathieson makes them right away.

"One gets himself set over by the door, where he can cover the whole room, and the other walks right over to Mathieson, this newspaper in his right hand, and sits right down in

[4]Farabundo Marti National Liberation Front, the principal leftist guerilla organization.

front of him and gives him this great big shit-eating grin. Tells Mathieson he's got to come with him and his friend on account he's got him covered with his pistol inside the newspaper.

"Mathieson doesn't change his expression and just blows the guy away with this .45 Lightweight Commander he'd had out under the table when he first saw these two come in. Puts three rounds right in the guy's breadbasket, kicks over the table and puts two more into his friend who's still trying to figure what the fuck had gone wrong with their fiendishly clever strategically flawless plan.

"Of course, after that, he was blown, everybody knew he was Agency, but he decides to stay on anyway. Everybody in fucking Salvador knew he was ours, but he didn't care. Met with Carranza[5] in public, helped trained some of his men. Told the Agency if you wanted to catch bears, you had to let them know where the honey was.

"He got in all kinds of scrapes, but people kept bringing him righteous information, which he used well. But Langley didn't want to risk him too much more after that. They wanted him back for a while, to put him closer to the controls, let him soak up some of their Big Picture shit. You know.

"Helms, Bissell, Colby, hell, everybody loved the guy. He was their Golden Boy, could do no wrong. Only trouble was, he wanted to be back in the field. Missed it like a setter misses bird season. Kept his edge all the time, even through eighteen months at a desk in Langley, pushing papers with the best of them. Every weekend, he'd go down to the Farm on the James, put in time on the range, get shit kicked out of him by our pet Korean unarmed combat guy, and generally keep the edge.

"Good thing, too, because he was going to need it. Because the next assignment was his first in the Middle East. They sent him to Egypt, to help train Sadat's bodyguards. At least that was the *surface* mission. What he was really there to do was give Langley an eyeball assessment of Sadat himself, see what he was made of, tell us if we could count

[5]Colonel Nicolas Carranza, head of the Treasury Police, most feared of the Salvadoran security forces.

on him—and see just what in hell he was doing with the four billion dollars we'd tossed him for military and internal security assistance.

"Well, Sadat, as you know, got himself blown away. So much for internal security. Those guys came across the track at him, right into the reviewing stand. Bodyguards were looking every which way but where the assholes were coming from."

Beeson looked off into the middle distance, squinting. "You heard about the rest. Phil helped round them up, the Egyptians gave them life sentences, they escaped, and when the SSI[6] bozos finally got them all back—one way or another—they scooped up a top Jihad planner along with them. Cat named Khalid Bakhit. Real bad news, old Bakhit.

"Phil wasn't too big on Egyptians. Said Sadat was first-rate, but they hadn't had much civilization since the pyramids, and people without civilization tend to go bad fast. Said they'd had lots of practice at going bad, last couple thousand years." Beeson stood up and stretched, examining the contents of his glass, now nearly empty.

"When Phil finally pulled up stakes in Egypt, they brought him back home to Langley, where Casey gave him another tin medal and made him spend some time with some senators, some congressmen. You know. The kind that like to say they're really plugged *in*.

"Then, he got the shit assignment of all time. Lebanon. He knew he was blown there. Beats the shit outa me why he went ahead, knowing what he knew. Loyalty, I guess. The Agency had been home to him, had been his father, his I don't know what. So he went. He went."

Staring down at his shoes, the general spoke softly. "The kid had balls. More balls than anybody on this side of the Potomac, that's for sure. Phil Mathieson didn't rattle easily. He wasn't the kind to pull the plug. No sir. No way."

Pretorius took a long sip on his malt whiskey, waiting for the rest. Beeson looked at him oddly, and said, "You been in the business for some time, haven't you?"

"I was with DIA awhile back, ONI before. Live in En-

[6]Egyptian State Security Investigations Department.

gland now, just over to take care of some personal stuff when I stumbled into this thing."

"Well, you might think about stumbling right out, you know what's good for you. Phil didn't do himself in, and he sure as shit wasn't any junkie. Therefore—something big is going down, something even Phil couldn't handle. And if *he* couldn't, *you* sure as shit can't. Anyway, it's Agency business, and none of yours. You stick to whatever the hell it is you do in England."

Pretorius stared back at the grizzled giant. "Things are a little different. Somebody's trying to make it my business. And everybody else is trying to warn me off."

General Beeson took a long drink and smiled. "You're not by any chance free-lancing, are you?"

Pretorius shook his head. "I'm out. Been out some time."

"Then walk away. Just walk away."

"Too late for that. Phil's dead and the Agency isn't doing a goddamned thing about it, except maybe have the IG's bloodhounds try and prove he was a junkie and a sometime double."

"What makes you so sure?" A last sip, looking down at Pretorius, over the edge of the glass, speculating.

Pretorius stood up. "Same reason as you're sure. Plus a few little interruptions to my life recently. Guys watching me who haven't got any business watching me. But you know, too. You worked for them. What makes *you* sure?"

Beeson leaned close, gun-metal eyes boring straight into Pretorius' own. "Because I've fucking well *been* there before. I was there, in Nam, when we finally got back Tucker Gouglemann's body. Every bone broken. *I mean every fucking bone in his body.* They could've got him back from Charlie. I know. But no, the Agency hung him out to dry like they hung Mathieson out to dry.

"Nobody *gives* a shit, lad. Not now. Now, it's all a matter of efficiencies, of cost/benefit ratios. And right now, they're on to new business, buddy boy. That's why they want you out of it. You're getting to be a liability. If you didn't have Hornbill as your rabbi, you'd have been long gone by now."

The thought startled Pretorius. Possibly Beeson was right. He'd heard of stranger things happening in the middle of sensitive situations. And this thing *had* to be sensitive, what with all the surveillance, the bugging of Miranda Mathieson's apartment. "General," he began quietly, "did Phil Mathieson kill himself, or didn't he? Did the job finally get to him?"

Beeson spat accurately into the grass, just missing the edge of the patio stonework. "Hell, man, you know the answer to that one. Some guys were *born* for this kind of shit. He was one of them."

"So what happened in Vienna, General?" said Pretorius, studying the older man intently.

Luther Calhoun Beeson returned the stare, taking Pretorius' measure, weighing him as he must have weighed other men over the years. Men he'd been about to send into a thousand variations of purgatory in the cause of flag or friendship or a crazy mixture of both. Finally he spoke. "Well, if you're so damned determined to find out, you'd better let Phil tell you all about that himself."

And into Pretorius' lap he tossed a single audio cassette.

_____ 16

Phillip's Story.

Left alone in Beeson's granary, Pretorius punched the black plastic tab of the portable cassette player.

The tape began its steady spooling from one hub to the other. The voice of Phillip Mathieson—rasping, sardonic—issued through the speaker.

You hang around in this business long enough, and sooner or later you're going to square the circle. Got to be.

First thing happens is they put out the hook for you—maybe in college, maybe in the service—and you're in like Flynn, you're CIA, you're one of the chosen. You're bulletproof, baby. Nobody's going to let anything happen to you.

There's some kind of invulnerable, gung ho feeling you get when you're a hunter, but out here the roles get reversed real fast. And so the getters get gotten. And the chances get nar-

rowed down more and more, and one morning comes a time you don't rise again from the dead.

You get out in the field, and you start to dig it fast. You see guys getting taken out, you figure, Shit, could've been me. And you know the desk jockeys in D.C. or Langley or wherever either don't know or don't care. They're throwing dice, they don't think half the time.

You know then you're not bulletproof. Never have been, never will be. You know you're never going to make it to retirement, not if you're a stand-up guy, not if you spend any kind of time in the field. You also begin to find out it is generally not the tradecraft nor lack thereof that kills people. It's the assholes back in Langley with their feet on their desks.

It's some jerk who decides you're going to go back to where you've been blown, to where they've got your picture on dartboards and in their police files and in the wrong people's wallets. And you go, like a fool you go, because they tell you, Hell, man, you're the best there is. Nobody knows the territory like you. You're the best, man. You're the best.

Yeah, you go. That's why I went every time. That's why every time Casey or Coldwell or some other Agency hotshot put his arm around me and said, Kid, get out there and do it to it, well, hell, I went. I'm human.

I think it really went back to Lebanon, to my second tour in Beirut. That's when I picked up the first trace on this thing. I was living, then, in the Al-Manara apartments, in West Beirut. Best pad in town, no question. Outstanding. Up on the eighth floor. You could look out my living room window one way over the Med, and look out another window over the Chouf Mountains. Couldn't beat the view.

We were trying to put a picture together of the Hizbollah, some kind of stab at seeing what their structure was, how their chain of command worked. You know how it goes, you get a couple names, you talk with some people, you let them know you know, and they give you another name, because they think you know more than you really do, or they want to show they've got more of the straight skinny than you do, or something. So you get more pieces, and you begin to fit more stuff into the picture.

But your exposure gets greater, too. People know you're asking these questions, and from the questions it would take a

real idiot not to know what you're after. And what we're after
would be dynamite.

So you start building up this mosaic, and that's what we
were doing in Beirut. The Hizbollah, you know, is one of the
tougher nuts to crack. They recruit all the time, they know how
to use cut-outs, and it's like sifting a fucking ton of sand to find
one little grain of gold.

I mean, they do this for a living, they're not just playing at
it. They're good at it.

So this one morning I got up, did some reps on the floor,
took a shower and shaved, made a little breakfast, got dressed.
Same-same, just like always.

I looked out the window, checked out the coast road for, oh,
five, maybe ten minutes. Nothing unusual. No repeaters, no
groups of guys in cars, no vans with funny windows.

I walk down the eight flights—elevators give you no room if
something goes down—say somebody opens the doors and
they're standing there with a sawed-off shotgun, well, what are
you going to do? Dial 911? I get downstairs to the basement
garage, check out the car. Everything kosher, so I get in. I put
the briefcase on the passenger side, secure it so I can flip up the
lid but the thing won't slide off if I brake fast.

Well, I'm going along the road, along that nice clear stretch
of coast, and all of a sudden, BLAM. These guys shoot out of
one of those side streets in this truck, and they ram my car.
Pros. Pinned the front fender right to the tire. Textbook.

Three ragheads scramble out, falling all over each other,
some kind of subguns coming up and I throw the son of a bitch
in reverse. Right away I hit this other car that had been moving
up behind me, and there's these two other guys in it.

The rubber's shrieking on the left front tire, dragging
against the metal, and it's smoking, but we're not too worried
about what the dealer's gonna say when we take it back, not
at this stage.

The briefcase's right there on the passenger seat, so I get out
the little H&K 9-mil. By this time the bad guys are realizing
they're not going to have a nice clean snatch, because this
turkey's gonna get the getters, and they're already committed.

These guys had extra wrappings, just eyes showing, so I
knew they wanted to keep me alive, to get what we knew, so
that kind of slowed them down at first.

But then this one raghead, big bastard, puts some rounds through the windshield. I get down, work open the attaché case, pop up with the H&K, and butt out the rest of the windshield so I can get a clean field of fire. They got two guys busting their chops trying to get the doors open, but they're locked, always locked, so it's just me and this big guy and I get off a three-round burst which erases the fucker's face.

I whip the steering wheel around and pull out. The god-damned tire is shrieking like a bastard and I know I've got three, maybe four blocks before it heats up enough to blow, and then I'll be in deep shit. Not a lot of traffic: it's about seven A.M. by that time, just a couple cars and trucks around.

The ragheads get back in their vehicles and it's Tom and Jerry time. We're moving like a son of a bitch, and the second car, the one that was trying to bracket me from behind, this car pulls up even with me and this guy hangs out this piece, I guess it must have been an Uzi, I don't know, so I fucking stand on the brakes and they go right past. Beautiful.

The first car now, it slams into the back of the Fiat, which by now is looking like something out of a demolition derby, and I decide to therefore get the hell out of there. I figure my only hope is to stay with the car, buy me some distance, so I floor it. I go around a corner and these guys haven't made the turn yet so I just park the damn car between two others, and get my head down fast. From down there under the dash, I heard the car go past, and then I grab the H&K and a spare 30-round mag, and run like a bastard into an alley that goes between these two stores.

Well, about halfway down the block these guys realize they've been suckered, so they grind it into reverse, and from where I've got down in the alleyway I hear them stop just about where my car would be and the doors open.

I knew they'd figure me for the alley, but probably for coming out the other end. Either way they'd have one guy take the other end with the car, and one guy go in to sweep the place.

I'm down behind this Dempster-dumpster thing, real thick iron, like a goddam tank, when the first guy finally starts coming down the alley. Darting one side to the other, hopping around like a goddam chicken. I can hear him, but I keep my head down. My back's exposed, so I know I don't have a whole hell of a lot of time before the guy with the car gets around back and they bracket me. No star, this guy. Probably learned everything from old John Wayne movies. Should have waited for his buddy with the car to come up the other end. But these Hizbollahs want to be heroes more than they want to be alive.

So I'm hunkered down there and the guy gets, I don't know, ten, maybe fifteen feet away, and I dodge out and give him a burst, right in the midsection. He had this surprised look, like, Hey, you're not supposed to be there, you're supposed to be—you know?

The thing nobody tells you in these things is, you don't have to be a star, you just got to be first. I never met anybody good enough, fast enough, to react to a man with gun and get the first rounds in. Doesn't work that way. You stay at the ready, you keep the variables down, and when you work the situation, you get there first.

You don't say, Pardon me, but I'm just about to blow your ass away, señor. You don't say, freeze, motherfucker. That's for the movies or when you file a report to city cops. You don't wait to see what happens, you just do the right thing. Better to be tried by twelve than carried by six.

But now I got one guy, and still his buddy's got to be at the back end of the alley in no time. So I drag the raghead who's down around to other side of the Dumpster and I get ready.

Only the fucking car doesn't come. It doesn't come. And I realize the second guy is smart, real smart. So I jump inside the damned Dumpster. And I sit tight. There, on top of more goddam garbage than I ever threw away in my whole fucking life.

Then I hear the footsteps. I almost don't hear them. Soft, real soft, guy's like a fucking cat. Then no sounds at all. He waits, waits maybe five, six minutes, I don't know.

He starts again. I hear his footsteps go to one side, to get a good angle on whatever's the other side of the Dumpster, right where I'd been at first.

Finally—and by this time I'm still doing real slow, real shallow breathing and my knee's starting to feel like somebody's slicing into it, just from squatting down waiting—finally the guy figures I'm long gone, I've split.

So he walks over to his buddy, and checks him out. I hear him moving the guy's subgun on the cement so I figure he's *only got one hand free now, so I up and pop him. Two bursts, almost on top of him.*

I get out of the Dumpster real fast, and I go through his pockets. Not much left of his face, but there's something about him that just didn't seem kosher. I mean, this guy was definitely not Hizbollah. Some kind of European, I thought. Big guy. Six foot two, three, maybe. Big-boned. His hair was wavy and medium brown, not black, and he was dressed in one of those safari jackets newspaper guys like to wear when they're playing soldier.

Got the wallet, flipped it open, and bingo. Guy's got Soviet consulate ID. Military attaché. Got a residential address on the Rue Hamra. So he's big ticket. But not, definitely not, one of Musawi's lads.

Finally I get back into the office and we start looking at the situation. We fire the photo from the guy's ID back to Langley, but even before we got a positive on him, one of our guys said, Yeah, that's Yakovlev, he's GRU.[1] He's one of Pyotr's people. Top class. Full marks, Mathieson. How you gonna explain this one, smartass?

So what was the GRU doing, involved up to its giznikits in the forcible abduction of a CIA officer? Especially now that all is sweetness and light between Gorby and George?

Of course, the GRU is a thing apart, anyway. Very little professional camaraderie between us and the GRU. Not like the KGB. I'd always had pretty clear lines open to the KGB, especially in Beirut. But then all of a sudden, some of the people I'd built up links with started disappearing. Just disappearing. A few got recalled to other places, don't know where. Others just—disappeared.

We figured it was the Hizbollah getting things screwed up as they usually do, because two of the vanishing acts had Hizbollah fingerprints all over them. I mean, the MO was the same. Vehicle intercepts, the whole thing. Maybe they thought they were getting Americans. Who the hell knows. At any rate, the guys never showed up in Beirut again. In fact, as far as KGB contacts were concerned, I had only two by this time.

I'd never gotten close to any of the GRU people in Beirut.

[1]Chief Directorate of Intelligence of the General Staff; military intelligence.

Hard, as always, to get close to GRU people at all. Thing was also I'd been given a lead on what looked like something big happening with the GRU, something one of my KGB contacts leaked. But nobody at Langley had the hots to do any kind of follow-up. Guess they figured it was bad for relations with the Russians, seeing as how we're all best friends now. They said I didn't have anything substantial, only shadows, only—supposition. Don't you love that fucking word?

So what was a GRU guy doing in this kind of snatch? Everything we knew about the Hizbollahs, they knew. So that couldn't be the idea. They wanted to turn me inside out, to see what our network is in Beirut, in the Mid-East? Hell, they can read a paper if they want to know that. Or just look at the embassy list, the consulate list. Look at the temps. No problem. So what was a GRU bozo doing trying a snatch on your friendly local CIA man? Got to be a renegade, got to be something off the books.

Couldn't figure it. Nobody else could either. I put it in my incident report, and try to forget it. But I couldn't. Didn't make sense. No way did it make sense.

I'm thinking, then, if I was a prime target, then I better get my ass the hell out of Lebanon. Either that, or change the rules on the bastards. That was when I decided to get hold of Dunayev. Officially, military attaché at the Sov Embassy. Realistically? Colonel, GRU.

The corpse had been his boy, so Dunayev was going to look pretty bad back in the USSR. He'd be curious to know just how his boy got greased, and maybe want to get an eyeball-to-eyeball with Yours Truly the old target here.

He agreed to meet me at Chez Emile, just off Martyr's Square. Small, dirty, but known far and wide for the poisonous quality of its Moroccan cuisine. We set the time for one o'-clock the next afternoon, and we both showed up a little after twelve, and we each found the place loaded with the other's people. Par for the course, right?

Now obviously I'm not about to try anything stupid, and he knows that, and I know he knows that, so I just walk over to him and sit down across from him, both of us grinning like bastards.

Well, we sit and we talk and we cover many interesting things including the weather and local problems and finally old

Dunayev says—check this out—the snatch was fucking unauthorized. Unauthorized, can you believe it?

I said, Well, if it wasn't, then what the hell was it all about, then? And what was his boy doing playing grab-ass with the Hizbollahs? And Dunayev, looking like somebody'd just chopped his pecker off, says it frankly beat the shit out of him.

So we look at each other long and quiet, and finally he says, We are looking into the matter in various ways, and he apologizes for this unfortunate incident and regrets the actions of the late Mr. Yakovlev, and it will most certainly not happen again. Well, I tell him, it sure as shit will not happen with Mr. Yakovlev again. At which he laughs, and I laugh, and everybody around us in this godforsaken trichinosis parlor starts to laugh. But a nervous laugh, and we both know everybody in old Emile's has got his finger around a trigger and we decide the conference is over.

We finish our dinner. I got the impression then and I really have it now that the good colonel was not shitting me, that Yakovlev was definitely doing something off the books and that Peter Yegorovich Dunayev was not a happy camper. There was also one other little thing: Dunayev wanted to set up another meeting with me, he said. Someplace not so public. And he starts asking me things about life in the U.S., things like how much money does it take to buy a nice house in the country.

Things then start to cook when Dunayev, five days after our little lunch, gets recalled to the Aquarium, mo sukoshi, *and his replacement scoots in late on a Friday night, on Aeroflot, in plain clothes.*

We already had a good picture on this replacement, from the feebies, because he'd been a very bad boy in California. He'd been working with a consular cover and had been observed to be spending lots of time around Palmdale, taking lots of tourist photos around some of California's ugliest real estate.

They couldn't pick him up for anything, but there were some leads that told them he'd been furnishing shady ladies to a couple of engineers doing sensitive things on the B-2. Before the feebies could set up anything, though, the guy vanishes. Like he had some kind of sixth sense, or somebody in his pocket at the local field office. And here he shows up on our doorstep.

This guy is an Armenian, a very smart lad, it turns out. Light colonel, GRU, ex-Spetsnaz,[2] ex-Frunze, ex-a bunch of other stuff, but a very current Viking—which, in the GRU, means he's one of the operational elite. A mean and capable dude, no mistake.

We find out just how mean when two days after the guy cruises in, on a Monday morning, one of my sources tells me the guy's laying heavy money around to do a snatch on me.

I am now finally getting more than a little tired of all this, and want to Have Myself a Merry Little Christmas at least one more time, so I give Langley the call and they pull me out of there, out on the last plane to Paris, on the manifest as George R. Rudley, of New Bremen, Ohio. So there's no signal on me at the airport.

Next thing I know I get a call in Paris from one of my guys back in Beirut, tells me they grabbed the driver our people sent to pick up my car. The driver happened to be my height, my coloring, so they grab the son of a bitch. Oh, and yes, the confirmation came—it was the fucking Armenian and his store-bought Syrians.

So now we know. GRU, and official. They'd just kept Dunayev out of the loop, is all. But back at Langley, I find nobody, but nobody, knows any special reason why the GRU wants Your Obed. Servant.

I get stuck for about a month to a paper-pushing job, while they make up their minds what to do with me. Then word comes through that I'm getting a real plum. Coldwell calls me up to the seventh floor, and I get my new assignment: Vienna.

Duty doesn't get any better than Vienna. Terrific city, the women are beautiful, and you're close enough to the borders to be able to recruit easily. Agents come by the carload in that part of the world. You get stuff offered to you every day that'd take you months to dig up anyplace else. A few interesting morsels come my way. There's always one thing or another about Waldheim: he's in the Mossad's pocket, he's in the Sicherheitdienst's pocket, he's in the SDECE's pocket, you know. We've been hearing all that for years, and nobody much gives a shit because the Austrians are going to keep him in no

[2]Special reconnaissance units.

matter what because he's the fucking president, schatzie, that's why.

But in the middle of all this shit, I keep hearing—like a steady whine in the background—some funny things going on with the GRU rezident, like he's wanting to come over, to defect. Little things. Nothing overt.

And—here's the big surprise, boys and girls—the current rezident turns out to be none other than our old friend, Colonel Dunayev.

So the Powers That Be decide nobody'd be better than good old Yours Truly to ferret out whether Dunayev wants to change coats, seeing as how we're old buddies, and all. Maybe, they say, he's pissed because Moscow was running an op around him, on his own turf, who the fuck knows.

That's why I came here, that's why I got myself into this mess. They told me—are you ready, sports fans?—they told me, You're the best, man, the best there is. There's nobody else we can really, uh, COUNT on, you know? Got me again. Zap.

So I get here, in the land of Harry Lime, and I start finding bread crumbs. Dunayev's been seen here. Dunayev's been seen there. Dunayev, it seems, is being served up on a plate without any work by anybody. This, I think, stinks like the socks on a Celtic center.

I tell Langley, I sense something definitely not kosher about old Dunayev this time. Bullshit, they tell me. You were wrong about him when he told you it wasn't a real GRU op. They tell me, You're getting too edgy about this damn thing. They tell me all kinds of shit, and so I say OK, OK, I'll bring him in.

But there's something about this, something that doesn't check out. There's a thing that's bigger behind this, somehow.

So I decide to get another lever working, and I get hold of a local ex-spook, a guy who used to work for Waldheim, but who's now retired, doing a little journalism, and trying to keep a very expensive lady on the side without his wife knowing. I offer the guy a couple of grand to find out everything he can about GRU people here and who they're dealing with back home.

And he comes up with some very interesting stuff. He tells me Dunayev is now very much in the good graces of Moscow, that he is in line for some very good career changes, and that he is about as likely to change coats as fly to the fucking moon.

I probe the guy. He tells me more, that the GRU is now running several parallel ops to KGB deals, but that the KGB either doesn't know or doesn't care.

He also tells me that back in Moscow a certain Army General Mescheryakov, one of the nomenklatura, *is taking a very hard line against the politburo, which is either just plain suicidal or a bid to move up into the hierarchy if he can orchestrate things to his liking.*

Turns out this Mescheryakov is a hawk, not just in the traditional sense that GRU generals and our own Joint Chiefs are hawks, but a hawk in the way that makes other hard-liners look like Rebecca of Sunnybrook Farm.

And, my source tells me further, he seems to have very heavy-duty backing in not only the Aquarium, but in the Kremlin as well. Source says quote, at least three rabbis of much, much power. Including one in the number two seat in the Defense Council.

So now we begin dealing with something a little more interesting than just the snatch of your friendly CIA man in Beirut. We are dealing with a runaway GRU something or other, an off-the-books operation of some size. But what? And, more important, why?

The tape continued to roll, but the last few minutes were blank. Pretorius punched the "off" tab. He leaned back in his chair, knuckling his eyes. *No,* he thought. *Phil was into something big here. And it was what got him killed. Hornbill ought to get this tape. Somebody ought to, and Hornbill's probably the only guy I could get to who's senior enough to keep it from getting buried.*

He punched the eject button, flipped the cassette over, and once again punched "play."

The Hell of it was, and is, the eerily disembodied voice continued, *that somehow I knew it was yet another setup, that they were going to have one more try at scooping up Yours Truly. But a part of me wanted to believe the opposite, that Langley really and truly—possibly for the first time in their whole lives—knew what they were doing.*

Old Dunayev was making all the right noises and all the right moves. And he would, by any of the conventional yardsticks we use to measure such things, have been a good catch.

The Station Head got everything set up: the passports—

Dunayev was to get three, one for each of three separate scenarios. They loved to talk about scenarios, the new boys. Ah, the movie possibilities. So Dunayev had a German passport, plus a Swiss and a British one.

The escape routes were set up nicely, too. The story to the mechanics was that a high Austrian government official who'd got caught with his hand in the till was being brought out, to go work for the Americans, and that we wanted a smooth exit for him, with no unpleasantness at airports or at the border. This appealed to the basically larcenous nature of our people, and so they worked diligently to prepare his departure.

He was to be driven to Linz, where we'd put him up in the Zum schwarzen Adler. In the morning he'd take a private plane into the Schwarzwald, to a small private landing strip. From there, a fast buzz up the Autobahn to Frankfurt, where he'd catch a Pan Am flight to New York.

We had three or four other plans, each of which we carefully laid out to Santa's helpers in Vienna. But none of them, once Dunayev got in the car to Linz, would be the one we'd use. Dunayev was too valuable to risk telling five or six people about, even if they didn't realize he was, in fact, Dunayev, Scourge of the GRU. No, there was always a hero or a double, even, who would see this as a grand opportunity for brownie points with the Austrian police or state security or their real case officer back in Czecho.

What we were going to do in fact was pull him out of the car just before Linz, put in an actor dolled up for the occasion, have the actor go through the whole bit with all the damn airplanes, and have good old Dunayev just drive all by his lonesome straight from Vienna over into Switzerland, and from there use his Swiss passport as Alois Schussel to catch a Swissair flight into New York, where we'd then put him onto a plane to Dulles, and then a quick drive to a safehouse in Middleburg, a big old antebellum mansion tucked out of sight with all kinds of good security, and let him talk his brains out, promising him women, money, all of it.

At least that was the theory.

The way it went down was something else.

I finally decided on an approach. We knew Dunayev was a camera buff, used one of the old Leica IIICs, and every so often—every couple of days—he used to go into that dealer in

*the Graben, to buy film, look at accessories, talk to the clerks
about Leicas. A real buff. So we had the Austrians put a
woman in there, attractive lady in her late thirties, and let the
owner know he was doing a terrific service for the state.*

*Comes a Tuesday afternoon, Dunayev is doing his prome-
nade, stops in front of the window, looks over the merchandise,
and walks in. Starts talking with the owner, who introduces
him to Gertrud, who—because of a world-class briefing two
days earlier—knows just about everything there is to know
about Leicas. Says her grandfather was Oscar Barnack or
somebody. Well, this gets old Dunayev excited.*

*Gertrud also tells him she's got one of granddad's cameras,
one of the original Model Ones, not a repro, and she's looking
to sell it, but not through the shop. She needs the money, she
says, because she's looking to move to America. All this, of
course, out of earshot of the proprietor, who by now has gone
discreetly into his darkroom or storeroom or whatever the hell
it was in back of his shop.*

*Dunayev, by now, thinks he's died and gone to heaven. They
make a date for dinner. He suggests one place, she suggests the
Café Landtmann, on the Ring near the Burgtheater instead.
Says it's the most romantic place in Vienna, which old Dunayev interprets as a signal she's hot to trot.*

*We're recording everything he and Gertrud are saying, all
the sweet nothings, all the stuff about the damned Leicas, and
then our guy in the third floor window across the street sees a
funny thing:*

*Two very heavy-looking gents are now outside and suddenly
seeming very interested in this little shop. Our guy radios in
their descriptions, and it turns out these two guys are local
GRU and that they are occasionally used for wet jobs. So we
ask ourselves, what the fuck are they doing shadowing our
boy? They're obviously not the usual walkers.*

*Do they know Dunayev is thinking about flying the coop?
And if they know, are they looking to see who comes to scoop
him up? Are they waiting for him to make some overt move
they can use for evidence in a court martial, once they truss
him up and get him back in the USSR? Stay tuned, sports fans.*

*So all right. We decide to let Gertrud and Dunayev have
their fun, meet in the Café Landtmann. But we make no
approach. Instead, we see if he's leaving any bread crumbs for*

these guys, or if they are in fact hostile to our fair-haired boy.

*Well, it turns out these guys are always about fifteen min-
utes behind, almost never within line-of-sight. Which means
our boy is wired, which means they're trolling with him, using
him for bait. Bait for us. For me, specifically.*

*Once again, the magic question—why me, Lord? Why the
fuck is the GRU so goddamned interested in me that they
mobilize all these people in Beirut and fucking Vienna?*

*Langley, we discover, is—surprise!—just as puzzled as we
are about this one. They say, Jeez, sorry, and they send over
a team to give me some clean backup, boys the Sovs have never
seen, couple of young kids straight out of The Farm who are
allegedly very, very good in the unarmed combat department,
who can shoot better than Wyatt Earp with a hard-on, and who
have been hand-picked by covert operations for This Very Job.*

*They are dead inside of three days of stepping off the fuck-
ing plane. Some couple walking along the Franz Josef Strasse
sees one, puffed up, blue as a flounder, floating face up in the
Danube Canal. Die Blaue Donau. Terrific.*

*The other two are spotted on a river bank the next day by
the cops, and all three have 9 mil wounds, some of those new
Israeli hollow points it looks like from the tissue damage, but
no rounds actually left in the bodies. One guy looks like he had
a couple rounds dug out of him already. Obviously they were
wasted by people who want to be very, very careful about not
getting linked with their work. Which points to the highest
level of pros being assigned to this one.*

*Shit, I think. These guys are fucking serious. But what's a
mother to do? I do the only thing I can do. We start setting up
the deal.*

*The fair Gertrud calls old Dunayev, gets him alone, says
she's working for the Americans and would he like to meet one
of their top intelligence people, a man who can give him safe
conduct, passports, money, three-window office at Langley,
women in Georgetown, the works. Man named Mathieson,
used to be in Beirut.*

*Dunayev at first acts like he's surprised, then like he's disap-
pointed Gertrud isn't interested in him just for his pale quiver-
ing body. But he starts asking questions, playing out his part.
Can he have a new identity? How much salary per year? Can*

*he live in the countryside and raise horses? All the bullshit, you
know, just like he's thinking it over for real.*

*Gertrud comes on like a trooper. Anything is possible for
you, dear Colonel, she says. You're a valued officer, a real hero
helping the cause of democracy. Someday, she says, your own
country will welcome you back with open arms and you will get
medals instead of scorn. Herr Mathieson will see to it, ja.
Gertrud, of course, has no idea this joker has zero plans for
coming West, or for doing anything else with us other than
getting Yours Truly on a stretcher into an Aeroflot straight to
Moscow.*

*No matter. Macht nichts. We set up a first meeting between
me and Dunayev.*

*And of course it goes smooth as a greased goose. We agree,
straightfaced, this whole thing has to handled with Great Sensitivity, with all the snaps and locks on. We shake hands, I tell
him we'll have it set up for him within ten days, and I'm smiling
like I'm about to wrap up this prize catch from the GRU,
although I know he's got anything but that on his mind, that
he's working out how they're going to grab your friendly local
CIA man instead.*

*You can tell he's under some pressure, because he balks at
the ten days. Says can't we get things moving right away, say
in two, three days. I make all kinds of negatory noises, but I
agree, because I want to see how this thing plays out. So we
say auf Wiedersehen, and we split.*

*We leave it like this: He's going to check and see when he's
in minimum contact with his people, which depends on lots of
things, you understand. Meantime he says he knows this town
not far from Vienna, a place named Eisenstadt that might be
just dandy for—as he put it—"effecting the transfer." Which
must have been a kind of slip, because nobody ever says that
in our trade unless he means an exchange of prisoners.*

*I counter by suggesting the Schönbrunn Palace. Good open
areas for visibility and coverage. Helicopter access to the big
front parking area. Enough windows and doors to position our
people in easily. And it's a nice, normal tourist attraction that
even a colonel of the GRU might logically want to go to—no
problem, none at all. Lots to recommend it. So why do I still
feel wrong about it, about the whole damn thing?*

You know how fucked up Langley can get in matters like

*this, and you know how the GRU is generally able to play
people like trout, which is certainly true in my case. They
pressed all the right buttons, both with me and with Langley.
Inevitable outcome, somebody's going to say if this op goes
south. So I wanted to have somebody, somewhere, clued in to
what's going down.*

*Right now I think the Agency is of a mind to whitewash all
its home office fuckups, and in a definite mood to let field
people hang out to dry. Coldwell is different, he's a stand-up
guy. But he's got a chief of staff who's an old lady with lots of
mid-level friends he likes to protect, cover for, keep them from
losing their pensions. You know. You've seen this movie.*

*We've got the Schönbrunn pretty well covered. Don't see
how things can go sour, but you never know. You never know.
The whole route's laid out for Dunayev and we've even got a
wire into his office, just in case we ought to be hearing something we're not.*

I'm putting this into the Post Amt *in an hour or so, then
we're going to put everything in place. So sayonara. If I call
you by April 2, that means everything went OK, no matter
what I talk about on the phone. If you don't hear from me by
then, well, then, you'll know what happened. I got a real rotten
feeling about this one, Luther, and I never got quite the same
feeling before, even back in Nam, out on the roads. Keep the
rubber side down, and enjoy yourself. Goodbye.*

A hiss of emptiness as the tape spooled to its end, and
Pretorius hit the off button.

He sat in silence, leaning forward in the chair, his head in
his hands. Outside, through the screen door, you could hear
things that sounded normal, that sounded real. Birds, in-
sects. Things like that.

Oh, God damn *it all,* he thought. *Why does this shit always
drag you down, always drag you right back in the middle of it?*
He shook his head and looked out through the door over the
fields. He tucked in his shirt and walked outside. The sun
was beginning to set. He went over to the bar and poured
himself another splash of Lagavulin while Beeson regarded
him with a dour look.

Pretorius gestured with his glass. "And was that all, just
that?"

Beeson nodded. "That's the last I ever got. That one tape,

and a note saying to hold on to it, that there'd be more once he got into it a little further."

"I guess he got into it a little further," Pretorius observed, a distant expression clouding his eyes.

"He did," Beeson confirmed. "Dunayev never showed, and Mathieson disappeared that afternoon. No contact until they scraped him off the sidewalk two days later. He was gotten by the getters. Once they make their minds up, your chances go distinctly down. No matter who you are. No matter how *good* you are. And Phil was goddam good, one of the best."

As Beeson spoke, Pretorius was looking out over the fields and saw the hunter take another fence, the rider seeming to flow with the horse's motions as they took to the air, then continued on the ground without breaking stride.

The general took in the determined chin, the set of Pretorius' eyes. "Don't even think about going over there," he finally offered. "Mathieson was the best I've seen. And I've seen a lot of them. Maybe you were good once, but you've been out a long time. Your chances just don't exist."

Pretorius turned to look at Beeson. "Maybe," he answered. "But you know I'm going, don't you."

Beeson stared. "I know. And I know the Agency isn't going to help you one goddamn bit. Nobody outside the IG's office is going to have anything to do with you. And they'll fix it so you'll have no help from *any* facility, not just theirs."

"I got the message. You can tell them you made it clear."

Beeson looked down at his spit-shined oxfords. "You're a real son of a bitch, Pretorius. Anybody ever tell you that?"

Pretorius grinned. He waited for what was inevitable, knowing what he knew about Beeson.

The general continued, "So I guess I'll hook you into somebody outside channels, somebody who can help you in Vienna. Because that's the only way you're ever going to have a chance of arriving back here other than in a box like your buddy." He turned on his heel, and together the two men began walking back to the house.

The Virginia sun was just beginning to set. The hunter and its rider were making one last circuit around the field.

17

Into the Fire.

Anyone who ever visited Arthur Hornbill's library left it only with infinite regret.

Mahogany shelves with carved moldings lined the room, laden with an eclectic, often eccentric selection of books. The few square feet of wall which escaped being bookcased were a deep and resonant green, but with a bluer hue than usual. To all of this, the brass of the reading lamps lent glistening accents.

Chairs for reading—deep, capacious, all-comforting chairs from which any reasonable reader would find it difficult to rise—were distributed around the room. The library comprised the combined parlor and dining room of Hornbill's brownstone, and every inch of space was thoughtfully crammed by its owner. Easily half Hornbill's government salary went for books, and his collection had long ago spilled over into the second and third bedrooms upstairs.

Even the kitchen and bathrooms were not spared. Each had its own complement of volumes, fiction and non-fiction, hardcover and paperback.

For this was Arthur Hornbill's vice: When he was not pursuing his chosen profession of spying, he was pursuing a good book.

Hornbill loved a good book more than anything else on earth. But if you asked him what he collected, he would reply unhesitatingly, "Quirky minds." By which he meant he loved nothing more than reading the product of a good contrarian intellect.

He was an omnivorous reader, consuming anything that appealed to the numerous nooks and crannies of his imagination. He read everything with the speed of a starving man facing his first Chateaubriand. He seldom, if ever, forgot anything he read.

At the end of a long and trying day, Hornbill would walk from his club on Fifth Avenue at 54th Street to his apartment at 55 East 77th, looking forward to opening one of his treasured books every step of the way.

But this evening was different, for Arthur Hornbill was waiting in his mahogany-lined lair for a telephone call from an old and dear friend, one also in Arthur's profession. Hornbill had been perched on his venerable green Chesterfield couch, all the better for being cracked and on the brink of bursting, when the call came through.

Hornbill's secure phone was of a Swiss design especially modified by DIA technicians. A chip within it regularly altered certain codes in the scrambling unit concealed behind the bookshelves. Only Hornbill knew the sequence of code changes, and he had never written it down.

The phone was bright red, with a single tiny red button just below and to the left of the touch-tone pad. This would activate the scrambler, and then Hornbill could proceed with the conversation.

In a lifetime of dealing with oft-failing mechanical devices, Hornbill trusted scramblers about as much as he trusted internal combustion engines. So Hornbill never said anything that could not be taken as ordinary conversation. No stilted code phrases, no specific words of military or espionage interest, and certainly no instructions in the clear which could, if an eavesdropper knew the identity of either conversationalist, betray an element of Hornbill's business.

Indeed, it had been known since the early seventies that certain foreign intelligence services had triggering mechanisms which could alert recorders to particular conversations in ordinary microwave relay, long-distance telephone calls, if an individual happened to say such words as "cruise missile" or "Stealth" or "Polaris."

He'd been aware this particular call would be made at this time, and that it was of a certain importance. Still, when the telephone warbled, Hornbill stared at it for a moment as if it had been a strange bird, as if he were wondering just what to do with it: capture it, cook it, or shoo it away.

After the third warble of the thing, he punched the scrambler button, picked up the receiver, and waited for the device to lock on before speaking.

He stared across at the books on the shelves and made a mental note to put them in some sort of order. Hornbill had been making precisely this same mental note for nearly twenty years, yet the jumble continued to grow. He wondered if it were because he actually preferred the appearance of chaos, or if it were simply a matter of so little consequence that he would forever ignore it.

After he heard the scrambler's characteristic click kicking in, he spoke. "Good evening," Hornbill intoned.

"Good evening yourself," replied Luther Beeson.

"I take it our lad's going as planned?"

"Arthur, you got one stubborn son of a bitch there. Predictable, but stubborn."

"Well, let's hope he can stay alive long enough. There's too much going on that we don't know the answers to, and the Agency's too likely, as usual, to shoot itself in the foot. What are the mullahs saying?"

"They've taken it away from the Savonarolas, which is a credit to their tiny minds. They're now convinced it's a wet job."

"Well, well. Maybe there's hope. Did you give our friend the bit we agreed on?"

"Oh, yes. He played the tape, just as we agreed—slightly edited, as Coldwell insisted. And Miranda obviously did her part to perfection. He's really gung ho now. Don't think we'll have any variations."

"Let us fervently hope not. I'll alert our man there, as well as a few other friends. This should be a most instructive few weeks."

"If he lives, it'll be instructive. If not, well, we'll all have a hell of a lot of back-pedaling to do. The senator is just waiting for some of our people to screw up somewhere."

"And every other idiot trying to make a national media name for himself. We should find him another hobbyhorse, something less damaging."

"How about corruption in government? I could point him toward a couple of his buddies in the Senate, but the bastard wouldn't ever barbecue a fellow lawyer."

"As someone once said, anybody who likes sausages or laws should never go to see either being made."

"By the way, Coldwell sent word out to the field that Mathieson was a junkie. If the GRU thinks we've swallowed the story, they won't disappear back into the woodwork."

"He's right. If they knew we'd tumbled that it was a killing, they'd pull a vanishing act until it was too late for us to do anything. We were so close before they wasted Phil. Damn, we were close. It's been a real setback. It's cost us too damn much time; things are more dangerous than ever. Feels like the Cuban missile days, only we don't have Mac to ride herd on the JCs[1]."

There was a pause on the line. Then: *"Are they stepping up things? Do you think they've advanced their schedule?"*

"I don't think we've seen the half of it. Obviously, what worries me is the JCs are likely to get spooked before we find whatever the hell is going on."

"They're straining at the bit already. Some of those people would go running into Red Square with bows and arrows, if that's all they had. Remember Collins in Saudi."

"Mm. Well, let's hope our lad draws out the opposition soon enough so we can finish the job."

"You've got the other people in place?"

"They've been set for the last three days. We'll get regular reports once things get moving again."

"And they're reliable?"

"As good as our own. Sometimes better."

Beeson reflected on this. *"Let's hope so, for all our sakes."*

"We'll keep in touch," Hornbill concluded. "I'll let you know if anything breaks at this end, but as far as we're both concerned, the clock is running, right?"

"Right," said Beeson. *"Take care."*

Hornbill replaced the red receiver and looked at it thoughtfully, rubbing his chin. *Pretorius, old friend, if you ever speak to me again, one way or the other, I shall be most agreeably surprised.*

And then he picked up his well-worn copy of St. Thomas Aquinas, and began searching for a few shreds of solace.

---

[1] Joint Chiefs of the Armed Forces.

18

M. E. Lockwood.

Kolya Sergeyevich Bychenko, Colonel, Chief Directorate of Intelligence of the General Staff, Army of the Union of Soviet Socialist Republics, had every reason to feel pleased. He lay on the big four-poster bed, hands behind his head, looking out at the first signs of a Maryland spring.

Bychenko had been driven here in the closed rear of a Lincoln limousine built for transporting people of his nature and importance. All windows in the rear passenger area were opaque, including the raised window between the rear and the front seat areas.

The Russian had no idea where the house was. He only knew he'd been driven at least one hour from Andrews Air Force Base. Then, the sound of crunching gravel, and approaching footsteps, and the door of the vehicle opened and he'd emerged, rubbing his eyes in the glare of floodlight.

The house, known simply as Tunbridge, was set high on a hill, approached by a winding roadway. Towering oaks dominated the grounds. Here and there "dependencies," subordinate buildings serving the many needs of a country estate, provided architectural echoes of the main house.

The house had been built by a wealthy Baltimore merchant in 1834. The family had lived here in fits and starts until 1986, when their genes had, at long last, reached a point of diminishing returns. Money and resourcefulness had run out.

In that year, the tax-beleaguered estate offered it to the National Parks Service, and the Parks Service accepted with alacrity.

But as quickly as Parks responded, a real estate specialist representing "a small division within the Defense Department" acted just as eagerly, offering an unusual arrangement: a lump sum to be used for its complete restoration, in exchange for using the house for national security purposes over the next seven years. After that, the house would pass, rehabilitated and pristine, to the ever-patient Parks Service.

The Central Intelligence Agency paid a staggering amount. This was applied to restore the home to the grandeur of setting and substance Tunbridge had known in the early nineteenth century.

The current and highly appreciative resident of Tunbridge now swung his feet off the bed, and snuggled them into a pair of American shoes.

Bychenko loved his luxuries, and well-made shoes ranked high among them. He made a mental note: he would bring at least three pairs of American and English shoes back with him.

He walked to the window and looked out. The sky was gray and forbidding. Low rain clouds were beginning to slide in from the East. He wondered if his hosts had thought to purchase him a raincoat. If they had, it would likely be either a Burberry, a London Fog, or an Aquascutum. The Americans never did things by halves.

Everything else had been thought of. Two dark suits, two sports jackets of an English cut, trousers, a selection of shirts, pajamas, socks, and underwear. Everything.

Below and to the left of the large front gate, a dark blue sedan occupied a strategic position. The gates were iron and could be shut electronically within seconds. But if they failed to do so, in the event of an armed incursion the car would block the gate and the men inside, armed with submachine guns, would effectively command the entrance.

Bychenko smiled and began pacing in the room, hands in pockets. The sounds of the house were the sounds of a large house waking up, people beginning to move, the clatter of the kitchen, a hundred other domestic noises. The smell from the kitchen, a smell of American bacon beginning to crisp, was maddeningly tempting.

Bychenko wondered what Coldwell, the Director of Central Intelligence, would be doing about his arrival, and who he would choose as the interrogator for his debriefing. According to the files at the Aquarium, the CIA's most effective interrogators were an M. E. Lockwood and someone called Odermatt.

Bychenko was, in fact, very much looking forward to his debriefing. He had been preparing for it over the past seven months, and like any soldier in a high state of readiness was charged with anticipation.

Much depended on his success. The operation could go ahead even if the Americans failed to believe him. But if they did, so much the better.

They had, after all, believed Penkovskiy, and it had allowed the Soviet Union to gain precious years in ICBM deployment. Colonel Oleg Penkovskiy had convinced his proud interrogators that the Soviet guidance systems were far inferior to those of the U.S., which caused Congress to reduce spending accordingly. The CIA, the Congress, and—most of all—the voting public, had believed others as well. For it was in the nature of Americans to *believe,* to trust. It was what amounted to a national religion, one eminently useful to people such as Bychenko.

A single knock on the door, which opened to reveal two clean-cut young men with the wide-open eyes that often betray lack of experience. "Yes?" Bychenko asked.

"Would you come downstairs with us, sir? Mr. Coldwell would like you to join him for breakfast."

So, wondered Bychenko. *The Director himself.*

At the bottom of the swirling spiral staircase, waiting, was a tall man in a navy blue suit, white shirt, and a red-and-black striped regimental tie. A wide smile creased his face, a smile much like Will Rogers'. Well-combed black hair, compromised by a cowlick that kept falling over his forehead.

"Colonel Bychenko, I'm Richard Coldwell, Director of Central Intelligence. Welcome to the United States."

Bychenko, although in civilian clothing and out of uniform, executed a crisp military bow. "Very kind of you, Director Coldwell. I am honored."

The wide smile got wider, and Coldwell gestured toward the open door of the dining room. "Well, let's get a little breakfast under our belts before we talk business, OK?"

"OK, as you say. The bacon, I could smell it all the way upstairs. It smelled delicious."

Coldwell smiled. "That's Albertine's cooking. She's what makes this place habitable."

Bychenko and Coldwell entered the big room, followed by the two young men, obviously Agency bodyguards. Bychenko guessed they were armed, from their unbuttoned jackets and the way they kept their right hands slightly open, thumbs slightly apart, ready.

A many-tiered crystal chandelier dominated a room proportioned as a perfect double cube. A small fire flickered in the fireplace, with an eighteenth-century portrait of a white-wigged man above the mantel.

A woman was standing just inside the room. She was tall, with long brunette hair and snappish dark eyes. Her cheekbones were high, well-defined. She seemed to appraise Bychenko at a single glance, taking in details, summing him up in a split-second. She stepped forward.

Coldwell made the introductions. "Dr. Lockwood, this is Colonel Bychenko. Colonel, this is your interviewer today, M. E. Lockwood."

They shook hands and Bychenko was surprised at the firmness of her grip. Her eyes once again had that strange appraising quality. *So this is the famous M. E. Lockwood,* Bychenko mused. *Odd that the Americans would have a woman as one of their top interrogators. Something else for the files.*

As they sat down, Coldwell asked, "Some coffee, Colonel? Albertine's coffee is famous for getting the heart started."

"Yes, please." A pause, then: "Your American coffee is quite good."

"It's Colombian. And we tend to make it fairly strong."

"Ah."

"Colonel, you'll be pleased to know your request for political asylum is now being considered at the highest levels. I'm authorized to tell you—could you pass the sugar, please? Good. Thanks. I'm authorized to tell you everyone is responding quite favorably, and you should have no difficulty."

"That's reassuring, Director Coldwell."

"Mr. Coldwell tells me you're originally from Brest-Litovsk, Colonel," said M. E. Lockwood, revealing perfect teeth and a soft, almost sensual smile. Bychenko was momentarily startled. *They must keep detailed files indeed to know the birthplace of an obscure colonel,* he noted. *Score one for the lady.*

"That's correct, Dr. Lockwood. But I'm afraid I remember very little of it. We moved to Moscow when I was ten months old. My father was part of the Ministry of Agriculture, and was promoted to the bureaucracy there."

"Really?" And the way she said it, Bychenko knew: *she's seen that my father was with the NKVD. She's wondering why I'm not mentioning that, why I should be masking it with the agricultural job.*

One of the young men entered the room with a steaming platter of scrambled eggs and Albertine's legendary bacon. A basket heaped with Maryland spoon bread was already on the table. "Please have some bacon and eggs, Colonel," Lockwood urged. "Unless you're watching your cholesterol?"

He laughed. "Cholesterol doesn't exist in the Soviet Union, Miss Lockwood. At least not officially. We don't have the luxury of choosing our foods to the degree you do here."

Coldwell watched as Bychenko heaped his plate high. "I hope your accommodations are to your liking, Colonel. You slept well?"

"That is one of the questions I won't be able to answer today, Director Coldwell," returned Bychenko with a straight face. "I can't remember a thing about it."

As M. E. Lockwood laughed, Bychenko noticed how clear and cream-white her skin was, how pleasing the contrast against her raven hair. *This is a woman of quality,* he mused. *How interesting she would be to get to know.* He crunched into his first crisp bit of bacon. "Your bacon is so very different from ours," he commented. "It's not just the slicing, is it?"

"You'll have to ask Albertine about that," replied Coldwell. "I think she does one or two things she doesn't talk about. Even she has her classified information."

And so the next half hour went, after which Coldwell said, "Well, it's time to get down to cases. I think you'll find the library more comfortable."

The library was not only more comfortable, it was in fact the central interrogation room. Next to the library, a room which had been a small study was now the lair of the technicians. The library itself had microphones concealed at strategic points, and not a whisper could be uttered without tape recorders collecting it faithfully.

The technicians waited until the small red light indicated the automatic locking door was closed and the three were inside. The door, which appeared to be simply one more of the house's beautifully grained mahogany doors, was actually a sandwich of mahogany and steel capable of withstanding high explosives and all but the most determined assaults. Dead bolts shot three inches into both sides of the door frame, a further deterrent to anyone wishing to rush the room and its occupants.

The chief engineer adjusted the position of his headset, then punched the two buttons that put the Studer deck into recording mode.

The reels began whirring obediently, and the thousand sounds that exist in a silent room began to be heard and stored by the greedy russet ribbon.

A chair being moved closer, hum of the ventilation system, a muted cough, wind entering a cracked window pane, birds outside, creak of the oak tree as it adjusted to yet another wind, coffee cup set down carefully, controlled steady breathing of the subject, scratching of a pencil, movements of the interrogator making herself comfortable. Then:

"Fourteen April, zero nine two five hours. Tape George, Delta, Victor, four oh seven nine seven six nine zero. Mark. Your name, rank, organization, and former responsibilities, please."

"Bychenko, Kolya Sergeyevich. Colonel, Chief Directorate of Intelligence of the General Staff. Until three days ago, on the staff of Army General Mescheryakov, responsible for liaison with the Central Committee."

"Colonel, for purposes of this interview, I should like you when at all possible to answer in complete sentences. Thus, if I were to ask you, for example, where did you live on the twenty-second of October in 1987, please respond by repeating the date, as in 'On the twenty-second of October, 1987, I lived on Nevsky Prospekt.' Is that clear?"

Bychenko smiled. Like all good interrogators, M. E. Lockwood was establishing her own orthodoxy, and therefore her control. He was also impressed that she *knew* where he lived in October of 1987. "Yes, clear," he replied.

"Good, then, we just have a few preliminary things to

cover. Would you give us the names of your parents, full names please?"

Bychenko answered this and other personal questions regarding his birthplace, schooling, relatives, which members of his immediate family were living and where, and then Lockwood began probing his military record. "You were assigned to *Spetsnaz* as a captain in June of 1979, yes?"

"That is correct."

"And you were sent to, what was it? To Zheltyye Vody for training?"

"Yes, that's true. Jump training. But what does that have to do with what I'm bringing you?"

"Be patient, Colonel. This is all just routine, as I'm sure you know."

Bychenko folded his arms and expelled a long, slow breath. "Continue, please. Let's get this over."

She smiled. She was getting to him, loosening his defenses as his emotions began to rise. "Colonel, no one would like to get this over as much as I would, not even you. If you simply cooperate, we'll both be better off. Agreed?"

He glared at her with a look calculated to turn younger officers to salt. In the case of M. E. Lockwood, however, all it produced was yet another dazzling smile.

This woman is exasperating! he fumed.

She continued to smile brightly. "In your own opinion, Colonel, was there a high proportion of homosexual behavior in the *Spetsnaz?* Our sources tell us the homosexual psychological profile—and that doesn't necessarily mean *practicing* homosexuals, you understand—is highly attracted to the kind of life offered by the *Spetsnaz."* This, followed by the most pleasant smile imaginable.

Across the big room, on the couch, Richard Coldwell was nearly convulsed. It took every ounce of reserve to hold in his laughter as he watched Colonel Bychenko contain his rage at Lockwood. She was, he realized, bringing Bychenko to the boil just before entering the main body of her interrogation. A dangerous game, one which could totally alienate the subject. But the cards were on her side.

"I have no idea of homosexuality in the *Spetsnaz,* Dr. Lockwood. In fact, the subject never arose throughout my five and a half years of service with the forces." He was grim-lipped, tense as a cat in the rain.

The initial questioning established the signposts of his career, including his promotion to staff officer in the 13th Army, his transfer to Carpathian Military District HQ, his later work recruiting agents in Austria and Germany, and finally his assignment to the general's staff in Moscow.

Most important, it established a pattern of factual question, factual response. As the interrogation continued, Lockwood walked around the circular library table at which Bychenko was seated, her hands in some sort of pockets which were in the folds of the pale blue silk dress she wore.

He thought her extremely attractive. As she passed behind him, her perfume caught on a current of air and he inhaled its delicacy. *No Moscow woman would ever wear such a perfume,* he thought. *Too delicate, and yet, at the same time, too sensual, too provocative.* He found himself wondering what the shape of her breasts beneath the dress would be like, freed from the brassiere, in bed—he stopped himself.

"I said, 'At Frunze, were you considered an excellent student, or simply competent?' " Lockwood repeated.

"I should say, excellent. If you won't think I'm boasting." He smiled at her and was rewarded by a flash of the beautiful teeth, the red, almost taunting smile.

"And your fellow students—did they regard you as—standoffish, friendly—what?" She was standing immediately behind him now. He tried to concentrate on the shelves of books. "They regarded me as slightly 'standoffish,' as you put it."

"Do you, yourself, feel you're that way?"

"Oh, yes, I suppose I am, at first."

"But then, once you get to know someone—?" she asked, waiting for him to complete the thought.

He paused. "Yes, I do warm up a bit. But I've never been regarded, even by my friends, as a—what do you call it? As a party boy?"

"No, I think we'd call it a 'good old boy,' " Lockwood corrected, laughing easily. "Now why did you suddenly decide," she said, rapidly shifting gears, "to ask for political asylum? Aren't things going well for you?"

"It was not a question of things not going well for me.

And as for 'suddenly' deciding, it was the culmination of a series of events which made it imperative that I communicate with your intelligence people."

"Imperative, Colonel? Why *imperative?*"

"Before we go any further, Miss Lockwood, may I ask if all my conditions have been met?"

Lockwood whirled suddenly and leaned over Bychenko, placing her hands on the arms of his chair, leveling her eyes straight into his own.

"Now I am an exceedingly patient woman, Colonel," she began, "and I have over the course of my limited career been exposed to all manner of bullshit artists and snake oil salesmen, each and every one of whom has said he has the real, the genuine, the one-and-only ever-loving True and Holy Grail.

"In your case, it appears you have some as-yet-to-be-defined, as-yet-to-be-revealed information which you seem to think is terribly important, but which might, and I hope sincerely to hell it doesn't, prove to be news to you but very tired old news to us. It happens that way, sometimes. A pity, but it does happen.

"That aside, you obviously do not wish to be screwed out of getting good value in this exchange, nor do we." She released her grip on the arms of his chair, and began pacing, looking out the tall windows as she did.

"We will give you political asylum, so you've got something on your account already. But we are not about to buy, as we say in the United States, a pig in a poke. We want to see the merchandise before we make any serious commitments.

"So therefore—" and here she took a deep breath— "kindly do not take up time with any talk about you show me yours and I'll show you mine. That is not in the cards, and never will be. We need to know precisely what you've got, and if what you've got happens to be worth it, you get your compensation. We are fair. You will not be cheated. You simply have to speak up and not be coy. Have I made myself clear?"

Bychenko had never been spoken to by any woman in this manner. "Of course," he said with elaborate casualness, attempting to conceal his inner fury. "You have been clear with me. I shall be quite as clear with you."

"Good," returned M. E. Lockwood. "Somehow I *felt* you were a man of logic and clarity." And she smiled her frosty small smile once again, the edges of her lips curving up slightly. "All right, then, let's see your cards, and I can tell you—here and now—what we're prepared to do."

Inside the adjoining room the technicians looked anxiously at the slowly revolving reels. Silence, and nothing but silence, was heard over the system. They adjusted their headsets. Then came Bychenko's carefully enunciated, accented syllables:

"From things I have observed in recent weeks it has become increasingly clear that unless someone takes decisive action, we are about to experience a nuclear holocaust. I believe I possess information which possibly may avert that eventuality."

Lockwood: "What were, as you say, these 'things I have observed'?"

"General Mescheryakov has been ordered by the president and Council of Ministers to implement a clandestine plan to go to full readiness for a generated thermonuclear attack on the United States."

A silence. Then:

"Have you seen evidence, hard evidence, that this directive is the result of an official decision, a policy decision, of the Council of Ministers itself?"

"I have. The directive was signed by a majority of members. I was not in a position to photograph this directive, as I was in the company of General Mescheryakov at the time I saw it. But it was official. And it was clear."

"What was the language of the directive? Can you be more specific?"

"I believe it included the phrase 'implement with all due caution consistent with the time constraints as previously outlined.' "

"What did the phrase 'time constraints as previously outlined' mean?"

"That was not clear. There was no mention of timing or scheduling in the document which I saw. But later General

Mescheryakov told me they would be breathing down his neck like wolves on the tundra."

Coldwell speaks once again: "Colonel, when precisely did you see this document?"

A pause. "The seventh of March. As this was an especially significant document, I made mental note of the date."

Lockwood: "Did anything subsequent to your viewing of this document give you an idea of the time frame to which it referred?"

A longer pause. "Not a *clear* idea. But General Mescheryakov, who obviously knew the time requirements, said to me—I think his words were 'Kolya Sergeyevich, when the first thaw comes, we shall either be under the earth or masters of it.' "

Lockwood: "And when does the first thaw generally come in Moscow?"

"Approximately three weeks from now."

_____ 19

Bye Bye Blackbird.

The man in the orange suit rushed toward the horizon at nearly four times the speed of sound. Ahead, indigo space hovered above a darkened earth, a corona of gold pulsing between.

One hundred thousand feet below, the snow-laced coast floated past. The SR-71 Blackbird was closing on its target: the submarine pens at Aleksandrovsk, on Sakhalin Island.

Ruled by its autopilot and astro-tracker, the Blackbird flew straight and true. At nearly Mach 4 the SR was unforgiving. If the pilot attempted hand-flying it, the aircraft would yaw or pitch out of control, shredding its titanium skin, shearing its structure, disintegrating in seconds.

The pilot, Alan Greenwalt, LTCOL, USAF, sat encased in his orange pressure suit as he hurtled forward at nearly thirty-five miles a minute. There was no sound other than the steady hiss of oxygen within the helmet.

He contented himself with checking the CRTs, the round dials, the readouts. He checked for stability augmentation, altitude, and attitude. He noted the Mach number, engine temperatures, oil pressure, and other life-and-death indicators. He was a touch bored.

Yet he kept his level of attention high. Among SR pilots, there's a belief that the aircraft "knows" when you look out the side window, and gets jealous of your attention. One backseater described life in the SR as times of boredom, interspersed with moments of stark terror. Despite this, the SRs had enjoyed a seventeen-year span without a single accident, a tribute both to the skill of its pilots and to the genius of Kelly Johnson, head of Lockheed's Skunkworks.

Greenwalt's SR had been "borrowed" especially for this mission, one of two kept in readiness at NASA for high-priority work. Two years back the Blackbird program had been scaled back, then grounded and mothballed. Until the deployment of the new top secret Mach-5, 150,000-foot-ceiling *Aurora,* the U-2s (sometimes spoken of as TR-1s to avoid the Gary Powers effect) would enjoy a monopoly in the reconnaissance aircraft program.

Except for now. Now was different. So they'd pulled in a favor from NASA, and Greenwalt was guiding the lone operational Blackbird toward its target.

Interrupting his vigil over the instruments, Greenwalt touched his gloved hand to the canopy's Plexiglas—and quickly yanked it away. Through the insulation of his glove, the plastic was searingly hot: Mach 4 friction heated it to 625 degrees Fahrenheit.

Even in the below-freezing air of this altitude, the flat epoxy-coated skin of the plane was heated even more, to 870 degrees: the temperature of a soldering iron.

Its normally black surface had slowly turned to blue from the friction of these speeds. Around the engine nacelles, the temperature reached 1,050° F. To prevent the SR from exploding at these scorching temperatures, JP-7 fuel, with a far higher flash point than the standard JP-4, is used in all SRs. No other aircraft in the world used it.

The SR-71 holds not only the world's altitude record, but

several of the world's speed records—including the record New York to London flight of one hour, forty-five minutes, and a few seconds.

What creates this astounding speed isn't the twin Pratt & Whitney J-58 turbo-ramjets. It's a pair of long cones called "spikes" moving in and out of the engine inlets, constantly fine-tuning the SR-71's diet of air.

For these and many other reasons, the SR is the most exotic aircraft in the world, the fastest and the highest-flying, and one of the least radar-detectible.

Yet the SR-71 is over a quarter-century old.

The first SRs began flying in 1966, after which Defense Secretary McNamara ordered the Blackbirds' tooling and dies destroyed. (An action, some claimed bitterly, to prevent the SR-71 from competing with a range of aircraft that would someday include both the F-111 and the B-2.)

The final blow came when—as a trade-off to save the B-2's ever shrinking budget—the Air Force canceled the entire twenty-aircraft Blackbird program. Nine became museum pieces in places like the Smithsonian and the Strategic Air Command Museum at Offutt AFB. Eight entered the oblivion of Air Force warehouses. The remaining three were transferred to NASA's Dryden Flight Center in California, to serve as flying research platforms.

Stripped down to their titanium skins, engines rebuilt to zero-compromise specifications, NASA's three Blackbirds became the world's most revered warplanes. They were virtually worshipped by their maintenance crews, acolytes in an arcane religion. It was one of these, pressed into National Reconnaissance Office crisis duty, that Greenwalt was now piloting.

He spoke through the helmet intercom to his RSO,[1] a young captain sitting directly behind him. "Time to target zone?"

A moment of silence. Then: "We've got eight minutes, ten seconds as of—now."

Greenwalt squinted through his visor at the horizon. On one side, the roughened edge of Sakhalin Island. On the other, the smooth ink-black curve of the Pacific.

---

[1]Reconnaissance Systems Officer.

Many SRs have flown penetration missions over Soviet territory, but none has ever been acknowledged. Flying at this speed, at this altitude, the SR was high above the ceiling of any MiG fighter, and faster than any interceptor.

Which was why, even with its extreme sophistication, its many abilities, the SR-71 Blackbird was unarmed. No guns or bombs. No missiles.

Despite its defenselessness, it looked uncommonly lethal. Although it could outfly anything in the sky, the Blackbird looked more like a manta ray—or even a cobra—than a bird. At Kadena Air Force Base on Okinawa, where the SR would return to offload its images, the plane was even called Habu, after a particularly venomous local black snake.

Greenwalt adjusted his position in the seat. The cameras beneath him in the tapered chines of the plane were now firing off their nine by nine frames, on a film strip 1,500 feet long.

The nine-inch resolution of the special Kodak reconnaissance thin-base film was stunning. For example, once processed in Okinawa, the prints would reveal every detail of the Soviet Delta-IV nuclear-powered strategic submarines, and the SS-N-23 nuclear-tipped missiles being loaded aboard them.

The Blackbird also activated its SLAR, side-looking airborne radar. Operating in any kind of weather, SLAR could record details when the finer-resolution photographic apparatus couldn't. The new digital capability added considerably to the SR as an intelligence platform, especially in gathering imagery of submarine pens. Today it was crucial the current status of the subs be determined, regardless of weather.

The first news of the missile step-up had come day before yesterday, and NRO ordered additional flights, at lower altitudes, for more detail. Which class SSBNs? Any Typhoons? Oscars? Delta IIIs? The new Delta IVs? In particular, what was the deployment of the Yankees armed with the newer 12 SS-NX-24 sea-launched cruise missiles?

Satellites, even the new LACROSSE, couldn't be altered from their routine paths so easily. Yet an SR-71 could take off from any point in the world, refuel several times in flight from a KC-135Q, run its mission, and deliver its pictures, all in less than ten hours.

Now the Blackbird slowed to its operational speed of just below Mach 3 and began its programmed descent to 50,000 feet.

Five minutes, twelve seconds to target.

Vassily Antonovich Levchenko, radarman of the VPVO (*Voyska Protivovozdushnoy Oborony,* Air Defense Troops) was the first to notice the flashing amber pinpoint on his Fan Song radar screen: probable penetration of Soviet airspace.

In 1983, near the naval base at Petropavlovsk, another radarman had detected a similar pinpoint. The speed, course, and RCS[2] indicated an American RC-135S (a subsonic reconnaissance plane based on the Boeing 707) on a reconnaissance flight. Which was, in fact, the reality.

The prospect of downing an American spy plane led his superiors to order a surface-to-air missile standby. And then, once they received authority from Soviet air command, the launch officer loosed his SAMs—bringing down a Korean Airlines 747 and with it, 269 bodies. A Japanese SIGINT unit on Wakkanai monitored the complete Soviet communications, commands and all.

The RC-135S had been using the Korean airliner as a blind, flying at approximately the same speed, on a parallel course that suited its needs.

Now, to avoid a similar mistake, Levchenko immediately called his superior officer. Within seconds, Lieutenant Petr Andreevich Cantacuzene was behind him, leaning over, peering intently at the screen.

"There. You see, Lieutenant? The one coming up from about 190, 195." Levchenko's voice was low, controlled, yet excited. This was what he'd been trained for.

Cantacuzene said nothing. Merely calculated how to best assess the threat, if indeed it *was* a threat. The object's course was directly toward Aleksandrovsk-Sakhalinskiy. The speed ruled out a lumbering U-2 or any civilian aircraft.

At an estimated 2,000 miles per hour, it had to be military. Most likely an interceptor, or—could it possibly be?—one of

---

[2]Radar Cross-Section.

the exotic American SR-71s. But the Americans had foolishly grounded their SRs, the most amazing of all aircraft in their armory.

Cantacuzene ordered the ZRV[3] units to standby alert. Again he leaned over Levchenko's console, dark eyes brooding over the rapidly closing blip.

He considered what the enemy aircraft's probable response would be if he launched his SAMs now. Obviously, the spy plane, with its sophisticated electronics, would detect the missiles almost instantly. The pilot, according to classic SR training, would then decrease speed somewhat, release the aircraft from autopilot control, pull back on the yoke, and escape to altitudes of up to 100,000 feet.

Therefore, Cantacuzene reasoned, his launching could be a waste of several of the *Rodina's* expensive surface-to-air missiles. Unless. Unless—he could have something waiting up there, when the spy plane's pilot pulled up his nose to escape.

Or—better yet—if he could have *several* somethings up there, waiting, distracting, finally overwhelming the SR.

Cantacuzene chewed his lower lip. Concentrating hard, he leaned on the back of Radarman Levchenko's seat.

Levchenko adjusted the contrast on the screen. The blip seemed even more menacing now. Brighter. Closer.

Greenwalt was now off to one side of Aleksandrovsk-Sakhalinskiy, cameras firing away, images being captured, stored, spooled. Later, touching down at Kadena, he would watch the chines being opened and their priceless cargo taken away to the windowless building for processing. Then, at long last, he would have his weekly beer.

He'd had a mild attack of diverticulitis several months ago, and the examining physician had warned him off alcohol, among other things. The doctor told him if it got worse, he might be grounded. Greenwalt missed his beer. He lost weight, and he had no more sharp abdominal pains, but he

---

[3]Zenityye Reketnyye Voyska, or Zenith Rocket Troops, responsible for the USSR's more than 10,000 surface-to-air missile (SAM) launchers.

missed his beer. So he allowed himself one after each mission.

Greenwalt had no idea of this mission's ultimate application. Only that it had been specially ordered by Bolling, and that the port facilities on Sakhalin were the target. Sakhalin generally meant subs.

The run was important; the briefing people were more tense than usual. His MENS (Mission Essential Needs Statement) included, this time, the Beretta 92F pistol with Knight sound suppressor he carried in a cross-strap holster. That meant somebody didn't want him taken alive.

He'd only a little practice with the 92F back at Kadena. The 5½-inch suppressor snapped onto the weapon easily, adding just six ounces to the weight. The front sight on the anodized aluminum "can" was a single shiny aluminum bead. The rear, an open square notch. A good sight picture for a silenced weapon. You could lock the slide to prevent recycling, which cut the sound down even further. Or flick it up, and fire semiautomatic. Greenwalt didn't want to think much about the kind of situations that might need either alternative.

His glance flicked over the readouts, resting on one of the two multi-image CRT screens which, in this specially prepared SR, had replaced several dozen round dials.

Even in autopilot, minus the demanding duties of handflying the aircraft, there'd been too much information to digest. Especially after more dials and readouts had been added for the newer sensors.

In back of Greenwalt, though, the RSO had even more to deal with. The backseater is in charge of the recon mission itself, as well as all electronic countermeasures in the event of an SAM or hostile aircraft threat. One of his key weapons is a sophisticated piece of electronic gadgetry which can deflect an attacking missile's course, turning it away from the SR, causing it to spend its hostile energy in empty air.

Greenwalt heard the backseater's voice through his bubblelike helmet. "We're getting famous."

"What've you got?"

"Ground to air radar lock. Looks like one of their SA-X-12 installations. New type, though. Different pulse."

"OK. Stand by. Advise if they launch."

"How close are we to the end of the run?"

Greenwalt looked at the film indicator, the computer readout that showed elapsed time, frames, and time to go at current airspeed. "Looks like—three more minutes."

"Roger."

The backseater, packed in among all his instruments, concentrated his attention on the screen. A slight sheen of sweat was beginning to distract him, despite the air conditioning within his pressure suit.

The mind of Petr Andreevich Cantacuzene was now racing. He snatched the telephone from its base and gave a crisp command.

The response was immediate.

Missile launchers were armed. Gammon SA-5 long-range, high-altitude SAMs were readied.

At Sikharovka Air Base, five specially modified MiG-25 Foxbat interceptors were activated by their crews. The side-hinged plastic canopies, like bulbous transparent coffin lids, closed slowly over the pilots. Upgraded, powerful Tumansky R-266 engines roared their eagerness. The Foxbats trembled under the tension. The pilots went through their final checklists, flicking the panel switches, excitement running high.

Finally, the signal was given, and the interceptors rumbled on their 4,500-foot takeoff runs, exploding into thunder as they swept past the squat concrete tower. As the planes began nosing up, the trees at the end of the runway shimmered and danced through the heat of the engines.

The Foxbats climbed at seven miles a minute, soaring easily toward 50,000 feet. The level of the American Blackbird heading straight toward them.

The RSO blanched as he saw—then heard—the radar lock from the Gammons. He flipped on his ECMs[4] and watched the screen.

"They've got us on a new frequency. Looks like four, five, maybe six launchers. Jesus!"

"Nice to know we're wanted," said Greenwalt laconically.

[4]Electronic Counter Measures.

"Well, let's take tearful leave of these guys. We've got enough." He eased back on the throttle, reducing the speed to hand-flying ability, and began nosing the SR up.

The backseater had his hands full. All his ECMs were going full tilt, but the chaff was showing zip. Zero. He checked all his circuits, which were quadruple-redundant. But nothing seemed out of place. Just that the decoy stuff wasn't there to decoy.

"Colonel," he intoned through Greenwalt's helmet headset. "We're showing no, repeat, *no* chaff."

Greenwalt reflected, mentally computing before replying. "Not to fret, Chalmers. We'll be at 100,000 in two minutes."

The backseater was not reassured. He tapped on the instruments. Nothing. The whine from the SAM radar lock intensified.

Lieutenant Cantacuzene smiled. Several phone calls had placed all the controls in his hands. He bent his concentration to the pale green objects moving slowly toward each other on the big screen.

Five of the objects were the Foxbats, as they began their second-stage climb and dispersal. They were rising fast, coming up from the 50,000-foot level.

One was the American SR spy plane, hurtling directly toward them, but still out of the Foxbats' radar range.

Lieutenant Cantacuzene watched the fast-closing objects on his VDU, scarcely able to believe his luck. *The single highest-flying, fastest aircraft on earth. The prize trophy of them all. And right there, within his reach. Within Soviet airspace.*

Pressing his telephone mouthpiece close to his chin, Cantacuzene held his breath. Then, sharply, quietly, one word. *Fire!*

Both Greenwalt and Chalmers heard it at the same moment. The Soviets' SAMs were rising, and the howl in the cabin became piercing. Chalmers scrabbled at his instruments, punching in new coordinates for the ECMs, watching the computer run its threat evaluation. But nothing. Still nothing.

Greenwalt, at the moment, was silently cursing the idiots

who ordered him on this particular overflight, and cursing the idiot who believed in his own indestructibility enough to accept these orders without question. *Ah, well,* thought Greenwalt. *Let's see what we can do about these guys.*

Greenwalt was, of course, aware that the Soviets' new SAM-5s had a maximum reported range of 85,000 feet. And he was now just about there and still climbing. But it was a footrace. A footrace that allowed for zero stumbling.

Suddenly Chalmers shouted over the headset. *"We got chaff! Hot damn, it's working!"*

Greenwalt grinned and shook his big head. Chalmers was a kid. Twenty-four years old. Thrilled all to hell to be a Habu Hotshot. And damned lucky to be one in peacetime, when the risks were fewer. Except for now. Except for this moment.

Chalmers' voice again broke through Greenwalt's musings. "Colonel, we count five threats—five new ones, look like Foxbats—approaching at zero-one-zero."

What the fuck? Greenwalt, his adrenaline now soaring, wondered. *Is this some special kind of sandbag op? Where did these guys come from?* And then he remembered: Sikharovka, near Vladivostok.

Of course. It was well known the Soviets stabled a dozen or more Foxbats there. For just this eventuality, he reminded himself grimly.

The range had to be a touch far for them. But there they were. On the scope they were closing steadily, head-on. Greenwalt banked the SR slightly, putting it into a turn and then nosing it sharply upward. He shoved the throttles forward and the big Pratt & Whitneys kicked in for all they were worth, which was considerable.

One way or another, Greenwalt and Chalmers were about to join the angels.

The Foxbats were screaming, engines at full output, yet the American SR was slowly pulling out of range. The Foxbats' wing commander, rigid with tension, willed his aircraft to climb beyond its textbook capabilities. On his scope he saw the SAMs fall away, one by one, from the invading spy plane. It was up to him. Solely up to him now.

The Russian punched new entries into his flight computer.

The readout showed less than forty-five seconds before he would reach his operational ceiling. Before he would flame out or simply slip into a stalling speed and begin falling like a meteor to earth.

Still the SR kept inching ahead. The other Foxbats, all except the wing commander's aircraft, were now far below, beginning their return to Sikharovka and what solace they could give each other.

But the wing commander had one advantage they did not have. His Foxbat had recently been converted to the newer Foxbat-E version, engines uprated to 30,865 pounds of thrust. Strategic sections of the welded nickel steel structure had also been lightened with titanium.

Still, his never-exceed combat speed was Mach 2.9. And the SR-71 pilot obviously knew that, staying just out of missile range, conserving fuel for the run back to Okinawa.

It was maddening. The wing commander knew he could never hold his Foxbat together if he red-lined the airspeed to get within range. But it was his only choice, his only option. Or else he would regret, to the end of his days, never knowing the answer to *What if?*

Until the SR-71 had broken both the altitude and speed records, both had been held by the MiG-25. So the duel was close. Too close, in the view of the Soviet pilot, to break off contact.

And so, with the expectation that he was destroying not only himself, but an extremely expensive piece of aircraft, the pilot increased his airspeed to Mach 3 and armed all four "Acrid" air-to-air missiles.

The missiles would be useless beyond the level he was nearing. He began closing fast. The indicator edged its way over, in millimeters, to rest at Mach 3.2. His thumb rested lightly on the firing switch.

Chalmers was first to notice it. *The impossible was happening; the goddam Foxbat under them was moving into range.* And then, unbelievingly, both Greenwalt and Chalmers heard the ear-piercing whine of an air-to-air missile lock.

The backseater punched in the commands for the diverter which would shift the missile away from the SR, and in a few seconds, the whine stopped, only to be replaced by the explosion of a missile behind them, too far away to do any damage.

The SR continued its climb, now gaining precious meters of distance. Then the nightmare, the recurring nightmare, of all SR pilots happened: the aircraft suddenly lurched, yawing to the left. Half the thrust of one engine was gone: *an 'un-start,'* Greenwalt realized. The inlet control system was temporarily out of balance.

But the automatic restart didn't activate.

Greenwalt flicked on the manual start, and the SR shifted momentarily, now again on its upward climb, when suddenly the whine began again and became louder and Greenwalt's head moved just slightly to one side before it and everything else in and around the Blackbird exploded in a mist of metal, blood, bone, ceramics, flesh, and plastics.

_____ 20

Devon and St. Wolfgang.

When Pretorius came to, he found himself eye to eye with David Lloyd George from a distance of nine inches.

The dog lay waiting with its front paws crossed. The pose suggested infinite reserves of canine patience, even with a master moronic enough to prang his motorcycle on this, the most idyllic of country lanes.

The 1935 Norton, its motor stilled, lay on its side. A long whitish scratch scarred the gas tank's dark green paint. Other than that, the tough old bike was unscathed, which was more than Pretorius could say.

At the back of his head, a large bump began to make itself unpleasant. His left trouser leg was shredded, revealing an abrasion reaching from the knee down to the lower shin.

Pretorius winced. Susannah would likely pour something sensibly alcoholic over both the bump and the leg. The sting was going to be unimaginable.

Slowly, very slowly, he brought himself to his feet. David

Lloyd George's gaze, still fixed firmly on Pretorius' face, revealed nothing of the dog's opinion. But Pretorius knew. Pretorius knew.

He lifted up the Norton and swung his right leg (which still boasted a complete trouser covering) over it. He gave a quick silent prayer, then kicked the bike into life. The ululating thunder of its motor sounded right; nothing out of kilter. But he'd have to use some rubbing compound on that scratch. Maybe even do some touch-up, in case the compound couldn't work its magic.

David Lloyd George, confident now that Pretorius could finally get the thing going, rose to all four feet and looked up inquiringly.

"All right, all right," muttered Pretorius. "We'll get going." He eased the Norton into first gear, and swung back onto the single-track country road, David Lloyd George padding along on determined stubby legs.

The Dreaded DLG loved these trips with Pretorius. It was just the two of them, even if the man did display more than his share of clumsiness. It was fine to be running in the open country. And the man, he knew, was careful not to let the motor go too fast. David Lloyd George's legs were powerful, but their lack of length made locomotion at almost any speed a vigorous event.

They were near Dittisham (pronounced *Dit-Sam* by the locals), passing by an ancient farm called Chipton. Then by the remnants of the iron-age settlement near Capton Cross, old even when the Romans had marched down this same road.

Pretorius often took the Norton over this way, enjoying not only the history, but the names of the places themselves: Tippity Van. Viper's Quay. Parson's Mud. And, of course, the farm intriguingly named Bosomzeal.

One of Pretorius' favorite pubs was coming up in a mile or so, and the thought of a having a pint outside in front, in the clean fresh air, was tempting.

Pretorius still had some thinking to do. Uncharacteristically, he'd been lost in thought when the motorcycle hit the pothole: He hadn't seen it coming. He'd been damned lucky he'd been going slow to let DLG keep up. If he'd been going at forty-five or fifty, as he usually did when alone, he could have broken his neck.

He parked the bike in front as David Lloyd George eyed him expectantly. Inside, the publican and a few of the people Pretorius knew from the area gave him a warm greeting, as well as a few choice comments about his trouser leg. He ordered a pint of bitter for himself, a half-pint in a bowl for DLG, and together they went outside to sit at one of the tables.

David Lloyd George drank noisily from his bowl, pausing from time to time to peer up at the reflective Pretorius. DLG loved his beer and looked forward to it when out on a run. (Once a cigarette-puffing matron had stopped to lecture Pretorius on the inadvisability of giving a dog a beer. Pretorius silenced the woman by citing statistics, composed on the moment, of lung cancer in dogs owned by smokers.)

Not many cars passed on this road, and you could look all the way across the fields from this rise, all the way down to the sea. You could see the billowing white triangles as sail-boats sensed the wind—each sail, each boat, each man or woman pulling on the lines part of a ritual reaching back before history itself.

It was hard to leave this, he realized, *to sink yourself back into something dark and ugly, all for the sake of somebody who wouldn't know whether you did anything or not, somebody under the dank black earth of a New England grave.*

He'd decided to take three or four days here at home before going on to Vienna. Susannah deserved and demanded it, and whatever or whoever it was that killed Phil Mathieson could wait.

He knew it would also help clear his mind. Beeson had given him a free-lance contact in Vienna, somebody who knew the territory. Beeson had also warned him that no U.S. government agency or officer would give him the time of day. Phil Mathieson was definitely on the IG's shit list, and anybody who took a sympathetic view of Mathieson's former activities was definitely *persona non grata.*

Which, of course, was all right with Pretorius. The last thing in the world he'd want under his feet would be some intel weenie from the U.S. Embassy, two or three years out of school, wanting to get close to some action.

He looked down at David Lloyd George lying happily at his feet. *Well, old beast,* he thought, *you're going to get some rest while I'm away. And you'll probably get most of it on the couch, and Susannah's going to have your hide tacked up over the fireplace if you get any more of your fur on her black dresses.*

He grinned at DLG, who seemed to smile back up at him. "All right," he said aloud. "Can't put it off forever. Let's get ourselves in gear."

And so the two started for home.

The speaker and the listener sat on the *Kaiserterrasse* of the hotel in St. Wolfgang, overlooking the Austrian lake called the Wolfgangsee. Both appeared to be German tourists.

The listener was a saturnine man of about forty, lean and fit. The speaker, who spoke in the soft accents of a *Süddeutscher,* was a rotund older man with a perpetually anxious expression.

"There appears to be some activity among the Americans now, something to do with their cousin who—retired."

The listener speared a chunk of *Weisswurst,* liberally daubed with Düsseldorf mustard, and began to eat.

"My source says his replacement may be coming soon, that he will be an experienced man, a man who essentially works alone."

The listener continued eating.

"There's no identification of the replacement, nothing we can work with. But," he added, "we should have it soon, including the arrival date. And it will, my source says, be within the week."

The listener chewed his sausage thoroughly before finally commenting. "Tell your source we will pay, and pay well for any news—I repeat, *any* news—of this American. *Klar?*"

"Clear," agreed the speaker greedily. "I will be talking with my source tonight in Vienna. We will redouble our efforts."

The listener nodded, looking through the window at the swans making soft ripples as they neared the dock for their evening bread. Already the tourists were gathered, children armed with plump brown Austrian rolls, waiting to pay homage to the elegant birds. The listener thought of the people he'd known in his life who would have gladly slit someone's throat for a morsel of stale bread. God alone knows what they've have done for a dinner of roast swan.

The speaker was getting uncomfortable. "Then if there's nothing else?" He paused, waiting.

"Nichts besonders," replied the other.

"Well, then," said the speaker, rising with some awkwardness from the table. "I shall be in contact within twenty-four hours. You may rely on us."

The listener's only response was a slight twisting of the lips, as close as he ever came to a smile.

He resumed watching the swans. And at a nearby table, a middle-aged couple, Japanese tourists, began busily photographing the scenery.

Susannah had just returned, bringing with her shopping bags filled in Dartmouth at her favorite grocer's, a man whose shop front had not altered in eighty years although his prices unfortunately had.

"Michael, darling," she laughed, "you look like something the cat dragged in, then decided to drag back out. What on earth *happened?"*

Pretorius, ensconced in his big leather wing chair reading a Dick Francis novel, looked surprised, having forgotten his left trouser leg was in shreds. David Lloyd George, for his part, was sound asleep in the middle of the living room floor, all four stubby legs pointed heavenward, twitching now and again as if in pursuit of the hated rabbits.

"Well," began Pretorius, "we had a small accident on the road over near Chipton Farm. Pothole jumped up at me."

"How very inconsiderate of the pothole. I daresay you gave it a good talking-to?"

Pretorius grinned. "A talking-to, a dressing-down, and a comeuppance to boot."

"Well done, sir," Susannah commended. "Now, how about a nice hot cup of tea?"

"Um. Some Lapsang, if we've got any, please."

"We've got eight boxes of the stuff, thanks to you. Can't you ever pass by a shop without buying out all their Lapsang Souchang?"

Pretorius made a face. "Comes from having a deprived

childhood. No Lapsang, no Bournvita, no Horlick's. You have no idea how difficult life was as a boy in America."

"You poor dear," she said over her shoulder, entering the kitchen.

Pretorius smiled to himself. *You are one extremely fortunate son of a bitch,* he thought. *How many men have a woman this wonderful to be with, every day, every night?*

David Lloyd George snuffled in his sleep, legs once again paddling furiously in the air. *You aren't too bad, either,* added Pretorius, looking at the dog fondly.

When he'd come back from the States and told Susannah of his plans to go to Vienna, to get to the bottom of Phillip Mathieson's murder, she'd been vehemently opposed.

Her eyes became red-rimmed and she sounded as if she were three days into a serious cold. But it was just the onset of her tears. "You *don't* really have to go to Vienna," she brooded. "They've got people who do this for a living, investigating murders. And they probably do it a bloody sight better than you!"

Pretorius held her in his arms, rocking her lightly, wondering how to explain it, how to make her realize. He smelled the clean warm fragrance of her hair and wondered himself why he had to go, why he had to go into the middle of it all again. And with little or no backup.

"I know about the people who are investigating it, darling. And they've got it in their heads that Phillip was a bent penny, that he's been working for the Russians. I know how they work. If they start from a bad premise, then they'll move heaven and earth to prove it. I owe it to his mother. Most of all, I owe it to him."

Susannah all but shouted, "But he's *dead,* damn it! He'll never know. And if you go there, whoever or whatever killed him is damn well likely to kill you, too! I've had too much of you putting your life on the line, and all for nothing. *Nothing!*"

Pretorius looked at the ceiling as he held her, knowing everything she said made perfect sense, and at the same time knowing that nothing could prevent him from going. It was something bred in him, something part of him. "Shhh, darling," he said. "I'll be back before you know it, all in one clumsy piece. And I'll bring you back a nice chocolate *Sa-*

cher torte. Then you'll be sorry. It'll blow your diet all to hell and you'll get fat and miserable and you'll have me to thank."

She moved closer to him, kissing his cheek, wondering if indeed this would be the time she'd lose him forever.

Well, he thought, *with any luck I'll have this thing over and done with in a couple of weeks, and then we can all get on with life.*

A few minutes later, Susannah materialized with an array of tea, hot scones, strawberry jam, and Devonshire clotted cream. David Lloyd George abruptly ended his dreaming, and sat at Susannah's knee with an air of extreme dedication.

At a telephone booth at the edge of St. Wolfgang, ten minutes' walk from the hotel, a middle-aged Japanese businessman placed a call to Vienna.

The conversation, conducted entirely in an Okinawan dialect, was three minutes' long, and dealt with very ordinary things. A few business items, some talk of a replacement product, the competition getting very active, that sort of thing.

At the conversation's end, the man walked back to the town's center and joined his wife in a local *Beisel* for a pleasant evening's meal. *The beer here is extraordinary,* he decided. *Someday we must come back under different circumstances.*

_____ 21

Dartmouth and Vienna.

Three days ago the black van had been parked outside the Cherub in Dartmouth.

The Cherub was built in 1380, just two years after the first English cookbook, *The Forme of Cury,* was written. Its proprietors took this tradition to heart, and specialized in En-

glish cookery in all its variations. This was why Pretorius
and Susannah considered the Cherub their favorite. It was
also why they celebrated every important occasion within it,
such as the discovering the Dreaded David Lloyd George in
a pet shop in Bath.

(The Cherub, it should be noted, isn't named after an
angel, but after a boat built on the Devon coast for carrying
wool. An appropriate name, for the Cherub itself began life
as a wool merchant's house.)

Upstairs in the inn's half-timbered, slightly leaning-for-
ward structure, Pretorius and Susannah were celebrating her
fortieth birthday. The actual, *technical* birthday would actually take place next week in Pretorius' absence. But Susannah was not about to miss spending her birthday with
Michael, even if it meant rearranging the Gregorian calen-
dar.

Susannah Kenney was one of those rare individuals who
celebrate, rather than mourn, their landmark birthdays. At
forty, Susannah was voluptuous yet still somehow vulnerable. She also had a disarming intelligence that could hold a
head of state in thrall. Listening to her throaty voice, looking
into Susannah's upside-down blue-green eyes, an admirer
could lose all sense of time and place. To this effect Michael
Pretorius was no exception.

Over lunch Pretorius toasted her not once, but many
times. Altogether they consumed a bottle and a half of
Veuve Clicquot, and as succulent a collection of local dishes
as the Cherub could concoct. The Cherub outdid itself that
afternoon with chilled fresh Salcombe oysters and River
Dart salmon, the latter seductively sautéed with honeyed
butter.

Dartmouth's deluge of tourists had not yet reached flood
tide, and most of the people at the neighboring tables knew
the couple at least by sight, raising glasses to them as often
as Pretorius and Susannah raised theirs.

It was a bubbly and lovely and deliciously dizzying lunch,
and then they said their reluctant goodbyes and went downstairs to step into the brilliance of a Devon afternoon.

The man in the back of the black van squeezed off twelve
shots.

Hastily developed, their quality was marginal. But the

prints were good enough for a positive ID when Pretorius stepped out of the Wien Schwechat airport terminal three days later.

On that day a determined drizzle was succeeding in making a gray day grayer. Pretorius squinted at the sky, turning up his raincoat collar. A Mercedes taxi drew up to the curb. The driver, a young man with improbably blond-white hair and the build of a steroidal weightlifter, tapped his hand on the leather-wrapped steering wheel, keeping time to jazz throbbing through the car's speakers.

Pretorius slid into the taxi and leaned forward. "Hotel Sacher, please." Although his German was fluent, he didn't care to advertise it. The driver nodded. The taxi slipped into the traffic stream, and they began the drive toward Vienna's *Zentrum*.

After a few minutes, the driver spoke, displaying an exhibit of white teeth in the mirror. "You are American, yes? Here for a little business?"

"I'm American, yes. But just here to relax, see a little of Vienna."

"You have not been to *Wien* before?"

"Once, years ago."

"Ach, so." This seemed to satisfy the driver's curiosity, and they continued in silence for a while.

Pretorius stared out at the industrial landscape surrounding Vienna, vast and leaden, a gray parade of mind-numbingly dull structures. The lineup was relieved now and then by neon corporate logos, like battalions in *feldgrau* waiting to be reviewed while wearing a few shiny medals.

The rain began pelting in earnest, merging the gray sky with the horizon. The whine of the engine and the hiss of tires on wet pavement began to lull Pretorius into thinking of the infinite green of Devon, and of the warmth of Susannah in the mornings.

The driver interrupted Pretorius' reverie. "You like jazz, yes?" More teeth in the mirror.

Pretorius nodded. "Yes, I like jazz."

"We have good jazz in Vienna. Many fine young musicians. And the best international musicians, they come here.

Last month we had Horace Silver. You know Horace Silver?" Teeth again.

"Not personally, but he's one of the best."

"Ja, gerne. And the Modern Jazz Quartet, they come here. Soon. How long will you be staying here? You stay long enough, and maybe you can hear the MJQ, *nicht wahr?"*

"I'll only be here a couple of days or so. Not long."

"Not long enough. You need at least a month to get to know Vienna. You need a guide? Car and driver to show you the real Vienna? Got good rates. Best in Vienna!"

Pretorius shook his head, smiling. "No, thanks. I'll be walking."

"Too bad. I could show you great stuff. Not just tourist stuff. Look, see over there? You see the big wheel at the Prater? Five minutes from there is the best restaurant in Vienna. No tourists know about it, just us Viennese. But I show you. You sure?"

"I'm sure. Thanks anyway."

And so went the conversation, every word broadcast on the car's two-way radio to the driver's case officer. By the time the taxi pulled up in front of Philharmonikerstrasse 4, the surveillance team was well in place.

All the Sacher's exits were covered, and Pretorius' room was under electronic surveillance as well.

Pretorius checked in, blissfully unaware of the attentions thus showered on him. He was pleased the old place hadn't been afflicted by the current generation of hotel interior designers. It was still the hotel that most reflected *das alte Wien.*

After the ancient bellboy bowed himself out of the room with an old-fashioned *"Servus!"* Pretorius sank into the depths of the room's one overstuffed chair.

He'd stayed at the Sacher years ago, but under a different identity. This was the first time he'd been in Vienna under his own name. He would behave as a tourist, as an American who genuinely loved Vienna, paying a nostalgic visit to the old *grand dame.* Which, in its way, and in the tradition of all good cover stories, was perfectly true.

Years ago, Pretorius remembered, one of the grandees at

McLean[1] described postwar Vienna as having "more spies than a foxhound has fleas."

This was the Vienna of Graham Greene's *The Third Man,* the Vienna of world powers squabbling over niggling details of the Occupation, the Vienna that raised black market manipulations to the level of a fine art. But always a Vienna in which intelligence people could meet more or less freely, exchanging the bits and pieces which were their stock in trade.

Nowadays, with the *rapprochement* between Warsaw Pact and NATO countries, the profusion of spies was nowhere near the postwar high. But spooks were here nevertheless, and in profusion.

Here, Pretorius had to pick up the unraveled ends of Mathieson's abruptly terminated life. To find out who—or what—had been so important, and so evil, as to have a senior U.S. intelligence officer snuffed out in so public a manner. It smacked of implacable, brooding evil. It stank of desperation.

He'd begin tomorrow, he thought. But at the moment Pretorius' stomach was rumbling like a disgruntled terrier's. He'd avoided the airline's portion-controlled horrors so he could later pay a visit to one of his favorite restaurants, the Stadtkrug, in the Weihburggasse.

Changing into a comfortable old Kinsley & Company tweed jacket and a pair of flannel trousers, Pretorius walked down the stairs and entered the tumult of Vienna at night. He headed up the Kärntnerstrasse, past the neon glare of the shops, and toward the Weihburggasse.

As he walked, he thought about the next few days. Beeson had given him a single name, August Kadmus, and a telephone number. He'd committed both to memory during his briefing. Kadmus, Beeson said, probably knew more about Vienna than did the KGB and CIA combined.

Kadmus had worked undercover for the Americans all through the war. As a young Waffen SS lieutenant, he'd been bright and presentable. He'd been hand-picked by the head

[1]McLean, Virginia. Long-time headquarters of the Defense Intelligence Agency (DIA) until the recent move to Bolling Air Force Base.

of the SS in Cologne, a politically astute *Sturmbannführer* named Dietrich Lephardt, as an aide-de-camp.

As more and more senior SS men were either killed or rotated in their duty assignments, Lephardt was ultimately assigned to the Vienna of the *Anschluss*. And with him, the slim and handsome August Kadmus.

Kadmus reported regularly to behind-the-lines OSS officers in Austria, bringing them intelligence on orders of battle, matériel movements, and, most important, psychological profiles of high Nazi leaders with whom Lephardt constantly socialized.

All went well until Lephardt, checking on the telephone calls and movements of his staff, found Kadmus making calls to the same number on the same day at the same time every week. Accordingly, he began to have wire recordings made, tapping into the line in the cellar with alligator clips.

The conversations seemed innocent enough, all with a girl Kadmus seemed to be seeing regularly. But there were a few too many veiled meanings, a bit too much tension in their voices.

Lephardt had the girl followed, and discovered a number of people who seemed to have a keen interest in such things as the rail system, the airport, the Wehrmacht's motor pool and local barracks, and other items of military significance.

Within twenty-four hours, the Gestapo net closed in on all the people the girl had been in contact with, as well as closing on the girl and Kadmus himself.

Under torture, Kadmus didn't break. The girl did—two hours before dying. Twelve people were executed or sent to Mauthausen, but Kadmus himself continued to be interrogated for over six months by the Gestapo, in hopes of catching larger fish.

He shrank from a robust and healthy young man of 175 pounds to a cadaverous 85. Still he retained his mind and the will to survive. At war's end, Kadmus was found in a detention cellar unconscious, lungs ravaged with pneumonia, teeth, fingernails, and toenails missing—removed in the course of interrogations.

The OSS had the emaciated Kadmus flown to Switzerland where he spent months in a special sanitorium set up for such cases, and where he was visited by no less a personage than Allen Dulles himself.

Finally, judged ready to resume a more or less normal life, Kadmus was released with 160 Swiss francs, a cardboard suitcase with a limited amount of clothing, and an overwhelming desire to make up for the life he'd lost in the interim.

Kadmus went directly to Vienna. His family had been wiped out in Dresden during the firebombings, and none of his remaining relatives seemed interested in a German who had spied for the Americans.

So Vienna, home to spies for generations, became August Kadmus's home as well.

At first Kadmus began making a living as a haberdasher, importing woolens from England, cravats from Italy, shirts and underwear from America, and having suits made to order by Jewish tailors lately released from the concentration camps.

But soon he entered a more profitable pursuit, the trading of information between intelligence services. And for the next four decades, Kadmus was regarded by intelligence officers of both Warsaw Pact and NATO nations as the one untouchable asset in all of Austria, the man to whom one could come when in need of something special—a name, an address, a key piece of information, background on certain groups on both sides of the Iron Curtain.

Once or twice, the *Bundespolizei* had been alerted to Kadmus's activities, and certain young officers had attempted to make names for themselves by setting up elaborate plans to capture Kadmus and his contacts on either side. But in each case, a single telephone call had the operation called off and the police officer in charge assigned to one of the more remote Alpine villages, with duties commensurate with his abilities.

This, then, was the man Pretorius was here to see. There was no description, nothing other than the telephone number. Pretorius was told only to use it after the third day, that Kadmus preferred to contact him, after a suitable period of surveillance.

Pretorius stopped, suddenly realizing where he was. *The Stephansplatz. Where would it have been—where was the win-*

*dow from which Phil had been pushed? And where would he
have died, reduced so suddenly to a bloody puddle of stilled
humanity?*

He looked for the number of the building and, finding it,
counted the six stories. The fifth- and sixth-floor windows
had ledges which projected somewhat farther than the floors
below. Baroque, with carved heads of mythological creatures, the building itself seemed suddenly sinister. But
Pretorius suspected it was only because he knew what had
happened here.

He shook off the uncomfortable feeling, and entered the
Weihburggasse.

In this winding and ancient street the Stadtkrug sits discreetly, as if reluctant to be discovered. The far more famous
Zu den Drei Husaren stands directly opposite, freshly
painted, always attended by a good crowd. But the Stadtkrug has something special, something restaurant writers are
never quite able to transfer to guidebooks and articles.

The Stadtkrug looks older than it actually is, and the food
tastes better than it actually is. Its curved ceilings and carved
timbers produce a feeling of great coziness, and the aging
waiters radiate an aura of floundering *gemütlichheit.* The
metallic whanging of the restaurant's piano is achieved by
tuning the instrument only once per decade.

It was one of Pretorius' favorite haunts in Vienna. The
Kellner, chin elevated, menu tucked under one arm, pre-
ceded Pretorius to a small table near the piano and gestured
imperiously toward the chair.

Once he'd been seated, Pretorius began leafing through
the menu, savoring the selections as literature, waiting until
the last moment to decide among them. He settled finally on
Rindfleisch and so informed the waiter, who gave his gravest,
most thoroughly considered approval of Pretorius' choice.

Across the room, one of the men who had killed Phillip
Mathieson a few weeks earlier looked briefly at the wine list,
found a tempting young *Heuriger,* thought better of it and
ordered a bottle of Apollonaris instead.

22

August Kadmus.

A servant brought Pretorius into the library with the air of a museum guard ushering someone into the presence of an odd though extremely valuable *Meisterstück*.

As Pretorius became accustomed to the gloom, he saw a man whose bulk overflowed a long-suffering leather lounge chair.

The eyes of August Kadmus regarded Pretorius over half spectacles. Eyes that revealed little, in that they never changed throughout the conversation, and revealed much, in that their sparkle spoke of a constant and vast inner amusement.

Kadmus was dressed immaculately, in the manner of most ex-haberdashers, even ex-haberdashers of his enormity. A three-piece suit of fine gray wool managed to encase its owner with fabric to spare. He was accordingly able to move without fear of catastrophe. His tie, a crisply knotted silk shantung, contrasted against an *eisblau* cotton shirt.

His shoes struck the sole discordant note. They could have been made for a dancer, for they were crafted of the thinnest, supplest glove leather, mounted on a sole only marginally more substantial.

After a few moments of the two men studying each other, Kadmus broke the silence in an oddly Oxonian English accent, softened by *Süd-Deutscher* sonorities.

"So," rumbled his voice from the depths. "It seems you are a highly popular young man here in Vienna."

Pretorius looked at the older man questioningly.

Kadmus eyed him and grumbled on. "You had friends waiting for you at the airport, a friend to drive you to your hotel, friends listening to your every sound in your room, and finally friends accompany you all around your promenades in Vienna. All without your knowledge, I can only assume."

He examined his hands with interest. "This marks you,

Herr Pretorius, as a man destined for political greatness. For only one with so many friends, and one in so radiant a condition of ignorance, could ever rise to be a great politician."

And Kadmus chortled, for Pretorius, well trained as he was, had not tumbled to any of the surveillance. The watchers were good. The watchers were, in fact, among the best.

Kadmus leaned forward, as if confiding a great secret. "Now, the interesting thing about all this, Mr. Pretorius, is how you managed to suddenly accumulate this, this great wealth of friends, most of whom, I assure you, do not work for me."

"Precisely who were these friends, then, as you put it?" asked Pretorius, drawing up a chair.

"Well, some of them appear to be Russian, and some of them do not. And this is what I find—*most* intriguing: I counted among them some old acquaintances of mine from the GRU, one from the KGB, some from the Japanese, and several from your own intelligence service. I refer of course to that semireluctant darling of the media, your CIA." And he pronounced the last three initials with a great show of exactness, signifying Kadmusian distaste.

"Now I realize you are here as a private party, as it were," Kadmus continued. "But I do find it a source of wonder that you've managed to furnish so much employment to so great a number of the intelligence community residing in our city." He shook his head, and three tiers of jowls shook in near unison.

Pretorius interrupted. "Herr Kadmus, this is all very interesting, and I do most sincerely appreciate your taking the time to enumerate my many friends. But General Beeson said you might be able to—"

"Nicht so schnell, mein Knabe; nicht so schnell. We will come to that, we will come to that. But first: I am a terrible host. Will you take some peppermint schnapps with old August, yes?" And he pointed toward a decanter on a sideboard.

"Certainly, Herr Kadmus. May I do the honors?" And Kadmus waved his gracious acceptance, for extracting himself from the cracked and cowering armchair would likely have involved a major feat of engineering.

Pretorius poured the clear liquid into two small crystal flutes. He handed one to his sizeable host. *"Prosit,"* he said, with an acceptable *Preuzener* accent, elongating the "r" into a slight "w" sound, omitting the sound of the "i."

Kadmus raised his glass delicately, downing it in a single draft. *Like a drop in the ocean,* Pretorius thought irreverently.

"So. We get down now to cases." Kadmus placed his glass carefully on the table next to his chair, and put both hands on his knees. Pretorius became aware of the lack of fingernails.

"You wish to know what happened to your unfortunate school chum, the man Mathieson. So do many other people. So the two of us will not feel at all lonely in this.

"We will discover what happened from a number of sources, and then we shall triangulate them. Like RDF, yes?"

(Kadmus was referring to radio direction finding, in which two mobile receivers measure their relative angles to each other and to a radio signal coming from a certain direction, establishing the precise location of the transmission. A method used with productive results in Nazi Germany when searching for clandestine radios, and in Laborite England when searching for unlicensed television sets.)

"And what do you think we shall find, *hein?"* Kadmus paused to flick an imaginary spot of dust off one lapel. "More than likely we shall find enigmas within riddles within mysteries, but we shall ultimately arrive at the truth. Yes! We always do." He relaxed and drew a deep breath, either of satisfaction or exhaustion.

"You haven't mentioned your fee," Pretorius pointed out, for Kadmus wasn't a government man, but an entrepreneur who earned his living dealing in information.

"Ah. No, I have not, that is quite true. But shall we say—seven thousand schillings?"

Pretorius winced. "Could we say, instead, four thousand five?"

The leviathan laughed copiously, chins again following suit. "By God, I like you, Yank." He shook his head in amusement, then steepled his fingers and looked very hard at

Pretorius. "Seven thousand. Did not Beeson tell you Kadmus is not a *Händler?*"

"I don't want to bargain, either. But I can do a fair amount of the legwork myself. I'm not a desk man."

Kadmus seemed to find this even more amusing. Recovering, he said "But *mein lieber Knabe,* you haven't been in the field in years. You don't really know Vienna, at least not the way it is today. You'd only be underfoot."

"Nevertheless," Pretorius argued, "I'm the only one who would be penalized; no one else. You can't lose."

This seemed to intrigue the older man. "You have a point. But I don't wish to be chasing shadows the rest of my now somewhat limited life, just because a burnt-out former American officer wanted to play spy in my backyard. *Und so,*" and here he took a deep breath and regarded the ceiling, "although I will not bargain with you, I offer the following compromise: five thousand schillings, but the time limit is two weeks. No more. If we haven't got to the bottom of this, haven't discovered precisely who is behind your friend's death, then, my dear boy, you walk. *Punkt. Auf wiedersehen, versteh'st?*"

Pretorius smiled and nodded. *"Versteh'st."*

Kadmus rubbed his hands. "Then why don't you pour us another *schnapps,* and we stop this talk and start work!"

An ornate Dutch tallcase clock in the corner began striking the hour. Kadmus plucked out his large pocket watch, examining it with great interest and winding the stem.

"I remember well that afternoon," he mused after returning the watch to its well-tailored home. "It is, of course, difficult for anyone to stage anything in Vienna without some little bird coming to tell me all about it."

"But how did they take Mathieson? And are you absolutely sure they took him?" Pretorius asked.

"Oh, yes, my dear friend. They took him, make no mistake. They were good, very good. Your friend was also good, and his plan was excellent. But they had made up their minds, you see. And it had been too long, with too many failed attempts, for them to miss on this particular occasion.

"Mathieson waited with his men about an hour and a half. Which, of course, is too long to wait for anyone in this business. Then he got in his car with his driver and started the drive back to the *Zentrum.* So far, so good. *Alles in Ordnung.* There was one car in back of Mathieson's own, actually a consulate car with regular Viennese plates so as not to attract attention. Mathieson had borrowed several cars from the American consulate for this operation. He did not have a good feeling about it, despite all the preparations, all the personnel involved.

"Halfway back to town, a large truck managed to insert itself between Mathieson's car and the consulate vehicle. Then two or three blocks later, a second truck came up behind the consulate car and they bracketed him, yes? Like two big steel bookends. Only when the driver, an inexperienced man, attempted to leave his two newly acquired acquaintances, they—crushed him. Like an insect that was becoming an annoyance.

"Mathieson may or may not have been aware all this was happening. We will, in all likelihood, never know. We do know his car was found at the end of—appropriately enough, the *Himmelstrasse,* just overlooking the *Wienerwald*—the driver dead behind the wheel. It appears no struggle took place in the car, no bruises or other marks on the driver. Only a hypodermic needle puncture in the neck, on the left side. These people seem to be quite clever with the needles, *nicht wahr?"*

Pretorius sat still, thinking it through, listening for the anomalies. "The trucks. How did you know about the trucks?"

"The *Polizei* had several motorists as witnesses. The trucks were traced, both were found to belong to a *Brauerei,* and both had been stolen the previous night. Good organization," said Kadmus in professional admiration.

"And how long before Mathieson's fall from the window ledge?"

"It was seven days later. At first, we, or at least the security service, wondered whether the body was actually that of Mathieson. It was almost too convenient to wrap up the case, too neat in its way. Easy enough to push an addict off a ledge, someone of Herr Mathieson's age, build, and coloring. The head, as you know, was damaged beyond recognition. But that was something that couldn't have been counted on. Unless they destroyed the head just before the fall. But then again, too many people were watching before he tumbled."

Kadmus was leaning back in his chair, fingers steepled. He was a man with a lifelong habit of considering all possibilities, no matter how remote. It was one of the many reasons he was still alive, in a business that permitted few mistakes.

"The security police, along with your own CIA, blanketed all the airports, rail stations, checked cars, even coffins and containers being shipped out of Austria. Everything." Kadmus' hands made an all-encompassing gesture. "But these people, these people were very good. It was as if Mathieson had never been here, had never existed. He was swallowed up. Until he was found on that sidewalk."

"No sightings of him in between? Nothing?"

"Not a glimpse. Whoever got him kept him under wraps, possibly for interrogation. One of my men who stopped by the morgue saw the hypodermic marks; he thought one looked as if an IV had been used for some time. The only purpose for an IV in our business is for sodium Amytal or Pentothal, or something stronger. It's not used for nourishment."

Pretorius winced, remembering a similar interrogation in his own not too distant past. "No, nourishment isn't the idea. And did the Agency send anyone here to check out the body?"

Kadmus' eyebrows arched. "I should have imagined you would have been told. Yes, there was such a man. Did routine dental matches, asked all the right questions. The identification was positive."

The two talked for another hour. Before Pretorius left, the older man got out of the chair (with an assist from his guest) and took him into the kitchen, where a flat black plastic box was lying on the scrubbed pine table.

"Go ahead," said Kadmus, gesturing toward the box. "Take it, it's yours. You may need it." And he waited for Pretorius' reaction when he opened the box.

He was not disappointed. Pretorius snapped off the plastic lid to reveal a factory-fresh Glock 19: possibly the world's ugliest but most efficient and effective semiautomatic, holding seventeen rounds of 9 mm. ammunition in its extended magazine.

As Pretorius hefted the compact piece, Kadmus chuckled. "A good Austrian pistol, *nein?* Anyway, I couldn't tell Arthur Hornbill I didn't furnish you with every assistance. So take it. But don't get involved with the *Polizei;* the serial numbers are for a gun that doesn't technically exist. Untraceable."

He also gave Pretorius a box of Remington plus-P-plus rounds, loaded to the upper limits of chamber pressure. Then he indicated it was time for his afternoon nap: "An old man's vice," he said ruefully. Pretorius shook the giant's hand. The servant appeared as if summoned by an inaudible bell, and showed him out.

After a pause to guarantee Pretorius would not return for something forgotten, Kadmus dialed a telephone number.

The woman who answered spoke in a slightly accented German, a Slavic—possibly even Russian—intonation. *"Hallo? Wer ist da?"*

Kadmus spoke quickly, in a monotone. As he talked he absentmindedly fingered a small brass object on the end of his watch fob. At the conversation's end, he replaced the receiver, looked at his watch, and expelled a long sigh.

"Pretorius, my friend," he said to himself, shaking his head, "You are about to become the most sought-after individual in all Vienna. I only hope you are good enough to survive the experience."

_____ 23

The Black Czar.

Immediately on entering the first room, you were assaulted by five large dogs, so you braced yourself for the turning of the knob.

You took care not to pay too much attention to the dogs as they became even more excited if you did. You entered and let Feliks' servant take your coat and hat, and then you waited and were subjected to the dogs' snuffling curiosities before being escorted into what Feliks' detractors called the Holy of Holies.

Feliks was seated in a Jacobean oak chair facing the entrance. He wore a black velvet cassock and held the ebony and silver staff he used as a walking stick. Sensitive, pallid pianist's hands emerged from voluminous sleeves. Long fingers dangled over the chair's arms, perpetually in motion as if the man were impatient, eager to move on.

But Feliks moved very little these days. Arthritis had severely crippled his joints, and even his limited expeditions around his rooms caused him great discomfort. This, compounded by an innate and unrelenting irascibility, made life Hell for his servant.

Feliks had one of those faces normally associated with medieval poisoners or certain saints. A waxen luminosity of the skin contrasted eerily against the eyes' pools of brooding agate blackness. The shaven head, hollow cheeks looming above a waist-length beard, completed the ascetic aspect.

Not wishing to limit the effect to his *corpus* alone, Feliks extended his aesthetic to everything around him.

All the walls were cassock black, and in this even the windowpanes were not exempt. These too were painted to forbid the intrusion of daylight, to provide wall space for a plague of icons and artifacts, and to confound real or imagined Chekist lipreaders and their high-powered telescopes.

Crucifixes with realistically punctured and dripping Christs were everywhere. Icons of every conceivable saint, every near or distant relation of the Holy Family were present. St. George the Dragon-Slayer glared fiercely from several vantage points. The relentless imagery was punctuated only by photographs of Feliks with a member of the Politburo, Feliks with a famous film director, Feliks with an admiral of the fleet, Feliks with the publisher of *Komsomolskaya Pravda,* Feliks with a glistening visiting dignitary from one of the developing nations.

Presiding over all, dignitaries, relics, and icons alike, was an evenly distributed layer of dust.

On meeting Feliks for the first time, one would assume him to be a canon, a bishop, some sort of high church official. And, indeed, Feliks had once served as a Russian Orthodox priest.

But his mission at this point in history was quite different.

For Feliks was the nominal and virtual head of *Ote-chestvo*, a movement which emerged from the Slavophilism of the 1840s. Under his considerable influence were several members of the Central Committee itself, a few from the Presidium, and many high-ranking officers of the Soviet military, including virtually all the GRU high command.

Predating Marxism by several decades, *Otechestvo* was fiercely dedicated to Russian traditions, to Russian thought and culture, and to Russian nationalism of the most uncompromising sort. *Otechestvo*, when the USSR was formed, believed the gathering of inferior nations under the mantle of the USSR would ultimately prove to weaken the Fatherland, Great Russia.

And now, on the eve of the economic disintegration of the Soviet Union, they were seeing the realization of their worst fears.

Great Russia was being drained of its lifeblood. The cost of maintaining the mongrel collection of Soviet republics had risen stratospherically. And much of the military budget—the money which should, by rights, be devoted to the defense of the Fatherland—was being bled and diverted to hold on to these bastard dependencies. As if it that weren't enough, money was being diverted to send good Russian men and matériel to the godforsaken so-called Third World countries.

The twelve men who came to Feliks' rooms this evening controlled the leverage that could restore Russia to its rightful position. A position abdicated in Gorbachev & Company's frenetic scrabbling for credits, their pandering to the big Western and Japanese banks, and forfeited in their drive to sustain a rag-tag bag of countries run by the *ni kulturny*, near savages.

They had already taken major steps, steps from which lesser men would shrink like boys. But they alone realized that Russia was on the brink of an abyss from which there would be no escape. And that they alone held the key to saving the Fatherland.

Feliks was deep in thought, lost in the wanderings of his formidable intellect. It was his prodigious mind which guided this complex movement, and which even now was playing out the endless variables, the moves and counter-moves of the endgame they were here to discuss. The voice of Petrosyants, the GRU strategic planner, rose above the murmur of the conversation, disturbing Feliks' musings.

"The Americans of course base their worst-case scenarios on what they wish to believe, not on what the actual probabilities are. They wish to believe one thing, therefore they construct an entire religion to support that belief."

The others were nodding in agreement. It was common knowledge that hope, more than reason, powered the machinery of American strategic defense.

Petrosyants pressed his argument, glaring through lenses thick as the bottoms of bottles. "Their Joint Chiefs of Staff have several pet scenarios on which they have concentrated, and it is these to which they will, in the first frenzied realization of a surprise attack, instinctively turn.

"Let us examine one of these," he pursued in his characteristic (and to Feliks distinctly annoying) professorial tone. "We can assume their force structure as based on 20 Trident submarines with over 3,800 warheads on their D-5 sea-launched ballistic missiles, 500 warheads among 50 rail-based garrisons of MX missiles, another 500 warheads in their SICBMs based in the American southwest, and their bombers carrying approximately 2,600 warheads.

"They realize we count heavily on the VPVO's surface-to-air missile defenses, which is why they've tried to push through their Stealth bomber. The B-2 can knock out many of our SAMs before its presence is pinpointed, clearing the way for B-52s. But fortunately their Congress has seen fit not to fund the B-2 in any realistic sense.

"Therefore, our SAMs can still be counted on in a U.S.-generated situation." The GRU man paused to sip delicately from a glass of hot tea. "They also still have very few B-1Bs at either their Whiteman or Dyess Air Force Bases, so we can assume their bomber force is still somewhat in the dark ages." A ripple of amused laughter throughout the room. The men looked at each other with knowing expressions.

"But gentlemen," Petrosyants continued, "even *they* know this doesn't really hold up well as a leg of their ICBM triad. So what does this leave us with?"

He looked around the room expectantly, even at Feliks,

who favored the man with a look that could freeze water in a glass.

Petrosyants pressed on undaunted. "It leaves us with the following sequence. They have seen our preparations—or rather what they *think* our preparations are—and they will, within the next week or so, confer endlessly among themselves, considering this option or that.

"But they will, in the end, believe we are ready to launch a surprise attack. And they will, accordingly, make their own preparations for a pre-emptive strike.

"Their non-alert Trident D-5s will have considerable mobility in a generated scenario versus a response to a surprise attack." He stroked his chin, staring at one of the icons which remarkably resembled Feliks himself.

"And they have other advantages if we force them to launch a first strike. But quite apart from those of us here, and those of us in our organization being quite unable to launch our own first strike, we still have the main advantage. For, gentlemen, we have *survivability.*"

From across the room Sergei Ilyushin, newly elected to the Congress of People's Deputies, regarded Petrosyants with mixed interest and revulsion. Petrosyants was well-regarded as a Chess Master and as one of the GRU's best and brightest strategic thinkers. Yet behind his logic there was an icy disregard for human life.

But even Ilyushin had to agree with the officer's assessment. In a nuclear exchange, the underground bunker system guaranteed the survival of not only Soviet leadership but much of the population.

What Ilyushin disagreed with was Petrosyants's premise that war was necessarily inevitable. Ilyushin had known many men like Petrosyants, and knew generals loved fighting as much as surgeons loved cutting. Everything in their training made armed conflict desirable, peace unendurable.

He interrupted Petrosyants's argument. "Agreed, Colonel-general, we do indeed have a perverted form of survivability, much as a bird when struck down from the sky, killed and allowed to decompose, still has its skeleton. But is it not better to avoid being struck down in the first place? Why accept merely being a skeleton, lost in the ashes of a largely uninhabitable world?"

Petrosyants smirked at what he considered to be Ilyushin's naivete. "With respect, Sergei Nikoleyevich, our best scientists have calculated the world after a nuclear exchange will be quite habitable, especially with our nationwide system of bunkers. You are mistaken in your assessment there.

"And as far as uninhabitability is concerned, consider what our lives would be like under the yoke of the Americans, or even—in the next century—*the Japanese.* This is not the dream our forefathers yielded their lives for. The obliteration of Russia? No, I think not. Better to dream and risk and achieve, than to ultimately grovel before the bloated plutocracy of the West and their Japanese masters."

The others, their eyes carefully watching Ilyushin, began to nod in assent. But Ilyushin persisted, hoping to provoke Petrosyants into an indiscretion: "Colonel-general, you are a man of war, much as I am a man of politics. Are you certain your zeal for war has not surpassed your love for Great Russia, great though that love may be?"

Petrosyants colored deeply to the edge of the thick military collar that bit into his neck. "With respect, Deputy, we are now at a moment in history which requires men of resolution, strong men. The time for politicians and mewling compromises is over. There is a price to be paid, and I as much as anyone know that price means the death of millions—not only the Americans, but our own people, who will in future be honored as heroes and martyrs of Father Russia!"

Feliks had been glowering darkly for some time, impatient with this exchange. His mind had already leaped ahead many stages. He regarded this dialogue as political prattle, empty echoes of a foregone conclusion.

He leveraged himself slowly to his feet and pounded the ebony and silver staff on the stone floor. The group was suddenly quiet. "Let us go in, my brothers," he intoned. "There is much to discuss, and much to decide."

His dogs rose from their accustomed places around his feet, and the men tossed down the remnants of their vodkas and began to wander toward the hall, following Feliks as if in some bizarre religious procession.

Several of the men were in army uniform, but most were in the sacklike suits that indicated their superior status as bureaucrats. They muttered to each other, commenting on Petrosyants's tirade, and of the necessity for strong measures in critical times.

It was bone-chillingly cold in the hall, and the great fire had been lit only a few moments. Three stories tall and built of huge blocks of quarried granite, the hall dated back to the days of Aleksandr Nevsky, a more vigorous and warlike time. As the men entered, they rubbed their hands together and looked longingly at the steaming salvers of meat and poultry and vegetables. There was *tefteli,* salmon *pojarski, blini, kulebiaka,* and an almost endless array of other Russian dishes. Such a feast was almost unthinkable in the Soviet Union of today. Yet Feliks' followers had managed it with ease, requisitioning much from army stores.

Feliks pointed wordlessly with his ebony staff, indicating the position each man should take at the huge trestle table. As the last man was seated, Feliks leaned the staff against the table, and raised his arms dramatically, eyes seeming to pierce the ceiling, to lance through the dark night's clouds and rise to the very heavens themselves.

"Almighty Father, God of Great Russia, protect us in this, our hour of peril. Give us the strength to smite our enemies, the courage to sacrifice what must be sacrificed. Grant that we, unlike those around us, may have the steel to conquer not only our enemies beyond our borders, but our even more dangerous enemies, our insidious foes within who would seek to destroy Great Russia. This we ask, in the name of the Father, the Son, and the Holy Spirit. Amen."

And Feliks sat down as the men around the table raised their eyes to look greedily at the feast before them.

An entire side of beef had been prepared for this night, and it had been roasted to perfection, sliced, and was now being passed around the table on huge porcelain salvers. Feliks, a vegetarian, declined it, but helped himself to heaping portions of the turnips, potatoes, cabbages, and leeks.

As he ate, his anthracite eyes glittered, stoked with righteousness. For this was his moment, the time he knew would come, when the fools around him would finally realize what was happening to Great Russia.

For years, he thought with a deep and dark satisfaction, he had been dismissed by the leadership as a crank nationalist, a harmless old fool whose ravings were mere echoes of a movement that died decades ago, long before the Georgian Stalin's ascent. But now—now the fools were seeing the results of their building on quicksand, of their attempting to hold a patchwork union together of so-called Soviet Republics, a union that was no more a union than a peasant's stew was a single perfect filet mignon.

All over Russia, movements allied with his were beginning to emerge and thrive. From the effete, intellectual Russian Federated Writers' Union, to the fiercely militant *Pamyat,* with their comical paramilitary trappings reminiscent of Yukio Mishima's private army.

Slowly, these movements had been coalescing, coming together, feeding on the disasters all around them—the Azerbaijani incidents, the Baltic states, the ignominious retreat from the foolish adventure of Afghanistan, all the follies, all the waste, all the trusting young skulls rotting in foreign soil.

Even the most senior members of the Politburo came to discreetly ask Feliks' advice on certain matters. And it was said, with some truth, that both the GRU and the *Oborony* (Defense Council) considered him Russia's one true leader, "the Black Czar," as one general—admiringly but dangerously—put it.

As Feliks ate, spearing huge chunks of potatoes drenched in butter, his coal-dark eyes assessed each of the men around the table. None here was his intellectual equal, but no matter. They would all be useful in the days ahead. For the days ahead only required loyalty to the cause, to *Otechestvo.* Too much thinking in time of crisis, too many intellectuals, could be fatal. And after all, intellectuals were the cause of the strangulation of Russian culture and Russian consciousness in 1918.

The wine and vodka had been flowing freely; tongues were now well lubricated. The men were pledging great friendships, blearily boasting of their commitment to the cause. Feliks judged it was time to speak.

He rose like a black dawn, an apocalyptic figure. His eyes, surmounted by great tufted wings of eyebrows, leveled at the seated men. All conversation stopped.

"We eat here tonight as if our nation were not being torn

apart." He paused to let this penetrate, to allow the men who were still chewing to finish, guilty expressions suddenly showing. "We laugh and we joke, as if after tonight there would still be a tomorrow.

"But our tomorrows are numbered. We are quite quickly running out of all our tomorrows, and out of money, and more catastrophically, out of the blood of true Russians. And why?

"Because after seven decades of being subjected to the madness of Marx and his fellow Jewish intelligentsia, Great Russia is beginning to emit a death rattle."

There were murmurs of protest from several of the men. But they were quieted with a single quick motion of Feliks' hand. "It is, after all, what they *wanted,* is it not? They have their Union of Soviet Socialist Republics, do they not? Their tottering Tower of Babel, spread across an entire continent? Then why not let them enjoy the fruits of their intellectual depravity, the spoils of their sins against you, against I, against every true son of Russia?"

He leaned forward, supporting himself on the tall silver and ebony staff, a sinister shepherd leading his flock to a dark destination. "I shall tell you why. Because now, *now* is the pivotal point in our history. *Now* at last they are unsuspecting and weakened. *Now* they are too absorbed in eviscerating their own Socialist Dybbuk to realize there are true Russians awakening to a great and glorious rallying call! We are creating a spiritual rebirth of Russia, a rekindling of the fires of revolution—but based on a *Russian* rather than a tainted internationalist precept."

He swept on. "As is well known, the internationalists surrounding Lenin hated Russia, and knew the clever way to conquer was to subvert. That is one of the fundamental precepts of Marx, himself, of course, a German Jew living in England, a man truly without a country. And so Russia in the Revolution was subverted, a subversion completed by Josef Stalin, the wily Georgian, and his terror squads under Lazar Kaganovich, who conducted Stalin's massacres so adroitly that they lost the cream of the nation, the genetic pool of our best and brightest.

"Our churches were profaned into museums of atheism, our women forced into factories, our families moved into the squalidness of indiscriminate industrialization, our beautiful villages raped and destroyed."

Feliks' eyes seemed quite literally to glow. Saliva sprayed as he gathered momentum.

"Yes, my brothers, we are paying the penalty. We have been paying the penalty ever since 1918 when we let them, yes, *let* them butcher our sainted Czar Nicholas II and the Imperial Family. We have been paying for it with the lives of millions of Russians.

"But is this enough? No, even now our 'President,' surrounded by his own Westernizers, is selling our birthright—trading petroleum, natural gas, even our forests—to foreigners, to Americans for wheat, to France for meat, to China for potatoes.

"He is trying to carve up Great Russia in tiny pieces, for American and Japanese credits. And what fate does he reserve for us, once his carving is complete?

"He wants us to be a pale pattern of the West, a caricature of capitalism, a kind of docile Disneyland of democracy for tourists to visit and litter and jeer at!"

Down toward the other end of the table, the seam that passed for Petrosyants's smile twisted bitterly. But as usual the eyes were unreadable behind the spectacles.

Feliks pointed in turn to each of the uniformed men at the table with a long, quavering finger. "The military is being dismembered. Our aircraft, our missiles, are being cut to pieces *by our own people, our own soldiers.* What the Americans couldn't do to us, we now do to ourselves, and gladly!

"If we are to live in the way our forefathers fought and died for—if we are to keep the flame of Russia alive and not allow it to be snuffed out by every momentary gust of wind, *we must be strong!* Surely you must realize that I of all people have Russia's future at heart. I do not believe, though, that Russia will *have* a future unless we act.

"The economic naïveté of the Marxists is now coming home to roost, like a vulture, ready to pluck out the entrails of Russia the instant—the very *instant* the last gasp of life leaves us.

"Already the bankers of America and Japan, the Shylocks of our own time, are rubbing their hands in glee. They cannot *wait* to begin our dismemberment. You have heard how these jackals take over companies, corporations, carve them up, sell off the pieces, and ultimately destroy those companies?

"Well, my brothers, imagine that happening to our entire country! The capitalists will take what they need for their ventures, replenishing nothing, until Russia itself is emptied of every natural resource, every factory, every working man. The supply house will change to a charnel house. And *that* is the legacy of indecision!"

Feliks towered over them, the candles of the chandelier guttering slightly, as a draft swept through the ancient hall. "But Great Russia is entrusted at this moment in history to *our* hands, to *our* minds, and to *our* hearts. The risks are great. There may be some among us who grow faint-hearted at what we must do to succeed. But the alternative . . . the alternative is *oblivion.*"

Feliks stared at each man in turn, the silence as he did so increasing in tension with every passing second. "I have invited Army General Mescheryakov here tonight, one of Russia's great heroes. He, and Colonel-general Petrosyants, have evolved what I believe to be the one path that can, at last, save Great Russia—save it for our sons and daughters—and for all the generations that follow after us!"

There was a startled silence, then a patter of applause. A tall, broad-shouldered general with GRU epaulets stood up and leaned forward on the table, supporting himself on the knuckles of his doubled fists. His head was bald as a billiard ball, and he had neither eyebrows nor eyelashes. He appeared to have some sort of genetic defect which prevented the growth of hair. His eyes were a penetrating, almost eery green.

He began speaking slowly and methodically, as if every word were too important to go unheard, as if he were patiently giving instructions to a cadre of young officers.

And as the general spoke, Ilyushin's complacency gave way to a mounting horror. Only now was he beginning to register what was happening here, in this room, in this citadel of centuries past. There was an anti-Semitism which, as in Hitler's Germany, would be used as a scapegoat, as a focus of fear. There was a hatred of outsiders which, as in many dictatorships long since past, would be fueled as long as it would bring the dictator to power, then would be turned inside, against those who still dared offer opposition.

But as fearful as all these things were, there was that which dwarfed all such fears in its sheer madness:

These men were calmly proposing to trigger thermonuclear war.

_____ 24

Dawn, Sikharovka.

Like sleek black porpoises they moved, out past the breakwater where the commitment begins. The sea was pushed and parted, churned by the screws turning astern, mimic windmills driving the great dark shapes before them.

On this dark morning, the men on the bridge of the Delta III sub were feeling the edge that begins every mission. It had been seventeen days since they'd put into Sikharovka, and now the throb of the engines transmitted an excitement through the steel to their boots on the deck, to their gloved hands on the cowling.

Lieutenant Gostev, absolved of his hangover and breathing clean salt air at last, leaned against the wind.

Setting out to sea in a submarine, he reflected, is like going out in no other vessel. Only the submarine commits itself to the deep, to the real sea that lies below the world of man. Lesser vessels press down on the sea's resistant surface but are refused, forbidden the mirror-image of flying that is the given privilege of the submarine.

Each mission, of course, has its own personality. The worst are routine. The best are those that face a portion, however small, of the unknown. These are the missions you live for, the reason you entered the service, and this one, Gostev realized, was that sort of mission.

It was even rumored the mission was a special project of Admiral Terpanichev's, that not even the Admiralty in Moscow was aware of it. Therefore, Gostev reasoned, it was likely Terpanichev's way to test the ASW hunter/killer teams. It was well known that once a mission was cleared by Moscow, many leaks seemed to occur, and ASW teams were often told their quarry's exact position and course.

Whatever the reason, this mission was special. All the signs were there. The night work, the extra provisioning, the security measures, even the infinitesimal differences in the captain's behavior. But Gostev was happy. Free from the constraints of the shore and about to be free from those of the surface, he was in his element.

He watched the gray rocks of the breakwater changing perspective as the boat swept past, salt spray spuming over them with a rhythmic certainty. The other submarines were moving at a barely restrained pace, eager to enter the realm below. The dim gray minutes before dawn were brightening fast. Too fast. Soon the American satellites would be able to see them, to even identify the rank on the officers' bridge coats.

The command came from below. "Clear the bridge."

"Bridge. Aye, aye," Gostev snapped back.

Gostev took one last look at the Sakhalin Island shoreline melting into the early morning mists, gray into gray. Then he and the others slid down the ladder to the world in which they were trained to live and thrive.

By the time the hatch was secure, the whitecaps were lapping the base of the steel sail and the boxy forward section where the big ICBMs were housed. The boat was going down to where its bulbous hull would be translated into a thing of gliding and surreal beauty.

Army General Mescheryakov, head of the GRU, calculated the votes he controlled within the Defense Council, the top military/industrial organ of the Soviet Union. Between his control of that organization and the GRU, he could now orchestrate the maneuvers necessary to launch his deception—the illusion of a great nation preparing to go to war.

If only the KGB didn't get too close, didn't awaken to the plan. And if events in Vienna did not again get out of hand. He began to think of the hated Dovgalevsky, now in complete charge of the *residentura* there. This was a weak spot, in a function in which a weak spot was utterly unacceptable.

He made a note to select a replacement for the Vienna *rezident*. But first there were other priorities.

He dialed the number of the head of the Air Defense Troops. Congratulations were in order for the first successful downing of an American SR-71. He would confide to the commander that the overflight had been part of what GRU intelligence had discovered was a large-scale preparation for war by the United States.

He would urge the commander to be ever more vigilant in the days ahead.

There were now seventy-three P-3C Orions in the Japanese Maritime Self-Defense forces, each equipped with a Magnetic Anomaly Detector (MAD), and the ability to monitor sixteen different sonobuoys at one time.

Three of the Orions had been monitoring the seas around Hokkaido since both the Marine Observation Satellite (MOS-1) and LANDSAT reported the imminent sailing of a large number of submarines from the Soviet pens on Sakhalin.

The intercept station at Wakkanai, twenty-seven miles across the La Perouse Strait from Sakhalin, also logged in a large number of signals, apparently between submarines and their base.

In a sleek new Orion recently delivered by Kawasaki Heavy Industries, Cho Kanagawa sat reading his copy of *The Bungeishunju*. Poring over the pictures of beautiful, successful people drinking Scotch whisky, wearing gold watches, using fountain pens, driving big automobiles, Kanagawa sighed and sipped from his can of Pocari.

He'd been on watch less than forty-five minutes. As a matter of training and habit, Kanagawa glanced over to the digital displays. Two had been activated. Moving quickly, he entered a new frequency in one of his receivers.

Suddenly he pressed his hands over the headphones, forcing them closer to his ears, shutting out the rumble of the big Orion P-3C aircraft. *The subs were moving into his sector*.

After the group of eight subs had been detected by the Orion off Hokkaido, the prime minister was kept informed of their progress on an hour-by-hour basis by Japan's senior intelligence service, *Naichó*.

The prime minister's mood was dark, his temper vicious, and his staff was careful not to add to his troubles until the crisis was resolved.

Baka! It all seemed crazy, the prime minister thought. *Hadn't we given them most of the credits they'd solicited from our banks? Hadn't both we and the Americans set up innumerable joint ventures with the Soviets? Had they been so duplicitous as only to pretend in Perestroika, to lull us into a false sense of security?*

The prime minister had several briefings over the last ten days, usually conducted by Naichó, but a few directly presented by Chobetsu,[1] the signals intelligence agency.

Chobetsu was set up in 1958. It now has over 1,200 employees and ten ground stations, including headquarters at Camp Ichigaya in Tokyo, and is mainly charged with collecting and analyzing communications of China, North Korea, and the Soviet Union.

Their YS-11A electronic intelligence aircraft had been flying regularly out of Machinoc Air Base near Misawa to gather transmissions from Sakhalin, collecting telephone conversations, communications between ships, headquarters signals to and from the subs, even car telephone communications of senior Soviet naval officers.

In the end, Chobetsu's work had been the most decisive in arriving at the conclusion: It was not merely a military exercise, not merely maneuvers. The Soviets were positioning themselves for the opening of hostilities. Even though Japan had the third most powerful military machine in the world, it would be powerless against a sub-launched nuclear attack.

The prime minister ran his hand through his thinning hair, and looked at the photo of his family in its frame on the desk. For the first time in his life, he was facing the possibility of never seeing them again. For there was enough nuclear destructive power in the sub's missile launchers to obliterate all Japan within seconds.

---

[1]Short for Chosa Bessbitsu; fully designated as The Annex Chamber, Second Section, Investigation Division, Ground Self-Defense Forces.

He tried to conceive of the horror that had been Hiroshima and Nagasaki, extended to every square centimeter of Japan, a limitless field of ashes.

It would mean the end of *Nihon minzoku,* the extinction of an entire people.

_____ 25

The Talking Dogs.

The chorus of voices, well intentioned though largely out of tune, reverberated among the walnut timbers, whitewashed plaster, and large marble plaques commemorating the Confederacy's dead.

All this conspired to produce a most satisfactory echo, encouraging even the tone-deaf to sing with ringing enthusiasm.

The Director of Central Intelligence was one of these. His booming baritone voice had never known the luxury of landing solidly on a note as written. Instead, it swooped down on the note, invariably missing it, only to rise and quaver uncertainly in the note's vicinity, much as a myopic hawk might attempt striking a sparrow in mid-flight, only to grab at empty air, and thereafter hover confusedly in the general area.

Nevertheless, the director persevered in his singing, considering it a duty. He was thus engaged when the young CIA bodyguard came up the aisle and whispered in his ear.

Up to this point, Coldwell had imagined St. Mark's as his one true sanctuary from The Job. He was accordingly annoyed until the aide explained the reason for the interruption. Coldwell spoke quietly to his wife, then rose and followed the man out into the bright Virginia sunshine.

People in Leesburg had gotten used to the Director of Central Intelligence being a visible part of the community. The town has always had more than its fair share of senior government officials, and it was therefore considered bad form to stare at the dark blue government Malibu with the two young men who were obviously either bodyguards or plainclothes detectives of some sort.

The driver was waiting by the right rear door. The director climbed in. He inserted his crypto ignition key into the mobile phone, a Motorola Dynasec 1000 Secure Voice/Data Cellular Terminal. Then he punched in the numbers. The "Fascinator" encryptor kicked in as soon as the connection was made.

It was the head of NPIC, Ken Nordstrom, with the most recent take from LACROSSE. The news wasn't good. Could they meet, say, two hours from now? Either Langley or NPIC?

Coldwell looked at his watch. He'd been looking forward to Sunday roast beef dinner with his family. *Well, that tears it,* he thought. *I won't be back home until dark. And if the take is really bad, then it means bringing more people in, maybe even briefing the White House.*

He spoke briefly: "Okay. We'll do it at the Agency, at 1:45. Let's keep it tight and small. You and I, and Felker. Keep the NSC out of it for now. They'll have enough to play with later."

He sat by himself in the car a while. Then he went back to his wife and children in time for the offering.

The tapes were chilling. Each of the sequences assembled by Tim Nagata had a time/date window burned into the lower edge of the frame. For twenty-three minutes the images on the big HDTV projection screen showed a steady evolution: the huge survival bunkers being provisioned, the Rocket Forces relocating and readying their launchers, the Navy preparing their attack submarines, the Air Force repositioning and arming their strategic bombers, the Soviets' rail- and truck-based missile garrisons gearing up.

Ken Nordstrom's introduction had been understated. The tapes told their own chilling tale. Coldwell had been informed of earlier activities in the Soviet Union. But until now he'd held onto the fragile hope that they were merely war game maneuvers, or some sort of bluff.

He remembered late 1983 when the Soviet Union, to intimidate Japan, sent thirty aircraft and a flotilla of missile-carrying cruisers and destroyers through the Strait of Tsu-shima. Soviet-Japanese relations had been deteriorating ever since, especially with the USSR's constant rebuffs to Japan's requests to return the Kurile Islands.

Earlier, Coldwell had been a young man when the Cuban missile crisis had been front page news. Khrushchev, like Gorbachev years later, had loudly announced conventional arms reductions only to beef up technology and create a far more lethal military machine. At the time Khrushchev reduced Soviet military manpower by 1.2 million, he was busily creating the Strategic Rocket Forces, making ICBM production his top priority, and starting the Soviets' own military space program.

Then he'd gambled on the U.S. being too intimidated to call his bluff when he positioned offensive MRBMs in Cuba. Kennedy had done it, and the missiles were removed. But it had been a near thing.

Coldwell furrowed his brow. *Was this merely another bluff, this time to both Japan and the United States? A reminder that Soviet military strength, despite conventional reductions to generate favorable press, was greater than ever?*

If so, what was the goal? Greater leverage in international economic discussions? But that would be ridiculous. Intimidation would gain nothing in those talks. And the Soviets had already gained virtually everything they'd wanted in arms reductions.

Reluctantly, as the images spooled past, as LACROSSE displayed its startling clarity and penetration, Coldwell was forced to agree with the Agency's conclusion: The odds were strongly in favor of a repositioning of forces prior to a generated attack on the United States, possibly even on Japan. War games were unlikely, especially as the Soviets, who usually announced such maneuvers to keep tensions low, had made no attempt to communicate.

After the lights went up in the NPIC screening room, Coldwell swiveled his chair around to face General Felker, the Defense Intelligence Agency head. "Sy? What's your net on all this? Are we looking at the real thing?"

Felker had been unusually quiet throughout Nordstrom's presentation, making notes on his pad as the images unfolded. He looked at Coldwell with a bleak expression, and said: "Does Pat Boone sleep with his white bucks on? There's no question, no question at all. We've got to take them out. Before they take us out."

Coldwell regarded him thoughtfully, then turned to NPIC's director. "Ken," he said in a low voice, "we're going to schedule this show for ExComm[1] tomorrow morning. Full court press; Talking Dogs and all."

The members of ExComm had each been personally selected by the president. Many had intelligence policy backgrounds; all were experienced in national security matters. Yet they were as diverse a group as could be imagined.

Part of the presentation was a "fast track" Special National Intelligence Estimate (SNIE), prepared for ExComm and the president by the Board of National Estimates. But the reconnaissance images were what had everyone sitting bolt upright.

The Agency's Talking Dogs, intelligence officers specially trained for presentations, launched into their presentation without a lengthy introduction. They were concise, accurate, and detailed. Like good Agency analysts, they veered carefully away from policy statements, but marshaled their arguments skillfully to support the conclusion.

In just forty-five minutes, the presentation was over, and questions from the ExComm members began to fly thick and fast.

Alfred Wolff, former head of Wolff-Burns, the New York investment banking house, was as usual in a contentious mood. Wolff had made a successful career out of playing devil's advocate, never actually embracing a conclusion, but attempting to appear Solon-wise by carping at anyone who dared voice a genuine opinion. The president had picked Wolff for ExComm reluctantly, and only after a White House aide had reminded him of Wolff's fund-raising ability for the upcoming election.

Pointing at one of the enlarged photographs of the bunkers, Wolff drawled in his New York honk, "This is all very interesting, Mr.—ah?"

[1] Executive Committee of the National Security Council.

"Wallace, sir. My name is Wallace."

"Yes. Very good. Well, you've got some dandy snapshots there, Mr. Wallace. But I fail to see the relationship between what is plainly a genuine civil defense measure and what you seem to characterize as the Russians actually gearing up for war."

"Sir, with respect," began the officer, "the offensive moves are not in regard to the bunkers, but in the images of the submarine pens on Sikharovka, which you just saw. We also have proof of more aggressive moves not only from our own sources, but from the monitoring efforts of our allies the Japanese."

"Well, you're going to have to do a lot more convincing to get me on your little bandwagon," Wolff replied. "My friend Marshal Karpov has assured me, only last week, that the Soviet Union and ourselves are now well launched in a new era of peace." He smiled smugly, and rocked back in his upholstered swivel chair.

The other members, well used to Wolff, ignored this exchange, and used their time to explore the most pivotal evidence revealed by the reconnaissance images.

"You say there was a large quantity of SS-N-23s loaded aboard in Alexandrovsk?" This from Admiral Howe, the National Security Agency's director.

"Yes, sir. The images indicate a full complement for each of the Delta IV-class boats. Thirty-two sea-launched ballistic missiles in all."

"Have you got anything on the Soviets' movements out of the Baltic?"

"No sir, not since the *Tbilisi* moved out last month. Very little activity," replied Wallace.

The admiral thought this over, then asked: "And what's been going on up at the Severodvinsk Yards?"

"Would somebody mind telling me what in hell are the Severwhatchamacallit, whatever it is, Yards?" interrupted Wolff.

Patiently, Admiral Howe explained: "Severodvinsk—they're the most crucial shipyards of the USSR, Mr. Wolff. Up in the Arctic. They built the Typhoons, they now build lots of the *Akula*-class boats—the new silent ones—and they're one of the most reliable indications of the direction of Soviet naval policy."

Wolff grunted, and stuck his pipe back in his mouth.

Wallace picked up the original question smoothly, "The activity at Severodvinsk has been pretty normal. That is, despite all the disarmament negotiations and the withdrawal of troops in Eastern Europe, the Soviets have still been pushing hard to produce more attack and cruise missile submarines."

He turned slightly toward Wolff. "The submarine has been, at least since Admiral Gorshkov's time, the capital ship of the Soviet Navy. Not the battleship, the cruiser, the aircraft carrier, nor anything else. So the Yards up there have been going full tilt for some time."

Howe nodded his affirmation of the Talking Dogs' assessment. The Soviets still possessed the only purely offensive Navy in the world, and their Admiralty held the more defensive orientation in great contempt.

"Any more questions?" This from Ken Nordstrom.

Richard Coldwell looked around the big oval mahogany table. All were sitting in silence, each absorbed with his own thoughts on what was now in place, only waiting to be touched off. "Gentlemen," said Coldwell to Nordstrom and the presentation team, "thank you very much. You've been extremely helpful."

As the doors closed, Coldwell looked around the room, and expelled a long, slow sigh. "Anybody here a Gilbert and Sullivan fan?" he asked.

Admiral Howe and General Felker looked as if someone had broken wind at a funeral. "What, may I ask, have Gilbert and Sullivan got to do with all this?" ventured Felker.

Coldwell smiled. "In one of their shows, they created a phrase that should be printed on the front of every intelligence digest. 'Things are seldom as they seem.' I think that's the case here." He got up and began pacing.

"You've seen some pretty convincing evidence that the Soviet Union is preparing for something that could only be interpreted, by any reasonable person, as preparation for thermonuclear war." He smiled incongruously. "But think about that for a moment. Consider that we are generally *known* to be reasonable people. Consider that this is what they, or anybody else, would *expect* us to conclude. Then consider why on earth anyone would *want* us to conclude that."

This sort of reasoning invariably made the military members of ExComm intensely uncomfortable. It was the "infinity of mirrors" thinking that was the special province of the intelligence analysts. Coldwell excelled at this. In fact, in his earlier days in the Defense Intelligence Agency before he was brought over to CIA, his superiors had often kept him muzzled, for fear of antagonizing military men who favored a more straightforward, predictable response to situations.

Admiral Howe spoke first. "I'd rather ask, *who* on earth would want us to think that."

Coldwell nodded appreciatively and picked up the thought. "There are, in fact, several people who might want us to believe the Soviet Union was preparing a generated attack."

"Qaddafi, for one," voiced Felker. "He'd like nothing better than for both of us to wipe each other out."

The men around the table smiled except for Wolff, who was feeling increasingly out of his depth.

"The Chinese leadership could conceivably reap some benefits from such an exchange," commented George Leotas, Under Secretary of Defense for Policy. "But the down side to them is too big."

"You seem to be leading us toward somebody in the Soviet leadership itself," observed Howe. "Am I correct, Dick?"

"I'm not sure I'm leading you anywhere. I just think the only people who might want us to think they were about to wage a nuclear war might be the Soviets themselves. It might be a prelude to something else, some other goal. Remember, they've used brinkmanship several times before, and they've never lost anything by it. Their gamble in Cuba didn't really cost them much of anything, even when they pulled the missiles out. But if Kennedy—with McCone's help—hadn't faced them down, it could've cost us plenty."

"Wait a minute, wait just a damn minute," interjected Wolff, waving one dismissive hand. "You're not standing there telling me the Russians actually *want* us to think they're about to blow us off the face of this earth?"

"No, but we've got to consider everything, considering how unorthodox the situation is. Why hasn't their leadership communicated to us anything about war games, or troop maneuvers? Wouldn't they realize we'd *know* what was going on, and that tensions would be building up?"

Wolff looked stricken. Coldwell pressed his argument. "That would be their normal response if they were genuinely about to generate an attack on a global scale. If they weren't, if they wanted to surprise us, well, they'd be falling all over themselves to get to the Hot Line, telling us about some new war games or tests of military equipment, anything to keep us nice and calm."

Admiral Howe was leaning back in his chair, fingers laced behind his head. "All right, then. And as I assume you want to defuse this situation early, before things get *too* out of hand, what do you propose we tell the president?"

Coldwell stood still for a moment, then said, "We tell him there's a chance, a real chance, we might have to stage a preemptive strike—in case this thing goes too far. We should begin preparations to go to an acceptable level of readiness in case the situation deteriorates, or in case we're just plain wrong, and the Soviets really *are* going to launch. We also tell him we already have a number of agents in place to determine what the real nature of this is."

The astonishment in the room was like a curtain suddenly snapping up. Coldwell sat down as six pairs of eyes stared at him in stunned surprise.

"Let me—let me just see if I've got this right," began General Felker heavily. "You've *already* put people in the field on this?"

Coldwell nodded. "That's right, Sy. We've had this thing on WATCHCON I[2] almost a month. We put people on the job three weeks ago. We're just starting to get information back, but it's nothing reliable, nothing to hang our hats on. But something big *is* going on. Big enough for them to terminate five of our people so far."

[2]Watch Condition One. The intelligence equivalent of Defense Conditions or DEFCONS. WATCHCON I is the highest priority.

Wolff exploded. "You've put *hostile agents* in the field in the Soviet Union, in this, the first chance we've ever had for a lasting peace? My God, man, don't you realize this could blow whatever trust the Soviets ever had in us? *Jesus!* We ought to get on the horn right now and apologize. God knows *what* they're thinking!"

The ExComm members stared at Wolff in disbelief. General Felker turned to him and said in an ominous tone, "You're not getting on any phone, you pompous son of a bitch, and you're not saying anything to *anyone*. If you even think about it, you'll be in a one-room cell in Leavenworth and the only people who'll ever know or even remember you're there will be the people in this room. Do I make myself sufficiently clear?"

Wolff went pale. His only response was a quick nod of assent as he began to scrupulously study the leather-bound notepad in front of him.

Coldwell looked around the room. "I think we've about covered everything. I'll have my staff draw up the recommendation for you to approve by this time tomorrow."

And the men filed out into what suddenly seemed to be a different world.

The following day, Richard Coldwell met with the president. The chief executive, never one for making a decision when he could defer it, had trouble digesting the ExComm recommendation. In the end, he asked Coldwell to detail the Soviet Union's probable responses for each potential U.S. action. Coldwell advised him of the time constraints, but agreed to return with the alternative scenarios within one week.

The U.S. Joint Chiefs of Staff, knowing a probable DEF-CON change would be implemented soon, discreetly let key theater commanders know sizeable redeployments would be forthcoming. The commanders redirected their forces to reflect the probable commitments, calling the movements exercises or maneuvers.

In this way, without resorting to the approval process of either the executive or the legislative branch, the U.S. military stepped up its readiness for war.

High overhead, a Soviet military surveillance satellite

took careful note of these changes, and fired its accumulated data downward to a relay station.

Three days after his meeting in Washington, Alfred Wolff had a power breakfast at the Regency Hotel in New York with several of his cronies. He hinted darkly at things he was not permitted to divulge, which reinforced his image of Great Unknowable Power. This trickle, small as it was, found its way to one Yuri Kaganovich, employed at Wolff-Burns under the name Robert Carlin Maxwell.

From a telephone booth at the corner of 53rd Street and Sixth Avenue, Kaganovich placed a call to the Soviet Union. He held a brief conversation with a man about the purchase of furs.

Two hours later, Alfred Wolff was delighted to receive a call from his old friend Marshal Karpov. Who, by a happy coincidence, would soon be visiting the United States under the terms of the recently concluded arms reduction treaty.

The two agreed to meet.

_____ **26**

The Residentura.

One does not apply to the GRU for employment. To the KGB, yes. But the KGB is by far the inferior service.

There are literally millions of volunteer employees in the KGB. None in the GRU. One can apply for employment quite easily in the KGB. Every factory, every apartment building, every government department, every organism in the Union of Soviet Socialist Republics has a unit of the KGB who will take you in quite easily.

But the GRU is another matter.

If you were to approach someone known to be GRU and as much as mention those three initials, you would most likely be arrested and interrogated. The GRU is an officially *secret* organization. It does not exist. The KGB exists, but not the GRU.

Therefore: *Why are you asking about that which does not exist? And who is paying you to do so?*

The two organizations are, by any standard, very different. The difference begins with ideology. The KGB exists to serve the Party and Communism. The GRU instead exists to serve the Fatherland, that which is eternal and unchanging, regardless of party, regardless of politicians. It is therefore the more patriotic of the two.

The difference sharpens with technology. In the past twenty years, the GRU has created the Soviet Union's only true cadres of technologically skilled espionage professionals.

Finally, in the highest arts of intelligence, especially in the creation and management of disinformation, no organization on earth rivals the GRU.

Vienna has always been one of the GRU's nerve centers. Its position near the Czechoslovakian and Hungarian borders once greatly eased making certain deliveries and exchanges. And though the lists showed the GRU to have the same number of personnel as ever, the truth was quite different.

For under the reinforced roof of the *residentura,* more than thirty GRU officers and men were at work—as well as a number of others under their sphere of influence. In the embassy portion, ten people with *Otechestvo* allegiances were positioned. The ambassador himself was an admirer of the *Otechestvo* leader, Feliks, and saw to it that the GRU and *Otechestvo* people had no interference.

Beyond its black wrought-iron fence, the Soviet Embassy building at Reisnerstrasse 45–47 begins with a three-story neo-Palladian facade. But this soon stretches back into a catch-all concatenation of stone and brick, and within this is the GRU *residentura* itself.

Entering from the embassy proper, one descends a flight of stairs and enters a small room with massively reinforced concrete walls. (These walls, in fact, run around the entire perimeter of the *residentura,* and can withstand virtually anything, including the nuclear devastation of Vienna.) In this small room, identification and passes are checked by a

GRU officer, *Spetsnaz*-trained and part of the Sixth Guards Tank Army.

The guard room for *Spetsnaz* officers is immediately across the corridor from the pass room, and there would normally be five or six officers reading, watching Viennese television, or inspecting their weapons.

The other rooms are nondescript, but include a photographic darkroom, the "Navigator"'s office (head of the GRU in Vienna), an officers' common room, offices for the First Deputy and other deputies, interception rooms for local surveillance, and so forth.

There is, of course, an extra entrance and exit to the *residentura,* kept locked at all times. Finally, there is a flight of stone steps leading down to the bunker—one of the most important areas of all.

The door to the bunker resembles a cross between a bank vault's door and the bulkhead hatch of a submarine. Constantly observed by surveillance cameras, one is admitted only after punching in the correct combination, a combination changed at irregular intervals.

Once inside, you are in the presence of a great communications center, signals received and transmitted to and from every portion of the world. From this bunker, hundreds of messages are exchanged daily with Vatutinki, the top-secret village near Moscow which is the GRU's main communications center.

Both security and communications are ideal. And, unlike virtually any installation within the Soviet Union itself, unwelcome visits by ranking politicians and senior KGB *apparatchiks* are at a distinct minimum.

The Vienna *residentura* was, for these and other reasons, chosen as the nerve center of the GRU/*Otechestvo* plan.

Personnel had been quietly tripled, and the financial center of the movement (a critical part of any revolutionary process) installed within the data processing area.

In Vienna, the KGB had been slowly subverted by the process of bringing in a new senior officer, then having him slowly—so as not to arouse suspicion—install his own people, all of whom would ultimately be part of the movement, all bought with promises of attractive posts once the new government was in place.

All but two KGB employees had been replaced. One, a cipher clerk, the other, a female officer who had valuable contacts among the Austrian diplomatic community. But they would be gone within the month, replaced by those loyal to the cause.

It was in the predawn hours of a Spring morning when events at the *residentura* began to collect momentum. It began with a call routed through Vatutinki at 4:25 Viennese time. The duty officer had difficulty getting the GRU's Vienna station head, Colonel-general Leonid Dovgalevsky, to respond to his knock. The young officer was fearful of the consequences.

A muffled curse was heard from somewhere in the room, then the reluctant shuffling of slippered feet toward the door. A crack opened and the duty officer looked down into the oddly light brown eyes of Dovgalevsky. The face surrounding them was creased and pouchy, bloated from too much drink, too much food, and, it was rumored, too much killing in the Afghanistan adventure.

"Kakovo khuya khochesh?" growled Dovgalevsky.

The young GRU captain stiffened to attention. "Colonel-general, there is an urgent telephone call from Army General Mescheryakov. It is requested the Colonel-general take it in the bunker."

This, of course, was only standard procedure. As was well known, calls from General Mescheryakov were never to be taken in the regular *residentura* living quarters, only in the GRU section, and then only in the ultra-secure communications bunker.

Colonel-general Dovgalevsky blinked. *"Blyad!"* he muttered. "Thank you, Ivan Vassileyevich. You have done your duty. Now go fuck yourself and tell the operator I shall be on the line in five minutes." And the door slammed in the captain's face.

The telephone conversation was long and exceedingly unpleasant for the Colonel-general. Army General Mescheryakov was not pleased that the Americans were still nosing around Vienna. He considered the abduction and death of the American spy, Mathieson, to have been too late and too clumsy. Especially when, after all that effort and the

American's interrogation by the Serbsky Institut's experts, it was still a mystery what, if anything, the Americans knew about GRU/*Otechestvo* activities in Vienna.

"And now they've sent this, this *specialist* over!" exploded Mescheryakov. "How will you get rid of *him,* Colonel-general? Will you let him collect a full dossier on all of us? Invite him over for a glass of tea? Why is this man still *alive,* you cretin?" The voice on the line dripped with venom.

Dovgalevsky exercised extreme internal discipline. His temper, legendary throughout the service, was held in check only by the fact that he was being dressed down by a man who, on a whim, could have his victim loaded alive, feet first, into the crematorium at GRU headquarters. It had happened before.

"Please be assured, General Mescheryakov, that all appropriate measures will be taken to contain the situation. We have the subject under surveillance, and by our best. They have orders, *strict* orders, to keep the American under observation until we can find out what they know."

Army General Mescheryakov made a disagreeable noise. "Under *observation,* Dovgalevsky? You will keep him under *observation?* What are you waiting for? Get *rid* of the man! Protect the *residentura* at all costs!"

Colonel-general Dovgalevsky bit his tongue, then asked in what he intended to be his politest possible tone: "But General, we don't want to draw any more attention—"

Mescheryakov exploded. *"Blyad!* You've already *got* attention! *Terminate* this spy! Don't let him have an instant's further opportunity! Do you hear me? Do you?"

There was a silence on the line. Then, from Dovgalevsky, in a voice barely under control: "I understand fully, General. Is there anything else I can help you with this evening?"

"Yes, you miserable *mat tvoyu,* you can keep your head out of your ass until I arrive there Tuesday. Do you think you can possibly manage that, Colonel-general?"

A great pause. Then Dovgalevsky managed to speak, in semi-strangled tones. "Yes, I think we might manage that, General Mescheryakov. You will be arriving at what time Tuesday?"

"We will touch down at 1500 hours precisely. Make sure there is good security from the airport, but nothing too noticeable. And make sure the American has been eradicated by the time I arrive."

"Yes, General. Good *night*, General."

"Good night, idiot."

Dovgalevsky slammed the receiver down. He fumbled in his bathrobe pocket for a pill, put it on his tongue, and made a terrible face. *Mother of God,* he thought. *Does a man grow more and more insane as he accumulates rank? Does he grow so intoxicated with power that he ultimately loses all judgment?*

He sighed and made his way through the corridor, then up the cement stairs and back to his bedroom.

Outside in the duty room, against all regulations for *residentura* staff, against all orders for duty officers in the Soviet Army in general and the GRU and *Spetsnaz* in particular, the young officer who had wakened the Navigator poured himself a very considerable tumbler of vodka.

Kadmus looked with heavy-lidded eyes at the man who sat across from him. "I find this difficult to believe. You say the GRU has six men employed *full time* watching only this American?"

The little man with the white hair shifted his weight uncomfortably. "Yes, Herr Kadmus. Apparently they regard him as a highly sensitive assignment."

"And are they permanent *residentura* staff, or new people brought in, or have they used any of the Chekists[1] to fill in?"

"No, Herr Kadmus. They are all permanent GRU staff. And that is another unusual thing. None of the KGB seems to be interested in this man. Only the GRU. *Unmöglich, nicht wahr?*"

Kadmus seemed for the moment to be lost in thought. "It does seem highly anomalous, Chico. Usually if anything's big to one, it's big to the other. The KGB is not known for being bashful in matters of this sort." He rubbed the back of his neck, wondering at this latest piece of information.

"One thing may I ask, Herr Kadmus?"

"Probably not, Chico. But try it on anyway."

[1] Referring to the KGB, which began life as the secret police organization known as the Cheka.

"What is this American after, precisely? He goes no place interesting, attempts no contacts, has no backup from his own people. But the GRU is all over him. *Was kann das heissen?*"

"I'm afraid I cannot tell you, dear Chico. I can only tell you this man is very, very special, and in a way, most especially dangerous. You would do well to stay well clear of both him and his GRU watchers. It may not prove beneficial to your health." He smiled benignly over his several chins, and sipped at his peppermint schnapps.

Chico nodded curtly, accepting Kadmus's judgment in the matter, and after a few minutes' conversation left by the kitchen door. Kadmus reset the locks and the alarm system, humming cheerily to himself.

That the KGB was not interested was no surprise. It was entirely natural, given the problem. That the GRU was being so circumspect was more interesting. Almost as they were *waiting* for Pretorius to find something or do something.

Well, thought Kadmus, *my little rumors of Pretorius' supposed importance should accelerate things. Let us just hope the response does not exceed our capacity to manage it.*

_____ 27

An Object of Curiosity.

Pretorius looked out the window from which Mathieson had fallen.

His eyes scanned the slate-gray rooftops, peaked and slanted shards of Vienna's urban archaeology. The rooftops told the history of the city, though little was left that spoke of the Turks. Their legacy was in the coffeehouses, in concoctions like *Kapuziner,* or Capuccino, brewed by *Kapuzin* monks who learned to gentle the strong Turkish coffee with cream.

Pretorius found himself wishing for a decent cup of coffee. He'd been up half the night wrestling with questions.

Who else had been here, in this room? Who had been here just before he plummeted, tumbling, gathering speed before the final impact? What had fleeted through his brain? And why was the Agency so anxious to write him off? What had he found out that made him dangerous? Senior CIA people generally don't get iced in your better Western democracies.

The housekeeper stood silent behind him. A small gray woman, hands twisting together beneath an immaculate starched white apron.

He'd said he was there on behalf of Mathieson's family, and slowly she'd begun to open up, to answer his questions.

No, she'd seen no one else enter or leave the apartment. Not a living soul, only the Herr Mathieson, as God is her witness. He seemed to have had no friends, took no deliveries.

True, her door was usually kept closed. But her ears were very keen, still very, *very* keen, she assured Pretorius. And they had to be, for didn't the gentleman know all sorts of things went on in Vienna these days? One scarcely knew if one would not be butchered in one's bed, wasn't it so?

And these young people, always trying to smuggle in girlfriends, boyfriends. Liquor, drugs even. But she would permit no such goings-on, not if her life depended on it. Her small eyes glittered with fervor.

Pretorius nodded, letting her chatter on as he examined the room minutely. After a while he interrupted the *recitatif* to compliment her on the room's cleanliness, which produced a fleeting smile and an oddly girlish curtsey. By the way: had anyone other than the police visited? Had anyone else been asking questions?

Yes, some Americans. Very rude they were too, begging your pardon, sir. Such a terrible business to begin with, the gentleman killing himself that way. It was not therefore necessary to make things even more unpleasant. But these men, who had been accompanied by an official from the *Bundespolizeidirektion,* had accused her of hiding things. Her! The daughter of a magistrate! Can you imagine?

Pretorius was interested. Did they show her any identification? No, only the police officer, in plain clothes, had shown her his papers. He translated the Americans' questions to her, and he was very embarrassed too.

She assured Pretorius that Herr Mathieson had been a model tenant, keeping regular hours, and being most civil to her. Once he had brought her flowers, and said it was because he thought she would like them. For no other reason.

Oh yes, and he always kept his room neat as a pin. Bed always made, towels hung in place, no cigarettes, no liquor. A very nice gentleman he was. *Es tut mir leid.* What could have made him so sad, that he would take his own life in such a way? Was the gentleman married? Perhaps his wife had left him? Was it money troubles? People are too concerned with money these days, don't you agree?

Pretorius agreed. "But tell me, Frau—?"

"Frau Wittgenstein, if you please, sir."

"Frau Wittgenstein, you must understand Herr Mathieson's family is understandably upset at the loss of their son. Was there possibly anything he might have left behind? Something that would not have been of interest to the police, but something personal, something his family might wish as a memento of their son?"

She fidgeted, uncomfortable under Pretorius' gaze. He knew then: there *was* something she'd kept from the police. Something that had eluded the sieve of investigation.

"Moment, bitte," and she scurried away downstairs. Pretorius paced the dimensions of the room.

He looked out the window again, peering down into the street. Kadmus had said the tags were good, so he couldn't expect to see a dark sedan with two heavies in front, or a trench-coated, movie-style character lurking just inside a doorway across the street.

No, they would be better than that. The time to flush them out would be after he left the apartment. He'd checked out the route earlier.

"Bitte, Herr Pretorius." She spoke from the door, holding out a somewhat shopworn book for his inspection. "He left only this, this *kinderbuch.* He asked me to keep it in my rooms, for what reason I don't know, but he gave it to me two days before—before his death. It was of no value I thought, and certainly of no use to the *Polizei.* But if his family would like it—?"

She left the question dangling, easing the fact she'd kept Mathieson's book from the police, and that she probably hadn't mentioned it to anyone. Otherwise it would be in a Pliofilm evidence bag at police headquarters.

"That would be very kind of you, Frau Wittgenstein. I'm sure his family will be very grateful." He smiled at her, a warm and assuring smile.

The book she handed over was a curious choice for Mathieson, a volume of Lewis Carroll's *Alice in Wonderland* in German, published by Heyne in München some years ago. He opened the flyleaf and saw a penciled inscription: *Ex libris Leon Alberti, 10/19/56.*

The name seemed oddly familiar. *Alberti. Was it somebody Phil had spoken about?* He shook his head and looked up.

"Well," he said. "You've been very helpful, Frau Wittgenstein. Sorry I had to intrude, but his family wanted to know how he had lived while he was here. I'll be happy to report he lived in a very nice place, and that you obviously made his last days pleasant."

She smiled and her wrinkles rearranged themselves. *"Danke schön, Herr Pretorius. Danke schön."*

"Bitte," Pretorius replied with a slight bow, and made his way down in the open elevator. As the noisy contrivance inched its way down the six stories, he looked up through the cast-iron grille. Frau Wittgenstein was still looking down at him.

Outside, the street looked normal for that hour of the morning. He paused briefly at the doorway, then turned right and hurried toward his hotel. One of the men in the office building opposite lowered his field glasses and spoke into a two-way radio. *"Er geht nun fort."*

"Wir beobachten ihn," crackled the reply.

A man in a gray windbreaker and wearing yellow-tinted aviator's glasses came out of a pastry shop. The man had what looked like a hearing aid, connected to the walkie-talkie under his jacket. He was careful to keep at least twenty meters behind the target. He'd been briefed. They were dealing with a professional.

When Pretorius suddenly stopped in front of a shoe store window, the man kept walking at his normal pace, coming within four meters before his quarry resumed walking. He slowed his pace gradually, turned at a corner, and let the man on the opposite side of the street take over the tag.

This was an older man. Gray hair, a pair of thickish horn-rimmed glasses. He too wore a hearing aid. At the next opportunity, the man crossed the street, dodging traffic athletically for a man of his years.

Pretorius knew the tags would be working the area now. *But what were they looking for? What did they want? If Phil cancelled his own ticket, why so much interest in a failed spy? Especially if—as the IG's people were obviously convinced— the spy was a junkie.*

He found the store he was looking for. A large, brightly lit record shop. He entered, turning to close the door and looking behind him as he did. Few salespeople ever approach you in a record shop offering to help, which allows you to remain unhindered, undistracted. The arrangement of the CDs and cassettes also permits you to wander, to look around in any direction.

Pretorius spotted the man in the thick horn-rimmed glasses who'd been behind him in the street. A quick glance was enough. Pretorius picked out a June Christy CD, *Something Cool,* and paid for it. He left the store without a backward glance.

As he walked he noticed the gray windbreaker in front of him. He was bracketed now: not a good sign. He crossed the street, watching the store windows to see if either man crossed as well. Neither did.

Pretorius began to pick up speed, accelerating just past the pace of the morning shoppers. Anyone else attempting that speed would now be more noticeable.

In five minutes he spotted two more tags. One, a woman in her early twenties. Sunglasses. Scarf over her head. He took note of her jacket and skirt: harder for her to ditch than the glasses and scarf.

The second was a young man in a tan raincoat, loose, unbuttoned. The man kept one hand in a pocket, closer to his body than needed. Conclusion: weapon, possibly subgun, slung from a strap over the shoulder, inside the coat.

Pretorius rounded the corner, hurrying through the crowds on Singerstrasse. He walked, head lowered, as if lost in thought. Gray Windbreaker paused at the corner and hit the PTT (press to talk) on the transceiver inside his jacket. He spoke quietly. The microphone just inside his collar picked up each syllable.

The transmission was picked up by a mustard-yellow Mercedes on Stubenbastei, one block away. The driver gunned the motor and shot ahead of the traffic. Two blocks later a couple got out of the car on the Wollzeile and crossed to the Luegerplatz. The woman wore a smart Tyrolean hat with a feather. The man, a crushed canvas rain hat.

As Pretorius emerged on the Wollzeile, he noticed the couple walking arm in arm, the man pointing at a store window. He looked closely at the woman's jacket and skirt. *Of course,* he thought. *Formerly Sunglasses and Scarf.* He continued in his original direction. The couple followed, their pace slightly increasing.

Another corner. Pretorius looked at his watch just as he turned. The couple followed by crossing the street first, then paralleling him on the opposite side.

Finally, Pretorius saw the door he wanted, and after first pressing one of the buttons on the door frame went inside. The couple continued on the other side of the street, not pausing, not breaking pace. Professionals.

Once inside, Pretorius ran through a long, poorly lit hallway and out a rear door, emerging into a cement courtyard in which several cars and vans were parked. He pulled a key from one pocket and got in an Opel sedan, putting on a soft loden hat as he did.

He was out of the courtyard and into Vienna traffic as Gray Windbreaker began checking the names on the buttons by the front door.

August Kadmus was enjoying himself. At the moment, he was ensconced in the rear region of a rented BMW 750 limousine, driven by a man whose knowledge of Vienna's streets was encyclopedic. Kadmus looked the archetypal Austrian industrialist, driven by his dutiful chauffeur. The men were monitoring the conversations of the GRU surveillance team on their receiver with some amusement.

When Gray Windbreaker reported to his masters that the subject had eluded them through the back courtyard, Kadmus slapped his leg in delight. "By God, that's good. That's really good. He's given them something to chew on, eh, Fritzl?"

The driver nodded somberly, and swung the big vehicle into position three cars behind the Mercedes.

"Some peppermint schnapps, then?" offered Kadmus, his eyebrows two tufted arches of inquiry.

"No, thanks," replied Pretorius. Having tried the liquid once, he was determined never to again. "So who were they? Embassy? Free-lancers?"

"Um. Exactly. They were, in fact, all from the *residentura,* all top people. No contract agents, no local talent. They're being very careful, Michael. Obviously, they consider you important. Although I can't, for the life of me, see why," he added mischievously.

"Seen any of them before?" asked Pretorius, settling down on, or more accurately, *in,* Kadmus's sagging chintz-covered sofa. "Anybody new, recently assigned here?"

"Yes, indeed. As a matter of interest, all the tags seemed to be new, with exception of the older man, the one with the horn-rimmed glasses. He's an old hand with the GRU in Vienna. A good one, too. Very experienced, very careful. Name's Radonicich. Pyotr Radonicich. You'd like this fellow."

"You've met him, then?"

"Oh, yes. This is a tight little community, my friend. Not like other cities. We help each other—a little here, a little there. All very friendly, all very professional. Saves a hell of a lot of time."

"How are your contacts in the KGB here?"

"About as good as my contacts with my dry cleaner and my wine shop."

"Who's the most knowledgeable man they have?"

Kadmus rumbled a laugh, huge chins jiggling. "Well, their *most* knowledgeable man would be most amused to hear you call her that."

"All right, all right," Pretorius grinned in embarrassment. "Who is she?"

"She's nominally the Soviets' cultural attaché here. Her name is Valentina Ene Verontsova. Born Kalinin, 1960.

Mother Estonian, father Russian. Not altogether terrible-looking, either." His eyes twinkled and he leaned back in his chair, hands interlaced on his stomach.

"How do I contact her?" asked Pretorius.

"You don't." Kadmus smiled benignly.

"I don't? What the hell does *that* mean?"

"It means I make the arrangements, then she gets in touch with you. What do you want? A handbook of my methods, a directory of my contacts? What is it you Yanks say? Get real? Yes, *get real,* Pretorius. And don't, for God's sake, be so damned touchy. Christ!" The big man shook his head in mock irritation.

Pretorius couldn't help smiling. It was seldom these days, you met a real pro, especially one with a sense of humor. "Sorry, August. Guess I'm a little edgy."

"Don't let it worry you. You'll relax as you get into it." Kadmus sipped at his schnapps, looking amused. "By the way, your first appointment with Valentina is tomorrow night. Eight o'clock sharp. Dinner at the Palais Schwarzenberg."

Pretorius looked up in surprise. "Always a step ahead. Well, thanks. I appreciate it."

"Don't worry," Kadmus chuckled. "You'll get the bill."

The watchers were gathered in the bunker beneath the Soviet Embassy, seated around the metal conference table. At the head of the table, Colonel-general Leonid Dovgalevsky stood over a still-damp pile of eight-by-ten photographic prints, fists planted angrily on hips.

"And still you don't see it. Still—still it evades your eyes," he said in a sardonic stage whisper.

All eyes were on the photos, then Horn-Rimmed Glasses spoke softly. "The book. He wasn't carrying a book when he went in, here, in the earlier shots. But see here? Now he's coming out, and he's carrying it in his hand."

"So what does that *mean,* students?" sneered Dovgalevsky. "That somewhere within that building, there's a lending library? A rare book shop? Perhaps an adult education class?" His eyes swept each of their faces in turn. He lit up a cigarette, the hollow-tubed *Troika* brand, and began generating acrid smoke. "It means obviously the police—

and everyone else—missed something of importance to this American. *Get that book! I want it on my desk by 0800 hours tomorrow morning."*

—————————————————————————— 28

Valentina Verontsova.

The Palais Schwarzenberg is, without question, every inch a Palace. Capital P.

It's also a hotel, a restaurant, and a garden. In all of these, the ancient ritual known as courting is still practiced by all ages of Viennese, as well as a few romantic *Ausländer*. For the Schwarzenberg is a world apart; only a few hundred meters beyond Vienna's Ring, it could easily be centuries away.

Pretorius had been waiting at his table half an hour. He was frowning at his watch when an elegant brunette entered, capturing every eye in the room.

The maitre d' escorted her to the table. Pretorius bolted to his feet, and for no apparent reason almost bowed. *Jesus,* he thought in embarrassment, *this place must be getting to me.*

As she was being seated, she spoke in a breathy, almost husky voice: "Mr. Pretorius? I'm Valentina Verontsova. Sorry I'm late, but my car is having a touch of spring fever." Which was followed by the flash of an eminently forgivable smile.

"No problem at all, really," said a momentarily stunned Pretorius. "I was just daydreaming. Good to meet you."

As she removed her gloves, Valentina Verontsova looked around the room appreciatively. Pretorius had a chance to take in the fashionable cut of her ebony hair, the velvet cocktail dress revealing the creamy whiteness of her skin. *And what is that perfume she's wearing?* he wondered.

"I love this place. I was *so* glad when August said you'd suggested it," she said with a smile that assaulted all Pretorius' defenses.

"Well, actually, August's being generous. He suggested it himself, and it *is* a beautiful place. I've only been here once, many years before, but frankly—well, it didn't enter my mind as a place to meet—to meet you."

"You mean to meet a potato-faced matron of the KGB, don't you, Commander?" she corrected, teasing.

Commander. How the hell does she know that? thought Pretorius. "Well, yes. You've got me there, Miss Verontsova—"

"Please," she interrupted. "Call me Valentina. And I shall call you Michael. Is that agreeable?"

"Not only agreeable, but preferable. Would you like something to drink?" He indicated the wine steward standing at modified attention some distance from the table.

She smiled. "I'm in your hands. Utterly in your hands."

He nodded to the steward who glided toward them. "Your wine list, please?"

The man produced it with a flourish. For some reason Pretorius turned immediately to the champagnes. He selected a vintage Veuve Clicquot, and watched the wine steward hurry off before returning his attention to Valentina.

She took the initiative. "August said you need some information. Your friend's death has caused—certain difficulties."

"Difficulties? No, 'difficulties' isn't the word," he began, leaning forward. "Phil Mathieson was a good friend, and his family was once pretty decent to me at a time when I really needed it. He got me out of a problem once. A real problem, when I was about to square the circle. And nothing about Phil Mathieson adds up to suicide or drugs. But certain people—both on your side and ours—seem pretty anxious to make it look that way."

"Lots of suicides," Verontsova said, "manage to convince their friends, even their families, that everything's just fine. Right up to the time they drink the thirty-five sleeping pills with their Stoli, or step in front of the five-thirty to Petropavlovsk."

Pretorius shook his head. "There's also some evidence to suggest he'd stumbled onto something. Something that could've gotten him killed."

She waited, one eyebrow raised almost imperceptibly.

"It appears," he continued, "to have something to do with your country. He was engaged in some—dealings with the GRU here. A man wanted to defect, or at least they thought that at first. But it didn't go down that way. What really happened is, unfortunately, anybody's guess."

She looked through the window out at the garden. "Seems so useless now, defecting, doesn't it? These days it's almost like being traded to another soccer team. Still, the people at the top take it fairly seriously."

The wine steward approached to position the wine bucket and open the bottle, and as the cork popped she clapped her hands like a little girl. "I *love* that sound: it's something we almost never get to hear at home. And yet my father sometimes used to manage to find a bottle for special occasions, when we were small, and he and mother used to toast each other."

"What does your father do?" asked Pretorius.

"Did. He's no longer alive. He was a battalion commander in Afghanistan. The *Rodina*'s Viet Nam."

"I'm sorry," Pretorius offered.

"Don't be," she said with the kindest of smiles. "He had a good life, a full life. I don't think he ever regretted a single moment. A good way to go out, no?"

"A good way to go out, yes," Pretorius agreed. "Let's drink to that."

Her eyes misted as she and Pretorius touched glasses. And Pretorius found himself thinking of Susannah, and feeling unaccountably guilty.

They talked of many things at dinner, which was a lavish succession of Viennese specialties nicely laced with the Palais chef's own creations.

Later, over coffee, Pretorius probed gently. "Have your people seen or heard anything that would be—potentially embarrassing to the GRU? Or even to the Soviet Union as a whole? Anything worth killing an American intelligence officer for?" He watched her eyes.

"These days?" she said skeptically. "You've got to be kidding. People are falling all over themselves trying to look helpful to the other services. Look at you and I."

"But the GRU's a different matter. They've never been

governed by the same rules as the KGB," he suggested. "And a lot of people are getting unglued by all this revisionism."

"You choose a Marxist word, *revisionism*. Are you suggesting the GRU may be advocating something . . . unofficial? Something contrary to our national interests?"

"I'm hardly in a position to answer that. But it's a possibility. I'm looking for something, *anything* that might tell me why Phillip Mathieson got wasted. So far I'm coming up empty-handed, although a lot of people seem to be interested in what—if anything—I turn up."

She looked at him across the table. This American was a good man, his nose a little bent out of shape. But handsome in a rugged, unconventional way. She wondered idly if he would be gentle in making love. The champagne was having its effect, she realized, and it must not cloud her judgment. Helping August out was one thing. Divulging sensitive information was quite another, especially with the changes in the KGB here in Vienna. The new KGB head here, who seemed to be on unusually cozy terms with the GRU *rezident,* had been systematically replacing everyone with his own creatures. She'd likely be next, and would be transferred away from Vienna. Still—

"Michael, you must know my organization is quite a large one, and that we have many sources of information."

"That's obvious. The KGB's network is well known; there's nothing else like it."

"You're being diplomatic again." She took another delicate sip, admiring the candlelight reflected in the crystal of her champagne glass. "But what I'm getting to is this: we have so many sources that at any one time, on any one topic, we may have literally *hundreds* of conflicting pieces of information."

"So what are you telling me?" asked Pretorius.

"I'm—I'm *trying* to tell you that yes, there have been rumors the GRU are doing something beyond their charter, something big. These rumors have been fairly consistent. Yet there are rumors, even official statements to the contrary. For example, the GRU's head, Army General Mescheryakov, has stated in the magazines *Kommunist*

Vooruzhennikh Sil and *Voennii Vestnik*[1] that a small group within the GRU has, indeed, been involved in what he describes as counter-revolutionary activities. Some of these relate to a highly militaristic nationalist group known as *Otechestvo*. But they are being investigated and the problem, he claims, has been contained."

Pretorius nodded. "Hardly seems worth killing a CIA officer for. Especially in such a visible way."

"No," replied Valentina, "I quite agree. But there are indications that more serious things, supposedly GRU-influenced, are under way.

"Such as—?"

"Such as certain forces being placed on an alert status far above anything directly authorized by the government, an action tantamount to ignoring civilian control. And far more responsibility being devolved to mid-level military commanders—especially in the Naval and Rocket forces than would be prudent, given the amount of nuclear weaponry now at their disposal."

Pretorius gave a long, low whistle. "That's dangerous stuff. Is the KGB investigating these, with a view to alerting your president?"

She looked once again into her champagne glass, rotating the thin stem between her fingers. "That I cannot say. But you may draw your own conclusions."

Pretorius thought this over. "How much of this do you think Mathieson turned up?"

"Oh, quite a lot, I'd say. And it appears there's something unusual going on here, in Vienna. It's not just your average GRU *residentura*. Your Mathieson had a number of local people working on the problem. So put it this way: if that many people knew, and we in the KGB knew, then surely the GRU would know. And they would react in a predictable fashion."

"By killing him."

"Exactly. But even they would not normally have done it in so—so public a fashion. Generally, anybody like Mathieson who was creating a disturbance would simply disappear.

---

[1] *Communist of the Armed Forces* Magazine and *Military Messenger* Magazine.

You'd never know where he went, or what became of him. This—this public 'suicide,' with the needle marks, was too anomalous, not good procedure. Quite out of character, even for the GRU. Unless, of course, something got out of hand."

"Have your people got any hard evidence it *was* the GRU?"

Her eyes seemed to cloud, to become opaque. "I can't discuss that with you. Obviously."

"But you're sure it *was* a GRU wet job."

"As certain as you and I are sitting here. And there was one thing more."

"Yes?"

"Mescheryakov. He arrived on Tuesday's Aeroflot from Moscow. And he's a man who seldom travels. So something's hot here. Put that together with a GRU assassination of your man, and there's obviously something going on here far beyond the ordinary."

Pretorius was thunderstruck. *What could be big enough to bring out Mescheryakov? And big enough to kill a ranking Agency officer on friendly soil?*

Verontsova looked at him with a tired smile, feeling she'd already said too much. "By the way, is there anything more in that wonderful bottle?"

She had only to glance toward the silver bucket, and the wine steward materialized to pour the last few drops in their glasses as if he were dispensing an 1851 Lafite to the Hapsburgs.

"Mmmmmm," Valentina purred with pleasure. "This has been wonderful. And you have been the perfect dinner companion, dear Michael."

"Well, I've got to admit my contacts with the KGB have never been—quite this cordial," he said.

She touched his glass with hers one last time. "To better times, then."

"To better times."

The evening was chill and clear, and the stars seemed to flood the skies. He walked her to her car, and leaned forward to kiss her goodnight. She turned her head, avoiding the kiss. "Too much champagne, Michael," she laughed. "Remember I have appearances to keep up. And this is a public place."

Embarrassed, he shook her gloved hand. "Absolutely right. Good night, Valentina. You've been really helpful."

She looked at him with an oddly intent expression. "Just be careful, Commander. These are not predictable people. No one is, these days. Not even me."

Pretorius nodded. As she drove away, one velvet-gloved hand waving out her window, he stood in the forecourt of the palace watching the tail lights of her little car blend into the myriad lights of the traffic just beyond. He looked at his watch: 12:15. He didn't feel at all sleepy. His spirits were up, and he felt invigorated by the night air.

He struck off at a good pace up the Schwarzenberg Strasse, hands in pockets, whistling. Pretorius was in a better mood than he'd been since his visit to Miranda Mathieson, when he'd begun to get committed to this damn thing. The wind was picking up and he shivered slightly as he waited at the light at Schubert-Ring. The traffic was fast and thick. He glanced up at the light, wishing it would turn.

He never knew just what made him sense the impending danger. Perhaps the slight extra illumination of headlights swinging toward him when none others had until that instant. Or the difference in sound of a suddenly accelerating engine. Or any of a number of inconsistencies in the flow of traffic.

Whatever it was, *something* made him suddenly look away from the traffic light to see a pair of glaring headlights tearing toward him, bearing down mercilessly.

The beams were on high, full bright, dazzling and hypnotic, as a surge of adrenaline rushed through his system. His legs, like suddenly released spring steel, catapulted him into the air as the car swerved into his body.

He felt the hood brush his feet and lower legs as he rolled over it. Cradling his head in his arms, he twisted to roll off before he could strike the windshield full force. The blur of two faces inside and the taxi light on top were all he remembered as he rolled.

Throughout this, which lasted two, perhaps three seconds, he felt as if he were in the eye of a hurricane, possessed with a strange calm and an eerily extended sense of time.

Then Pretorius hit the pavement, continuing his roll as he'd been trained long ago, ending on his feet, converting the energy into short sprinting steps. The car, a Mercedes taxi, shrieked to a halt, a thing infuriated at being deprived of its prey, then slammed into reverse, white backup lights betraying the driver's deadly intent.

Pretorius jumped to one side, drawing the automatic from its high-ride holster, slamming it into a two-hand hold, locking on target with a cold and determined accuracy.

A fact universally ignored by film producers is that a pistol is a next-to-useless weapon against an automobile. No pistol has ever shot a tire instantly flat, unless it was a specially modified monster capable of firing a high-velocity rifle round or shotgun slug. Pistol rounds are also difficult to place through auto glass, as even a minor divergence from a ninety-degree angle can send the round skittering off the glass, causing only a web-patterned cracking of the safety glass but seldom penetrating anything except the atmosphere.

Having been trained to avoid wasting ammunition in such a situation, Pretorius held his fire until the car had overshot its mark and the driver's window was directly opposite him at a distance of one and half feet.

He stitched three rapid-fire nine millimeter rounds through the window, almost like the three-round burst of a submachine gun: *blamblamblam.*

He needed only one good hit. One good hit was what he got. A single round met the glass perfectly, splintered through and entered the driver's temple with consummate ease. The hollow-point slug expanded as it ripped through the man's skull and brain, driving fragments of bone and tissue before it, leaving an exit wound the diameter of a golf ball. Brains and blood exploded in the car's well-appointed interior, spattering the man on the passenger side as the Mercedes rammed forward, the dead driver's foot still determinedly mashed against the accelerator.

His weapon still holding on the car's receding shape, Pretorius watched it speeding, jolting up over the curb, racing along the sidewalk. Pedestrians scattered as the machine threatened to reduce them to bloodied smears on the pavement. Traffic on the Ring was in chaos as drivers gaped at the sight. Three cars collided in rapid succession.

The Mercedes veered toward a glistening line of shop windows and smashed into a chemist's front window, shattering it before finally halting, horn blaring, as the man in the passenger side was thrown head first through the front windshield into a tidily arranged wall of cosmetics.

Pretorius reholstered and walked away at a normal pace. The efficient Viennese police would be there *schnell,* and the last thing he wanted was to explain why he'd decided, on a nice spring evening, to shoot a taxi driver in the head at point-blank range.

He spotted two couples walking together, and crossed the street with them so it looked like a group of five. He kept close to them for the next few blocks despite some hard glances by the two men, which he returned with what he hoped was an ingratiating smile.

The people following Pretorius had not interfered. There was no time, even if they'd wanted to. Besides, only one had any standing instructions to give Pretorius protection if needed. The others had been expressly told not to reveal their presence in any way, even if it meant the death of the subject they'd been flown here to tail.

There were three people in all. Kadmus's ever-patient Chico, and a young Japanese couple.

The boy looked no older than twenty. The girl was certainly not over eighteen. The two were well dressed: Both wore the exaggerated wide-shouldered jackets popular among the young, and ballooned trousers almost in the Turkish style. Her hair was gathered in a long ponytail. His haircut was more extreme: clipped very short—almost shaved—all around to just above the ears, the hair on top moussed into a spiked arrangement.

They walked with their arms around each other, young tourists in love, out for an evening's walk in old Vienna. They had, of course, spotted Chico at once. Although his photograph had not been among those in their briefings, it was obvious the small white-haired man was part of somebody's surveillance team. *But whose? From which source? The Russians? The Americans?*

Chico had been too shaken by the incident at the Schubert-Ring to consider the Japanese couple. He'd seen them, of course. But his mind had rejected them as threats or even players in this scenario. He plodded on behind Pretorius, fingers encircling the grip of the little Mauser automatic in his pocket. The Japanese remained about ten meters behind Chico, varying their pace, often stopping to look in this window or that, the girl giggling convincingly.

Pretorius entered the Sacher, and picked up his key at the desk. He asked for his box from the hotel safe, used the tiny key and withdrew the book. He might as well use the time to try and remember why the name in the inscription was so familiar.

When he entered his room, he stood frozen for an instant.

Everything was turned over, pulled out, or ripped apart. The mattress had been flipped off the bed and long slashes showed someone had more than an academic interest in its construction and contents. Every drawer in both chests had been emptied. Shirts, socks, everything lay in a tangle on the floor.

He checked the bathroom. Toothpaste tube hadn't been cut open. Shaving cream untouched. What they were looking for had to be a medium-sized object, nothing small. He looked down at the book in his hand, and knew his instincts had once again been correct. He dialed the front desk. "Hello, this is Pretorius, room 401. I haven't been robbed, so it's no matter for the police. But somebody's done some damage."

While the house detective and night manager rummaged and blundered around the room with apologies and tongue-clickings, Pretorius packed his bag.

Things were starting to heat up.

Forty-five minutes later, after a conversation with Kadmus from a secure telephone booth, Pretorius was safely placed in a two-room flat above a tiny *beisel*[2] in the Fleischmarkt.

The *beisel* dated back to 1397, and resembled a five-story cuckoo clock. The owner was a friend of Kadmus, and

---

[2]The Austrian equivalent of a bistro.

Pretorius was reassured by the curiously elaborate security system installed in the old building.

His rooms were clean and well furnished, and the bed was a huge four-poster with a feather comforter. It looked inviting. But Pretorius was too wired to sleep.

The people who'd ransacked his room at the Sacher obviously were after something they hadn't found. And nothing of his was missing. So it had to be the book.

He pulled it out of his canvas bag and sat in one of the deep and comfortable chairs. He read the inscription again: *Ex libris Leon Alberti, 10/19/56.*

Alberti. Somebody from college, a faculty member maybe? No, nobody comes to mind. He rubbed the back of his neck. *OK, then. Somebody in the Agency Phil had talked about? Alberti, Alberti. Who the hell is Leon Alberti? Phil loved riddles. And Lewis Carroll was his favorite author. So who is this Alberti?*

He got up and paced the room. It was now 2:30 in the morning, but the city's neon signs were still blazing. He sat on the window seat and looked down toward the Rotenturmstrasse.

Vienna by night, he thought, *is a hell of a lot different than it was in Mozart's time. But he would've appreciated the quality of CD recordings. Almost as good as the real thing.*

He was reminded of this by a series of concentric blue neon circles, rippling in and out, advertising Philips CD recordings. He stared at the sign. *Alberti, Alberti, wherefore art thou—oh, sweet Jesus!* And he was thunderstruck as he suddenly realized the answer, from something he'd read studying codes and ciphers at DIA.

In the fifteenth century or thereabouts, Alberti, Leon Battista Alberti, invented a substitution cipher using two rotating concentric circles—the same principle on which the Nazis based *Enigma,* the military enciphering machine which used a series of resettable discs to generate what was, for years, an unbreakable code. The WWII Japanese *Purple* machine was based on the same idea.

He opened the book and looked at the inscription again: *Ex libris Leon Alberti, 10/19/56. From the library of Leon Alberti, October 19, 1956. If the name had been a riddle, was the date also a riddle? What the hell happened on October 19, 1956?*

He couldn't think of a thing. Obviously, many things happened on that date. But none so important they came to mind without looking it up in a reference book. Phil Mathieson had obviously been planting something as a key to what he'd found, in case he got zapped.

Pretorius stretched. Tonight's events were at last beginning to tell on him. He was suddenly bone-tired, and fell into the four-poster for a deep and dreamless sleep.

The hammering on the door grew too insistent to be ignored. No chambermaid, even with the Austrian passion for neatness, would be that adamant about getting in to clean the room.

Pretorius lurched across the room, stumbling over his open canvas bag before coming to rest against the door. He opened it a crack to find, peering up at him, a miniature man with a shock of white hair. "Herr Kadmus would like you to come by his house. As soon as possible."

"What's up?" Pretorius yawned, pushing his hair away from his eyes.

"The lady you were having dinner with last night?"

"Yes?"

"They found her this morning. In the Danube Canal."

_____ 29

Messages.

Near Moscow, the town of Vatutinki doesn't exist.

It is the GRU's top-secret communications center and appears on few maps except those of the military. Isolated by its own security, it nevertheless has everything to satisfy the needs of its inhabitants: shops, pubs, restaurants, sports, theaters, luxury apartments. It is, in many ways, ideal.

It has one drawback: once a man's assigned to Vatutinki,

he's attached to it for life. He is its captive, its creature, no matter if he's assigned to Afghanistan or Iran, to Uzbekistan or Oman. He will always return, again and again, to Vatutinki. For it is very difficult to clear people for duty in such a sensitive place, and once an individual is cleared, it is convenient to recall him again and again.

For this reason, Radioman Valerian Kharkov was now serving his second tour of duty in Vatutinki. He would, in all, complete eight tours there before dying and being duly consigned to Vatutinki's cemetery, which is also considered secret.

Leather-padded headphones clamped to his ears, Kharkov took down the message. The code was unfamiliar. In any case, it was none of his concern. Within three minutes the transmission from Vienna was complete, and Radioman Kharkov tore off the top three sheets, placing them in an envelope, marking it for General Mescheryakov's Eyes Only.

It was considered too sensitive for even Army General Mescheryakov's cipher clerks. Using a one-time gamma pad, Colonel-general Dovgalevsky had written a short situation report to his superior at the Aquarium. It was necessary that the general himself decipher the contents.

Kharkov signaled for the *Spetsnaz* orderly, who raced down the corridor to the elevator.

Five minutes later, Mescheryakov, having traced out the message from his pad, felt the heat rising within him. It was increasingly difficult to breathe.

He was confident, Dovgalevsky explained in the message, *once the general realized the danger of the Vienna operation being compromised, the action taken last night regarding the female KGB officer would be entirely justified. The American Pretorius will be found shortly,* he assured the general. *He would be terminated quietly long before any revelations gained from his KGB informant could be passed.*

The general tore at his collar, scarcely able to speak through the red haze of his rage.

"Blyad!" he exploded. "That—that cretin! He will get us all shot! How in the name of God was such a moron ever promoted to Colonel-general? Tulchin! Get in here!"

Mescheryakov paced the room angrily, striding from one

end to the other as his stiff-spined orderly took down every
syllable.

"To: Dovgalevsky, L. R., Colonel-general, Commanding
Officer, GRU *Residentura* Vienna. From: Mescheryakov,
V.I., Army General, Director, GRU. Subject: Reassignment. Message reads as follows: Immediately and upon receipt of these orders you will consider yourself relieved of
command of GRU Station Vienna and will proceed directly
to GRU Headquarters, Moscow, for reassignment to duty at
a place and function to be decided at some point in the
future by the undersigned. You are to cease forthwith any
activities with regard to non-Soviet individuals within the
Vienna sphere of operations and will engage in no conversations regarding this matter with any military or civilian personnel whatsoever. Signed, Mescheryakov. Got that,
Tulchin? Read it back."

The aide read back the order precisely, as Mescheryakov
stared out the window at the smokestack. *Dovgalevsky, my
friend, I am going to personally send you up in smoke within
fifteen minutes of your arrival here. I am going to take the
greatest personal pleasure in this. It may, in fact, be the single
most satisfying act of my military career.*

The female found in the river had no identification, but
Russian factory labels in her underclothing prompted the
police investigators to check with the Soviet Embassy. Female Russian tourists are few, and this one seemed exceptionally well dressed, even fashionable.

A Second Secretary came to the morgue and identified the
body, blanching as he realized this was not some trade mission assistant, but a ranking KGB officer.

The attendant pointed out the cause of death: a single 9
mm. bullet to the base of the skull.

The man had arranged himself in one of Kadmus's more
comfortable chairs. His pale, almost colorless hair was long
but carefully combed. He wore a light tan tweed suit with a
vest. His eyes were red-rimmed, slightly watery. Pretorius
guessed him to be about thirty.

"I don't think you gentlemen have met," Kadmus intoned. "Mr. Pretorius, Mr. Carter. John Carter."

Carter didn't rise or attempt to shake hands. Pretorius knew he was Agency at once, and that his name was not likely to be John Carter nor anything like it.

"Mr. Carter," Kadmus added in an attempt at humor, "is with your consulate here."

Pretorius merely nodded and took a seat. Carter was used to people falling all over themselves to explain their actions. But Pretorius had seen this act before.

Studiously arranging the silk handkerchief in his jacket pocket, Carter drawled, "You've begun to make yourself unwelcome in Vienna, Mr. Pretorius." A flat observation, designed to provoke a response.

Pretorius declined comment.

Carter's watery eyes glanced at him. He continued. "You very nearly created the worst possible sort of incident last night. If our people hadn't been on the scene and quieted things down, there'd have been a manhunt for you throughout Vienna. All points bulletins. Worst kind of publicity." He finally finished the handkerchief arranging and looked at Pretorius as if examining a new species.

Pretorius was obviously being called on to offer some sort of explanation. The Agency man stared at him, waiting.

Carter made a small *moue* of distaste as he realized Pretorius wasn't going to react predictably. "We could send you home, have you declared *persona non grata,* of course. But that sort of thing tends to get around, and that's bad for everybody's image. So we're telling you to back off this one. To wrap it up and leave. Completely. Is that understood?"

Pretorius smiled and leaned back in his chair. He was not going to engage in a debate. He had no idea how senior Carter was. He suspected he was middle level and following orders from somebody serious. "You'll have to reconsider that request, Carter," he said quietly.

"Request? Oh, it's not a request, Mr. Pretorius. We're *telling* you to wrap up your little game here. You've got a return ticket to London. We suggest you use it. We'd prefer this afternoon, in fact."

"Or what, Carter?"

Carter colored briefly. "Or we can't guarantee your safety, Mr. Pretorius."

"You haven't been able to guarantee my safety so far, it

seems. And you don't appear to have gotten anywhere with the Mathieson investigation, either. Just precisely what is it you do here, Carter? It can't be work."

"Now look," Carter sputtered, "your friend Mathieson was poking into matters totally unauthorized by the Agency. And as for you, I've had just about—"

He was interrupted as Pretorius suddenly crossed the room to lean over him in the chair. "No, I don't think you've had enough quite yet," Pretorius said in controlled fury. "You haven't had enough sense to tell a murder from a suicide. You haven't done enough work to know what's going on here with the GRU. And you haven't been smart enough to head off one murder last night, to say nothing of a second attempted one. I'd say you people haven't *had* enough, *done* enough, or *been* enough of anything."

Carter clenched his chair arms, staring up at Pretorius, knowing the wrong word at this moment could produce highly unpleasant consequences. Consequences which might have to be explained to his superiors.

"Now then," said Pretorius at length, "I suggest you people just go back to your paper-shuffling, or whatever it is you're able to do well, and let the rest of us get on with this."

Throughout this exchange, August Kadmus sat with his fingers interlaced on his stomach, looking from one man to the other as if he were a spectator at a mildly interesting tennis match.

Carter stood up glaring. "I'd suggest you take great care where you put your nose in the next few days, Pretorius."

Pretorius' only reply was a smile. Carter left, adjusting his vest, leaving Kadmus's door open behind him.

"Well, well. You don't appear to make friends easily, Michael," remarked the older man, pouring a generous beaker of *schnapps*. "You must try to be more diplomatic. And then, of course, go right ahead and do whatever it was you'd originally intended."

Pretorius smiled. "Diplomacy's never been a strong point with me. Besides, like absolute power, it also corrupts absolutely."

"But you know, the young man has a point. Things have gotten to the point where you're becoming a distinct liability to my operation here. In my business, I don't want too many inquiries. Do you follow me?"

"I follow. But the only way it's going to be wrapped up is if I stick to it. To idiots like Carter, the killers don't officially exist. Hell, CIA wants the whole thing buried with Phil."

Kadmus nodded. He looked at his glass speculatively, then tossed back the *schnapps.* "So it seems. Still, you're taking on a hell of a job by yourself."

"Look," said Pretorius, "we've obviously got the bastards stirred up, maybe even panicked enough to tip their hand. That's more than the Agency's done since Phil got wasted. I think we're on to something big. Big enough for the GRU to justify killing both a senior CIA man *and* a KGB officer."

"But why kill *her?*" asked Kadmus. "It doesn't figure. You, yes. But not the lady."

Pretorius brooded, staring at the intricate pattern of the carpet. Then: "They must have thought I'd tumbled on to whatever they're doing here, that I'd told Valentina, as a KGB officer, about it. Told her so she'd contact Moscow KGB, and pull the plug on them. So she was terminated."

Kadmus, getting restless, shifted his bulk. "It fits. But it still tells us nothing about their plans, dear boy. So far we've got very little information at a very high price, *nicht wahr?*"

Pretorius winced.

"But tell me," continued Kadmus, "you said Valentina thought the GRU was doing something against their national policy, something that seemed to be unusually active here?"

"That was what she felt," Pretorius answered. "I had the feeling the KGB was already working on the problem, and regarded it as sensitive."

"Hmpf," Kadmus grunted, looking out the window at the people walking by. "I think we've got enough now to get the Agency involved. After last night, they can't still insist Mathieson's death was the suicide of a junkie. Even *they* would recognize there's something big going on here."

Pretorius brooded on this for a moment, then said, "No, I think we'll find out faster if we pursue it on our own—just for a day or two. No more."

Kadmus looked at him curiously. "You're *verrückte,* you know. You'll find out, all right. You'll find out how it feels

to be floating in the Danube, like the rest of your friends."
He shook his head in exasperation.

"Just two days, August. Two days more."

Kadmus was once again looking out his window. "God
save me from cowboys," he muttered.

The GRU lieutenant brought the encoded message directly
to Colonel-general Dovgalevsky, who ripped open the envelope once the door was closed. He was amazed to see the
reply from the Aquarium was in the clear. He read it slowly,
holding it in both hands. A cold feeling began creeping up
his spine as the words penetrated.

This is my death sentence, he realized. *All the work, all the
sacrifices for this goddamned plan, and now this lily-livered,
fucking Moscow desk general decides to start pointing fingers,
to cozy up to his faggot friends in the KGB.* Chevo Nada!
*We're so close, and if somebody blows the whistle on us now,
we're all dead men. Hell, I'm dead anyway, if I go back to the
Aquarium. Might as well be a dead hero than a dead coward.*

He sat down at his desk and adjusted the Army-issue
lamp. *The American must be killed immediately,* he concluded. *Why on earth hadn't his people been able to handle so
simple a task? A single American, working alone, without
backup, without an organization behind him? It was unthinkable. And yet this one American could put them all out of
business if he got to the KGB or to his own government.*

Dovgalevsky leaned back in his chair and crossed his arms
over his tunic, fuming at the injustice of it all. To his mind,
he was a man betrayed both by his superiors and by fate,
which had so far denied him the promotions and honors he
had earned a hundred times over.

Well, we'll see, he thought. *More has been gained by dis-
obeying orders than by following them. The American General
MacArthur said that,* he remembered.

The irony made him smile.

30

Riddle Me This.

He closed the thin volume and weighed it in his hands, thinking of the Phillip Mathieson he'd known so long ago at New Haven.

A lean and lanky, awkwardly arranged frame, surmounted by a mile-wide smile, a tangle of reddish hair eluding comb or brush, Oxford blue button-down shirt, tan chino slacks. But most of all, a razor-sharp intellect, kept constantly honed with mathematics and riddles and puzzles.

Mathieson had a non-linear mind. He believed the most important breakthroughs in mathematics and physics came from leaps of the imagination, from letting the mind race unhindered, unfettered by the lower forms of logic. A higher logic would be furnished by the mind, he used to say. The endless storage capability of the mind would be, in a limber mind, called into play in a way that would humble linear logic.

To demonstrate his point, even the riddles he constructed depended on unconventional solutions. "Beyond the nine dot square," he called it, referring to the puzzle in which you had to connect all nine dots forming a square using only three straight lines. Once you did it, it seemed obvious. But some would struggle with it for hours until Phillip pointed out the solution.

So, thought Pretorius. *What kind of riddle would Phil leave if he wanted to conceal something critical, something important?*

The choice of Leon Alberti seemed strange. Although Phil was fascinated by the many techniques of encipherment, he always believed codebreakers could easily be foiled by something nonmathematical in nature. Something that depended on a broader, less expected interpretation.

Pretorius remembered Phil had admired Poe's short story, *The Purloined Letter,* in which the letter was "concealed" by being left in plain sight on a table. Just where nobody would think to look for it.

Where nobody would think to look for it. He paused and reflected. *The obvious thing here would be a literal interpretation of the Alberti cipher, which would lead you to look for a disk machine à la Enigma, or to think strictly along the lines of the mathematical relationships of 19/10/56 or 10/19/56 in an alphabet substitution process. But Phil would've known this, and would think differently.*

So what did he do? Pretorius looked at the book again. *Alice in Wonderland. In itself, a book of riddles, a book of altered perceptions. Leon Alberti, Leon Alberti. Now what would a fifteenth-century mathematician have to do with Alice? Well, Lewis Carroll—Charles Lutwidge Dodgson— had taught mathematics and logic at Oxford. So maybe it was a mathematical puzzle. Everything seemed to point to that.*

But maybe it's simpler. Remember—in plain view, where nobody would notice it. So what's in plain view here? The inscription? The book title? OK, Alberti's name was your first clue. It told you there was a puzzle, a riddle, something concealing something else. What's so obvious, it's ridiculous?

Remember the inscription—ex libris—from the library of. Where was Alberti's library? Rome? Milan? Florence? Bologna? Too obtuse.

He opened the book and riffled through the pages, holding them sideways to the tiny table lamp, to try and see if any irregularities existed, any pinholes over certain letters, any gelatin overlays, any anomalous inks. He looked closely at the surfaces of pages ten, nineteen, and fifty-six.

Nothing.

He expelled a long, slow breath and rubbed his eyes. *Obvious, what's so obvious nobody—including me, maybe— would ever notice it?*

Pretorius looked out the window, over toward the blue Philips CD sign. *All Phil was doing with the Alberti name was announcing a riddle. Probably as simple as that. He was counting on the cipher clerks—in case the GRU had gotten their hands on it—to be led off in endless, meaningless technical permutations and combinations. So what's the absolute reverse of that? What's the reductio ad absurdum?*

Then he knew: *The story itself.* Something in the story of

Alice in Wonderland would tell him what Phil had wanted to pass on.

He sat back in the room's much-worn chintz-covered chair and began to read.

A half hour later, he closed *Alice,* leaned back and smiled. The solution was as he suspected. So obvious, all the experts would've gone right past it.

He looked at his watch. Just enough time before they stopped serving.

_____ 31

The Queen of Hearts.

The first and almost overwhelming impression was one of smell, not sight. Six feet from the entrance, the chef presided over a squadron of bubbling cauldrons, producing an aroma so thick and tempting you could almost imagine tucking into it with a spoon.

It was like walking into a kitchen instead of a restaurant. The room accommodated only five tables, the rest of the space taken up by a large black cooking range, two ovens, the chef's wooden preparation table, and the chef himself. He was a tall, sharp-featured man with the sort of face usually seen only on people who work outdoors, leathery and seamed. He wore a small pair of wire-rimmed glasses, which gave him the aspect of an academic cattle wrangler.

Pretorius heard a shrill small voice somewhere around him. When the voice repeated itself, he looked down to see a miniature woman, perfectly proportioned, just below four feet tall. She was not a dwarf, and was in fact quite pretty. She seemed to be in her early thirties.

"Table for one, please," he managed to say, trying to keep the surprise out of his voice.

"Zu Befehl," replied the doll-like creature, leading him to a table toward the rear. As he sat down, she bestowed a smile on him, and handed him a menu. "Is this all right?" she

asked in perfectly accented English, indicating with a slight nod of her head the close proximity to the chef, now furiously slicing vegetables not two feet from Pretorius.

"Perfect," replied Pretorius. *"Ganz gut."*

The doll inclined her head pertly. *"Servus!"* she said, and bustled off into a back room.

Pretorius looked around him and saw a cleverly decorated small room, warm and cozy, a white Portuguese-tiled fireplace opposite the chef's area.

Around the walls a foot below the ceiling ran a wooden ledge, filled with porcelain platters and pitchers, wooden butter molds, tin gelatin molds, earthenware pots and mugs, all decorated with hearts, even a few heart-shaped glass bottles. The menu, he noticed, had a pattern of white-on-white hearts delicately embossed along the edges.

The few other tables in the little restaurant were occupied by young couples, casually dressed. From their easy manner and the way they talked and joked with the tiny *Königin,* Pretorius guessed they were regulars.

In other circumstances, he would be relaxed, enjoying the unique atmosphere of the place. But he knew he was nearing the answer he'd been searching for ever since his meeting with Miranda Mathieson.

He browsed through the eight-page menu, lettered in elegant though legible calligraphy, featuring plain and hearty Austrian country cooking. The wine list displayed a few of the more sought-after *heuriger* wines, describing their various qualities in an intelligent, accurate, yet not wine-geek-precious style.

The regal miniature materialized at his table. "Would the gentleman care to order now, or would he like to take a few more minutes?"

Pretorius looked up from his menu and was met by a pair of china-doll blue eyes, clear and large. Her hair was blonde, cut short, layered neatly. And her dimpled smile was disarming. He found himself wondering if she had difficulty meeting men who matched her perfect miniature scale. He suddenly felt awkward, ungainly.

She waited with an expectant expression, amused by his hesitation. "I'm sorry," he said at last. "I was just trying to decide. How is your *Schweinepfeffer* tonight?"

The dimpled smile broadened to reveal a set of perfect small teeth. "Exactly the same as it is every other night, sir. Very good. But a bit peppery if you're not used to it."

Pretorius, in spite of himself, relaxed and laughed. "Sounds good. I was raised on spicy dishes, so I think I'll survive. But could I have a glass of your house *Rotwein,* please? Just to give me courage?"

She laughed and took his menu, curtseying before she turned to address the bespectacled chef, towering nearly three feet above her.

The wine was delicious and the *Schweinepfeffer* better than he'd had even in Germany. The vegetables were nicely selected, and not overcooked, the meat superbly prepared. Pretorius made a mental note of the spices he thought he detected in the stew; he'd have to try this when—and if—he got back to Devon.

He thought of how simple Mathieson's riddle had been, once he looked for the obvious. *Ex libris Leon Alberti, 10/19/56.*

On page ten was Alice's jar of orange marmalade. On nineteen, pig and pepper. Which could only be *Schweinepfeffer.* And there, on page fifty-six, the key to it all:

The Queen of Hearts—*auf Deutsch, Die Herzenkönigin.* A well-known little restaurant in this neighborhood, just around the corner from the Rennweg, not far from the Soviet Embassy on Reisnerstrasse. He'd remembered passing it several times on one of his visits years ago.

When she removed his dishes and asked if he'd like some dessert, Pretorius decided to ask the question. "Have you any pancakes with *Orangenmarmelade?* A friend in the United States introduced me to it." He waited expectantly. Her answer would tell him whether he'd misread Mathieson's riddle or not.

The Queen of Hearts' expression was unchanged. But she paused thoughtfully, tapping the end of the mechanical pencil against her teeth. "Oh, and who was your friend, sir? I once knew someone like that."

Pretorius looked into the blue eyes and saw nothing that gave anything away. "His name was Phillip," he replied quietly. "Phillip Mathieson."

Her blue eyes were neutral, noncommittal. "Hmm. The

name isn't all that familiar. At any rate, I'm afraid we ran out of marmalade at breakfast. *Es tut mir leid."* And she gave a small mock pout, and smiled. "Will that be all, then?"

Pretorius looked at her incredulously. He'd been certain when she asked about the "friend" that he'd connected. But perhaps he'd just been too optimistic. He tried to smile. "Yes, thanks," he said. "It was all really delicious, and I've eaten much too much. *Nur die Rechnung, bitte."*

She curtseyed quickly and totaled up the bill. She placed it face down on the table and with a smile said, "We hope you enjoyed your dinner. Come again, sir."

Pretorius sipped slowly at his wine, thinking of how he could have misinterpreted Mathieson's riddle. Yet it all fit. It fit so well. He shook his head and turned over the bill.

Please do not speak further but tomorrow morning at six-thirty go to Gate Two of the Zentralfriedhof and wait for someone who will identify himself as Baumann. He will have what you need.

> *Schweinepfeffer Platte*
> *Zwei gl. Rotwein*
> *290 Sch.*

Pretorius looked over to the tiny figure now busying herself at a neighboring table. He turned the bill back over, put a fifty mark note on top of it, and left.

The shots spat out so suddenly the expressions on the two as they fell were of surprise, not of anger.

The hour was 11:27 P.M., Vienna time.

The girl had been pacing outside the telephone booth, hands jammed deep in the white monkey-fur jacket. The young man inside had been waiting for the Tokyo duty officer to get on the phone. The proper codes had been entered, the identity sequence confirmed.

Neither noticed the van until it was broadside, until the heavy door slid back and sixty-four rounds erupted from the silenced submachine guns, suppressors enshrouding the sounds. Only the shattering of glass in the booth caused people to turn.

The girl fell and was a puff of white fur on the sidewalk, a scarlet pool flooding beneath her.

The man was dead in milliseconds, sliding to a sitting position in the bottom of the booth, smearing a trail of crimson on the metal and the scattered shards of glass which were still hanging in the booth.

From the receiver dangling, slowly spinning on its cord, the voice of the duty officer, metallic, mechanical, spoke above the torn and bloodied head.

Beneath the California sun, in the building called the Big Blue Cube, the engineers bent low over their consoles.

The data had been checked, cross-checked, fed into a computer simulation model. Everything responded as expected. No anomalies were detected. The new mission trajectory would be relatively easy, the changeover seamless.

Finally the stream of data was released, fired off to the eye in a single burst.

As the eye sped over southern California on its practiced orbit, the new data was received and routed into the appropriate navigation subroutine. The old data remained within the original E-programmed chip, but the new data now became the onboard command source.

At first the satellite appeared unaffected. But as it began to approach denied territory, the new program began to take over.

Surfaces on the satellite itself began to rise slightly. The speed slowed as the eye edged toward its new orbit, 286 miles above the earth, inclined fifty-seven degrees to the equator.

In complementary course to the eye, a Soyuz weather satellite also picked up the new stream of data, and relayed it back to earth, to Tyuratam and a select group of analysts.

For the collection and transmission of weather data was not the Soyuz' primary mission, only its publicly announced one. This satellite was, in the language of reconnaissance, a ferret. Its object in life was to monitor streams of telemetry from U.S.-launched satellites, shuttles, and rockets, then retransmit the data back to earth where it would be analyzed.

In the event of war, such ELINT[1] would then be used to

[1]Electronic Intelligence.

either jam the functions of enemy satellites, or even reprogram them to either change their courses or destroy themselves in electronic *hara-kiri*.

The eye came closer to its point of entry to the new orbit, but seemed to be hesitating. Below, in the Big Blue Cube, its masters stared at their screens of data. A few anomalies showed. Then more.

A couple of supervisors came down from their monitors to visit the on-line consoles, offering suggestions.

The satellite was not entering the new orbit properly, despite the new program's flawless performance in the computer simulation.

Ray Halkins Myers, the Satellite Control Center's ranking engineer, took over the master console, fitting on the headphones, adjusting his seat. He began punching in commands, and several different displays filled the screen. He began a low, throaty grumbling to himself, a dialogue with his tools, with the multibillion-dollar collection of hardware and software that commanded LACROSSE.

Several of the screens showed all in order. But a third, then a fourth, showed data entering the satellite's programs that wasn't originating from the Big Blue Cube. "Gentlemen," he rumbled to those watching his screens, "we've been ferreted. Let's resend the new coordinates."

And he quickly punched in the codes, sending the new datastream a second time. He leaned back in his seat and knuckled his eyes. "Let's get a reading on what else is up there, around our guy," he ordered.

A young man with a bound book of computer printouts materialized behind him. "Sir, we show a Soyuz weather tracker dogging LACROSSE for the last forty-eight hours. Correlation is way high. Too high to be coincidence."

"Get NRO at the Pentagon. See what they've got, if anything, on this so-called weatherbird."

"We're on the case." A man at the next console punched at a telephone's number pad.

"Now," the big man at the master console drawled, "let's see just how smart this bird really is." And he began entering a code sequence that existed in only four places: his own memory, the safe at the Big Blue Cube, the safe at the NRO's suite at the Pentagon, and the safe of the Secretary of Defense.

Punching in the last number, he paused, then rapidly entered the command sequence. A high speed burst of data was shot up to the satellite on a new frequency, 18 gigahertz.

"I want a frequency sweep on that weatherbird. Get me a lock and let's see what he's doing up there."

Behind him, an Air Force lieutenant colonel, wearing a telephone headset, relayed the order to the NSA[2] at Fort George G. Meade, Maryland. Within two minutes Meade came back: the Soyuz was found transmitting on the original command frequency for LACROSSE.

"OK, now tell those weenies to keep the sweep going and tell me if they get anywhere near the new code-lock."

The officer behind him relayed the order. The room was absolutely still. Myers kept his eyes on the screen.

LACROSSE was still not in its orbit, but not behaving dangerously. Not yet.

Feliks brought the crowd to its feet, transforming it into a single terrifying being, devoid of cogency, invested with the venom of mindless rage. Just as others had done since epochs unrecorded, Feliks directed their fears, their gut-churning madnesses into a single vortex of power against a single enemy. A thousand mouths writhed as one, chanting in unison—*Death to the Betrayers! Death to the Betrayers! Death to the Betrayers!*

And who were the Betrayers? *The Betrayers,* roared Feliks, *were all around them, in the politicians and generals who groveled for the pittances the Western and Japanese banks were willing to toss them in exchange for Russia's birthright. The Betrayers were the Soviet Socialist Republics who were draining the Fatherland like blood-sucking leeches. The Betrayers were the Jews, the Atheists, the Russians who failed to speak out against Russia's enemies, who failed to fight on the side of the New Russia—a Russia that shall, once again, be* Great *Russia.*

The intoxication swept through the thousands like a gasoline fire, sucking away the breath and the reason, spreading terror in the seconds before it engulfed all in the holocaust of hatred.

And now the crowd pressed closer and closer to the stand, eager to see a last glimpse of Feliks as his bodyguards, supplied from one of the GRU's *Spetsnaz* battalions, bundled him into the long Zil limousine, roaring their fear, their love, their unspent frenzy.

Time raced forward.

32

The Other Viennese.

The gray light changed to gold, and the gold gave a new geometry to the monuments. Sliced by the trees and by other monuments into neat Viennese sections, the sunlight produced triangles, parallelograms, and other forms against gray stone. The gravestone of Adolf Loos, a stark and simple cube, became a singular screen for these patterns, geometry against geometry.

As the sun climbed, the patterns shifted downward, backlighting the dew-flecked grass among the graves. Jeweled spiderwebs revealed an orderliness surpassing even the orderly Viennese.

Here in the *Zentralfriedhof,* the Central Cemetery, lay what the Viennese called "the Other Viennese." And here, 120 meters from Gate Number Two, also lay Michael Pretorius.

He'd been concealed nearly three hours, with the resolve of the hunter who knows it is motion, not form, that alerts the quarry. He was not bored. Lying motionless in one of the older *gräbergruppen,* he saw the wildlife tentatively venture among the stones. Hares shredding the flowers strewn on the graves. Pheasants pecking at invisibilities on the ground, necks rhythmically bobbing for balance.

As in all forests, there was much to see. For Pretorius,

there was the added impetus that what he did *not* see could kill him.

Something fell lightly, almost gracefully, onto his collar from a tree above. He felt its weight, felt it move in microscopic procession. A worm? Centipede? He tried to remember if centipede bites were poisonous. Or—more important—if such bites were painful enough to make him move suddenly and betray his presence.

Resolutely, with all due dignity, the worm marched along Pretorius' collar. It stepped down onto his neck. It paused, sensing the warmth and moisture of his skin as favorable territory, and continued its progress.

Pretorius summoned all his control to avoid shivering as the worm crawled beneath his collar, inching toward his spine.

Then they came through the gate.

There were three of them. Two were heavy, each carrying a canvas bag. The third was thin, tall, wearing a dark raincoat and hat. Pretorius guessed the bags contained weapons, most likely submachine guns with suppressors. Without words the first two dispersed in different directions.

The third stood stock still, shoulders hunched against the chill morning air. As the light grew lighter, Pretorius saw the man wore steel-rimmed glasses. *Of course,* he realized with a shock. *The chef.*

Then he remembered the woman's words: *He will give you what you need.* Right.

In this light, the glasses gave the eyes a colder aspect than they'd possessed last night in the restaurant. The stare was reptilian. The eyes swept the area in the way of professional hunters of men, the procedure of policemen, assassins, and certain soldiers.

The focus, beginning at the far left perimeter, moved out, then in, then shifted to the right slightly. Then out again, then in. And so on until every centimeter of cover was inspected. And then a final overall look at the field of fire.

Twice the eyes swept past Pretorius. Twice the basilisk stare met the recumbent bundle of leaves and branches that broke up his outline. Twice the brain behind the eyes made a decision, and moved on. Twice Pretorius felt the fetid breath of death come close.

Beneath his shirt, along the moist warmth of Pretorius' skin, the worm progressed downward, crossing the puckered, jagged seam of scar tissue Pretorius had earned once, a very long time ago, along the former East German border.

Pretorius willed his muscles to relax. The worm, uncaring of his host, continued his march.

Finally, the tall thin man moved, his measured pace seeking his own position of advantage. From time to time, he would stop and look back toward the gate, expressionless. Pretorius was reminded of the way a ferret will suddenly stand upright on two feet, motionless, looking toward a potential source of danger, or a possible source of food.

The man looked out toward the Simmeringer Hauptstrasse and nodded in satisfaction. The sun would outline anyone coming through the stone pillars within the next hour.

The two gunmen now established their positions as Pretorius had earlier. They were back about thirty meters, concealed behind two rather baroque large monuments. The weapons were removed from the bags, an H&K MP-5 submachine gun and what appeared to be a cut-down AKM. A single burst from either weapon could destroy most vital organs in a split second.

Pretorius had picked his spot with care in the moonlit hours before. The perfect spot, in the end, would have been the worst, for it could also be the spot chosen by the killers. A less expected spot, off to one side, offered greater advantage.

It also gave Pretorius a full field of fire covering all three men, while affording good concealment.

Pretorius' body angled around a large boulder, vines of vegetation snaking over the mossy surface. He lay on his side, pistol hand outstretched on the ground toward the probable field of fire, leaves and small branches covering the arm. The Glock 19 was fitted with a suppressor and a full magazine of the new Israeli subsonic blue-tip rounds. Charcoal darkened Pretorius' face. A watch cap clustered with leaves concealed his hair.

The worm began a new trail, away from Pretorius' spine.

Wire-Rimmed Glasses paused again, turned, and took his final sighting on the entrance. Then he walked slowly forward, as if greeting someone. Pretorius realized he was rehearsing. It was now a half hour until the time of the rendezvous.

Into the sheltering curve and warmth of Pretorius' right underarm, the worm progressed. Microscopic feet lifted and trod on warm, moist skin.

No sounds came from the men concealed behind the monuments. Wire Rims was slowly walking backward from a certain spot he'd chosen for greeting Pretorius, if Pretorius had come as agreed.

The mist was beginning to lighten as the sun emerged from the clouds, warming the area. Wire Rims was motionless, except for a slight shifting of his weight from one leg to another.

Pretorius stifled an impulse to make a sound, any sound, to relieve the unbearable tingling as the worm made its way along the inside of his upper forearm, along the biceps.

He saw the man in the wire-rimmed glasses stiffen, suddenly alert.

Then he heard the sound of footsteps on the gravel leading from the gate. *One man, walking slowly.*

Wire Rims made a small motion with one hand along his trouser leg, a signal to the men hidden in the underbrush. One hand remained in his raincoat pocket.

The walker came into view. A man dressed in a black trenchcoat, much like the one Pretorius wore until today. The sun was behind him, his face impossible to see.

At that moment, the centipede elected to close the pincers on either side of its mouth around the soft, moist skin of one of Pretorius' biceps. The pain was like an electric shock, and Pretorius couldn't suppress the involuntary movement of his arm.

Wire Rims squinted toward Pretorius, the light dazzling his vision, then made a short, swift chopping motion with his free hand. Nothing happened. He half turned to look behind him, puzzled. It was then that the walker framed in the gate spoke. Quietly, and with an authority that knew no options lay open for the man it addressed.

"You may not count on your men. They have been silenced. Now take your right hand out of your pocket.

Slowly. Or you will be killed. You are covered from several directions."

Wire Rims hesitated. Then, in a movement so swift Pretorius couldn't be sure it had actually been made, the hand came out of the pocket, and with it, a large-frame automatic.

Before the pistol could be raised to fire, the man seemed to quiver slightly, like a tree struck by the first blow of an axe.

And slowly, ever so slowly, fall face forward into the damp black earth.

_____ 33

The Visitor.

The steel haft of a crossbow bolt was centered between the shoulder blades beneath Wire Rims' raincoat, the crimson blossom around it thickening, blackening fast.

Pretorius tightened his finger around the trigger, at the same time raising the barrel with its suppressor. Then a voice behind him counseled, "Really, *mein Knabe,* you don't want that thing to go off. Put the weapon away, and allow me to introduce you to someone."

Kadmus, Pretorius realized. *What in hell was Kadmus doing here?*

Slowly he raised himself, breaking up the minor thicket of leaves and branches with which he'd covered himself. "I must admit," remarked Kadmus, his rotundity wrapped in a trenchcoat resembling a tent with buckles, "we didn't see you until just a minute or so ago. Judging from your appearance, we were better off, *nicht wahr?"*

Kadmus's men came in from the trees and joined them. The two thugs with subguns had been dispatched in the same manner as Wire Rims—swiftly, silently.

As Pretorius had lain concealed, Kadmus's men moved through the cemetery in wraithlike silence. They weren't merely trained men; they were part of a *Jäger* tradition that reached back through the centuries.

Threading their way through the labyrinth of granite and marble, the hunters found their prey. The two thugs with automatic weapons hadn't bothered to conceal themselves from the rear, an indiscretion which would prove costly.

The hunters steadied their crossbows by bracing their forearms against the monuments, waiting for the signal.

The crossbow is one of the most powerful, silent, and deadly of all hunting weapons. In the use of the crossbow, one-shot accuracy is paramount. Reloads are, to put it mildly, inadvisable.

When the man in the black trenchcoat had come through the gate, Wire Rims and his assassins were totally focused on the lone figure. At that precise moment, August Kadmus pressed a transmitter in his pocket. A receiver in each hunter's trouser pocket vibrated silently, much like trembler pagers carried by physicians in the United States.

The hunters' forefingers pressed against the crossbow triggers, disengaging the steel bolts which sped like silent messengers of death itself. Each bolt instantly penetrated the soft flesh in the back of its target's neck, severing the spinal cord as a butcher's cleaver might sever the stripped neck of a fowl.

All was over in a moment, and it was a surprised Pretorius that Kadmus grasped in his bearlike embrace. "I know, I know," said the jovial German. "You're angry we spoiled your rendezvous. But really, Michael, these chaps are not the kind to go after singlehandedly. You could easily have gotten yourself killed. Besides," he added playfully, "I still haven't given you my bill for services rendered."

Pretorius laughed in spite of himself. "Nice to know I'm wanted," he said, dusting off some of the debris from his jacket.

"You'd be surprised, *mein Knabe*," smiled Kadmus, "But as I said, there's a gentleman I think you should meet." He gestured toward the man in the black trenchcoat who'd entered the gates.

The man was, in all respects, outwardly unremarkable. Colorless, no distinguishing features. He might have been a moderately competent accountant, attorney, or physician.

For despite the man's lack of distinction or difference, there was an air of professionalism about him.

Pretorius knew instinctively the man had to be someone very senior in intelligence. He'd met several such men over the years, and their only common denominator was their lack of coloration, their absence of memorable visual qualities.

"May I introduce Colonel V. S. Volynskiy of the KGB? Colonel, this is Michael Pretorius." Kadmus arched his eyebrows expectantly.

Volynskiy smiled, yet the eyes held no humor, sizing up Pretorius quickly. The two men shook hands. Volynskiy was first to speak. "Well. It appears the GRU has decided you're in season, Commander."

Pretorius laughed, the big German and the Russian joining in. August Kadmus clapped a big paw on the back of Pretorius. "You know, if you don't mind," Kadmus said, "I'd rather have this conversation somewhere other than in a cemetery."

Together the men walked out into the clarity of a fine Viennese spring morning, and got into the car waiting on the shoulder of the Simmeringer Hauptstrasse.

As they pulled out into the traffic, they were watched from the gate by two men who appeared to be Japanese.

Thirty minutes later the three were in one of Vienna's oldest coffeehouses, the Café Lauman. The place was owned by an old friend of Kadmus who'd worked for the Gehlen Organization before retiring. The man opened the tiny café for the three morning visitors, made them generous cups of *Kaffee mit Schlag,* then locked the doors for their privacy.

Pretorius now had an opportunity to observe Volynskiy at close range. The man seemed to adapt himself, even his accent, to whomever he was talking to at the moment.

The language of choice among the three was English. Yet when speaking to Kadmus, Volynskiy's sentence structure was oddly elliptical, his consonants clipped, like the German's. When speaking with Pretorius, he spoke in an easy, offhand way, in English as accentless as a Californian's.

Pretorius recognized this chameleonlike facility. Many in

the trade had it. He occasionally used it himself, to relax the other person.

Volynskiy's eyes were unblinking and gray. In certain light they could be mistaken for blue, or even for green. His hair was a mousy brown going to gray, and his skin was ashen, although not so pale as to be remembered as anything unusual. He was, indeed, a chameleon, a creature utterly suited to his calling.

"You see, Michael," said the ponderous Kadmus, opening the conversation, "things have been accelerating quite a lot. Two Japanese intelligence agents were killed last night, and it had all the fingermarks of your GRU friends. A bystander happened to see one of them before the door slammed shut, and he was wearing a gray windbreaker and the sort of aviator glasses—yellow-tinted—your GRU tail was wearing.

"We'd also found your little friend, the Queen of Hearts, although by other means than you did," Kadmus explained. "She'd replaced the real—and considerably taller—young proprietress after the GRU discovered Mathieson had been close with the original. Mathieson's friend had been tortured, and revealed that a replacement would likely come to be briefed by her in the event of Mathieson's death.

"And there you were, blithely ordering your—*wie heisst es auf Englisch?* Pig and Pepper?—and asking for your marmalade. We'd had the place staked out, and after your dinner there we stuck very close to you. Four men were with you here, all night."

Pretorius squinted in the sunlight at Kadmus, not relishing this *recitatif*. Kadmus continued blithely, "But to your credit, Michael, you used good tradecraft in anticipating something going wrong, in testing out the contact first. They were all set to execute you quietly. They'd even excavated, or *re*-excavated, a grave, a recently filled one, to make you disappear without a trace. Good thorough people. But, fortunately for us, not quite thorough enough, *nicht wahr?*"

Kadmus took a deep draft of his coffee, which resulted in a dollop of whipped cream resolutely clinging to the tip of his nose. He mopped it off and nodded toward the Russian.

"After the death of Valentina, the KGB's Moscow Center

decided to investigate and sent Colonel Volynskiy here. The
Colonel is with the Third Chief Directorate."[1]

Colonel Volynskiy nodded. "As you might imagine, we
regretted the loss of Comrade Verontsova. We'd also had
her investigating some unusual phenomena at the GRU *residentura,* without the knowledge of her superior here. A sensitive task to say the least.

"She was good, very good. And she'd just begun to turn
up some useable material when she was killed." He paused
and looked into Pretorius' eyes. "Did she pass on any information to you that evening? It might be invaluable to us. The
last report from her was five days before her death."

Pretorius downed the rest of his *Kaffee mit Schlag,* and
rested the heavy cup on the marble tabletop. "I'm sorry
about her death too, Colonel. But she didn't really pass on
much, other than the GRU seemed to have some connection
with *Otechestvo,* the Russian nationalist movement, and
that a General Mescheryakov was now in Vienna, visiting
the Navigator here."

Volynskiy frowned. "Mescheryakov himself—he's supposed to be on maneuvers with the *Spetsnaz.* Interesting.
Most interesting. But did she know anything about what
he's doing here?"

Pretorius shook his head. "She hadn't found out yet. That
was her priority, but security at the *residentura* was tight as
a drum. She felt something was just about to happen, but
didn't have a direction on what it was. Mescheryakov travels
rarely outside the Soviet Union, so this visit was felt to have
significance."

Oh, it would, mused Volynskiy. *It most certainly would
have significance.*

Drumming his fingers on the marble tabletop, the KGB
man brooded about the possibilities, and wondered how
much to tell the two Westerners. Much hung in the balance.
And time was growing short.

The CIA man, Carter, was angry. Twice his reports on
Pretorius' unwarranted interference had gone unanswered.

[1]Military Counterintelligence.

He bristled at his desk, wondering if the Japanese murders last night had anything to do with Pretorius.

More than likely, he thought. *How in God's name do they think I'm going to handle things here if they don't even acknowledge the problem? Here we've got a loose cannon, an ex-DIA hotshot who's going to give us a real live international incident. And right now we don't need any more bad press. So why doesn't somebody yank this joker out?*

He glared at the telephone, then looked at his watch. *Well, here goes nothing. Might as well know one way or the other.* And he stabbed at the numbers with his forefinger, wondering whether or not calling the head of station was prudent.

A few moments waiting until the connection was made and the scrambler activated. He spoke to the Langley secure operator and was rewarded with a two-minute wait, at the end of which an extremely irritated head of station, Vienna, snapped, "Well, Carter? Something important?"

Carter launched into a recital of complaints about the ex-DIA officer causing all sorts of unpleasantness, including a number of public incidents which could embarrass the Agency presence in Vienna.

The man at the other end listened patiently, letting the junior officer complete his list of reasons why the "washed-up DIA spook" should be quietly scourged and sent back to wherever it was he belonged.

At the conclusion of Carter's monologue, a few seconds' silence hung in the air between Vienna and Langley.

Then the young officer received a reaming-out that, in a long and undistinguished career in government service, he was never to forget.

Carter replaced the receiver gently, and wondered at the perfidy of the trade in which he'd placed himself. Then he took his jacket off the back of his office door and went out to a neighboring *Weinstube* for something to restore his lacerated ego. It was going to take some doing.

Lieutenant Gostev, resting in his bunk aboard the big Delta III sub, thought it odd. Why, after such an ambitious provisioning, should they now be lying motionless on the bottom of the Tsushima Strait? Only a few miles off the Japanese coast, Gostev knew they might easily be detected by Japan's sophisticated SOSUS equipment once they started up. The Japanese were understandably nervous about such things, and considered the presence of Soviet vessels in the straits as outright provocation. Previous exercises had never followed this pattern. *Which, of course,* Gostev reminded himself, *would be precisely why Admiral Terpanichev might order such a move.*

They'd surfaced only occasionally, and then only at night when the photographic satellites would be blinded, and when the radar-imaging satellites would be least likely to note the oblong shape.

Rumors, of course, were running like furtive minnows throughout the boat. *They were going to test-launch a new missile, firing it into a pre-determined spot in the ocean . . . they were at war and no radio contact was permitted while they waited everything out . . . they were positioning themselves to monitor the sonar signature of a new silent-running American boomer.*

Whatever the rumor, whatever the reason, Gostev was happy. He was at sea, he was in his beloved submarine, and above all he was away, far, far, away from his harridan of a wife, Nastasya, and her carping tongue.

Yes, life was good down here, he thought. *A decent, sensible, logical life. Not at all like the craziness above.*

Then he felt the engines start up.

_____ 34

Mescheryakov.

On the morning after Army General Mescheryakov's arrival in Vienna, an oblong pine packing case was loaded onto an Aeroflot Tupolev at the Vienna-Schwechat cargo terminal.

Stenciled "Diplomatic Files," the case rode up the rubber conveyor belt to disappear within the belly of the big plane.

No files, in fact, were within the wooden crate. But what was in it had indeed once been a useful repository of information. For the crate contained the body of Colonel-general Leonid Dovgalevsky.

The body was sheathed within a plastic and canvas body bag kept by the *residentura* for such eventualities. The skull was wrapped in an additional layer of plastic. It had unfortunately been shattered by a large-caliber bullet fired into it at close quarters.

The execution of Dovgalevsky was Mescheryakov's first act on arrival at Reisnerstrasse 45–47, after learning of the debacle at the *Zentralfriedhof.*

Mescheryakov now placed highest priority on the termination of the American. It was imperative to contain whatever damage had been done to the Vienna *residentura.* With Dovgalevsky's bungling, the American had been permitted to run free for several days. God alone knew what he knew about the *residentura*—or who he had passed it on to.

The *Spetsnaz* cadre reported the American had contracted for operational support with August Kadmus, something of an institution among the intelligence community here in Vienna. It had been Kadmus's men who had been responsible for killing the GRU "wet" team in the *Zentralfriedhof.* Therefore whatever the American knew, Kadmus and his people also would likely know.

"The only course is obvious," Mescheryakov snapped to the senior man. "Wipe out Kadmus and his men. Treat this as you would an infection, like gangrene. You don't *play* with it, you *eradicate* it. Getting rid of one element accomplishes nothing. You must act quickly, decisively. But most of all, you do it *thoroughly.* My God, haven't you children learned anything of the lessons of Beria?"

The *Spetsnaz* officer with the aviator glasses nodded sharply in response.

August Kadmus was seldom known to leave the house on Schubertgasse. First, because his bulk made it difficult. And second, because Kadmus didn't believe in making his memorable figure even more visible, considering his profession.

Yet Kadmus had one weakness which required him to leave his *sanctum sanctorum:* a deep and abiding love of food.

Kadmus was one of Vienna's true gourmands. If Brillat-

Savarin and Escoffier had been alive today, Kadmus would be their objective. His palate for both food and wines was equally astonishing. He could tell the precise composition of any sauce from a single taste. He could discern the vineyard and vintage of any red Bordeaux predating 1983, as well as that of most red Burgundies.

Being a member of the intelligence trade, Kadmus had a habit of avoiding habits. He seldom took the same route anywhere, and seldom did anything outside his home at the same time at regular intervals.

With one exception.

In the pursuit of food, August Kadmus was attracted once a month to a restaurant in Oberdöbling.

The restaurant was called Die Rote Kappelle. It was presided over by a jovial Bavarian, Paul Gutschow, whose mission in life was the preparation of the finest German cuisine imaginable.

As all great restauranteurs are also great impresarios, Gutschow required an appreciative audience, and found it in August Kadmus.

On the night of May 15, Kadmus and his four friends were seated around the table enjoying *Drei Mignons à la Berliner* (three cutlets of beef, veal, and lamb) and comparing the '59 Chateau Palmer with the same vintage of Chateau Montrose, when a man of medium height, wearing dark glasses and a tan raincoat, entered the restaurant and walked directly to the table where Kadmus and his friends were eating.

Without a word, the man opened his raincoat and withdrew a curious weapon: a Walther PP "Sport" model pistol with an old-fashioned six-inch Maxim suppressor screwed to the muzzle. Taking calm and deliberate aim, he fired five shots directly into the face of August Kadmus. The only sounds were soft pops, like small balloons exploding.

Throughout the shooting, all movement and noise in the restaurant seemed suspended. Then, realizing what had happened before their eyes, the customers and staff dissolved into a cacophony of shouts and screams.

But by then the gunman had vanished through the back door. The sound of an automobile door slamming and a rapidly accelerating engine were noted by one of the waiters.

The car sounded like a large one, he said later when quizzed by the *Bundespolizei*.

The body of August Kadmus sagged forward onto the table, his ruined head cracking one of the plates of Meissen porcelain the proprietor reserved for Kadmus and his circle of friends.

Propelled both by his friends in high places and by his own considerable charisma, Feliks gathered great momentum. As the nominal head of *Otechestvo,* he represented a force which the president was reluctant to squash, as he—and both the Defense Council and the GRU, which seemed to support his oddball movement—served as a useful counter-balance against the once all-powerful KGB.

But now the president, at the urging of several of his ministers, was watching the third in a series of telecasts by the apocalyptic figure.

The face of Feliks distorted as he neared the end of his two-hour-long tirade. All over the Soviet Union, the night-marish face filled television screens, beamed down from the *Molniya* satellite to several dozen ground stations.

Although the energy generated by Feliks when addressing a crowd was powerful, his power on television was electrify-ing. Proof, as General Mescheryakov himself once said, that television is not a looking glass, but a *magnifying* glass.

The lips twisted as Feliks pronounced the names of the president, certain members of the politburo, Central Com-mittee, and secretariat. "These—*jackals* who masquerade as men are savaging the throat of a prostrate Russia. And yet we call them not only *men,* but *leaders. Leaders!*

"Yes, they are *leaders,* if you accept them leading us to prostration before the Western capitalists and the Japanese. Yes, they are *leaders* if you, the people of once-Great Russia, are willing to be led like so many millions of lemmings to the precipice of ruin. Leaders, if you wish to see the Fatherland led to whimpering oblivion.

"In czarist Russia, such men would have been shot down in the street like the curs and jackals they are. In czarist Russia, such men would have never been permitted to live and to breathe the same air as real Russians.

"But *today,* in the Russia that is the legacy of decades of profligacy and prostitution of our great nation, today we watch helplessly as these jackals feed on our own flesh and that of our families.

"Russians! We must *arise,* arise and rid ourselves of the jackals. We must once again create a truly *Great* Russia, a Russia that recalls our days of triumph and grandeur—before the Bolsheviks, before the Mensheviks, before the scavengers that came to prey on the people!"

The screen cut to the crowd, standing now. They screamed, cheered, clapped their hands high above their heads. The chanting began: *"Feliks! Feliks! Feliks!"*

Back to the stark and ascetic face, the face of a zealot of Rasputinlike power. Dark circles under the glittering eyes tell of a tortured imagination, but one of genius.

He waits like a conductor until the crowd becomes hushed and expectant, eager for more. Then, in a voice low and compelling, he seduces them further.

"How many of you will join me?" The crowd murmurs. "How many of you will join me in ridding Russia of the jackals?" The crowd begins to growl, then to roar in a tumult like thousands of angered animals. *"And how many of you will join me in rising, in destroying, and then finally creating a new Great Russia?"*

The crowd is beyond any control other than the control which issues from the timbre of Feliks' voice. The camera pulls back slowly, leaving the close-up of the face, tracking back from the black robe, the silver staff, the tall apocalyptic figure. And then pulls back even more to reveal an enormous black flag with a central blood-red and white device—a graphic, modern version of the double eagle of Imperial Russia.

A click, and the screen goes black.

The others in the room wait for the president to speak. He passes his hand over his bald head, grimaces, then sits motionless nearly a minute. The silence in the room has a brooding, touchable presence of its own. Then finally: *"Arrest him. Use whatever force is necessary. I want him in the Lubyanka by morning."*

The KGB general in the room smiles, and leaves the room soundlessly. He has been waiting for this moment nearly two years.

• • •

Chico, telephoned by the owner of Die Rote Kappelle, had rushed to the safehouse in the Fleischmarkt to warn Pretorius. *"Mein Gott,* he said it was terrible," the distraught Chico managed to say as he struggled to get his breath. "The man fired directly into Herr Kadmus's face. He never had a chance. And no one could give a description afterward— everyone had a different version of the way the man looked!"

"Were you followed here?" asked Pretorius, looking down at the street through the room's one small window.

"What? No, no. At least I don't think so," stammered the little man.

"Then make sure, *absolutely sure* you don't return to August's apartment, or to anywhere you or your friends are known, until all this is over. OK?"

"Ja, gern. Oh Jesus, this is horrible. That someone should do this. That anyone should kill Herr Kadmus."

Pretorius had the impression that, as shocking as the death of August Kadmus was to Chico, he was at least as shocked that an unwritten rule had been violated in Vienna's intelligence community. Kadmus had been, until tonight, untouchable. *Der Alte,* he'd been known as by all sides. He'd seemed, in some ways, almost immortal.

"Chico, there's a back entrance to the *beisel* downstairs. When you leave, don't go out the front. Go through the inside door into the *beisel,* then out the back. Get out of Vienna. Leave the rest of this to me, right?"

"Richtig, richtig," said an utterly unnerved Chico. "I know a place in the hills above Salzburg, a farm—Frau Herzl—"

"Don't even tell me about it. Just *go. Now!"*

The small white-haired man disappeared, making Pretorius think of the white rabbit in *Alice,* going down the rabbit hole saying again and again, "I'm late, I'm late."

Pretorius looked at his watch. He was now on his own. And now he had an even larger debt to repay.

35

Dragonfly.

He lit a cigarette in the gloom. He was trying to quit and was experimenting with a number of evil-tasting brands in an effort to discourage his habit.

He inhaled deeply and winced. *These,* he decided, *hinted of the bouquet of smoldering bicycle tires. Yes. These might just do the job.*

The sun drifted deep behind the buildings across the street, merging the colors in the room to a continuum of blue, the corners going to indigo. *The French had a phrase for this hour,* he recalled. *L'heure bleue.*

The room in which he brooded was one of perhaps a dozen throughout Japan reserved for his occasional use. To the staff on this floor who worked for the *gurupu,* he was a senior financial officer, a dedicated older man who liked to look in on the affairs of the companies. He had many names, but the one name that identified him to the small circle of his seniors was "Dragonfly."

Both cover and location were convenient for his purposes. Shifting location was better security, and senior officers seldom had to explain their presence or activities.

He took another drag on the cigarette and stared out the window at the building across the street. The windows of his office were double-glazed and equipped with low frequency generators to nullify voice vibrations. A parabolic microphone aimed at the glass from a nearby roof, for example, would retrieve nothing.

It was unlikely this building would be under surveillance by the Soviets or anyone else. But the level of security surrounding him dictated the cancellation of chance. The Soviets were always curious, and their methods often surprisingly successful.

From Dragonfly's early days in *Nibetsu,* the Soviets had been his special concern, his occupational specialty. In 1956, he had been sent to the Soviet Union for three years as a graduate student, controlled by his case officer in the Second Section.

Since then, his Soviet researches had increased in scope and intensity. No one in Japan understood the Soviet threat more than he. And his accomplishments had gained the respect of *Shachokai,* the Council.

Dragonfly had also done what no other Japanese intelligence officer had been able to do: *penetrate both the American CIA and the DIA simultaneously, and at an extremely high level.*

For years, he'd had direct access to one of the top people in the Defense Intelligence Agency, as well as to another who sat on several of the CIA's senior operating committees.

The arrangement was dangerous, certainly. The *quid pro quo* had been to furnish these same Americans with information on the progress of certain Japanese technologies. Involving such areas as the development of massive parallel processing (MPP) within the Fifth Generation computer project, these technologies would have great impact on military planning for the coming century.

The American intelligence people were no fools. Their government could not, or would not, produce the funding for such technologies. And so the intelligence community had set about procuring them in the way it knew best. As an additional benefit, it had helped the careers of the conspirators on both sides immensely.

Still, it worried him. It worried him that in a certain way, he had betrayed his country. But *Dai Sen Rikyu,* the Great Strategy, had to be protected at all costs. Compared to that objective, his own risk was irrelevant.

Only the Americans could furnish the intelligence needed to counter the Soviet threat, which could destroy everything Japan had worked so hard for since the war's end.

Dragonfly had great distrust of the Soviets, as did almost anyone in Japan who'd been an adult in the last days of the Second World War. Joining against Japan only days after the annihilation of Hiroshima, the Soviets had been anxious to pick Japan's bones clean. And, like jackals sneaking in after the lion's kill, they stole Japan's Kurile Islands beneath the noses of the Americans.

For this, and many other reasons, many in *Nibetsu* regarded the Soviets as Japan's most implacable enemy.

The current Soviet emphasis on restructuring and police-state democracy did nothing to allay Dragonfly's fears, any more than Khrushchev's de-Stalinization and military reductions had in the 1960s. At first, many Japanese were encouraged by Gorbachev's much-trumpeted *perestroika*. But then, as the Soviet military buildup continued to accelerate in the Far East—with no signs of "restructuring for peace"—the mood of Japanese observers darkened once more.

In early 1990, both Japanese and American intelligence uncovered ample evidence that, if anything, the Soviets had gained a quantum leap in efficiency. Especially in the Navy and the Rocket Forces.

Current events were now even more discouraging: in the Soviet Union itself, the militant *Otechestvo* movement was gathering momentum, rapidly adding new activities to their agenda.

Otechestvo was no longer purely political. It had entered a military phase. *A dangerous, inflammable stage,* he judged. *Too weak for stability, too strong for disengagement.*

The GRU's activities in Vienna also worried him. Japanese intelligence, watching the American CIA officer Mathieson since his arrival, had known of Mathieson's abduction by the GRU. When the American had plummeted to his death, a *Nibetsu* agent had been on surveillance outside Mathieson's building.

Subsequent investigation, passed on by Dragonfly's special sources in U.S. intelligence, revealed the killing had been on the orders of the GRU "Navigator" in Vienna, Colonel-general Leonid Dovgalevsky.

Since then, Vienna held special interest for Japanese intelligence. Too much was going on which was unexplained:

The GRU staff there had been increased by 300% in the past six months. Communications monitored between Vatutinki and Vienna multiplied far beyond normal needs. Agents had reported Army General Mescheryakov had flown to Vienna and personally executed Colonel-general Dovgalevsky. Mescheryakov was a dangerous man, a man capable of anything.

Mescheryakov was also a close friend of Zaikov, the powerful First Deputy Secretary of the Defense Council. The combination of Mescheryakov and Zaikov was threatening.

The man in the darkened office ran his fingers through his hair and stretched. In the last week, the GRU's activities in Vienna had reached a new peak.

It seemed to have been triggered by the American who had recently arrived to investigate Mathieson's death. The GRU had attempted his murder and failed. But they killed a female KGB officer with whom the American had met earlier that evening.

This, too, was curious: the KGB officer, a woman who had been executed by a single bullet to the base of the skull and fished out of the Danube Canal, had been reported by her superior as accidentally drowned. This same KGB superior was reported to have unusually strong links to the GRU.

Following the deployment of a *Nibetsu* team to complete a surveillance on the Vienna GRU *residentura* and the activities of the American, the team had been brutally murdered. Shot in public as they were contacting Tokyo Center by telephone.

What had they discovered? he wondered. *What had been so incredibly sensitive that the execution of two Japanese in public was necessary?*

Throughout the Soviet Union itself there was also now a full-fledged, increasingly public commitment between the GRU and *Otechestvo*. The GRU was particularly dangerous. Not because it had its fingers on many pulses, as any good intelligence organization should. And not just because of the nature of Army General Mescheryakov.

But because the GRU possessed the most dangerous military striking force in the Soviet Union, the shock troops known as the *Spetsnaz*.

Added to that, HUMINT reports had been received from Moscow, as well as from many military installations across the Soviet Union, that showed a significant correlation between the more active bases (in terms of current preparations) and the GRU.

Dragonfly switched on the small desk lamp. Things were accelerating quickly; too quickly for thoughtful analysis.

The collection sources were generating a flood of raw intelligence. One by one, he scanned the NSDs, the National Security Digests:

At Wakkanai, Miho, and Higashi Chitose, signals indicating massive redeployments were intercepted from the Soviets' Molniya 1 and Molniya 3 military communications satellites as well as from the newer, higher altitude Raduga 26 milcom satellites.

From Iwakuni Air Base, the Maritime Self-Defense Forces EP-2J signals intelligence aircraft were now flying around the clock, intercepting the communications between Sakhalin and the subs deployed in the Sea of Japan.

On the west coast of Hokkaido, the new *Chobetsu* facility was monitoring an increased volume of military communications from Siberia.

From Japan's underseas listening devices on the ocean bottom at the entrances to the Tsushima, Soya, and Tsugaru straits, more movements of Soviet submarines were detected.

His high-level reports from U.S. intelligence also confirmed an equally threatening level of activity among Soviet military facilities throughout the world.

Were the Soviets massing for a first-strike scenario against the United States, with possible side-strike intentions toward Dai Nippon as well? And if that were true, how long would it be before the U.S. decided to launch first?

Much of the activity seemed to be at odds with the Kremlin leadership. But didn't seem at all out of character with what was known of Zaikov and Mescheryakov. And now Mescheryakov was in Vienna, where unexplained activity of a different sort was taking place. *Could Vienna in some way be linked with the Soviets' aggressive maneuvers?*

He crushed out the acrid, rank-tasting cigarette. *A new team, more experienced, should be sent to discover what was going on in Vienna.*

Dragonfly switched off the lamp. The only light in the room was now reflected, pulsing, from the neon of the insurance company sign on the roof opposite.

In the building across the street, the small figures were still working under the fluorescent glare. He looked at his watch and lit another cigarette, the flame illuminating his face for an instant.

If the Soviets decided to deliver a hail of intermediate range ballistic missiles against Japan, he realized, there was no defense. And although the GRU/*Otechestvo* movement seemed directed solely against the United States, the people behind it were crazy enough to erase their financial debts to the Japanese—which were now considerable—at the same time.

In the Japanese Century, the Soviets and the Koreans would be the only ones to offer serious threats to Japan. The Koreans through their competitiveness and rapidly advancing technology base, and the Soviets with their constant and obviously increasing enmity toward the Japanese people.

But, he reflected darkly, *at this moment the probability is that none of us may reach the next century, let alone meet our enemies in it.*

Dragonfly stood in the darkness and took one last look across at the windows of the insurance company. The tiny figures, all white-shirted, were moving as if in a dance, their movements almost programmed as they carried out the perfectly normal duties of perfectly normal people, secure in their *wa,* their dedication to the group, their subjugation of the individual.

He envied them.

_____ 36

Jotò Island.

The drums couldn't be heard at first, so great was their size, so deep their tone. Instead, their force was first *felt*—a thing ancient, primeval—before, finally, the distant thunder would actually be heard.

In ancient Japan the *o-daiko,* gigantic drums struck by men wielding wooden clubs, set the boundaries of villages.

As far as the *o-daiko* could be heard, the land belonged to the village.

On the island of Jotò this night, the giant drums were resounding. Wearing only the briefest of loincloths, the drummers were already streaming with perspiration. Their bodies glistened as they bent themselves to their task. Their work was important: the boundaries they were changing were far beyond the village, beyond the island itself.

Officially, Jotò was listed as a Japanese Marine Self-Defense Forces artillery test site. In reality, it was a highly secured private retreat. Its ownership was lost in a maze of corporations, holding companies, and other devices for diverting unwelcome enquiry. Those who managed to prick the surface of this carapace were distinctly discouraged. Further questions, they were informed, would result in criminal charges.

Tonight the security surrounding Jotò was airtight. No air traffic or marine navigation was permitted near the island. MSDF patrol boats bobbed in the darkness offshore, radar screens sweeping, searching the moonless night.

The architecture on the island was remarkable, even considering the resources of those who owned Jotò. Three ancient Japanese farmhouses, complete with a dozen or so outbuildings, had been removed to Jotò and reassembled. Living quarters for the staff were in far more modern buildings recessed in the woods, clean horizontal lines gentled by plantings.

The gardens of Jotò were without parallel. A duplicate of the Jòju-In pond and island garden at Kiyomizu-Dera, in Kyoto, had been created in the island's interior. Other, less ambitious gardens were to be seen here and there, including a number of traditional tea gardens. One in the style of the tea-master Sen no Rikyù was especially revered.

It was a pity Jotò could not be spoken of in the outside world, for it held a microcosm of Japanese values, perfect and whole. It also held, from time to time, the center of power of Japan itself.

For the power of Japan is not military, although the Japanese defense budget is the third largest in the world. Nor is it purely financial, although the ten largest banks in the world are Japanese.

The power of Japan resides in the *gurupu,* the giant industrial/financial groups that dictate all national strategy, all economic activity. These evolved from the conglomerates known as the *zaibatsu,* the principal difference being the addition of independent financial capability. Behind the *gurupu* are the families which have been the power behind not only the throne, but behind all Japanese government, corporate, and military life.

What holds the great families together, even more than their long history of intermarriage, is a cohesive oneness, a homogeneity, binding individuals together as individual grains of rice are bound together in warmth and moisture.

This uniquely Japanese oneness is known as *nihonjinron.* An awareness and appreciation of being one people, almost one infinitely celled organism. Which is why the power of the families is able to penetrate every sphere of Japanese life.

Their power also extends to the emperor himself, for the great families had been part of the Japanese court for over a century. Since the Emperor Meiji, the personal fortunes of every emperor had been within their control. The families provided close counsel in the Meiji, Taisho Jidai, and Showa reigns. Between the wars, two indistinguishable political parties financed by the *zaibatsu* ran Japan. Mitsui bankrolled Seiyukai; Mitsubishi funded Minseito.

The Mitsuis, the Sumitomos, the Iwakasakis of Mitsubishi—these and a few other families directed the destinies of the Japanese people over the decades. In the 1930s the *zaibatsu* they controlled goaded the government into the military conquest of markets, rather than the mere penetration of them by commercial means. A strategy that ended in the ashes of Hiroshima and Nagasaki.

At the close of World War II, the personal fortune of the emperor showed significant holdings in Mitsubishi. The great families felt no sense of awkwardness about this. The well-being of the descendants of *Amaterasu,* the Sun Goddess, was as much their responsibility as the *gurupu.* It was simply another means of fulfilling the destiny of *Nihon minzoku,* the Japanese race.

Now, in the decade before the Japanese Century, the families had grown more sophisticated than ever. They had achieved by "strategic" trade what war had failed to achieve by bloodshed. And they would be ever more successful as the years rolled on.

In the past forty-eight hours a number of private aircraft had landed on the island's airstrip. None had filed flight plans for Jotò. But this discrepancy had been discreetly handled in the civil aviation authority's mainframe, avoiding the confusion of planes being mistakenly reported lost.

Each plane's passengers were greeted by *gurupu* executives in strict protocol according to rank and station. An outsider might guess this to be some sort of reunion for military officers of flag rank, each of whom had chosen to arrive in civilian clothes.

The arrivals were ushered into black limousines, which murmured along the roads of Jotò, bringing the visitors to their quarters. A small staff of servants awaited each, briefed on preferences in food, drink, and other amenities.

In all, eighteen such guests had now arrived on Jotò. And one of these was a man known only as Dragonfly.

Although not related to any of the great families, Dragonfly was considered one of their number. Few intelligence officers had any direct contact with the families, but Dragonfly met with them frequently. He was, in effect, the sum and substance of what was called *Renraku Bu,* the Liaison Bureau. He was the Council's only interface with Japan's many intelligence services.

Dragonfly was valued greatly for the quality of his analyses of intelligence, and for his remarkable sources. Since the early 1960s, he'd developed his own personal window into the Western intelligence communities. Many wondered at this, as Dragonfly's flow of intelligence seemed almost miraculous.

Since the early 1950s, much of Japan's intelligence community has been engaged in trade and industrial espionage. This includes, among others, several units within MITI (Ministry of International Trade and Industry) and JETRO (Japanese Export Trade Organization). As chief of *Renraku Bu,* Dragonfly was responsible for briefing the Council on the intelligence product of these organs, for which he was greatly respected. But on this weekend his briefing would be devoted to political and military matters: most particularly the current situation within Russia, and its possible linkage with the odd occurrences in the Soviet Union's Vienna *residentura.*

Although he felt economic and trade intelligence was of far greater long-run benefit to Japan, Dragonfly's personal specialty was Soviet military intelligence. And in this, his American contacts had been usually helpful.

For example, he had been able to give the prime minister as well as two important industrialists warning of the Cuban Missile Crisis before even the American Congress knew of the Russian missiles off America's shores.

In the years since, he produced an unbroken stream of intelligence breakthroughs, most of which dealt with current Soviet military capabilities. Only the Americans had more up-to-date information.

Indeed, it was said admiringly that Dragonfly could not produce more detailed and accurate intelligence if he were sitting in on every major meeting of both the CIA and the DIA.

And now, he was called on to evaluate the threat posed by the new Soviet military preparations. Few things could threaten the long-term success of *Dai Sen Ryaku,* the Great Strategy, than what was now on the horizon: the possibility of a thermonuclear exchange between the two great military powers.

This was why Dragonfly was on Jotò, to present an intelligence estimate of that danger.

Much depended on the Council's decisions. Not only the future of *Nihon minzoku,* but that of other populations measured in the millions, populations which fueled the success of the Great Strategy.

For these were the millions who had been slowly converted into markets for the *gurupu.* Millions who would grow ever more dependent, until the central economic power on earth, the power which could crush any threat to peace, would be *Dai Nippon.*

Only in this way could the threat of nuclear annihilation be countered. Not by blustering and bullying, nor threats of massive retaliation. Nor the games-playing of arms reduction talks and the deceit such games inevitably engendered.

Only by collecting and centering economic power could

they, the one nation that had known the reality of nuclear ruin, guarantee their survival for all time.

Most of the chamber was sheathed in the same gold leaf as the wall behind the Council. The design was at once both ancient and modern. The long horizontal lines of traditional Japanese architecture harmonized well with more modern elements. It was above all, Japanese, and the overriding impression was one of enormous, limitless power.

Six *kanji* characters were carved deeply into the gold-leafed wall. A literal translation might read:

> Amid the wind and the rain
> hidden deep in the mountains
> a reclining dragon waits.

These were not the words of an ancient poet. They were the words of former Prime Minister Yasuhiro Nakasone, and they were spoken at the graduation ceremony of the Japanese Defense Academy's Class of 1985.

As with most Japanese public utterances, they held both ceremonial pretense *(tatemae)* and deeper intent *(honne)*.

The *tatemae* was that Japan's Self-Defense Forces were prepared for any conflict, any emergency. But anyone who took this to be the only meaning would be thought a fool. For the *honne* was that Japan, under a hail of unfair calumnies from a weaker and unsuspecting West, is now all-powerful, and awaits the opportunity to assert its destiny.

Dragonfly bowed deeply on entering, and the servant accompanying him backed out of the chamber, still bowing, before silently sliding the big *shoji* shut.

He kept his head lowered until a voice bid him to come and be seated. A single *zabuton* was positioned five meters in front of the long low council table. The table itself was a lacquer creation of exquisite design, and behind it sat the eight members of the Council on their cushions.

The actions of politicians and generals were petty compared to the power of the Council. Any of its eight members could buy and sell a Prime Minister as easily as placing an order on the Tokyo Stock Exchange.

The man in the center was quite old, possibly in his late

nineties. A few wisps of white hair gave contrast to a deep tan, and his face seemed to reflect a great solace, an understanding that transcended momentary triumphs and tragedies. A face not merely of wisdom, but of an all-seeing certainty that could turn any event, any occurrence, to advantage.

The others ranged in age from one in his late thirties to men in their sixties. All seemed to radiate a curious, undefinable strength seldom seen in everyday life.

Dragonfly took his place and bowed once again deeply.

"We are greatly pleased to see you again, our brother," began the elder at the center. "We trust you are in good health, and that your excellent work is not proving too great a burden."

Dragonfly bowed his head and replied in a formal way, expressing his appreciation of the honor of being in their presence.

Another spoke, an exceedingly thin man in his mid-sixties. Dragonfly recognized him as head of the largest heavy-industry group. "Your position is critical as you must realize, Dragonfly. *Dai Sen Ryaku* has but one weakness, and that is the foolishness of others. For the actions of fools cannot be predicted, and in that way they are the most formidable of enemies."

The others at the table listened intently as the thin man continued. "The use of logic forever fails against fools. Yet it is only through logic that we can form a position from which to defend our interests. But logic, as you well know, depends on the uses of intelligence, on the determination of the several truths of a situation.

"You who are in daily contact with the events which concern us—can you offer your views on the current situation, as well as its probabilities?"

Dragonfly then began his briefing of the Council members, a concise and exact presentation which stopped short of recommending specific action, but which left no doubt as to the current degree of danger and the inevitable outcome if no action were to be taken.

At its conclusion, he bowed his head once, quickly, and waited for the questions.

There was a silence of great length as the councilors gathered their thoughts. Finally the youngest of the Council spoke. He was the first son *(chònan)* of a man who was the head of a sizeable electronics conglomerate.

"Your analysis is well formed," the young man said to Dragonfly. "Forgive me if I belabor a point for clarity: If we understand you correctly, do you mean we face the possibility of nuclear war between the Soviet Union and the Americans within the next few weeks?"

Dragonfly did not waver in his reply. "I estimate the probability at better than eight to one. I do not expect either side to stage a generated attack earlier than two weeks from today. But you must know either side is capable of anything."

Each man knew how mercurial American foreign policy had been in the past. Sudden unilateral action, with little or no attempt to involve allies in deliberation, had been the rule. This unsettling history, combined with the known volatility of the Soviets, was alarming to the Council.

Then, from the eldest: "You will have by this time given some thought to our alternatives. We have not intervened in any crisis up to this point, and it is obviously in our interests not to appear to do so at this moment in history. Yet we face a grave threat to our plans. What are your thoughts?"

Dragonfly bowed his head and paused a few moments before beginning. When he did, it was in a voice of uncommon resolution and strength. All seemed to lean forward to listen.

"Sir, I am only an intelligence officer, trained in one thing: the collection and analysis of information." He chose his words carefully, watching the grave faces on the other side of the table.

"Determining policy is something I am neither prepared nor inclined to do. However, as you have asked what I believe our alternatives to be, I shall tell you to the best of my limited ability. But the choice of those alternatives, even the *weighing* of those alternatives, I must respectfully decline."

He then outlined several courses of action.

All were well reasoned. All contained some expectation of success, or at least more success than would be gained by waiting for the completion of a nuclear exchange, and then attempting to reconstruct *Dai Sen Ryaku* in a radically altered world market.

But one of the alternatives was not, in the strictest sense, entirely logical. It was a uniquely Japanese approach to the problem. It called for a highly personal commitment and participation by Dragonfly himself, based only on a *feeling* about the situation and its causes.

When he had finished, the eldest congratulated him, and said they would call for him upon the conclusion of their deliberations.

As he left the chamber, bowing low, Dragonfly knew the next few hours would determine a world of peace, or a wasteland of ashes. It was then that the memory of another time sought its way into his consciousness, much as an ancient mountain stream forces its way through the rocks.

BOOK TWO

BOOK TWO

37

Little Boy.

06 August 1945.
Could it be? Could anyone possibly be as lucky as he?

Imperial Naval Ensign Kenji Nomura looked out from his window toward the hills. Beyond these hills lived his beloved Michiko, not eight miles distant.

Before dawn began to wash the green of the hills, even before the crows began to voice their territorial claims, he'd pedaled his bicycle home.

Kenji had been given only one day's leave between graduating from the midshipman academy at Etajima and reporting to duty at the Yokosuka Naval Base. His instructors had marked him for great things, and awarded him a greatly desired posting: the intelligence staff of Vice Admiral Tozuka. Even now, his newly sewn ensign's stripes betraying his inexperience, Kenji was filled with pride. He would serve the emperor as well as any son of *Dai Nippon*.

The enemy was on the brink of invading the home island. A few nights ago, the naval base at nearby Kure had endured a devastating bombardment. Some of the officers killed were from a class which had graduated only six months before his own. He'd known many of them: proud, patriotic young ensigns like himself. Powerless to respond to the B-29s as the aircraft dropped their deadly eggs in the night, illuminated by searchlights below.

But it would be different when the Americans attempted to invade the home island. For here, they would be surely defeated by the sheer courage and ferocity of the Japanese people. It was Japan's greatest opportunity, and would prove to be their greatest moment. Had not General Tojo said so himself?

So far, the Americans had spared Michiko's city. Probably because, it was rumored, the city was so beautiful the would-be conquerors wanted to reserve it for their own personal pleasure, untouched, unscathed. But there were other rumors. That President Truman had a relative living in Hiroshima and would never jeopardize the city. Or, more disconcertingly, that the Americans were reserving the city for a special and terrible fate.

Well, ran his dark unspoken thoughts, *they would soon see their folly. They would see it reflected in the blood of their sudden, astonishing defeat.*

His thoughts turned to more pleasant things, to Michiko and her family. He'd left them at ten o'clock last night, after spending the evening at their home. After dinner with her parents, Kenji and Michiko had walked together through the garden, lost in their thoughts and their shyness.

The scent of blossoms borne on the breeze seemed to surround them. From the house came the sounds of *samisen* and *koto* from her father's radio. From time to time, a shrilling, strident voice intruded. Now, with the American invasion of the home island so imminent, politicians were ever more on the radio, exhorting all citizens to fight to the final glorious victory.

Kenji and Michiko moved further into the garden, crossing the tiny bridge that led to her father's carefully constructed teahouse.

Michiko's father, although a senior and greatly feared colonel in the Western Military District, was a scholar and devotee of *cha no yu.*[1] He had built this teahouse in the style of Nagamasa Kuroda, a tea master of centuries past. And in the moonlight, in this soft and tranquil evening of August, one could almost imagine being transported to that time.

Michiko had met Kenji in one of the rare social events at the Etajima Naval Academy. Chaperoned by her mother, she had been one of thirty-five girls, all from good families, invited to the spring cotillion held for the soon-to-be-graduating midshipmen.

Kenji had been dazzled by her soft beauty, the delicacy of her every movement. He felt inadequate in her presence, and tongue-tied. After their first meeting he wrote to her, apolo-

[1]The Way of Tea.

gizing for his inability to express himself the night of the dance. He took great pains with the letter, and Michiko had kept it ever since, touched by the young midshipman's sensitivity.

Since then, they'd arranged to meet three times, always in the company of her parents. And this night was the first they were permitted to walk unchaperoned in the garden.

Lanterns shone pale yellow light on their path, reflected in the glistening *sanro*,[2] a traditional sprinkling of water on stones to catch the lantern light. Michiko's wooden clogs made soft clopping sounds, and the crickets contributed their chorus.

Together they walked toward the teahouse on the stepping stones set in a meandering *chidori* (plover) pattern, emulating the tracks the bird makes in the sand of the seashore.

They entered the miniature building through the low entrance way, leaving their footwear on the large stone outside. Near the stone the snow-lantern shone over a perpetually flowing seascape of raked gravel.

Inside, the soft light from the tripod candlestick cast shifting shadows. The chirricking of crickets made a music of evanescent delicacy.

Michiko stared down at her two pale hands, placed symmetrically on her knees. The rich thick masses of her hair, arranged in the traditional style, were even more beautiful as her head tilted forward. Her kimono was the palest color of cream and peach. Her obi, the darkened hue of ripening plums.

"You seem so quiet, so very sad tonight," he ventured.

"Oh no, no. Not at all!" returned Michiko, almost too swiftly. "You are—I don't know. I'm a bit overwhelmed, I think." And she lowered her eyes again. And again he was struck by how lovely was the halo of her hair.

"Please, I hope I haven't offended you," Kenji said, wondering what he had done, what he had said to upset her.

"I don't mean it in any accusing way," she said after a moment's pause. "I mean only—well, you make me think of so many things at once, I hardly know which of my thoughts

[2]Literally, the three dews.

to say to you. So I—I say nothing. I must seem such a fool!"

"Michiko, you're everything to me. And none of it fool-ish!" Kenji blurted out. "I can't begin to tell you how much I—"

As soon as the words escaped his lips, he regretted them. He now saw clearly how he had offended her. He was behaving like a peasant, gushing out his innermost thoughts, reckless and boorish, devoid of delicacy. No wonder Michiko Hirota, daughter of a respected colonel, probably thought him crude, unacceptable.

As he looked on her beauty, on the pale, almost luminous skin and the lotus-soft lips, he felt unworthy of such a creature as she. He knew now, for a certainty, he could never be deserving of touching where the curve of her neck entered her silken kimono, could never kiss the petal-softness of her lips, could never be the father of her children, could never—

"But you're so magnificent, Kenji! You're my—" Michiko said.

He held his breath.

Her eyes were suddenly downcast. "I've said too much," she whispered. "Far too much. Please forgive me."

The silence in the room seemed to fill it to bursting. He looked across the low table to where she sat, like himself, on her heels tucked in behind her. Her head was lowered in shame.

He fixed his gaze on the *tokonoma* behind her, which sheltered a Chinese scroll painting of mountains rising in conelike formations through the mist.

He focused his thoughts with a supreme effort, the joy rising within him threatening to conquer all rational thought.

"Michiko," he began in a voice that seemed to belong to someone else, a stranger, "I can't begin to offer you wealth or position, as some could. I'm only an ensign, a new one at that. But I'll serve the emperor as well as anyone, even of far higher rank. And it's my greatest wish that someday—"

He halted, amazed that he had been so bold. Her eyes were now raised to him, spellbinding in their ineffable brown softness. Kenji steeled himself and plunged on, now knowing what he must say or be forever ashamed of this night. One way or another, he must *know*.

"Michiko, once I arrive at Yokosuka and am given liberty, I should like very much—if you'll allow me—the great honor of returning here, and asking your father the colonel for—your hand in marriage."

At the finish of this, Kenji quickly cast his eyes downward and bowed his head. He could not wait for her reply while looking in her eyes. It would be too much to ask that she reply in the next few moments. Too much, by far, for a poor naval ensign to expect from a great colonel's daughter.

But the silence continued past endurance.

And still he knelt with his head bowed, listening for any sound, any signal of refusal, or—dare he even dream of it?—of acceptance.

Slowly, without breathing, he raised his head. His eyes marveled at the beauty of Michiko as his gaze moved upward, past the delicacy of her neck accented by the silk of her kimono, to the softly sculpted chin, upward farther to the full lips that promised an infinity of wonders, to the perfect nose, and finally to her eyes—where he saw a pearl-like tear forming and beginning to trickle down one dimpled cheek.

"Oh, my dear Kenji," she cried when she regained her voice. "How can I tell you how honored I feel, at this, the most beautiful moment of my life?"

Looking out across the hills, Ensign Kenji Nomura could still see her as she was at that moment, as indeed he had been reliving the memory again and again, all through the night. Once more, his heart leaped within him, as a golden carp leaps to the sunlight which gives it its color.

At that moment, from an American aircraft eight miles distant, Little Boy tumbled out, a black oblong object released from metal claws, drifting earthward, swinging lazily beneath its parachute in the morning sunlight of August 6, 1945.

And then, 1,850 feet over Hiroshima, at 8:16 A.M., Little Boy detonated.

Even eight miles away, Kenji saw the ozone blue-white flash, outlining all things, even those brightly lit by the sun, for the thinnest sliver of a millisecond, and his hearing was assaulted by a deep and ominous explosion. All the windows, although miles from the bomb, shattered inward.

A roiling cloud of black smoke sprouted upward three miles, where it blossomed into a ball of scarlet flame, a voluminous, poisonous flower riding high above a lethal black mushroom.

The mushroom seemed to be slowly feeding on itself, the edges ever folding inward, the column changing in menacing majesty.

The sighting-point of the drop, the Aioi Bridge—a T-shaped cement and steel structure linking three islands of the city—whipped up and down, thrashing like a beast in torment, the slabs of its roadbed separating, crashing down upon the structure, only to flail up and down again and again.

The city of Hiroshima was converted into ash, lifted up to the heavens, and then dropped.

Michiko, Michiko, was the only word that could materialize in Kenji Nomura's mind. *Michiko!*

Kenji, an infinity of thin glass slivers shimmering in his uniform, leaped to his bicycle. He began pedaling toward Hiroshima, the one word stabbing through his consciousness, again and again, as if it were the central fact of his existence.

In the city itself, within a half mile of the blast, girders of metal melted into lyrical shapes. Never before seen, though, were the courses of brick that melted, slowly oozing downward to cool and adhere at odd angles to sections of brick still intact below.

In the seven rivers that reached like searching fingers toward the sea, whirlwinds whipped the water into swaying spouts, moving from side to side, dervishes conjured from Hell.

As Kenji bent all his strength into pedaling, the sky above turned black, and a rain began to fall that had never been known. For the drops were large and black, and uncannily cold for what had been a sunny summer's day. They splashed on Kenji's hands gripping the handlebars. They pelted his uniform, forming tiny deposits of ash and sand, radioactive relics of the vaporized city.

A flood of refugees surged past in the opposite direction, back toward Rakuraku-en. And as they fled, a great wind swept down the road like an avenging creature, driving the black rain before it, forcing the people to cower in their terror.

His eyes compressed against the wind and rain, Kenji had to dismount from the bicycle and push it alongside him for a few miles. Then, as the road got wider entering the city, he was able to climb back on and ride toward the Hirotas' home where Michiko would be waiting for him, her arms outstretched.

Then he realized: *Michiko would not be home, nor would she be in school.*

Like almost all girls of her age, she would have been clearing fire paths, in case of bombings, to save as much of the city's center as possible. How pointless it had all been, he saw now. As pointless as the little bamboo rafts the people of Hiroshima kept near their futons as they slept, in case the American bombers destroyed the dams high in the hills, and the waters came surging down into the city.

Suddenly, the black rain and terrifying wind stopped. The roaring and the darkness parted to reveal, once again, the brightness of a fine summer's day. As if, in this eternity of a morning, all humanity had not been served notice of its nearing extinction. As if over a hundred thousand of Hiroshima's own citizens were not now carrying the seeds of their own decay within them, in a parody of pregnancy in which death, not birth, was the biological goal.

He prayed as he rode that she was still alive. She had to be alive. She *must* be alive.

Terror and dread filled him with a flooding weakness, invading every cell of his body like a scurrying cancer. The silence of the city was punctuated by the crackling of flames, and by soft *whooooom* as rice paper and wood dwellings would suddenly explode into flames and disintegrate within minutes. The soft cries of the still living were like the cries of animals, tortured, subjected to a punishment so severe as to remove any sense of connection to cause.

Later, when men would point to Pearl Harbor as the cause of Hiroshima, heads would nod. When historians would cite the greed of the great *gurupu* as the motivation for conquest, men would agree.

And then, from the serenity of decades' distance, they would feel themselves superior to the long-ago politicians and generals who could not see as they, the armchair experts, could see now. And they would put the chance of it ever happening again as remote, very remote indeed.

But such considerations might be happening on the moon, so remote were they from the concerns of Hiroshima on this morning of lethal sunshine, and deadly rain, and killing winds. This was a thing of infinite inhuman force, unleashed much as a *tsunami* or an earthquake might be set loose by forces that simply *are,* that have causes equally remote and irrelevant to the immediacy of survival.

As Kenji penetrated farther into the wasteland that had been Hiroshima, he wondered if the lucky ones were the dead, the carbonized caricatures of flesh in the rubble.

Even the streets themselves were gone. The blocks where buildings had been were devoid of structures, except for a few large concrete and metal shells which, although still standing, were burning brightly. The once-proud trees were transformed into a few charred posts, skeletal fingers pointing accusingly at a cerulean sky.

He began to see blackened people, hair falling out in tufts, sheets of skin flapping from their backs like wet newspaper. He saw a trio of soldiers with the insignia of the Western Second Corps, hanging on to each other, crying for a little water, a little water—*mizu, mizu!* And then he saw that their eyes were only sockets. They must have been staring upward at the moment of detonation.

He was now passing through the district called Shiroshima, about a mile from the explosion, and he saw the derailed electric trains, filled with passengers, all dead, motionless, as if waiting for the cars to start up once more. The West Parade Ground, where he had marched as a midshipman less than two months ago, was littered with corpses. He saw half a dozen dead cavalry horses, their entrails exposed, pink casings still bubbling, blackened by the heat.

And now he looked into every face of every girl, every woman passing, looking for some indication that a face, a shape, might be Michiko's, yet hoping none of them would be. It occurred to him that he was now an utter outsider, an intact human being, a freak in the midst of such devastation. He unbuttoned the sweat-soaked uniform jacket and threw it away.

As he neared the center, passing the inferno of the Hall of Industry near the Aioi Bridge, he saw blackened outlines pressed into the cement in the shape of human beings: cinders of extinguished humanity.

And finally he came to the Hirotas' garden, where only the night before he'd walked with his Michiko, and sat with her in the teahouse near the snow-lantern, and regarded the beauty of the three-stone arrangement, the gravel raked around it in a pattern of lapping waves.

The snow-lantern that had stood outside the teahouse was toppled on its side, the ancient surface blackened on the top and one side. The three-stone arrangement was still intact, the gravel only slightly disarrayed. But the *nandin* tree, which only last night had borne its tiny red berries so bountifully on every branch, was this morning a single blackened, shriveled stick.

Of the teahouse itself, there was no trace. Nor was there even the slightest vestige of the Hirotas' home.

At first, he thought the stones and the snow-lantern had merely been lifted to some other place, and that some distance away he would discover the colonel's house, intact as always.

But soon he realized the worst. The place where only this morning it had stood was stripped, denuded as a desert. The blast had hammered almost directly down on it, consuming all in its omnivorous power, sucking up and lifting the dust and ashes to fall far away on green fields, and on the ever-shifting sea.

He stopped the bicycle and stood beside it, great sobs racking his body. The shame of being among the living corroded his conscience; guilt embittered his soul.

And in that embattled moment, in that shattered place, Kenji Nomura entered into a covenant with the man, the self that was yet to be.

38

Hibakusha.

09 August 1945.

She thought it was a cat. Then she realized: *it's my own voice, it's me.* She couldn't see individual things, yet her eyes sensed light, and the rest of her sensed pain.

She fought back her tears, stifling her whimpers. She listened intently. The only sounds now were the crackling of embers, reluctantly yielding the last of their energy.

From time to time, as if drifting in and out of a mist, she heard voices. Muttering, masculine utterances, low and impersonal. Would they find her? *Did anyone know she was alive?* Tentatively she moved her fingers, then one arm. And then the other.

Her face felt swollen, oddly immobile, as if covered with river mud which had then dried. *Perhaps that was why she couldn't see—mud had somehow gotten on her face. Yes. She must get to water. She must wash it off.*

With great care, she took a deep breath, gathered her strength, and tried to sit upright. And then fell back, exhausted by this so trivial an effort. *What was happening? Why was she—*

Blissfully, surrounded by a serene and flooding warmth, she slipped into a dreamless sleep.

An unknown time passed. A hand touched her forearm and she heard a voice: *She will be fine. Really, just fine. There will be work to do, you see, as with all of them, but she will live. She will not be as she was. Not ever. But she's really—most fortunate.*

Then the endearing, heartbreakingly familiar voice: *Michiko, Michiko.* Her father, his gruff, military growl breaking in unaccustomed emotion. *Michiko, my beautiful Michiko, what have they done?*

She'd been one of hundreds of girls cleaning up the firebreak areas in the city. At the moment of the detonation, she heard no sound, and only momentarily registered the enormous electric blue flash, the shimmering of the sky, before falling unconscious.

Those farther out had both seen the flash and heard the detonation. They had called the bomb *pikadon:* literally, flash-bang. But those like Michiko, nearer the center, saw only the flash, and heard nothing.

Strangely, the thin white cloth of her long-sleeved blouse and trousers had protected much of her skin. But her survival was due to a three-story wooden building which had stood—for a few tottering moments—between her and the fireball.

Her friend Eiko had been twelve feet farther out in the street, and her shadow had been imprinted on the stone wall directly opposite. The shadow remained, captured as a photograph at one moment for all time, at the same angle to the light that had reached 300,000 degrees centigrade.

But of Eiko, there was no sign, not even a charred lump of flesh.

Had Michiko seen her friend's black shadow and realized its meaning, she would have lost her mind. As it was, she had no awareness of where she was, nor of what had happened, for more than two weeks.

15 August 1945.

The NHK announcer spoke in rounded tones of solemnity: "A broadcast of the highest importance is about to be made. All listeners will please rise."

The young officers in the room rose in a clatter of uncertainty. The announcer continued, "His Majesty the Emperor will now read His Imperial Rescript to the people of Japan. We respectfully transmit His voice."

Through the speaker of the shattered portable radio, the national anthem, Kimigayo, shrilled. And then, after a few moments' pause, the recording of the reedy, high-pitched voice began, a voice never before heard by the people. It was, after all, the voice of a god on earth.

"To Our good and loyal subjects," the voice began in syllables of archaic court Japanese. On this early afternoon of August 15, 1945, it spoke of many things. But most of all, it spoke of the impossibility of continuing to endure the unendurable.

The words, painfully etched in air, seemed unearthly, unreal. The seeming impossibility of the words' being spoken made one concentrate on their sound, delaying comprehension.

And then, even before the listeners realized their great and awful meaning, the words ended, and the music began once again, and the truth was laid bare and unassailable:

The war had ended. Dai Nippon had lost.

Kenji Nomura, like so many other young officers in the BOQ, had been thinking long and hard of *seppuku*. His life had been his family, then his service to the emperor and his honor as an officer in the Imperial Navy, and, finally, to his Michiko. To Michiko, who had been wiped from existence by the *pikadon*.

When he had finally collapsed in the ruins after two days of searching, he'd been picked up and sent to the Naval Base at Yokosuka. Michiko's father had sent a message to him by special army courier.

I regret to inform you that our daughter Michiko and my wife have passed into eternity in the recent bombing. I know you share my grief and I offer you my heartfelt sympathy both as a fellow officer and as one who knows of your respect and your affections toward our family. Okitsugu S. Hirota, Colonel, Second General Army, Western Military Command, Hiroshima.

So all that he had loved was gone. His own family, the honor of Japan, his beloved Michiko. But why could he not commit *seppuku*, why could he not seek the final, undeniable honor of ending a life without reason, an existence without purpose?

That was the final agony. He knew he was not a coward. He knew, knew as deeply as he knew anything, that he could plunge the short sword in by its sharkskin haft, and rip it across his abdomen, looking down at the thin-lipped red smile that would cheat the world of its victory.

But something deeper within him burned brightly. Revenge? Hatred? No, something different—something of a nature he could not name, could not define in any conventional terms.

He knew he would not, *could not* be beaten. He would survive and strengthen himself until the horror would be cleansed, and would be replaced with a greater destiny than the fields of rubble and skulls, the legacy and litter of militarism.

He realized he was alone in the room now, his brother officers having shambled out to consider the emperor's message in whatever privacy they could find.

Kenji Nomura bowed his head briefly, and then stood, tempered in the crucible of defeat, a weapon of destiny, strengthened beyond measure.

27 September 1945.

They had taken the bandages from her eyes, and she was permitted to sit up for small amounts of time.

She could see things held close to her eyes. Her arms, she saw clearly, were starting to form scar tissue over the open wounds. The right hand, exposed directly to the blinding light of the *pikadon,* had been baked into a cramped claw, the skin pink, with mottled purple patches, stretched shiny as a new plum's skin.

Every day, her father brushed the wounds with oil, as the doctors had advised. Later he would massage the scars, once the wounds stopped suppurating. The doctors were very hopeful, they said. She was lucky to be alive. If she had not been so close to the sheltering presence of that building, she would not be here today.

Her mother had met a merciful end, her father said. She'd been at home, near the epicenter of the blast. She couldn't have felt anything, he said. She would be in heaven smiling down upon them. They must both, therefore, be strong and conduct themselves with honor, especially in their present situation.

He also spoke of the pink-faced Americans who were unexpectedly gentle, even respectful. To her questions about the *pikadon,* he was evasive. But bit by bit she eked out the information that many thousands of people had been killed, and even more thousands badly hurt, some even more badly than herself.

Several times she asked her father of news about Kenji. He had been evasive, and would not answer her. She sensed something ominous in his manner, as if concealing something terrible that had happened to Kenji.

Finally, one day, her father told her: Kenji had been missing since the *pikadon*. It was likely that he had been killed. If so, it had been for the honor of Japan, and for the glory of the emperor. It would be better now if she would concentrate only on getting well, on adapting to a new life.

The glass of the windows in her new room was the pebbled, translucent sort one sees in doctor's offices. But she could raise the sash and look out. Their new home was a small farm building fifty miles southwest of Hiroshima, which her father had repaired and made liveable, although without electricity.

When her father would visit her, usually two or three times a day, he seemed oddly shambling, humbled, older. Like most demobilized men of the Imperial Army, he still wore elements of his uniform, the shirt and trousers, and sometimes the tunic, but never the cap. All were neatly pressed, devoid of insignia, but showing wear. A few months before, had one of his junior officers appeared before him in such array, the subaltern would have been severely reprimanded.

There were many changes in her father's manner. Greeting her, he would smile nervously, the manner of a man concealing something. For some reason, this worried Michiko more than anything.

She was also made nervous by the fact that no mirrors were in her room, and when she would ask for one to comb her hair and make herself presentable, they would say "There are no more mirrors, they have all been broken." But it was not true. She knew it was not true.

They told her never to touch her face, as there was great danger of infection at this early stage. But she wanted to see. *What must she look like?* she wondered, a cold terror gripping her stomach. *She could not be—normal, not with her arm and hand so damaged. What must her face look like?*

She nearly fainted at the thought. But she must know. Somehow she must *see*.

The white glass doorknob rotated quietly, almost silently, and she composed herself to look as unconcerned as possible. She leaned back against the pillows.

Her father brought in the tray with her bowl of *miso shiru,* and her medicine, bought illegally from U.S. Army medical corpsmen in the town's occupation barracks.

He sat opposite her as she first took the spoonful of her medicine and then, with difficulty, finished her soup.

He smiled, and spoke of the colder weather now coming in from the East, of the American medical people who were now beginning at last to help the *hibakusha,* people like herself, damaged by the explosions in Hiroshima and Nagasaki.

Hibakusha. She was now one of a people apart, a group singled out, a collection of freaks among normal people.

Her fingers curled into fists of tension. She did not want her father to sense her fear, her cold unreasoning panic. Things seemed hard enough for him. She must be strong. They must both survive. Not as animals, but with honor, as human beings.

Hibakusha. Hibakusha. Unreasonably, the word continued to haunt her.

The sound of her father's voice, asking her a question, interrupted her introspection.

"What, Father? Forgive me; I was distracted."

He smiled, tired and wan, his face creased into more lines than ever. "My daughter, you must not be worried. We will survive this, and there will be a tomorrow in which we will look back on this as a bad dream; nothing more. For now, you must think of nothing but getting well."

"I'm not worried, Father," she said, forcing her voice to sound calm and sweet. "I know you are with me, and we are fortunate to have each other. And Mother and Kenji are in heaven, looking down on us."

Her father, seated on the edge of the small stool next to her bed, looked down at the floor in silence. She wondered for a moment if he were praying, but when he looked up she saw his face contorted in anguish. He struggled to regain control.

He got to his feet, hiding his face in his hands. "Forgive me, child. Forgive me!" And he rushed from the room, stumbling as he closed the door.

She looked at the closed door and thought of how hard it must be for her poor father, burdened with an invalid, deprived of his wife, robbed of the honor and pride that had been his as a ranking officer of the Imperial Army. She must think of ways to make his life easier, to lighten the unbearable sadness.

And then she saw he had forgotten to remove her medicine bottle and spoon.

She sighed, leaning back on her pillows, her eyes tracing, for the thousandth time, the dimensions of the room. Everything had been whitewashed. The room was clean and cheerful. She knew every centimeter by heart; every aspect, every particle of the room.

Her eyes returned again to the bottle and the spoon. The shiny metal of the spoon was reflecting a ray of morning light from the open top of the window, throwing it onto the white wall in a starlike pattern. *How beautiful,* she thought. *Like an origami star. When I am well, I shall make many beautiful things for my father in our home. I shall always have flowers, beautiful flowers for us, arranged in many beautiful ways, in* ikebana. *And I shall wear lotus blossoms in my hair—* And at this thought her lips began to quiver in bitter regret.

Aiee, she thought. *My hair—will it ever again be the way it was?* For her long and luxuriant hair, in the first five days after the *pikadon,* had fallen out in hanks on her pillow. Only now was a light fuzz beginning to make its appearance, like the down of a newly hatched chick.

She closed her eyes, clenching her fists again. The left hand, the one fused into a parody of a hand, pulsed with pain. She willed herself to relax, opening her eyes, staring at the ceiling as she had so many times in the past month. Once again, the starlike pattern on the wall drew her attention.

And then she knew how she could at last see herself.

With her right hand, the one still smooth, that still had the opalescent character all her skin once had, she reached carefully toward the spoon. She twisted her body to make the last bit of distance, and her fingers closed on the spoon. She drew it to her, and, exhausted by the effort, sank back into the pillows, closing her eyes.

With her eyes still closed, she moved the spoon in front of her. Her thoughts were in turmoil, her fear gripping every molecule in a viselike grip. *But I must know, I must know,* ran the litany in her head.

And then she opened her eyes, and stared into the convex back of the spoon. What she saw there, she could not believe. It could not be so. It could not be *her*.

Frantically, she twisted over in the bed and reached out for the medicine bottle. With her fingernails, she clawed the paper glued around it, the pharmacy's label that hid the reflective glass surface.

Her nails scraped and tore at the firmly-fastened paper. But small shreds detached themselves, and then rips appeared, and then whole sections came away, even as her fingertips stained the paper red with blood.

She scrabbled at the few remaining bits of paper still obscuring the surface, hastily wiping off the blood with a corner of the sheet wrapped around her purpled hand.

And stared deeply into the glass as she brought it closer to her ruined face.

And then the screaming began.

_____ **39**

Yokosuka.

12 September 1945.
The tall windows were shut, muffling the rumbling of trucks below. Three pieces of furniture set the stage. A small scarred table, a chair for the interrogator, and a second chair opposite, for the prisoner.

Arthur Devies Hornbill, United States Counter Intelligence Corps (CIC), entered the room. His eyes, set in a deceptively cherubic face, took in the interrogation room at a glance. Like all the rooms on the second floor, this one had a tall ceiling, a parade of multipaned windows resembling French doors, a waxed parquet oak floor.

What had this room been? Hornbill wondered. *An admiral's office? Conference room? A reception room for social occasions? Classroom?* He walked to the window nearest the little desk, and stared out at the bay.

Part of the Imperial Naval Base administration complex, the building was one of many such monuments the Japanese raised in the 1920s, reflecting no architectural style other than that of bureaucracies everywhere. Hornbill looked at his watch. Two minutes until the next prisoner.

On a near–assembly line basis, he'd interrogated Japanese naval officers of all ranks in the last few days. The uniform Hornbill wore was that of a U.S. Marine Corps officer. His rank was selected according to the rank of the prisoner. Hornbill had been a major twice in the past two days, a captain seven times, a lieutenant ten.

On the whole Hornbill preferred being a major, as it gave him better seating in the officers' mess. Its only drawback was the need to return salutes more frequently, distracting to a man as introspective as Hornbill.

The next prisoner would be a young ensign attached to Vice Admiral Tozuka's intelligence staff. Hornbill, accordingly, wore the bright brass bars of a second lieutenant.

Hornbill's Marine Corps uniform was crisply pressed; the prisoner's clothes would be crumpled, soiled. Hornbill was freshly shaved and clean; the prisoner would have perhaps a three days' growth of beard. He would also, by now, be smelling like the bottom of a birdcage.

He sat down carefully, pulling up the knees of his trousers to preserve their crease. He stared across at the door and drummed his fingers on the small table. Finally, after a few moments, the corridor outside rang with the heels of two men. One tall and heavy, Hornbill noted, the other small, light. Their rapid approach told him both were young.

A sharp rap on the door, and an overstuffed Shore Patrol lieutenant, khaki-encased stomach bulging over a wide white web pistol belt, propelled the prisoner into the room.

The young Japanese officer came to attention instantly, and the MP left. Hornbill gestured to the empty chair. The man made an almost imperceptible bowing movement, walked to the chair, and sat down. Hornbill noticed the uniform was pressed and bore no trace of dirt. Unusual.

Hornbill kept no file on the table. He'd memorized each file in all the interrogations. Blessed with a near-photographic memory, he found never having to refer to paperwork gave him an edge. This man, Nomura, was aged twenty, a recent naval academy graduate placed on Admiral Tozuka's intelligence staff a month ago. Too new to be associated with Colonel Kubota, or any of the other people of the Nakano Spy School.[1] Unlikely to yield anything of substance.

Still, Hornbill took in the prisoner's appearance more analytically. He saw an uncharacteristically tall young Japanese with unblinking eyes. A quiet, almost frightening strength seemed to reside there. Hornbill had seen this only twice before:

Recently, when he'd been one of several young officers introduced to General Douglas MacArthur in the ward room of the *Missouri,* after the surrender ceremony. And earlier, when he'd first met John Moses Sharpless, the man known to the intelligence community as The Fisherman.

There was no fear in these eyes. Neither was there the sour aura of humiliation that marked most of the officers he'd interrogated here. Again, unusual.

To a Japanese officer, being a prisoner was far worse than it would have been to an American. In the Japanese prison camps, American, English, and Australian prisoners of every rank were accorded less respect than a dog. Fighting to the death was the only honorable way for an officer to behave. It was not only *bushido,*[2] it was manliness itself.

Hornbill let the silence work for him, as it had done so often before. Two or three minutes of it generally unsettled most men, especially those who knew their fate depended on the whim of the interrogator.

But this one, this Nomura, seemed to relish the silence. Even to draw sustenance from it. Another anomaly. This one would be difficult, even though the information here would be of a low grade, and likely worthless.

Hornbill spoke in Japanese. "You are from Rakuraku-en?"

No reply. Still, something flickered in the eyes.

"I have only a few questions to ask you," continued Hornbill. "They will be of a routine nature, and they will in no

[1] Military spy school which selected officers and noncoms for espionage, commando-style warfare, and special survival training.
[2] Samurai code of behavior.

way compromise you, nor cause you dishonor. You are considered a civilian now, and you will be treated as well as we can manage in these difficult times."

The eyes—deep, brown, expressionless—regarded Hornbill across the small table.

Hornbill decided to provoke the beginning of a dialogue, if only on a cursory level. Three more officers, all more senior, were waiting their turns, and this one was allocated only a half hour.

"Please forgive my poor use of your language. You must understand that I, like yourself, am not accustomed to this situation, and my preparation was necessarily limited. You *can* understand me, can't you?" Accompanied by an anxious, solicitous expression, as if concerned that the man might, in fact, be deaf.

A pause. Then a nod in return. Brief, reluctant. But the beginning of communication.

"Good. Now, were you planning a career in the Imperial Navy, or were you going to serve only until the end of the conflict?"

An interminable silence. Hornbill waiting. The other's eyes finally wavering, for the thinnest flicker of an instant. Then:

"It was to have been my career."

This time, a nod from Hornbill. "I've seen your records. You showed remarkable promise at the Academy. No wonder Admiral Tozuka's people chose you for his staff."

The eyes continued their unblinking stare. Hornbill began to wonder if the young man were in shock. But no, the skin appeared dry, the eyes quite focused.

"What are your plans, now that the war is over?"

A smile of infinite bitterness. Another flicker of the eyes. "I have no plans."

"No plans at all?" Hornbill looked at Nomura quizzically. "Will you not return home to Rakuraku-en, to your aunt, to help in the rebuilding?"

No reply.

Too much time was going by. Hornbill decided to press his case, to get through the short agenda. "And what were your specific duties with Admiral Tozuka's staff?"

Another pause. "You will have seen from the records that I was a junior officer on his planning staff."

"Yes, an intelligence officer. We know that. But what were your *specific* duties?"

"I was assigned to help the senior staff officers complete their analysis of the fleet's readiness for defending the home island against the ultimate invasion, given the destruction of the air force."

"And was the analysis completed?"

"It was."

"And where is it now?"

The eyes behind the mask veiled. Then: "Destroyed. It was destroyed on completion."

"But why?"

"The analysis concluded defense would be hopeless. Impossible, except for a few days' delaying action. If we had submitted it to Admiral Tozuka, he would have been bound by duty to forward it to War Minister Anami. The admiral would then have forfeited his head for defeatism."

Hornbill smiled at the candor. "Then you've learned one of the most difficult lessons of intelligence work, that we're often engaged in producing unpopular information. We are the Greek messengers of our own time."

Nomura, in response, did not smile. He merely nodded at this obvious truth.

Hornbill watched him intently. "One final question, then you may return to your quarters. Has anyone—from any military, paramilitary, guerrilla, underground, or unlawful intelligence organization—attempted to recruit you for postwar activities?"

This produced an almost startled look from the young ensign, which Hornbill interpreted to mean the thought had never occurred to Nomura. The look disappeared as rapidly as it arrived. "No sir," came the clipped reply. "Am I to understand I am now dismissed?"

"You're dismissed. But you're ordered to stay within the administration compound area unless and until otherwise directed by the Occupation authorities."

"Very well, sir." Nomura stood, bowed quickly, and left the room. On the other side of the door, Hornbill could hear the big SP officer speaking to the young ensign, and finally their footsteps receding down the long corridor.

Hornbill sat very still, thinking rapidly. Something about Nomura bothered him. Something that seemed like a barely contained violence, or a suppressed passion.

Then he stood and once again looked out the window facing the water. A remarkable time in which to be alive, he reflected.

Out there, the morning of September 2, less than a month after Little Boy's detonation over Hiroshima, 258 Allied warships had been riding at anchor, lazing in the gentle swells of Tokyo Bay. One of these, the battleship *Missouri,* was anchored just four and a half miles from where Commodore Perry's flagship had been in 1853.

Allen Dulles had agreed to young Hornbill's request to be assigned TDY to the occupation of Japan. Hornbill's CIC duties in Europe had become more or less clerical, and there was concern throughout CIC that extremist military groups would be forming in Japan, recruiting young officers, especially those previously tapped for intelligence duties.

Besides, Hornbill wanted to see this portion of history in person. His command of Japanese, while minimal, was at least functional for the purposes of the interrogations. And so the staff of SCAP[3] agreed to take on the young Marine intelligence officer for at least the next six months, as their resources were strained by the sheer numbers of officer-prisoners awaiting exit interrogations.

He'd been invited aboard the *Missouri* by Admiral Badger, and had sat far above the ceremonies, his legs dangling over the edge of the roof of the bridge.

There, below on the holystoned, bleached teak of the main deck, Hornbill saw a tableau he'd never forget. At 0856, sideboys piped the Japanese delegation aboard, civilians in formal morning dress, the military in badly tailored uniforms.

He recognized one of the latter—General Yoshijiro Umezu, chief of the Army's General Staff—from his briefing a few days earlier in Yokosuka.

---

[3]Supreme Commander Allied Powers for the occupation of Japan, General of the Army Douglas MacArthur.

Umezu had been a bitter opponent to surrender, agreeing only to participate in the ceremonies after the emperor himself had requested his involvement. He noticed Umezu's scowling examination of the tiny Japanese flags painted on the *Missouri's* bridge: proudly displayed symbols of destroyed Japanese ships and aircraft.

The table with the documents was just to the left of the *Missouri's* number-two turret. Beneath the turret stood a number of generals and admirals who'd been prominent in the war against Japan.

And then MacArthur walked onto the deck with Admiral Chester Nimitz and "Bull" Halsey, positioning himself before the microphones and scanning the faces before him. All the officers including MacArthur were dressed informally, in khakis without neckties.

The young Hornbill was fascinated by MacArthur. The general wore no medals. If he had, as one young sailor near Hornbill put it, "They'd a gone clear over his shoulder and down both his front and back."

Looking at MacArthur now, on the decks of the battle-weary *Missouri,* Hornbill realized he was looking at one of the pivotal figures of history.

Hornbill saw with a shock the tall, desiccated form of Lieutenant General Jonathan Wainwright at MacArthur's side: frail and wraithlike, as if the dead had returned to serve judgment. Wainwright had surrendered the Philippines to the Japanese in 1942. In their prison camps he'd endured rigors unknown to captured general officers, even under the Nazis.

There, too, was Lieutenant General Sir Arthur Percival, who surrendered Singapore in that same year of shame. Both Percival and Wainwright had been flown directly from their prison camps in Manchuria to witness the surrender of their tormentors. Hornbill watched Umezu's expression carefully, but the Japanese general seemed not to recognize the two.

He became aware, then, of MacArthur's words ringing across the deck, echoing in metallic resonance through the public address system.

". . . my earnest hope, indeed the hope of all mankind, that from this solemn occasion a better world shall emerge out of

*the blood and carnage of the past, a world founded upon faith
and understanding, a world dedicated to the dignity of man and
the fulfillment of his most cherished wish for freedom, toler-
ance, and justice."*

Hornbill felt a thickening in his throat, and a welling of
moistness in his eyes, and knew he would never forget this
scene among men who for nearly four years had faced each
other in turbulence and slaughter. And who, in this moment
of final confrontation, were now facing the reality—strange
and unreal after so much death and so much anger—of
peace.

A low, ominous rumble was heard as the final documents
were signed and the ceremony seemed about to end.

Then suddenly, the rumble translated itself into a shattering roar as 450 aircraft, launched from the Allied carriers
waiting outside the bay, swept in low over the flotilla of
peace.

All this Hornbill replayed in his mind as he looked out
over the water, noticing for the first time the low, brooding
clouds carrying rain across the bay. The pelting of the rain
swept toward the land, visible only by the changing surface
of the water on which it fell.

He unfastened the snaps securing the lieutenant's bars on
his epaulet straps, and felt in his tunic pocket for the set of
major's oak leaves.

The next prisoner would be a lieutenant commander.

───────────────────────────────────── 40

Michiko's Hope.

15 March 1955.
Michiko huddled in the dank and darkened theater, lost in
the gaudy images floating across the screen. The theater was
cold. Few people chose to go at this hour, in this weather.
But she liked going, even if she'd seen the film before, even
if the film itself were not worth seeing. For it was a way of

being among people without watching them wince at the ruin that was her face.

Michiko would go to the theater early and sit in the first row, so no one could turn around to notice her.

It had been almost ten years since Hiroshima. She didn't want to return, although others were there like her, other *hibakusha*. She didn't want to see the wreckage of the dream she still treasured, still carried in her heart. Didn't want to distort the memory of the small green mountains ringing the city, the wide boulevards with their magnificent overarching trees, the beautiful homes, the temples, all her forever laughing, forever young friends.

No, she wanted to carry those images as they were, as they had been before. For the only things permanent are memories. And Michiko's memories were, at this time in her life, all she possessed that was beautiful.

The noise of a rolling bottle on the cement floor startled her. She wondered if it had been set on its course by one of the rats that infested older theaters. She tried once again to concentrate on the screen, to lose herself in the reverie of its impossible romance. On the screen above her, Gary Cooper rose thirty feet tall to embrace a girl with long black hair. They spoke in English. The screen scrolled *kanji* subtitles in rhythm to their speech.

Michiko's glorious hair had returned, slowly, within a year after the bombing. She washed and brushed it every night to glossy perfection. Whenever she left her small apartment she combed it to cover part of her face, as if carelessly arranged.

She imagined herself the girl on the screen, intact and lovely once more, yielding herself to the tall stranger. It was not difficult. More and more of her life had become dependent on her imagination, on the nurturing of her dreams.

Gary Cooper was telling the woman of his love, of his determination to make a better life for them both. Michiko believed him, believed that life on his ranch would indeed be peaceful and beautiful, and that they would someday have children and—

The lights came on in the theater, and the audience began shuffling out. Quickly Michiko looked down at the small book she always carried for this purpose. Her lovely hair fell in two black raven's wings on either side of her face, and no one could see it without being directly in front.

In a few moments, the sounds of the departing audience quietened, and the theater was still. The cleaning staff knew her, had seen her face, had learned to smile at her in a friendly fashion, for which Michiko was grateful. She adjusted the white 'flu mask on her face before she left the theater. To others, it would seem as if she were just a normal girl who had a cold. Unless they noticed that in the wind, part of the mask pressed itself back against flesh that was not there.

Outside the streets were streaked with rain which had fallen during the movie. The neon signs were winking, beckoning to passersby to play pachinko, to eat delicious food, to have exotic cocktails, to enjoy the curvaceous bar girls.

But this was a world Michiko would never know, the world of lights and people. Still, she had her own world, and as it was largely of her own making, there were comforts and pleasures which were unique. She read a very great deal. She mused on life as it was when she was a girl, when her parents would take her on the boat across to Miajima, and how the great red *tori* was reflected, dancing in the ripples of the Inland Sea.

It was winter now. A gust of wind knifed through her thin cotton-batting coat, and she shivered involuntarily. Only two blocks until home, but she must first stop by Itoh-san's to pick up her mail and a few groceries which he'd been so kind to pick up for her.

Itoh-san's shop front was dark, but she knew he would be just behind the curtain inside, sewing until the small hours of the morning. She rapped lightly on the wood frame of his door. A shift in the darkness, the flicker of a light, and soon the round smiling face of Itoh-san revealed itself at the crack between the door and its scarred frame.

"Come in, come in, child. You must be chilled as a sparrow." He gestured grandly, as if his small shop were instead the entry way to a great *daimyo*'s castle. "Come have a good hot cup of *o-cha* and talk with old Itoh. I grow lonely here at night, with only other people's clothing to talk with."

Michiko loved this old man. His face was creased into a thousand lines, all of them seeming to smile at once. She thought his name singularly appropriate to his work, for in Japanese *itoh* means thread. Michiko often wondered if his name had pre-ordained his trade. She knew little of him before meeting him four years ago, bringing her father's old uniform to be patched, dyed, and altered into a suit coat and trousers.

She could not know, and would not know, that Itoh had once been a proud captain of cavalry in the Second General Army, and was once headquartered in Hiroshima Castle itself. And that he had been an acquaintance of her father's, secretly enjoined to watch over Michiko in the event of her father's death.

Itoh, like Michiko Hirota, had never returned to Hiroshima, preferring to live as a tailor in this small village twenty miles distant. He never mentioned his other life, and she never mentioned hers—except to speak of her father, who still lived in the farmhouse they'd moved to after the war.

Together the two shared a bond not only of loneliness, but of a delight in the imagination, the ineffable beauty of things dreamed but never seen. Michiko earned extra money by sewing the simpler things which Itoh let her take home. The rest of her income came from taking in laundry from several families in her neighborhood, in addition to a small amount of money her father sent, despite her protestations.

Behind the curtain leading from the shop front, a single bare electric bulb illumined the room in which Itoh lived. An iron teakettle, its surface dotted in the hailstone pattern, nestled over a charcoal brazier which was the room's only source of heat.

Michiko sat opposite the old man, not fearing to hide her face, for she felt that somehow, for whatever reason, Itoh-san did not find her features repellent. Which was indeed true. For, like the wise who see the soul while seeming to look at the surface, Itoh thought her quite beautiful.

"You have a letter, just arrived in the afternoon post," Itoh said softly. Then he added: "Not from your father."

Michiko was puzzled. *No one knew of her here, other than her father. Could he be ill?* She reached for the thin blue envelope with anxious fingers.

It was from a doctor in Fukushima, a place unfamiliar to

her. Had her father traveled and fallen sick in a strange place? Holding the letter tightly, she read the careful brush strokes with dread. But—*no!*

The letter was about her, about Michiko. And about a medical program someone, or some religious group, had recently created to help *hibakusha* like herself.

She continued reading, relieved her father had not become ill. He was old now, even older than Itoh-san, and she worried about him living alone in the drafty farmhouse, tending his meager crops when weather would permit. He was frail, bent with rheumatism, and susceptible to lung infections.

Now she bit her lip in concentration. Although there had been relief organizations for *hibakusha,* they had been handouts, scraps of succor doled out as if the victims were blind beggars, and not for her.

But this seemed different. This was about the new plastic surgery some doctors had developed in America, perfecting their techniques so keloid scars could be dealt with intelligently. The letter was careful not to promise too much, only that certain young women of Hiroshima would be selected for a special program, and that they would be flown to the United States for special surgery. She, Michiko, had been proposed by the physician who had treated her years before. Would she be interested in being interviewed?

She crushed the letter in both her hands and stared up into the bare bulb's flickering light, tears streaming down her ruined cheeks.

*Would there be a chance? Would she—*could *she—ever be normal, ever be—pretty?* She bit her lip, not daring to hope, not venturing to yearn for the impossible.

One hand flew to her face, the fingers lightly touching the scar tissue.

Itoh leaned forward, touching her shoulder, concern crumpling his features into even more lines than before. *"Dear child! What is the matter—is it your father?"*

"No, no, Itoh-san!" She struggled to find the words in the torment of her thoughts. "It's something—something about helping people such as I—"

Itoh carefully took the crumpled ball of blue paper from between her fingers. Carefully, very slowly, he pressed it out on the low table which held their tea things, and, placing his spectacles on his wrinkled face, read the letter.

Soundlessly his lips formed the words as he read, his eyebrows lifting as he saw the words of tentatively extended hope, of caring.

"But—but this is wonderful!" he finally stammered, placing the letter down on the table again. "This is a chance to see if something can be done, an opportunity to see the finest surgeons in all the world—"

Michiko hid her face behind her hands, tears coursing between her fingers. Her shoulders shook as she nodded her understanding, but not her acceptance. Her emotions, tangled as the roots of cypresses, rose above her logic, and she wished—paradoxically—to have nothing to do with it.

Itoh waited patiently, smiling his wonderful smile, leaning forward as if ready to offer comfort, should Michiko ask it. Finally, she wiped the tears from her face, and accomplished what, to her, was a pleasant expression.

"What is there to be grieved about, child?" asked Itoh finally. "This seems a blessing."

"It's just that—that—I don't want to be—*I don't know!*"

Itoh looked down at his hands and thought a moment. "Is it that you feel you might be treated as some sort of—exhibit for the *gaijin* physicians?"

Once again she covered her face and nodded. "Like in a circus, like some sort of—of experimental object, a laboratory animal!"

"Child, child, you must bury your pride. These are people who want to help."

"But are the Americans doing it out of guilt? Will they want to parade us around, before and after—like trophies?" Her eyes searched his, wide with confusion.

"Michiko," he began, taking both her hands in his. "It's not just that, is it?" And he smiled his wide, wise, myriad-wrinkled smile. "It's something else, something deeper."

Michiko stared at Itoh, aware that he had seen into her very soul. "Yes, Itoh-san. It is—that my world is so very different now. I have only been a woman this way," and here she gestured at her face. "I do not know how to even *think* of myself any other way. I can live this way, I have my dreams, I have my—"

Itoh closed his eyes and spoke gently, almost inaudibly. "You have your own world, do you not?"

Her only reply was a silent nodding, her head cast downward, ashamed.

"Oh, my dear Michiko, you have retreated so far—*too* far into your world of dreams, your imagination. If there is hope, you must—you must at least *try!* Even though, in this, you may have to be even braver than you have been before."

She collapsed into his arms, sobbing, tears falling onto the small lacquer table. Itoh felt his heart swell within him. He could not trust himself to speak.

_____ 41

Return to Hiroshima.

12 April 1955.
The colonel and Michiko stepped off the train carefully, trying to avoid the rush of workers exploding from the train, each face in the crowd intent on a mission in which every sliver of time was precious.

Emerging from the station, Colonel Hirota saw the streetcars directly in front. *The same type that had been here that day.*

He remembered walking past this place just twenty minutes after the bombing. Remembered seeing the corpses still waiting inside the blistered streetcars, conveyances and corpses never to move until they were physically taken apart days later. Four of Hiroshima's seven streetcar lines still came to this station; likely the cars were made from parts of the same blistered streetcars, rebuilt and repainted, now carrying the living in a considerably changed world.

As father and daughter walked through the streets of Hiroshima, they looked for anything familiar, anything to reassure them that this was, in fact, the city in which they had once lived and laughed and enjoyed their existence.

There was, of course, the Palace of Industry, its once-beautiful dome now a tangled skeleton of melted girders renamed the A-Bomb Dome. And the seven fingers of the Ota were still there, although concrete walls now confined the river to neat geometric channels.

Little else seemed familiar. They had not seen Hiroshima in ten years and the change was staggering. New buildings were everywhere, and more were being built.

They walked toward the Hiroshima Citizens' Hospital, the colonel carrying a small canvas bag in case Michiko was asked to travel immediately to the United States. Michiko had not bought any Western clothes, as they still had to face being accepted by both the Japanese and the American doctors.

They had eaten their small *bento* lunch on the train. Still, the street vendors' carts smelled tempting, tempura sizzling on skillets in the fresh spring air. They hurried on, anxious to get to the hospital.

It was said that an American publisher, Norman Cousins, had started the idea of selecting a number of Hiroshima maidens for plastic surgery in the United States. Much discussion had taken place in Japan over this.

Was it insulting to Japan's own physicians and surgeons? Was it a publicity device for Cousins's magazine? Was it a way for the Americans to relieve their guilt? Or was it simply an openhanded, generous effort to help the maidens? Hiroshima's leading daily newspaper, *Chugoku Shimbun,* expressed its concern that the maidens not be made objects of international curiosity, like creatures in a zoo.

No matter. The thing that counted was the possibility of help. In the case of Michiko, as with many other girls, the Japanese doctors had given up after the first experimental skin grafts. The thick keloid scars were extensive, and she was too radically damaged for their skills to help.

But here, possibly, was a way. It was known that the American medical profession was the best in the world. And plastic surgery had advanced considerably in the past five or six years; everyone said so.

So when Michiko and her father arrived in the big reception hall of the Hiroshima Citizen's Hospital, their anticipation was great.

They were to wait nearly three hours before Michiko was

called, her name echoing with hollow resonance in the tall
and now nearly empty room. Michiko was examined minutely in a nearby room, sitting naked on a table, her face
uncovered, the tragedy of her exposure all too evident to the
physicians.

After a half hour of examination and questions, she was
asked to put on her clothing and mask again, and she was
met by her father and a young intern, stethoscope worn like
a medal. The intern escorted them into a large room in which
a number of physicians and one nurse sat on one side of a
table. The colonel was reminded of a court-martial. Two of
the doctors were *gaijin,* likely Americans, as was the lone
nurse.

One of the Japanese doctors, a round-faced man in his
thirties, wearing a white lab coat, began speaking.

"You realize, of course, we have very many applicants
and only a few openings in this program, *ne?* We therefore
have to apply certain standards, standards which are to
ensure that the young women chosen are suitable, both
physically and emotionally, for what lies ahead."

He looked down at his small hands, plump as partridges,
clasped together in front of him. Then he leaned forward,
looking into Michiko's eyes intently. "All the world will be
watching you. This is not a private affair.

"That is why," he continued in a softer tone, "We must
tell you everything about what may occur in the process of
the surgery."

Itoh-san stitched the trouser bottoms carefully, making sure
none of the seams could be tugged loose. His thoughts wan-
dered, as they often did these past few days, to Michiko and
to the trip to the United States:

Would they be able to help her, truly help her? he wondered.
*It had been nearly ten years. Had the damage become irrevers-
ible?* He looked at the cheap wool of the trousers and stroked
it with his fingers. His nails had the long and defined stria-
tions of the old. They were kept immaculately clean, and cut
perfectly.

Looking after himself was a source of pride with Itoh.
After all, if he were unable to look after himself, who would?
He smiled. *Michiko would,* he thought to himself. *But, with*

any luck, Michiko will soon be on her way to the United States. And to a new way of life, leaving her life as a hibakusha behind her, like the ugly shucked carapace a pupa leaves behind as it transcends itself, and becomes a butterfly.

It was getting cold in the little room. He drew his old cardigan sweater around him more closely, and picked up the next garment to repair.

The colonel took the news calmly, although his heart seemed as if it were tearing itself apart in anguish.

It was not fair! Especially when she needed it so!

The young doctor had asked to see him separately, a kindly expression on the round and understanding face. "Mr. Hirota," he began gently, "we have examined your daughter very carefully and we cannot, in good conscience, ask her to be subjected to what would be, in her case, of extremely limited value."

"What do you mean?" asked Hirota, alarmed.

"I mean—" and here the doctor looked down at his highly polished black shoes, as if he could not look her father in the face. "I mean her case is too—severe to yield successfully to surgery, or at least the state of development in which reconstructive surgery is today."

Colonel Hirota stared at the doctor, not seeing, thinking only of what Michiko would say when her dream is denied, knowing that she would be consigned, forever, to a life in the shadows.

"This is not to say that someday, perhaps, there will be hope. But at this point, we would only be subjecting her to unnecessary torment, with little chance of improvement. Her best course is to continue to try to adjust, and perhaps someday advances in surgery will—" He spread his hands to indicate an unknown possibility, an uncertain hope.

Colonel Hirota stood silently, looking beyond the young doctor at the wall. *The world was once so simple,* he thought. *So shining and pure, with only the emperor and honor and one's family to serve and protect and, yes, love. I do not know this new world; I have been educated and trained never to think as a victim, yet—yet it suddenly seems we are in the grip of something we have set loose which we cannot put back ever again.* His mind played back images of that day in Hiroshima, minutes after the explosion. The corpses in the street-cars. The horses lying among their riders in the parade ground. The houses collapsed and burning.

"Sir?" The young doctor was looking at the colonel with a worried expression. "Mr. Hirota, are you all right?"

"Yes, I'm—fine. Only somewhat disappointed, as you may imagine."

"Would you prefer that I tell your daughter? Sometimes parents find it too difficult, whereas I as a physician—"

Hirota dismissed the thought with a wave of his hand. "No, no. I must tell her. It will be easier for her if I tell her."

"As you wish, sir," said the young doctor, bowing briefly before leaving.

Colonel Hirota thought, oddly enough, of his wife—dead these ten years. *Thank goodness this was never part of her life, that she was taken before having knowledge of any of this!* He walked to the window and looked out. From here, he could see the empty blocks where homes had not yet been rebuilt. On some of them boys were playing the now-popular game of baseball, running and tumbling into each other, laughing as if they had no cares. And, of course, they didn't.

He turned to go and tell his Michiko.

42

The Gamble.

17 November 1959.
The line of black umbrellas bobbed uncertainly as the small procession picked its way through the gravestones, heading back toward the dirt road.

The smell of the woods was sweet and dusky. Rain underscored the scent as drops fell on leaves or made miniature brown craters in the dust.

Michiko was heavily veiled, her silent tears unseen, unshared. She leaned forward as Itoh supported her with one thin arm, the other marshaling a waxed paper umbrella above. His eyes brimmed with sorrow, for he felt her grief as if it were his own. In losing her father, this child, this woman who had suffered so much, had lost the final fragile thread of family, a part of the continuum of self.

Tonight, thought Itoh, *I shall speak to her of her father and tell of the agreement he and I had. It will perhaps calm her, and give her a sense of security. Perhaps. But I am old, and she knows I cannot live more than ten, perhaps twelve years, even if nothing untoward happens. Still it may help. It may get her over this time.*

Later in the train going back to their village, Itoh commented on the passing scenery. Rice paddies, open fields, and small pockets of woods were giving way to new gray factories. *A new Japan will emerge,* he said to Michiko, *and the Japanese people will never be poor again.*

Her only response had been a soft nodding agreement. And this, he knew, was only out of her respect for him, for he knew she wished to retreat ever more within herself, to lose herself among her memories. He feared for her. Building a world solely of dreams and memories, he knew, would lead to insanity. He'd seen it in the war, seen it too many times.

She must not retreat completely into that world, he resolved. He must not allow it. But what would connect her to reality in a positive way, what would give her a reason to live beyond her play-world of memories—memories already made more beautiful than they had been in reality.

The world outside the train rushed past in dizzying flashes, and it hurt his eyes trying to distinguish individual trees, buildings, rice paddies, trains stopped on tracks alongside them. It was, he thought, just as the world itself was slipping past, too fast for him to comprehend. Japan was changing, absorbing new ideas, and creating its own.

But Itoh himself was now only a spectator, and the progress, although slow to the participants, was too accelerated for him to comprehend.

Itoh looked over at the now-sleeping Michiko and sighed. He removed his wire-rimmed spectacles and polished the lenses. Then he placed them carefully in their tin case, closed his eyes, and drifted off into his own imaginings.

• • •

In the offices of Mitsuko Electric, Kenji Nomura put the finishing touches to his report. He had not slept for forty-six hours and the thought of going home to lay himself down on the softness of a *futon* seemed a luxury beyond imagining.

His life since the end of the war had been filled with work, and although his monthly take-home pay as a *salaryman* was only 14,500 yen,[1] the management had treated him well, and promoted him regularly. It was said he was being groomed for greater things, and indeed it was unusual among his fellows that he was invited to dinner with the families of the higher-ups. He often felt ashamed of his poor clothing, but always managed to present a neat appearance, even if the edges of his cuffs were frayed, even if the points of his collars too often confounded the efforts of the heavy starching to keep them neat and in place.

He was, he knew, included sometimes because these families were constantly recruiting eligible bachelors of his age for the attentions of their daughters. The right marriage, he knew, would assure his future.

But although he was stirred now and again by the beauty of some, the idea of pursuing marriage, of choosing one of these coy, carefully prepared packages seemed somehow distasteful. Almost as if it were without honor.

It was eleven o'clock before he finally slid open the door of his one-room apartment, and saw the envelope placed on the low table.

Few letters came to him, for he lived a monklike life, working hard at Mitsuko, spending his few outside hours studying the Soviet Union, training in the *dojo* of his friend Sen Mori, and, of course, in the meetings of which he could never speak. For he had been recruited for what was then known simply as the Second Section, or *Nibetsu*. The job with Mitsuko was a necessary cover until the organization could have a more official status. It was also his main source of income.

The envelope was of a poor tan paper and bore the postmark of a small village to the west of Hiroshima. He hadn't

---

[1] Or about $40 U.S., at the then prevailing exchange rate of 360 yen to the dollar.

heard or read of the village since he was a child, in Rakuraku-en, living with his aunt.

He opened it with care, and read the *kanji*, painstakingly lettered in the old-fashioned way. And as he read, his heart became liquid, then fire, then a living, beating, breathing heart once more.

He could not believe it.

He wanted to shout, but knew not what to shout. Joy welled up within him like a liquid under extreme pressure, and he felt a great and unbounded strength surging through his being.

He pressed his knuckles to his mouth for fear of making a sound the others in the rooming house would hear. Tears ran down his bronzed cheeks, the first tears in five long years.

Alive! She is alive, after all!

He reread the letter a dozen or more times, concentrating on every word. It broke his heart that she had suffered the agony of being a *hibakusha,* and cursed himself that he could not have been with her, to help her, to console and share with her.

But he would make up for those years. He would devote his life to making hers once again beautiful and joyful. Itoh's letter told him of her disfigurement, and in plain and honest terms. The old man obviously wanted him to decide before she would even know of Kenji's existence, lest she suffer yet another disappointment, or see him register disgust at seeing her face the first time. But Kenji smiled at this. His love for Michiko would withstand all tests.

That night, for the first time since he was a boy, Kenji prayed and gave thanks. In the morning he would post a letter to Itoh and arrange to meet him.

As he fell asleep in the softness and warmth of his *futon,* Kenji Nomura felt blessed, and complete.

Had he made a tragic mistake? Had he gambled the few remaining shreds of this girl's self-respect on the imagined response of what may be only a callow boy?

Itoh was racked with worry and self-reproach. The sticks had been thrown, and all would be known by next week. Perhaps the boy would not respond at all. Perhaps he would be repulsed, disgusted at the idea of Michiko's disfigurement, and simply ignore the matter.

But then something somewhere within him told Itoh: *No, this one will be honorable.*

He had, of course, kept careful track of the young man ever since the colonel had begun to decline in his final illness, ever since the colonel had told him of the young man's existence and of his own deception in keeping it from Michiko.

The colonel had, Itoh realized, only been solicitous of Michiko's happiness. Although he knew how very much the girl loved Nomura, he was too fearful of the consequences of their meeting, and of the young man's facing the horror of her once-lovely countenance.

Itoh's decision in writing the young man had come only after days of deliberation, and of weighing all alternatives. She had nothing left to live for other than her memories, and she was retreating ever more swiftly into that shadow world which, in the end, would be indistinguishable from reality.

And so Itoh had taken his terrible gamble.

_____ **43**

Choices.

01 December 1960.
The rain, it seemed, would not let up. It had been pouring steadily since the pre-dawn hours and looked as if it would rain the whole day.

The short projection of tiles sheltering Itoh's doorway amplified the spatter of the raindrops. The sound was comforting. Itoh opened his door and peered out. No one was in the street. Puddles were forming: the raindrops were coming thicker and faster now.

A dog, coat sodden, tail lowered, ran zigzag from the butcher's doorway to the front of the public bathhouse. Itoh closed the door and shivered. The little stove made the front room warm, but he put on a worn and heavily mended cardigan. *Michiko,* he remembered every time he put on the sweater, *laughed that there was more thread in the repairs than in the fabric of the sweater itself.*

Michiko. When he'd told her Kenji was still alive, he was afraid she'd stopped breathing. Her hand had flown to her face and she'd been suddenly still, so still that Itoh had been frightened.

"How—how do you *know?*" she finally managed to whisper.

He'd told her of his agreement with her father, how the colonel had bound him with an oath of silence. But now Itoh felt she needed someone, someone who could care for her more than he, Itoh, could in his clumsy way.

She was silent for a time. "Where does he live?" she asked. "What does he do?"

This seemed to Itoh a good sign. At least she wasn't closing off all talk, as he'd feared. He said Kenji worked for a large electronics company in Tokyo, had remained unmarried, and that he now knew she, too, was alive.

At this, she once again became silent. Then, finally: "Does he know about—about the way I am?"

Itoh nodded mutely.

She looked down at her hands, unconsciously covering the one purpled hand with the other. "It would have been better if he'd continued to think of me as no longer alive."

Itoh snapped, *"No!* Never *say that!"* He grasped her tiny hands in his and looked into her face earnestly. "You are a wonderful woman, Michiko, far more wonderful than you know. Be grateful you are alive, and that *he* is alive, and that—regardless of what you've been through—the two of you may yet find some small happiness!"

One glistening tear formed. Then another. And another. And then the torrent began as the tears of hope and fear, of joy and tragedy, traced their way down her scarred cheek. Michiko collapsed into the old man's arms and he patted her softly on the back as one would a baby, listening to her sobs, feeling the release of so much emotion he was afraid she'd be unable to stop.

Michiko, my Michiko, he yearned to cry, *you who have*

*been more to me than if you'd been my own child, let this come
to be, and let you find what you so greatly need at last!*

Gently he rocked her in his spindly arms, listening to the
dwindling whimper of her torment, his heart aching as if
pierced. He looked around the tiny room with its meager
furnishings, and thought of the equally sparse room where
she lived and did her sewing, in the small house down the
street.

At length he spoke to her. "Kenji wants to see you. He will
come here soon, the day after tomorrow. If you wish it."

She drew back from Itoh and looked at him with her
tear-streaked face. And the wail of agony that issued from
her was like the cry of a dying thing, so great was its torment.
"Hush, child!" he said gently.

"But he cannot see me, not *this* me! No, it is better that he
forget about me, that he remember me the way—the way I
once was, one night in Hiroshima!" And she sought the
comfort of Itoh's careworn cardigan once more, as he
stroked the lovely raven hair.

"At many times life is more difficult than death," Itoh said
softly, feeling her sobs against his old chest. "The choices of
life are many. The choices of death but one. You are a lone
venturer in your journey, child, and only you can choose
which of many paths to take. But the risk of denial is *always*
worth accepting, especially when what hangs in the balance
is the chance to begin a life together—where before there was
none."

He held her away from him and looked into her eyes. "Let
him come to you, Michiko. Give to him what he will give to
you. Accept the risk. It is life itself."

She felt as if there was no more life within her, nothing
with which to tell this old man how very much she owed him.

But somehow, from deep within her, Michiko Hirota,
hibakusha, produced a smile which was to the old tailor an
expression of infinite beauty.

Kenji Nomura sat across from the tailor in the tiny restaurant. *The old man sits tall,* he observed silently. *He must have
been an officer.*

Itoh grasped the porcelain bottle and poured more *sake*
into the two cups. "And so you now work for an electronics

company?" he probed, wishing to know more of this young man.

"A very minor position, Itoh-sama, but I hope I am worthy. I do accounts and a little administration. I know nothing of electronics, other than it is a growing industry and that Japan is investing heavily in its future."

"That is true, that is true. We see more electronic gadgets in the shops every day," Itoh agreed, downing his cup in a single draft, his eyes narrowing. He realized there was something behind the young man's self-dismissing comments. *What was this young man concealing?* It bothered him.

"You knew the Hirotas before, in the old days?" asked Kenji.

The old tailor nodded, smiling. "Yes, they had a beautiful home. The colonel's family was greatly respected; his great grandfather had been a *samurai*. Then, unusual for one of his class, he became a successful merchant, trading with the Portuguese."

Kenji raised his eyebrows. He'd never known how the Hirotas became wealthy, and it would have been unthinkable to ask. "The colonel was a formidable man," he said.

"Formidable?" Itoh laughed. "No, I'd rather call him *terrifying*. He cultivated it, you know, with that deep voice, his commanding presence. He became a full colonel at the age of thirty, it was said, because his superiors were afraid *not* to promote him."

Kenji Nomura laughed, hiding his teeth politely with his hand. "I remember being in such awe of him the first time, I could not speak. I'm sure he thought me an idiot."

"No, no, I happen to know he thought a great deal of you. But he had you thoroughly investigated before you were invited to their home, you know."

"Really?" Kenji was surprised. Not that it was odd. It was what he would have done himself.

Itoh nodded. "Yes, and he was impressed that you'd been chosen for Admiral Tozuka's intelligence staff." He watched Kenji carefully for a reaction. There was none.

Kenji sipped at his *sake* reflectively, thinking of how to bring the conversation around to what was really on both their minds. "Do you—" he began falteringly, "do you think Michiko is *ready* to see me?"

Itoh's eyes were clear and direct. It was as if the old tailor were looking into Kenji's soul as he spoke. "I think, instead, it is more a question of whether or not she thinks *you* are ready to see *her*."

The young man's head bowed. He studied his empty cup. Itoh leaned forward to refill it, one hand lifting the sleeve of his *yukata* to keep it clear. A silence fell. They were the only two customers in this small room, which was why Itoh had chosen it. The proprietress stayed discreetly out of earshot, waiting for Itoh to summon her.

Kenji nodded. He took a careful sip of the *sake,* and felt its warmth gentle his nerves. "I have done nothing but think of her since I received your letter, Itoh-sama. Had I not received your letter, I doubt that I would ever have married. I have carried my thoughts of her in my heart ever since I met her, and even after I thought she—thought she'd been killed."

He looked intently across the low table to the tailor. *"Nothing is more important to me, Itoh-sama. She is my life, and what she has gone through only endears her to me all the more. I shall ask her to share her life with me, to become my wife."*

Itoh's face became even more serious as he leaned across the table and placed his wrinkled hand on the young man's shoulder. "But you must ask yourself the cruelest of questions, and you must answer yourself honestly: *Can you look at the face of Michiko every day for the rest of your life, and see what is, and what always will be, a living, breathing horror? Can you?"*

Kenji Nomura sat with his hands palms up, looking with clear brown eyes into those of the old man. "I have thought long and hard, and questioned myself, looking for any reservations within any crevice of my soul. *I know, as do you, that to offer her hope, and then to withdraw it because I could not bear to look at her, nor to touch her—would be worse than criminal.*

"I am at peace with myself in the knowledge that the Michiko *within* is the Michiko I shall see, regardless of what the war, the world outside, has done to her face. I tell you this, knowing how much she means to you as well. I want to see her. I want to *be* with her."

And he closed his eyes, waiting for what the old man would say.

Itoh passed a hand across his wrinkled brow, as if willing the difficulty of this away. "Nomura-san," he began in a low and tremulous voice, "I hope you can sustain the burden you have chosen. Few men would be able to. But then, few men would be worthy of the love of a woman such as Michiko. I hope the two of you will be happy. I wish it more than anything I have ever hoped for in my life."

And the two men, the tailor and the spy, embraced each other and wept.

_____ **44**

Washington, D.C.

13 August 1962.
The creation of Robert Strange McNamara's new Defense Intelligence Agency hadn't been without its birth pangs.

Hornbill, dragooned from CIA by McNamara, was considered a keystone in the new DIA architecture. His World War II record in military intelligence was distinguished. And in his postwar role on MacArthur's staff, he'd made friendships with many who later became Pentagon powers.

Although Hornbill saw no genuine need for the DIA (considering all intelligence work to have military implications and the spin-off detrimental to a truly central intelligence agency), McNamara couldn't be talked out of it.

Hornbill reasoned it would be better to be part of the new agency and help with the liaison with CIA, than let some ex-Ford Motor Company crony play Spook-for-a-Day. His closest friend, John Moses Sharpless, CIA's counterintelligence chief, agreed.

So Arthur Devies Hornbill turned over his CIA desk to yet another new, well-scrubbed face, and began the job of building a new Washington entity with all the headaches that came with it.

Recruiting seasoned people from CIA was not unthink-able. But Hornbill preferred to avoid it, dipping into the three military intelligence agencies as much as possible, with a few forays into State's Bureau of Information and Re-search.

He was also able to bring in a few hands who'd either retired from the Agency or quit to teach or write or sit on the board of a defense contractor at an inflated salary. Despite all their grumblings, the old war-horses missed the trade. Besides, Hornbill was able to promise hefty government pensions after only a few years' service.

In this way, Hornbill put together a competent intelli-gence agency in record time, without too much raiding of Allen Dulles's zealously defended structure.

Six months into the new job, Hornbill was able at last to have a night off. In a town where women outnumbered men by nine to one, Hornbill was considered a catch, and was relentlessly invited to D.C. cocktail parties.

He usually deferred the invitations with consummate skill. But on this night, feeling restless, he decided to go.

The party was held at a mansion near Dumbarton Oaks, a house which seemed to be only slightly larger than Mon-tana.

By the time he arrived, the party was already going at a great pace. People were spilling out of every room, with waiters circulating like bees in a disturbed hive.

The guests seemed to be exceptionally international, even for a Foggy Bottom soirée. Hornbill noticed two or three Agency faces. A fair number of Orientals were also in at-tendance, smiles the order of the evening.

He was extracting himself from the attentions of his amo-rous hostess when he caught a glimpse of a face that seemed oddly familiar.

The face disappeared behind a group of animated French diplomats. Hornbill moved toward them only to discover the man had vanished.

The face tugged at his memory, yet he couldn't quite place it. *A Japanese, yes, but from where?* Hornbill had put in seven months with SCAP, and had met thousands of Japa-nese who would be this man's age by now. Still, the image didn't connect.

This worried Hornbill. Generally, when he remembered a face, it was for a reason. Nothing went into Hornbill's memory without a purpose, and he had the uncanny feeling this one was special. But *who?*

Despite discreetly covering all the rooms in the place, Hornbill never saw the man again. He wondered if the man had recognized himself, Hornbill, and disappeared because of it. Such occurrences were not uncommon in his business.

It was only while riding back to his Anacostia apartment in the taxi that he realized: *Yokosuka. He'd interviewed the man in Yokosuka! Who was he? Young naval officer, ensign, intelligence. Assigned to whatshisname's staff—Tozuka—just before V-J Day. Right.*

He paid the driver distractedly, tipping the man far too much, and climbed the stairs to his rooms. Still the memory dogged him, tugging at his imagination. *What was the man doing here? Was he here with a diplomatic cover?*

It was axiomatic in any nation, even among the Japanese, that once you've been tapped for intelligence work, you're in it for life. Unless, of course, you screw up unconscionably.

So the odds were this man was Japanese intelligence. *Interesting,* thought Hornbill. *In the morning, we'll put some salt on his tail and see what we discover.*

In the morning, Hornbill had a friend from State request his hostess' invitation list "just to see who's sociable in this town, and who's not." If somebody from DIA, especially Arthur Hornbill, requested it, the news would be all over D.C. by nightfall.

Of the five Japanese appearing on the list, three were senior embassy staff and two were spouses. None corresponded to Hornbill's description of the Japanese naval officer he'd interviewed seventeen years ago. Undaunted, Hornbill called a friend at ONI and requested the files on detainees in Yokosuka interviewed by CIC in September of 1945.

It took three days of rummaging before a rumpled, disgruntled, and cursing Chief Yeoman extracted it from a tottering stack of unfiled reports.

The face on the black-and-white photo was, indeed, the

face Hornbill had seen at the party. Younger, and unlined. But the same face.

Nomura, Kenji. Ensign, Hornbill read aloud. *Assigned to Intelligence Staff, ADM Tozuka, IJN. BOQ Yokosuka. 20 years old. Considerably above average intelligence according to IN files. Projects confidence not often seen in so junior an officer. Reports no previous contact of insurgent elements. Released 05 October 1945, stated intention to return to Rak-raku-en, to care for elderly aunt and seek employment. Recommend yearly confirm. Detainee may be candidate for subseq. recruitment by rev. groups, Soc/Comms. ADH, CAPT USMC (CIC).*

Next Hornbill had the picture sketched, adding on the years, and circulated to three State Department employees who had been at the party and who had sufficient security clearances and smarts to keep silent.

Two hadn't noticed the Japanese. One recalled she'd been introduced to him, and said his name was "something like Yamato, Yamamoto, something like that." She said he'd been invited at the last minute by the Commercial Attaché at the Japanese Embassy. The man represented a manufacturer of electronic parts "looking for a marketing partner in the United States," someone to distribute their line of capacitors, resistors, and transistors.

Bingo, thought Hornbill. A check was made of commercial visas issued within the last three months and turned up one Hideo Yamashita, representing the Mitsuko Electric Company of Yokohama. A check through Immigration showed him entering the country July 30 in San Francisco.

Three hotels were favored by Japanese commercial travelers staying in Washington. A discreet check showed no one answering Nomura/Yamashita's description as being currently registered.

Then, two days after Hornbill's initial probe, a call from Immigration. The man calling himself Yamashita had exited the United States in New York, taking a Pan Am flight to Tokyo yesterday.

Damn! Hornbill exploded, slamming his fist into his desk and wincing. *He must've seen me. I blew it. Now what was he doing that was so sensitive that one recognition would have caused him to cancel his plans?*

He pressed the lowest button on his intercom. "Lulu?"
"Sir?"
"Get me Guinness Ross on the phone, over at FBI. I want to set up a lunch date. Stay on the line after we're connected. We may have some follow-up to do."
"Yes, Mr. Hornbill."

The visas and entry declarations of Japanese heading for Washington were subjected to intense scrutiny for the next two months, for it was felt that if *Naichò* or any of the other Japanese intelligence agencies were involved in anything serious in D.C., then Nomura's replacement would soon be arriving.

Hornbill was right. On October 1, 1962, a young Japanese businessman calling himself Hironori Funakoshi entered the United States, and took a small apartment for himself in Washington, intending, as stated on his visa issued in Tokyo, to "set up joint ventures between numerous U.S. and Japanese firms interested in the photographic accessories market."

The FBI—in one of those rare moments in which Hoover's people actually liaised with the CIA—reported Funakoshi as being an agent of *Nibetsu,* the Second Section, Investigation Division, Ground Self-Defense Forces. *Nibetsu* was then, and is now, largely engaged in collecting military intelligence from the dozens of Japanese military attachés posted around the globe.

More interestingly, Funakoshi also proved to be a graduate of the Nakano Spy School, a Japanese Army unit that continued clandestinely after the war's end. Nakano was notorious for producing not only skilled espionage agents but guerrilla leaders as well.

The man was not alerted nor interfered with in any way. But the surveillance on him was the beginning of a project which was to last for several decades: the monitoring of Japanese intelligence activities in Washington.

In the meantime, Hornbill was still intrigued with the whereabouts and status of Kenji Nomura.

45

The Moss Garden.

16 October 1989.

In the slanted shafts of sunlight, silhouetted women bent low over the flawless moss, picking up fallen tiny red maple leaves.

They were the widows of World War II military men. Some wore scarves, securely tied beneath aging chins. Others wore a sort of bonnet, large and white, obscuring most if not all of their faces.

Hornbill followed the tall monk along the *roji,* the random stepping stones of the traditional "dewy path."

The monk was robed in rough brown cloth. The shoulders were broad, yet sloped downward in the way of weight lifters and practitioners of certain martial arts. Hornbill noted the man's hands: calloused not only along the edges of the palms, but on the fingertips as well.

No one else was on the path, which now followed a stream in a gentle series of curves, each created to draw attention to a particular view: a group of stones, an unusual tree, a planting of flowers.

At one point the stream flowed through a series of stepped beds of lilies, each bed bound with bamboo. One led down to another, the water following its course, each cerulean rectangle receiving its water in turn.

As he followed the path, Hornbill suddenly found himself inches from a second monk who, expressionless, patted him down for weapons. Satisfied, the man nodded for him to pass. The monk had materialized so suddenly, soundlessly, Hornbill couldn't have responded even if he'd wanted to.

The first man, oblivious to the second's appearance, kept walking ahead. Hornbill was now fully alert, beginning to notice small things:

Perimeter defense antennae sprouting near the path. A small surveillance camera, lurking in the shadows of a rock formation. Hornbill realized he was moving into an area of extreme security.

Finally the monk stopped, motioning Hornbill forward, pointing to a view of cherry blossom trees across a lake. "You will find him there," he said. "Go to the moss garden beyond the trees, near the stream, and wait."

Hornbill nodded and walked along the edge of the lake, noting how the sky's reflection seemed a part of the garden's design. When he reached the opposite side, the ground sloped upward. Here, too, the maple trees left their tiny red leaves in contrast against green moss. He was fascinated by the play of color against color, texture against texture.

Then he saw Nomura standing at the edge of the clearing, in gray robes.

At first it was hard to reconcile this man with the youth he'd questioned at Yokosuka decades before. The frame had thickened and broadened, the head shaven, the face engraved with age. But it was the same man.

"And so we meet again, Lieutenant Hornbill," the imposing figure said.

Hornbill smiled. "We meet again, Ensign Nomura."

It was, in fact, the first time the two men had actually seen each other since the State Department party in 1962, when Hornbill had recognized Nomura. It had taken Hornbill seventeen months to discover that the mysterious figure known as Dragonfly had, in fact, arisen from the identity of the former naval ensign from Yokosuka.

Since then, through intermediaries, Hornbill and Nomura had reached an accommodation—sharing intelligence to each other's benefit, without the knowledge of either's government. Such arrangements in the intelligence trade are commonplace, but potentially explosive.

Nomura sat down on the moss and, with an odd, palm-up gesture, indicated that Hornbill do the same. The sound of running water, coming from a small stream just beyond their vision, gave the place a quantum of tranquility.

Hornbill saw a man with a contained tension, like a spring under compression. He knew Nomura had risen high within Japan's intelligence hierarchy. Hornbill's people had even reported that the *gurupu* supplemented the government's budget for Nomura, and that he had frequent contact with every element of Japan's industrial, military, intelligence, and public leadership.

Yet few knew Nomura's face. And almost none knew his history.

At the same moment Nomura was quietly studying Hornbill, watching, wondering: *Will this man, this odd Westerner in a tweed suit, understand what I'm about to tell him without thinking me a traitor to my own people?*

"Do you remember," Nomura began, "what Hiroshima was like?"

"Yes," said Hornbill, reliving the scene in his mind. "SCAP had an inspection tour after I arrived in Japan. It was a little over a month after the bombing, two days before my interview with you."

The Japanese cast his eyes downward, and placed a hand on the ineffable softness of the moss. "No, I mean, had you seen Hiroshima as it was—before?"

Hornbill said quietly, "No. I never knew the old Hiroshima."

The other nodded. "It was known for its beauty, for the seven fingers of the river Ota. For its beautiful trees and gardens. We thought, all of us who lived there in the war, that it was being spared because of its beauty." He smiled, but the smile was without humor.

When he raised his head, the eyes that met Hornbill's were like those of a dead man. The voice was curiously flat. "I was there one hour after the detonation. And I still carry the memory of Hiroshima with me. It is the central fact of my existence."

"Obviously difficult for anyone who was there to erase the memory," observed Hornbill.

An egret lifted from the lake, a blurred flurry of white, an awkwardness become graceful in flight. "My wife was three hundred meters from Ground Zero that day," Nomura said unexpectedly.

Hornbill was stunned. "I didn't realize—"

"I thought she'd been killed then," Nomura continued, almost as if the other hadn't spoken. "She was—she is—a *hibakusha*. We found each other only years afterward. You saw those widows near the entrance? She works with them whenever we are here. It gives her comfort.

"She is, in many ways, my conscience." He fixed Hornbill with a piercing, almost challenging stare. "If it were not for her, I would be so submerged in the *wa* of everyday existence, I would be incapable of thinking of what I wish to propose to you today."

Nomura closed his eyes and drew a deep breath. Then, more gently, he continued.

"In the early 1930s, many Japanese began to believe our national destiny could only be fulfilled through conquest, for we as an island were too dependent upon the resources of others, particularly petroleum. The great *zaibatsu*, too, felt their markets could be more easily conquered militarily than by economics."

Hornbill nodded in agreement. He'd often heard the giant cartels had goaded the government into war.

"So," continued Nomura, "we began the military adventures that led to the shame of Hiroshima and Nagasaki. Our successes had always been over weak enemies, in easy circumstances. We were surprised by the magnitude of the victory at Pearl Harbor. For the first time, we had vanquished a formidable opponent.

"But Pearl Harbor became the seed of our defeat. For there we threw away our honor, our birthright of island integrity. And of course, once honor is thrown away, it can never be regained.

"The harvest of Hiroshima was the result. Forces were set in motion which lost more than our national integrity; the innocence of mankind itself was lost on a global scale."

To Hornbill, it was odd to hear a Japanese place the responsibility for Hiroshima on Japan's own aggression. The Japanese press and many of the Japanese intelligentsia had begun to view the fate of Hiroshima as part of the increasing mythology of the victimization of Japan, as if war were visited upon her from a vague, unspecified alien cause—almost an act of God—and not the direct result of Japan's decision to wage aggressive, large-scale war.

Nomura's voice became softer as he thought back. "As I walked among the ashes of Hiroshima, and felt the rain of death as it struck my shoulders, I began to taste the bitter tea of—of something more than defeat.

"This was an abandonment of the soul itself, a loss of all

honor in any conventional sense." He paused to draw a hand across his bronzed forehead.

"The concept of *territory* vanished once the bomb detonated over Hiroshima. We all became vulnerable, regardless of which borders we barricaded ourselves behind, regardless of which flags we attempted to wrap around ourselves. War, as a solution to political problems, became both unthinkable and impractical."

The intensity of the man's feeling was like a laser fired through darkest space, pure and undeniable. Hornbill remembered the same quality in the young officer he'd interviewed at Yokosuka, and remembered wondering where that intensity would lead.

Nomura, suddenly restless, got to his feet. He motioned to Hornbill to follow him. They passed an open sarcophagus, ancient and moss-covered, the lid open for passersby to sit on.

In a few minutes the path led sharply upward. The steps became a combination of lichen-accented stones and tree roots. From their profusion, Hornbill guessed many of the roots had been taken from trees elsewhere and carefully positioned on this path.

This was obviously a place of great importance. Everything about it spoke of Zen traditions and training, especially the man in front of him, who seemed to take the steep path without the slightest strain. Hornbill's own muscles were beginning to feel the climb.

Just when the path seemed to be at its steepest, Nomura turned toward Hornbill. With the same strange palm-up gesture as before, he indicated what lay just ahead. . . .

_____ 46

Bitter Tea.

Rising out of the morning mist, the structure seemed ancient and immutable. It was as if no human agency had constructed it, but as if, instead, it had risen from somewhere within the hill itself.

A large flat stone lay in front of the small entrance, flanked by a stone basin into which a bamboo pipe spilled water. The two men entered through the low doorway, and found themselves in a seventeenth-century teahouse in the style of Katagiri Sekishù.

Hornbill was intrigued by paintings of flying cranes on a frieze running around the upper walls next to the ceiling. They seemed to be alive, coursing in swift silence as they sought—what? Refuge from a relentless winter? Immortality?

Nomura took his seat in front of a low table on which were placed the implements for *cha no yu,* the ancient ceremony of tea imported from China in centuries past.

Hornbill sat opposite, looking beyond Nomura at the ancient scroll in the *tokonoma,* and the gnarled yet oddly graceful wooden bough forming one upright of the recess.

A kettle sat over a small charcoal brazier, a wisp of steam curling upward from its spout. Nomura poured hot water from it into a tea bowl of crude ceramic material.

Hornbill recognized the form. Echoing rustic rural pottery, it was, in fact, a valuable and rare Iga bowl.

In the bowl Nomura swirled a small whisk, and replaced the ladle on top of the kettle. The movements were practiced, economical. He emptied the tea bowl, and wiped it, leaving the cloth on top of the kettle's lid.

Next, with a tiny scoop fashioned of bamboo, he placed two spoonsful of tea in the tea bowl and ladled hot water over it. He took the whisk again and swirled it briskly, spinning the green tea in tiny eddies. Then he placed the whisk to the right of the tea caddy.

A pause, in which his eyes closed briefly. Finally, he lifted the tea bowl with his left hand, and offered it to Hornbill with his right. Hornbill accepted the tea with a slight nod. Rotating the bowl slightly, he sipped.

He smiled at Nomura. "Your tea is excellent, Ensign Nomura," he said, smiling. He handed the bowl back, waiting for him to continue.

When Nomura did, it was with great delicacy. Too often Westerners and Japanese exchanged thoughts without first making allowances for major cultural differences. When that happened—particularly in political negotiations—one party or the other misconstrued the intent or the degree of commitment, and disaster ensued.

Considering the nature of what Nomura was about to propose, it was vital that Hornbill fully understand the context.

"As you're well aware, at the war's end, our two nations began a curious relationship," Nomura began. "Although we were conquered and occupied by the United States, we felt a great admiration. You were all-powerful economically, industrially. You extended your hand in friendship and helped us build a new Japan. You taught us to believe in democracy and in the worth of a manufacturing economy."

Hornbill nodded, accepting the bowl of tea once again.

"But then," said Nomura, "you, who had everything, began to let it all slide away. Like the tiny stones that are the starting signals of an avalanche.

"You began throwing away your tradition of engineering excellence, and let your companies be run by financial men, not product men. You forgot that long term, the consumer is the master—not the investor. Economically speaking, it is the *consumer* who decides who lives or dies. And it is the product on which the consumer bases his or her decision.

"You curse us for buying Rockefeller Center, yet you buy a Japanese car instead of an American one. You are angered at Sony for buying CBS Records, yet you buy a Sony Walkman instead of an American cassette player. You feel threatened when the ten biggest banks in the world are Japanese, yet you spend your money on Japanese microwaves, Japanese musical instruments, Japanese cameras—" He paused, shaking his head.

"You have only one television-set manufacturer left. You will soon have none. And why? Because we spent so many years improving, perfecting, using research United States' electronic engineers created but which your managers thought so little of, so driven were they to keep costs down short term and keep earnings up.

"You still have your aircraft industry, the best in the world. You still have the greater edge of technology for military uses, but it is slipping. You have superiority in many areas of the computer sciences, but we are about to pass you, and will do so within the next decade. It is not a boast. It is a certainty."

Hornbill knew what the man was saying was true. He leaned forward, and, wiping the rim of the bowl of tea, passed it back to Nomura. Then, watching for some sort of reaction from the older man, asked Nomura the question which had been at the back of his mind. "Then are you—are the *gurupu* trying for world domination? Do you regard this as economic war?"

When Nomura finally spoke, it was in a voice so low as to be nearly inaudible. "We do not wish to be anyone's masters, nor do we wish any nation to have power over us as they have had in the past. Most especially, we do not wish another Hiroshima.

"The only way we can guarantee that is to become the dominant economic power on earth. So, partly by your own election, you will become more and more the brood cows, merely markets for our manufacturing. And so, in time, will Europe, and the rest of Asia. This is the strategy we call *Dai Sen Ryaku*. But it is not merely a strategy. It is an *inevitability*.

"Within fifteen years our military technologies will be dominant. Yours will be obsolete, for your government will not invest in that which is a necessity. Despite your superior aircraft of today, despite what little else you still possess, you will wake up one morning and realize you are at the world's mercy.

"And will you be the worse for it? I think not. At least you will be among the living, and not among the ashes of the aftermath of yet another war. You will be using our VCRs, and driving our cars, and watching our movies, and working in our factories, and using our banks, and you will know harder work, but you will not know poverty. It will be a different world, and you will learn, as the British have learned, to live without being masters."

He paused to wipe the rim of the bowl of bitter tea, refilled it, and offered it to Hornbill.

Nomura leaned forward, his words urgent. "In the next ten years, we run the highest risk of thermonuclear war. The Soviet government is far from stable. Many nations now have intermediate range missiles: Iraq has the capability of launching a missile from Baghdad straight into the heart of London. China is still under the control of old men on the verge of madness.

"America, though, still holds the key to survival in this next critical decade. The key is in your own defense technologies, in both intelligence and weaponry. Although we in Japan now have the world's third largest defense budget, we are still far behind. We have great need of what you have today, especially in those technologies and intelligence systems which will enable us to react in time to save ourselves from an armed conflict.

"If we can survive the next decade, there is a possibility that peace may be assured for all time.

"What I wish to suggest to you is a trade: *America's help to let us survive the next decade—in exchange for Japan's help to let you survive the next century.*"

And in the next hour, Kenji Nomura was to propose a plan that would lead both to treason, and lead one to death.

_____ 47

Flashpoint.

It was difficult to assess the damage.

Tim Nagata tried to remember all he had told Kazuko, all that the microphones and sensors implanted in her apartment had captured. The interrogation team, although sympathetic to what he had suffered, still had the job of cataloguing what had been transmitted to Japanese intelligence.

The debriefing had taken three weeks. Nagata told and retold his story until it began to sound, even to his own ears, as if it had happened to someone else, a stranger.

Finally the team was satisfied, and he was permitted to go home. DIA assigned a psychiatrist with whom he met Tuesday and Thursday afternoons for post-trauma therapy.

NPIC wanted him to resume work part-time, slowly working up to full days.

And so Tim Nagata began to piece together the shattered bits of his life. His battered Honda was once again seen making its way to the drab tan building at First and M.

At first he felt curiously empty, as if he had been gutted, as if a void existed in place of his psyche. But then, slowly at first, his work began to heal the wound, even more than his sessions with the psychiatrist.

LACROSSE was now NPIC's oracle, and Tim Nagata its high priest. Even the bunkers, the gigantic survival shelters that ranged across the Soviet Union, were being taken seriously. Bunkerphobes were no longer in vogue. Most important, LACROSSE was proving invaluable in assessing the increased Soviet military activity throughout the world.

Director Coldwell was doing his best to convince the president of the accelerating danger of the situation, and the Talking Dogs were now regular visitors to Tim's console.

The president, though, was caught between his inclination to defer decisions and his need to ride any groundswell of public opinion. Coldwell, to bring the president to a decision, arranged a leak to *The New York Times* about the Soviets' increasingly belligerent maneuvers.

The Soviet president countered by issuing a statement that the "repositioning," as he called it, was not intended as inflammatory, but was only a "showing of the flag" as well as a "reassertion of Soviet peace-keeping power."

To armchair Kremlinologists, the explanation was simple: The Soviet leader was trapped between carrying forward his programs of democratization, and showing the hard-liners he was as tough a leader as any they could field themselves.

The truth, unfortunately, was more complex.

Only Director Coldwell and his Executive Assistant knew the delicate line the Soviet president was treading. Coldwell had a top-level source, positioned in the Kremlin, who revealed that Mescheryakov, head of the GRU, and Zaikov, First Deputy Chairman of the powerful Soviet Defense Council, were part of *Otechestvo*'s hierarchy.

Both men were advocating a return to a more militant strategic position against the West, a stronger, more vital military presence. The "repositionings," as they were being called, could not be rescinded without risking Zaikov and Mescheryakov's wrath.

With Kryuchkov, head of the KGB, looking for a fatal chink in the president's armor, the supreme Soviet leader could not afford to alienate the only organs of the state powerful enough to counterbalance the KGB.

The Soviet moves were becoming bolder now, as the new images from the AFP-731 reconnaissance satellite were proving. The new KH-12 (KEYHOLE) technology produced razor-sharp images of Soviet installations.

Weighing 37,300 pounds and placed in orbit 62 degrees above and below the equator, the satellite captured every detail of the Soviet SS-25 ICBMs being readied, right down to all the markings on the monsters' cylindrical sides, markings which would be vaporized as the huge missiles incinerated Los Angeles, San Francisco, Dallas, Chicago, Detroit, Boston, New York, Philadelphia, Baltimore, Washington, Atlanta, Miami—as well as underground ICBM silos in places few Americans had ever heard of, often farm villages of less than 6,000 population.

What the AFP-731 missed under cover of night, LA-CROSSE picked up and faithfully transmitted. Both satellites, although technically under the aegis of the National Reconnaissance Office, were now the exclusive creatures of Dr. Timothy Winslow Nagata. His stewardship of the reconnaissance satellites had now become legendary; his knowledge of their product was encyclopedic.

When any of the CIA's mullahs wanted the latest interpretation of the Soviet "repositionings," it was Tim Nagata who was consulted, and no one else.

And, in truth, it was his mind that had collated all the infinite bits of data his creatures had uncovered, that had integrated the overt military threats with the far more powerful threat of survivability within the gigantic bunkers encircling Russia's cities and military installations.

Probably no one in the building at First and M, whether DIA or CIA, had so completely grasped the truth of what lay before them, as seen through the eyes in the sky, as Tim Nagata.

• • •

The trains all left on schedule. Except for the number of load-bearing steel wheels under two of the boxcars, each looked like a commercial freight train.

They departed from their storage igloos in Dyess Air Force Base in Texas, Fairchild in Washington, Wurtsmith in Michigan, Grand Forks in North Dakota, Barksdale in Louisiana, and six other air force bases around the U.S.

They were now speeding along with two 89-foot-long missile launch cars (MLCs), each with a tube containing the 200,000 pound, ten-warhead MX Peacekeeper missile. Besides a locomotive and the MLCs, the train included two security cars, a missile launch car, and a maintenance car.

The trains, now sharing tracks with normal passenger and freight traffic, would proceed to randomly selected positions. Upon the appropriate codes being communicated to the launch car, the top of the MLCs would open, and the tube would slowly rise up to a near-vertical position. The missile's roar would be heard for miles, and the plume of smoke would arc up into the clouds, well out of sight until it returned, once more, to earth.

High above the state of Michigan, the Soviet Almaz large radar imaging spacecraft swung in its lazy orbit. On either side of the massive cylinder, fifty-foot radar panels extended slowly.

It watched a United States missile rail garrison car leaving its igloo to join other cars in the train on the tracks outside. The image was transmitted to a building in Tyuratam not very different from NPIC's in Washington. The image came up on the screen, blooming into a flare until the technician dialed it down.

Although definition was hazy, the image was decisive. The Americans were not known to use these trains in exercises. This had to be a prelude to war.

The technician signaled to his supervisor.

48

In the Floriangasse.

The *Naichò* agent had been in his car more than six hours, sipping at lukewarm tea poured from a thermos. He reflected on the fact that in surveillance, the capacity of the bladder was at least as important as the quality of the brain.

When the small man with the white hair entered and left the building within ten minutes, the agent used his two-way radio to report in.

And when a few minutes later Pretorius also left hurriedly, it was obvious things were beginning to accelerate. The man in the car reported this too, then locked and left the vehicle, following on foot.

The American led the agent through a maze of more than a mile of back streets. The American was well trained, almost losing the tag with a series of double-backs and other tricks. At one point the American walked alongside a parked closed van, stopped short, then reversed his steps to the van's rear, looking across the street to check if anybody appeared confused when he failed to emerge by the van's front.

But the *Naichò* man, too, was highly trained. Being on the counterintelligence side meant experience following people who'd every reason to believe they'd be followed.

On they went, the American surging through the nighttime crowds in the Opernring, cutting across the traffic of the Mariahilfer Strasse, the *Naichò* agent keeping a distance of fifty meters or more.

Finally, fifteen minutes later, the Japanese saw the American enter an elegant nineteenth-century apartment building in Floriangasse. Instead of following the American inside or being visible standing on the street, he found a drugstore opposite and several doors down.

He bought a tube of toothpaste and a toothbrush to placate the clerk, then stood inside near the glass door, looking through to the windows opposite. *The American would not be so foolish as to turn a light on, or to draw the curtains. But he might just look out a window to check the street.*

Which was, to the *Naichò* agent's credit, precisely what happened. For a split second, the Japanese saw the flash of a dark blond head at a fourth-floor window. He waited a minute more, looking at his watch as if he might be meeting someone in the neighborhood.

He looked across again, noting the floors which were lighted immediately above and below to see where the apartments divided. Then he left the drugstore, crossing the street to a point directly beneath the window in question, counting his paces as he walked to the entrance.

A short length of flexible steel, slid between the inner lobby door and its frame, slipped the lock effortlessly.

He glided up the stairway in silence, and glanced down the fourth-floor corridor. Then he paced off the distance and noted the number of the apartment. *Four Twelve.*

The *Naichò* agent left the building and found a telephone booth. He called in and waited for a relief man.

On the thirty-eighth floor of the Wall Street firm, the receptionist looked disapprovingly at the three standing before her.

Not the sort of men who do business with Wolff-Burns, she concluded. *Certainly not important-looking enough to see Mr. Wolff himself.*

The tall one had asked, "Is Mr. Alfred Wolff in this morning, Miss?"

"I'm sorry," she replied in a drawl she affected when discouraging unwelcome visitors. "But do you gentlemen have an appointment?"

"Well, no, I'm afraid we don't," said the older man, reaching into his jacket.

Pulling out yet another business card, she thought. *This makes eight today. Terrific.* She smiled frostily. "Then I'm sorry. You must realize Mr. Wolff is a very important man, and you'll have to—" And then she froze.

At that moment the FBI agent had his ID nine inches from her nose. "I think Mr. Wolff will see us, Miss. And if you don't mind, don't buzz either him or his secretary. Just take us to his office, please."

The young woman swallowed hard. *Was this one of those insider-trading things?* But she rose and showed them to the waiting area for the corner office, guarded by a female dragon of forbidding aspect.

"Mrs. Melcher, these gentlemen are from the Federal Bureau of Investigation. They'd like to see Mr. Wolff."

The older woman was not impressed. "You'll have to come back another time, gentlemen. Mr. Wolff is giving an interview to the press just now," she said, scarcely lifting an eyebrow. She'd dealt with cops before. She considered them on a level somewhere between cleaning people and slum landlords. Despite their badges and their guns, she wasn't impressed. She looked at them curiously once again, as if amazed they were still there.

"How soon will Mr. Wolff's interview be over?" asked one of the agents politely.

"Well, in about ten to fifteen minutes. But I'm afraid you'll have to make an appointment for a more convenient time. Or perhaps you could talk with one of his assistants. You see, Mr. Wolff has a *very* heavy schedule the next few days, and—"

The tallest of the FBI men, Special Agent Rumbelow, produced a folded series of papers bound in a pale-blue cover and looking official. "Mrs. Melcher. This is a federal warrant for the arrest of Alfred Wolff on some fairly substantial charges. I think it would be best if he saw us immediately after his interview."

Mrs. Melcher's for-once-impressed gaze went from the papers to Rumbelow's expression, then to the receptionist, then to Wolff's impressive mahogany door, and then, finding nothing of solace or refuge in any of these things, finally back to the FBI agent.

"I think that will be fine," she managed to force out in a tone of wounded *lèse-majesté*.

It could have served as a museum for *Jugendstil* furniture, or a gallery for the Vienna Secessionist painters. Within its walls was a wealth of the decorative arts. Pretorius recognized two Egon Schiele paintings and one Klimt sketch he'd seen in books before, works which had been identified only as "from a private collection." He also saw no less than nine examples of Josef Hoffman's furniture.

If you've got to hole up in Vienna, he observed, *you can't do too much better than this.*

The arrangement had been that if an emergency jeopardized either Kadmus's apartment or the safehouse in the Fleischmarkt, they would use this.

Pretorius arranged himself on the sofa in what he supposed was the living room, although several other rooms in the huge apartment seemed adequate for that function. This room was simply the largest.

The apartment belonged to a woman Pretorius believed must have been one of Kadmus's loves in years long past. Kadmus said she spent this part of the year in the south of France.

In one extremely feminine bedroom he discovered a photograph of a thin young Kadmus in German uniform, his arm around a petite brunette. Pretorius wouldn't have recognized him if it hadn't been for another framed picture of Kadmus as a young man, on a table in the apartment in the Schubertstrasse.

In the rooms throughout the house, the same woman appeared in other photographs taken over the decades. Even in her eighties, as she must be by now, she still looked striking. The photographs showed a small but dramatic-looking woman, with dark brooding eyes and high, almost Scandinavian cheekbones.

He thought she must have been an actress, a singer, or an entertainer of some sort. Kadmus referred to her as *Vögelein,* the little bird. Pretorius wondered how she would learn of Kadmus's death, and how she would take it.

He pondered his next move. *It was time,* he thought, *to take the action to the enemy.* For too long he'd been a sitting duck, waiting for the Russians to strike next as he tried to discover what was behind the killing of Phillip Mathieson.

Pretorius paced in the darkness. And as he paced, Victor S. Volynskiy, Colonel, KGB, turned the corner and began walking toward the building in the Floriangasse.

Army General Mescheryakov looked down at the small man strapped on the stretcher, the IV connected to his right forearm. The man's eyes were glazed, his skin an ashen gray. "How much have you given him?" Mescheryakov asked the *Spetsnaz* medic.

"Enough to make him tell you his life story and those of all his friends, if you get him started," replied the medic smugly. "But don't take too long. At his age, depending on his heart, we could lose him."

"As long as he tells us what we wish first, losing him doesn't concern me." Mescheryakov pulled up a stool next to the stretcher and lit a cigar.

"Now then, old man," he began easily. "Just how is it that you are called Chico?"

—————————————————————— 49

The Czar Falls.

Mescheryakov ordered everyone except one cipher clerk out of the bunker beneath Reisnerstrasse 45–47.

My Christ, he thought grimly, *what a time for this to break loose.*

The news from Vatutinki couldn't have been worse. Feliks had turned a television rally into the beginning of a full-scale armed rebellion. And now, he'd disappeared. With the whole damned KGB after him like a pack of wolves.

He shook his head. *If Feliks is caught, and if Kryuchkov[1] puts the screws to him, more heads will roll than in Stalin's time. And one of them will be mine.*

Think, think, think! he exhorted himself. *How to turn this into a strategic advantage, how to convert this into a victory?*

The lights on the board came alive. The cipher clerk was receiving another signal from Vatutinki, one hand pressed to his left earphone, the other scribbling, struggling to keep up with the message. Mescheryakov went over to stand behind him.

[1]General Vladimir Kryuchkov, Chairman of the KGB.

Earlier he'd instructed the clerk to send a coded message to a certain major at the Aquarium, GRU headquarters. The major had the responsibility of maintaining contact with Feliks, should anything extraordinary occur. And this was certainly extraordinary. Feliks knew this major well: He would be the emergency link between himself and Vienna Center. And now Mescheryakov was waiting for the officer's response, waiting to see if Feliks had made contact.

The clerk finished copying down the message, signaled his receipt, and signed off. He started to ask the general something, but Mescheryakov swept the papers off the clerk's table and strode briskly to the adjoining duty officer's cubicle.

There, squinting under the pale yellowish light of a gooseneck lamp, Mescheryakov laboriously transferred the message to a one-time gamma pad.

In five minutes, the thing was done.

Feliks had made contact. He was hiding with a small group of his senior supporters in Leningrad, concealed within a disused, sealed-up wing of the Hermitage museum. He was requesting military support from Mescheryakov, hoping for a Spetsnaz battalion to be placed under his personal command.

Mescheryakov balled up the message in his fist, then placed it in the huge marble ashtray and used his cigar lighter to ignite it.

As the flames burned and the black ashes lifted, he thought. *We have a number of scenarios. One, the dreamland scenario: The entire country rises up to support Feliks, we take over, we avoid the risks of a thermonuclear exchange. Two: Feliks is taken by the KGB or by regular troops, he spills the entire plan, and I am trussed up and delivered to Kryuchkov for gutting.*

Mescheryakov frowned and looked at the remnants of the note in the ashtray, crushing the ashes with the brass handle of a letter opener.

No, no, he mused, *we have not come this far to let one maniac destroy everything in a moment. If only the bastard could've waited, if only he could have subjugated that massive ego to the plan. Then all would be well. But still—still there must be way, a third option.*

Mescheryakov reflected on the nature of Feliks: *In the*

creature is the key. He does have great charisma. How can we use that? He is in great danger. How can we use that?

And then he broke into a broad smile.

The decision was obvious.

Leaning on his silver-headed staff, Feliks brooded over the events that had backed him into this corner. He shivered involuntarily. The marble walls were cold and dank. In this section the heat had been turned off for years, for here were stored some of the Fatherland's greatest treasures, the personal effects of the Czar Nicholas, including many of his court uniforms.

The Bolsheviks had left it all here to rot, to decay and dissolve while they presided over the decay and dissolution of Russia itself. Over the years the silken costumes had been gnawed by the rats in the hunger and cold of the Russian winters.

Feliks stared at the imperial robes, hanging in tatters in the cases. *By rights,* he thought, *it is I who should be wearing these now. For it is I who am the spiritual heir of the czars. Myself, and no one else.*

Carefully he lifted one of the long velvet robes from its armature. The rich thick blue velvet had darkened, the gold brocade tarnished to black. He slipped one arm into the wide boyarlike sleeves, then the other. He adjusted the weight of the collar around his thin neck. He looked around for a mirror, but found none.

It feels—it feels as if it belongs. Yes. It feels as if I'd worn this before, as if I'd lived this way in another life. Feliks was nothing if not mystic.

He walked down to the end of the huge gallery hall, adjusting his halting, arthritic stride to the sweep of the long robe. And there, by the light of the enormous waxen candles placed on the floor by his bodyguards, he saw himself reflected in the glass of a window shuttered on the outside.

Feliks had always been in love with his own image. It was, in fact, regarded by many as the reason he'd entered the church. But now, as he looked upon himself in the robe of Nicholas, Czar of All the Russias, his joy knew no bounds. He turned, admiring the swirl of the velvet as it too turned, following his motion. He imagined the effect on others. He lifted one arm in a regal motion.

And then the huge double doors burst open.

The big GRU captain fronting the group of armed soldiers recognized the strange figure at once. "Feliks Mikhailovich Sosnovsky, I arrest you in the name of the People. You are charged with crimes of treason against the Union of Soviet Socialist Republics." He signaled the soldiers behind him to take the bizarre robed figure away.

Feliks stood rooted to the spot, immobilized by the—the *effrontery* of these *peasants!* He made a quick, dismissive gesture, the sort of gesture he imagined to be imperial. "Out!" he began. "Remove yourselves from—"

But the sentence was never completed. A ferret-faced young corporal, his finger nervously caressing the trigger of his AKM, confused the gesture in the near-darkness with what he'd expected, that the old man would go for a weapon.

With an ear-shattering series of explosions, gunfire erupted in the ancient marble hall, ripping through the velvet and into the graying flesh. The body was thrown back several feet with the impact of eight 7.62 mm. rounds fired in slightly over two seconds.

A short amount of time, almost insignificant.

But, as Army General Mescheryakov was later to observe, sufficient to create a martyr.

_____ 50

In the Darkness.

The doorbell rang. Pretorius slipped off the sofa, moving to the door in silence.

The bell jangled again. As Pretorius stood listening, he heard a soft *whssssh*. A note slid under the door and over the polished floor, coming to rest against his foot.

Standing to one side of the door, he hesitated before picking the paper up. He remembered something one of his Marine instructors said, centuries ago in DIA training:

"When somebody wants you near a door, all they've got to do is ring the bell and slide something under it. Nine out of ten fools will pick it up, and someday, standing on the other of the door, there's going to be some smart bastard who's going to put some rounds through the bottom of that door and into your dumb skull, and at that precise moment you'll wish to hell you'd listened to your poor ole Drill Sergeant McNally."

He looked around and saw a cane standing in an umbrella stand nearby. Lifting it out, he placed its rubber tip on the note, edged it over to the side of the door, and picked it up.

Pretorius, the note read, *Must talk with you at once. I shall wait until you open. Urgent.—Volynskiy.*

There was no sound from the other side of the door. Pretorius edged soundlessly down the hallway into the kitchen. He found the service door in the darkness, and with exquisite slowness turned first the lock, then the doorknob, again staying to one side of the door.

He expelled the breath he'd been holding and slipped the 9 mm. Glock out of its high-ride belt holster.

Using one hand on the knob, Pretorius slowly, ever so slowly, pulled it toward him, praying no squeak would issue from a protesting nineteenth-century hinge.

After an eternity, the door was open. He removed his hand from the knob and placed it over his other for a two-handed hold on the pistol. Then he jumped out into the hallway, front sight perfectly aligned with the center of mass of Colonel Viktor Sergei Volynskiy, KGB.

Volynskiy wheeled at the sound like a startled cat. For the space of a breath his hand almost went for the weapon beneath the raincoat.

"Sorry, Colonel," said Pretorius, reholstering. "Wasn't sure it was you. How the hell did you track me down?"

Volynskiy smiled and shook his head. "Kadmus has been paying for this apartment for years; there was a bill in his desk from the management company. The woman who lives here must be his *Schatzie,* I suppose. I realized it would be a perfect place for you to go to ground. But Jesus, you did scare hell out of me."

"Sorry, Colonel," replied Pretorius, laughing. "Next time

let me know when you're planning a visit." They entered the apartment and went into the darkened living room. Volynskiy removed his black raincoat and smiled, just visible in the scant light from the doorway leading to the kitchen. Pretorius was in shadow, sitting on the sofa again. "Now how can I help you?"

"We'll get to that in a moment," said the colonel, checking the street outside. "Well, you seem to be moving up in the world. The last time we met you were lying in a cemetery."

"I only wish it hadn't been necessary to come here," Pretorius said. "I'll miss old August. He was one of a kind."

Volynskiy nodded, his eyes unblinking. "I'd only known him since the night before the *Zentralfriedhof,* but he was a classic. He must have been something in the old days."

Pretorius got up and headed toward the kitchen. "I'm being a godawful host, Colonel. Let me get you a drink. There's some vodka back here. Not your state-distilled cleaning fluid, of course, but—"

"Don't move," Volynskiy's voice commanded from behind in a steady monotone. "Above all, don't go for your weapon."

The light flicked on as Pretorius turned to see the KGB Colonel covering him with a Makarov, one of the few fully automatic handguns ever made, a favorite with a few senior Chekists.

"Now turn around and lace your fingers in back of your head." Pretorius did as ordered.

"Stay—just—like *that."* From the sound of Volynskiy's voice, Pretorius could tell he was moving toward the door. He heard the lock being snicked back, the door opening. He heard several men enter the room.

"Vot ghaspada," said Volynskiy, *"on yest vash!"*[1]

Hands still behind his head, Pretorius turned carefully. He recognized two of the three men as GRU. One was the man in the gray windbreaker, with yellow-lensed aviator glasses. The other was the older man in horn-rimmed glasses. The third was new: squat and heavyset, thick with muscle.

For a heavy man, the third one moved quickly. Pretorius' hands were snatched down from behind his head and bound

[1] "Well, gentlemen, he's all yours."

behind his back in an instant. The Russian used plastic detention straps, faster and easier than cuffing, removable only with a knife.

Volynskiy smiled sadly. "I'm afraid, Mr. Pretorius, you've been had. You were a little too curious for your own good. And as they say in the West, curiosity killed the cat. Rules of the game."

The man in the yellow aviator glasses had his pistol leveled at Pretorius' gut, watching his charge's eyes carefully. *A pro,* Pretorius noted. *You can see the intention in the prisoner's eyes before it telegraphs to the body.*

The gray-haired man in horn-rimmed glasses, keeping his hands in his overcoat pockets, moved between Pretorius and the windows. Volynskiy slipped the Makarov back in its shoulder holster and put on his raincoat. The man in the yellow aviator glasses gestured toward the door with his pistol.

As Pretorius turned to go, he heard the older man come up behind him and felt a tiny pinprick in a neck muscle.

Then the floor soared up to slam him in the face.

There were demonstrations in all the cities, torchlight parades searing the night. Huge portraits and posters of Feliks materialized everywhere. Underground presses began to churn out copies of Feliks' venomous speeches. Attendance in the churches nearly doubled, and the sermons started to take on a sharply nationalistic, anti-Western, anti-Japanese, and anti-Semitic tone.

The KGB was extremely edgy. Their powerbase was threatened, and even the president sought to distance himself from them. In a public interview the morning after Feliks' death, he described the incident as "immensely regrettable."

The corporal who shot Feliks was court-martialed for several breaches of military discipline and publicly sentenced to ten years' solitary confinement. The KGB officer in charge of the arresting unit was broken to lieutenant and posted to what amounted to jailer's duty in the Gulag.

Sergei Ilyushin, the journalist member of the Congress of People's Deputies, wrote a scathing editorial in *Pravitel'st-*

vennii Vestnik, in which he took exception to the floodgates of hate Feliks' martyrdom had opened. Two days after the piece appeared, Ilyushin was set upon by a gang of youths and left for dead in an alley off the Nevsky Prospekt.

_____ 51

View to a Kill.

For three hours Pretorius had been lying face down on the van's floor, a sizeable Russian foot planted in the small of his back. The grit on the floor grated against his face. He had no idea where they were going, only that they'd been going uphill the last half hour.

He opened one eye to note the woven fabric of a trouser leg at close range. Beyond that, a canvas bag. He closed the eye. "Good morning," boomed an accented voice above him. "You have made a good rest? Yes?"

He opened both eyes and turned his head. Seated on a padded bench near him, holding a pistol, Yellow Aviator Glasses was speaking. Pretorius didn't reply. In the front passenger seat, the squat heavyweight twisted around, peering back with porcine eyes. The third man, the older one, drove in silence.

The gray light coming through the van's front windows was beginning to brighten. Pretorius guessed it must be around five, maybe five-thirty. The plastic straps on his wrists hurt like hell. He wondered whether the straps had shrunk or his wrists had swollen. He flexed his fingers, trying to pump up the circulation. The foot pressed hard on his back to discourage further motion. A laugh came from above, abruptly dissolving into a cough.

The van turned to the right and the ride got rougher. *A country road, maybe a track to a farm, or a field, or a quarry,* he thought. *They wouldn't drive all this way just to kill me. On the other hand, they wouldn't do it without a blindfold if they were going to let me live, either.*

It was not a comforting thought.

The van slowed. The Russians were quiet, looking around. Pretorius had the feeling they'd never been here, that they were searching for a signpost, a landmark.

Another turn, this one to the left. The road got worse. With every rut and dip, the straps cut deeper into his wrists.

Finally the van lurched to a halt. The driver killed the ignition. Nobody got out for a couple of minutes. They sat in silence, listening in the stillness of the dawn. Then Yellow Aviator Glasses slid open the side door with a rattling metallic clangor.

"Get out, Yank. You've got a long day ahead," he said. The fat one laughed.

Pretorius struggled to his feet, hands strapped behind him, somehow managing to stumble out without falling. What he saw took his breath away.

They were parked on a dirt track in front of a wooden Alpine hut, facing a vista of incomparable beauty. The snowy slopes of the Austrian Alps soared steeply into the morning mists, white rising into white, heaven and earth blending improbably.

All three Russians had their weapons out, scanning the area. When they finally seemed satisfied, Yellow Aviator Glasses opened the hut's planked door, motioning with the pistol for Pretorius to go in.

The walls inside were logs, stripped and scrubbed to near whiteness. A blue-and-white enameled stove nestled within a fieldstone fireplace.

"Over there," said the Russian, indicating a heavy wooden chair made of what looked like small pine logs. "Sit down."

"Can you cut off the straps? They're tighter than hell; the circulation's stopped."

"Don't be stupid," smirked his captor. "You're not here for a holiday, Yank. Sit *down.*"

Pretorius complied, flexing the protesting wrists.

"Aleks! In here," the Russian shouted. The heavyset thug waddled in, an unpleasant smile on the blubbery face. "Get this bastard secured to the chair," ordered Yellow Aviator Glasses, standing well back. The muzzle of the pistol was once again leveled at Pretorius' gut.

As the squat Russian used more of the plastic bands to strap him in, Pretorius slowly rotated his forearms to get maximum distance between them and the chair's wooden arms. The Russian jerked the bands tight. Pretorius drew in his breath sharply.

Aviator Glasses tapped him on the nose with the pistol barrel, and smiled. "There, Yank. You will wait. But do not try anything. *Panimayete?*"

Pretorius watched him without expression.

Arthur Hornbill drew back the draperies of his room in the Palais Schwarzenberg, looked down into the gardens, and considered the ironies of his chosen trade.

If I hadn't volunteered for duty in Japan forty-seven years ago, he reflected, *I wouldn't be here in Austria today. If Phillip Mathieson hadn't been pushed off a ledge by a GRU lunatic, Michael Pretorius wouldn't be here today.*

Hornbill had arrived on the morning Pan Am from New York, relaxed and restored. Airplanes, to Hornbill, were the perfect retreat from a pressured professional existence. No telephones, telexes, or faxes to intrude; no career-carving assistants to conjure up crises.

He considered airplanes as airborne cylinders of serenity, made imperfect only by the inedibility of their rations and the zealousness of their stewardesses. When flying, Hornbill took care to pin a small, carefully lettered sign on the airline blanket: *Do not awaken or disturb unless aircraft stops suddenly. Above all, I do not wish to be fed.*

Hornbill's adrenaline was running high. Everything had gone according to plan, except, regrettably, for the death of August Kadmus. But at least Mescheryakov had been drawn out and was now in Vienna, and Feliks was no longer in the picture. Things were looking up.

Possibly, just possibly, the operation would be wrapped up this week.

The heavyset thug sitting across the hut from Pretorius stared at him unblinkingly. Pretorius found himself wondering if the guard was able to doze with his eyes wide open. He'd known somebody at college with that uncanny talent, and in certain classes had envied him greatly.

The others were outside somewhere, covering the perimeter. With infinite care, Pretorius tried rotating his forearms to see if he'd gained any looseness.

A sharp bark outside, seeming to come from a great distance, and the guard stood up to look through the gingham-curtained window. Pretorius experimented and found he'd gotten a quarter-inch of play between his forearms and the chair.

Unable to see anything outside, the squat Russian returned to his chair.

Pretorius knew these men were professionals. That, in its way, was reassuring. Pros had their own kind of predictability. Even so, these men seemed edgy, as if they were waiting for somebody big to show.

Who the hell is coming? he wondered. *Who's so important they had to drive way the hell out here? Or*—came the more ominous thought—*what are they planning that requires so much privacy?*

Two rifle shots in the distance. The Russian moved to the door with surprising speed, slamming it open, his pistol drawn and at the ready. Pretorius used the opportunity to test pulling his arm back and forth.

A shout from outside, apparently from the oldest of the three, answered in a surly tone by the fat one.

Pretorius wondered what the shots had been. *A hiker venturing too near? A hunter shooting a rabbit? Whatever it was, it was hardly likely to improve his position.*

In a moment the guard stomped back into the hut, followed by Yellow Sunglasses. Covering Pretorius with the pistol, Yellow Sunglasses ordered his partner to cut off the straps.

When the fat one finished slicing off the straps, he moved well away from Pretorius. Yellow Sunglasses motioned to the door. "Outside," he said. "Go slow. No fast movements."

It was midday. The panorama was if anything even more breathtaking. The Alps now stood in relief against an impossibly blue sky, their whiteness dreamlike, remote.

Just outside the hut the Russian with gray hair stood motionless, a 7.62 NATO sniper's rifle languishing in the crook of his arm.

Seventy meters down the hill from the hut lay a body in a blue nylon jacket. As Pretorius approached with Yellow Sunglasses, he saw the young face, eyes open, staring sightlessly into the grass. The face was Japanese, obviously a hiker who'd come on the Russians by mistake.

Two bullet holes, each outlined in a darkening scarlet circle of blood, contrasted against the sky-blue nylon. Next to the body stood a spade, blade jabbed into the ground.

Yellow Sunglasses looked at Pretorius without expression. "You've got work to do, Yank. Dig two graves."

_____ 52

Night Moves.

By late afternoon both graves were dug—damp, fresh earth neatly heaped by each.

Into one the Russians dumped the hiker, grabbing the feet and hands, throwing the corpse in like a sack of grain. Pretorius had to shovel the earth back, covering the still-surprised young face, then the rest of the body, finally filling the grave and tamping down the surface.

The other remained empty. *Well,* Pretorius thought, *either they're using it to bury me or to intimidate me. These people are nothing if not practical.* He shook his head and looked into the distance.

The nearing sunset had begun to wash the Alps with a rose-violet light, warming their coolness with color.

Even the three guards were momentarily distracted by the vision. For a fraction of an instant, Pretorius considered flinging the spade at the head of the nearest, the older Russian, then grabbing the Stechkin and—then he noticed Aviator Glasses smiling at him, shaking his head slowly. *Pros,* thought Pretorius. *The pros always think like the prisoner.*

He stuck the spade in the mound beside the second grave and walked back up the slope to the hut.

• • •

Mescheryakov's Mercedes coursed along the Autobahn in near silence. A second car in front and a third behind provided security. Still, the man next to the driver in front cradled a full-automatic AKM in his lap under a blanket, concealed from passing truck drivers who peered down into cars' interiors, hoping for a glimpse of feminine skin. An assault rifle would not reward their curiosity in quite the anticipated way.

Smoking his cigar as he lounged in the sedan's plush interior, the general was pleased with events.

Feliks is in heaven, where he always thought he belonged and where he is less of a menace. The American is in hand, his protectors terminated. Now we'll find out what the bastard knows, if anything, about Vienna Center.

He rubbed a big hand over his bald dome. He found the loose-fitting suit uncomfortable compared to his well-tailored general's uniform. Like some ex-lawmen miss wearing a gun, Mescheryakov missed the uniform.

We should be there in under two hours, he calculated. *Too bad we'll miss the sunset.* Looking at his wristwatch he thought of how long it would take to extract the information from the American, added three hours, and decided he'd be safely back in the *residentura* by morning.

The pig farmer's dog had been the only problem.

Finally they stopped its barking by tempting it with a piece of dried beef, ensnaring the dog with a rappeling line, and injecting it with a mild narcotic.

The men in black could then advance in total silence. The images in their night-vision binoculars were of two guards covering the two primary sectors. One had a scoped military sniper's rifle; the other a machine pistol of archaic design. They knew a third armed man would be inside, guarding the prisoner.

They'd plotted their approach earlier with a map, planning lines of infiltration which would use as much cover as possible. Now, as they neared the objective, the danger increased a thousandfold.

The guard with the yellow glasses seemed the most vulnerable of the two outside. He'd often rubbed his eyes, probably feeling a lack of sleep, and several times set down his weapon to stretch.

Finally in position, the men in black awaited the cars.

Pretorius' man dozed, chair leaning back on two rear legs, melonlike head propped against the scrubbed log wall. After trying the straps any number of ways, Pretorius realized there was no give. Zero. Nothing.

The chair, though, the chair had possibilities. The chair was portable. It could be moved, albeit with him in it—but nonetheless *moved*.

Snores came from the Russian's open mouth. The lips, like nervous caterpillars, fluttered with his breathing. Pretorius tried pushing sideways with his feet, to push the chair toward the wooden sink on which rested a bread knife. A quarter-inch at a time, the chair actually progressed. And no sound. At least not yet.

Pretorius wondered if any of the two outside would check through the window. He assumed so. He had no alternative but to do precisely what he was doing.

Over the course of a half hour he progressed perhaps two feet. If the squat Russian woke up, the distance would be noticeable, and the attempt would be ended. But it was all Pretorius had. So he pushed again, edging ever closer in an inchworm's race against time.

A gray moth entered the hut through an open window. It begin to circumnavigate the interior, buzzing, investigating. It lit on the brass kerosene lamp near the window and rested, cleaning its legs. It took off again on another exploratory mission.

Pretorius was now within six inches of the knife. He now leaned forward, and attempted to stand, the chair bound to his legs, arms, and chest. He held his breath. Slowly, ever so slowly, he turned around, positioning his left hand near the knife.

The thug suddenly stopped his snoring. Pretorius tried to will his heart to stop beating so loudly. The Russian rubbed his face, eyes still shut, and soon resumed his nasal serenade.

The knife was now in Pretorius' fingers, blade backwards. He sat the chair back down on the floor, getting his breath

again, and began forcing the blade against the strap, sawing
back and forth.

After an eternity, the plastic began to separate, and the
strap fell from his wrist, hitting the floor with a tiny slap.
Pretorius froze. The snoring continued, uninterrupted.

He reversed the blade in his one free hand and snicked
through the remaining straps quietly, holding each so none
dropped to the floor.

As the last strap was freed from Pretorius' ankle, the moth
decided to attempt a precision six-point landing on a smooth
and inviting surface: the Russian's upturned forehead.

_____ 53

The Trap Springs.

A howl of stunned surprise and outrage, a flurry of thick
arms swatting at the moth, now soaring to new altitudes
with a speed hitherto unknown to his species, and the Russian was on his feet.

But before the man could get his bearings, Pretorius was
across the room with the blade in the knife-fighter's move
known as *flechette*.

The cuts were quick and decisive; the fat on the man was
what spared him at first. Piercing the abdomen and slicing
down into a thick gray layer of fat, the first cut failed to
reach its target. So did the second, slashing up from the chest
toward the throat.

The thug's head jerked back and his hand grabbed for the
knife, only to be sliced across the palm, a red line suddenly
rippling with scarlet bubbles.

Pretorius heard a flurry of running outside as he faced the
Russian in a fencer's position, legs braced for the lunge. The
man, his coolness lost in rage, came at him with the sudden-
ness of an angered bull and Pretorius at the same time
stepped aside, angling the blade up, positioning it so the
man, quite literally, cut his own throat.

The door slammed open and Pretorius found himself facing the muzzle of Yellow Aviator Glasses' pistol.

He dropped the blade instantly and raised his hands. Below at his feet came the burbling of lungs, expelling their last into a welling reservoir of blood where before there had only been air.

"Blyad!" the Russian swore, his trigger finger hesitating. "Back! Get *back* from him!"

The third ran into the hut and quickly bent down to the fallen guard. He placed his index and middle finger against the carotid artery and waited. Then he looked up, gray eyes cold with malice. "You are fortunate, Yank. Fortunate that we have other plans for you."

Then Yellow Glasses snapped out, *"Up against that post! Hands behind your back, legs spread!"*

Pretorius was pushed against one of the hut's big supporting timbers. He felt wire being tightened around his wrists, cutting deeply enough to draw blood. His ankles were secured next, wired so tightly together the two knobby bones on the inside of his ankles hurt.

His breath came hard as he listened to them discussing what to do. Finally they pulled the other outside, leaving a bloodied smear on the scrubbed pine floor.

Then they waited.

Outside, in cloud-enshrouded darkness, the men in black heard the shouts and the noises from inside the hut, saw the two guards run in. The team's leader, a tall Japanese with a closely trimmed moustache, raised a cautioning hand to the others behind him.

He sensed some of the men might react without thinking, might seize this as a chance to take the site.

But doing that now would nullify the real objective of the mission: to capture alive the senior Russian officer who was, at this moment, less than three minutes away.

The sounds from inside died down. The door opened and two of the men carried a third out and threw him to the ground.

Above, the moon began edging out from behind the clouds, bathing the slopes in an eery gray-blue light. Someone with the right training might distinguish eight forms

clouds, bathing the slopes in an eery gray-blue light. Someone with the right training might distinguish eight forms
lying in various positions. The leader was glad both guards
were inside now. He was concerned about the other Russians
who would soon be coming up the road.

At Wien-Schwechat airport, the UH-60 Blackhawk was
thundering, blades beating against the thick ground-level
air, anxious to break the bond with the earth.

The military/assault version of Sikorsky's S-70 helicopter,
the Blackhawk was specially fitted out for night special operations. Although it bore U.S. Army markings, this particular Blackhawk was assigned to DIA operations in Germany
and Austria, and based primarily at the big USAF base at
Wiesbaden.

Inside were seven men, cramped and packed in with
equipment: the pilot, his gunner, three young Japanese in
dark military clothing, a gaunt American with a physician's
satchel, and one older gentleman curiously dressed in a
three-piece tweed suit.

The pilot scanned his readouts. He'd been told this was
not a training mission, that it involved a landing on the side
of a mountain near Salzburg with a strong possibility of
hostile fire. He, like his ship, was anxious to be off.

Finally the tower crackled its clearance through the heavy
padded headphones. The ship separated itself from the tar-
mac, the tail lifting first, then the nose. As they rose into the
moonlit sky, the tail slowly arced around with dragonfly
grace.

The lights below slid by with maddening slowness. The
helicopter was covering the miles quickly, but it seemed slow
at this height. Hornbill looked down, trying to find the lights
of the *Prater,* with its big Ferris wheel.

The Japanese behind him checked their straps and the
equipment they carried in the pockets of their nightsuits.
Each carried a specially modified 9 mm. Smith & Wesson
469, oversized sights slotted with luminous material. The
pistols were sheathed in cross-strap shoulder holsters. The
main weapons in any emergency would be their CAR-15s,
fitted with the new 90-round drums of 5.56 mm. hollow
point ammo.

The gunner was perched by the open hatchway with his machine gun. He watched and nervously chewed the web of his hand. He would be the most exposed initially. The open hatchway was what they all went for, knowing the gunner would be there, just inside. The flash of his rounds would attract everything. His gunner's helmet, Kevlar vest and crotch protector would help, but he'd known guys blown to Burgerbits even with heavy-duty armor plating.

Technology, he well knew, wasn't a hell of a lot of comfort when people are trying to shoot holes in you.

It had been years since the pilot flew into a hostile LZ. He hoped it would be years before he did it again. He had two kids to get through college, an ex-wife with expensive tastes and a larcenous heart, and a German fiancée who wished he'd leave his boring job with the Army and maybe start a commuter air service in America, once they were married.

The lights below began to thin out. The pilot brought up his night-vision goggles and began adjusting the levels.

Every time he shifted position, Pretorius gritted his teeth with the pain of the wire. The feeling in his hands and feet had vanished.

He tried to wiggle his toes and his fingers and didn't know whether he was actually doing it or not. He hoped there was enough circulation so gangrene couldn't take hold later. *Having no hands and no feet would be a hell of a way to wrap it up. It all depended on how long they kept him here, and what they had in mind for him.*

With his head turned to one side, cheek to the floor, he was able to see both Russians clearly. They were standing now, moving around but still watching him, weapons in hand, ready. Whatever was about to happen was near.

The leader was the first to see the headlights inching up the hill, dipping and bouncing with the roughness of the track. He raised one hand to signal the others. The moon had gone behind the clouds again, but their night vision was now at optimum level. Each saw his alerting motion clearly.

The men checked their weapons, CAR-15s topped with night vision scopes, able to delineate a target in total darkness out to 200 meters.

Then they looked back down the hill to the lights. Each was thinking the same: *Three cars. The front and rear would be security. The middle car would have their man.*

Inside the black Mercedes, Army General Mescheryakov was relishing this moment. *Soon, very soon, he would meet the bastard who had caused so much trouble to the Center, and to Otechestvo. Soon he would know everything the man knew, and then he would have the very personal, the very deep pleasure of killing him slowly. As slowly as his imagination would devise. And that, he decided, would be very slow indeed.*

As they pulled up in front, the door of the hut opened and Lieutenant Oleg Ulanov emerged, machine pistol in hand. Mescheryakov recognized Ulanov's yellow American-style sunglasses.

Mescheryakov's driver stepped out and opened the big car's door, lighting up the interior, revealing the general in civilian clothes. The security men were already out of the other two cars and began fanning out in the area.

Almost immediately one of them, a young *Spetsnaz* trooper, squinted hard at an outline he thought he saw next to a boulder set in the hillside. He stopped in his tracks, trying to get his night vision. At that moment, the moon once again emerged from a cloudbank, and the trooper saw the unmistakable outline of a man and raised his AKM quickly.

The leader's hand dropped.

His snipers took out three of the *Spetsnaz* security men and the general's driver. Each was dead before hitting the ground.

Ulanov dived out of the light spilling through the open door and fired at the flashes coming from one side and slightly up the slope. He rolled over to a tree stump just beside the hut and took cover behind it, breathing coming fast, heart pumping hard.

Mescheryakov jumped back into the car and into the driver's seat, slamming the door to kill the overhead light. One of his security men, AKM in hand, jerked open the other door and landed inside.

The attackers heard the engine start, and despite the five remaining *Spetsnaz*'s firing, began running toward the vehicle as it reversed down the track, its side shredding metal against the side of the security car which had been just behind it.

Inside the hut, Pretorius watched the gray-haired Russian who throughout the uproar outside kept a pistol trained on his chest, calm and unwavering.

The remaining three *Spetsnaz* were returning fire with great accuracy. Two of the black-clad Japanese took disabling rounds and fell. Another raised his CAR-15 and placed a quick burst into one of the *Spetsnaz,* severing the man's vocal cords as well as disintegrating two cervical vertebrae. The young Russian dropped his weapon, sinking to his knees, hands vainly trying to hold his throat together before dying.

As Mescheryakov reversed down the hill, his security man smashed through the passenger side window with his AKM's butt and began firing at the spectral figures running toward them in the moonlight. One tumbled over and didn't rise. The others kept coming, but the bumpiness of the track, made worse by Mescheryakov's frantic speed, made deliberate aim impossible.

The leader shouted to one of his men in Japanese. Wordlessly, a tall figure turned and raced straight down the slope, weapon held high across his chest. The leader stopped and fired a burst into the windshield of the retreating vehicle, shattering the glass.

Inside the car, glass shards sprayed over the two Russians, but the rounds failed to take either man. Mescheryakov hit the brake pedal and tried to turn the vehicle around.

The leader took aim again, but went wide of the mark. The adrenaline was pumping hard, electrifying his body. His hands had the shakes now; holding the CAR-15 steady was getting not only hard, but impossible.

The remaining *Spetsnaz* were running down the hill. The Japanese turned, dropping to the ground and firing carefully as they could. The rounds spat through the night air and took down three more of the Russians. One kept coming, firing from the waist. The leader took a round in the shoulder and felt the impact like a shock of electricity.

The Japanese centered his barrel on the lone *Spetsnaz,* and squeezed, the effort sending pain knifing through his shoulder. Five rounds erupted, and the Russian toppled. The leader dropped his weapon and rolled over in pain.

Mescheryakov now had the vehicle under control. The Mercedes wallowed back onto the track and began speeding downhill over the track at nearly sixty miles an hour, bouncing high over the ruts.

The security man abandoned any thought of shooting. He braced both hands against the roof and closed his eyes against the slivers of glass that rushed past from the shattered windshield.

Beside him the general drove like a madman, forcing everything from his mind, everything except keeping the elusive track in his headlights as the big car struck every rut created by the Austrian winter as it had thawed and refrozen and thawed again.

A figure materialized in the headlights, nearly unseen as the car bounced two or more feet in the air. A black-clothed figure, leveling a rifle directly at them, sparks spitting from the muzzle, rounds sizzling past Mescheryakov.

The security man was hit: he sagged to one side, head lolling lifelessly. They drove directly into the wraithlike apparition, feeling the impact hard, Mescheryakov alone seeing the Japanese's face as the body slammed head-first back through the jagged open windshield and into the seat beside him.

Mescheryakov fought for control as the Mercedes veered off the track, its suspension built more for *Autobahnen* than for these circumstances. A frozen moment as the car upended on both its left wheels, hanging in space, then, finally, rolling over and over down the hill, before coming to rest against a lone pine.

Pretorius felt the Russian going through the wires on his wrists with the cutters, and then felt the circular imprint of the pistol's muzzle pressed hard against his skull.

"I'm cutting through the wire on your ankles, bastard, because you're coming with me. But one move—*only one move out of the ordinary*—and you're dead."

The voice was impersonal, neutral, almost offhand. This was no panicked amateur. This was a professional determined to get on with the job at any cost. Including the cost of his life.

Rubbing his bleeding wrists, Pretorius struggled to his feet—and almost fell over when he couldn't sense anything below his ankles. He leaned against the post for a moment as the Russian backed away from him, the pistol leveled at Pretorius' belly. He could feel the circulation beginning to return to his feet. But they hurt. They hurt like holy hell.

Outside the sounds had died down. Pretorius wondered what had happened.

The Russian nodded toward the open door and said evenly: "Out there. But move slowly. And stay in the light until I tell you otherwise."

As Pretorius moved outside, his eyes adjusted to the dark and he began to make out the forms of bodies lying on the slope. Some in civilian clothing, others in the black battle dress used in certain special ops.

He felt the muzzle again, hard against the base of his skull, pushing him to walk ahead, away from the hut. *Mistake,* he noted mentally.

Suddenly he twisted to one side, and his elbow struck the Russian sharply in the abdomen. The man first began to sag, then recovered with a sharp second-knuckles-forward jab at Pretorius' throat, connecting with unbelievable power.

Pretorius gagged, but spun and delivered a snap side kick, a *yoko-geri keage,* to the Russian's groin. The man was rocked back, then came once again at Pretorius, hands curled in the "tiger claw" position.

Pretorius danced back out of reach. He knew certain Russians groomed for special operations had been schooled in a few of the more arcane Chinese martial arts, in the days before the Sino-Soviet split. He'd never come up against anybody trained in *fu-jow pai,* though, and was uncertain about the defenses.

He probed the other with a sudden *tobi-geri,* a jump kick aimed for the Russian's neck. But the man was startlingly fast, whirling around to land the side of his shoe against Pretorius' kidney area.

Pretorius was immobilized by the pain. The Russian came at him full force, hands curled once more in the tiger claw style. Dazed, Pretorius felt the man's left hand strike his chin, the right strike his groin. He doubled over in pain, collapsing to the ground.

As the Russian lifted one foot to crush the exposed larynx, Pretorius rolled over, snapping his leg out, sweeping his attacker off balance. The man fell onto Pretorius, who grabbed him behind one elbow, seized his wrist with the other, and snapped the arm.

A scream of pain tore from the Russian's mouth and Pretorius followed up by taking the other wrist, twisting it so his opponent was leveraged helpless against the ground.

As he stood there, the stillness of the night was gradually transformed into a shattering roar. The light of a moving blue-white sun illuminated the area around the hut, throwing everything into stark contrast.

Pretorius squinted through the blinding light to see a helicopter, its tail arcing around, scorpionlike, as it settled slowly onto the canted ground. *"Freeze!"* a voice shouted over a loudspeaker. *"Don't go for a weapon. Stay right there, heads behind your head."*

Lying on the bed was Army General Mescheryakov, head swathed in bandages, left arm extended in an inflated rubber splint. The eyes glared in hatred at others in the room. Over the supine Russian, a tall and almost skeletal figure watched, feeling the pulse, counting against the wristwatch.

"He's in bad shape," the physician observed to Hornbill and Pretorius. "But if you're asking me will he survive, I'd put the odds at five to one in favor. If you're asking me will he survive with the sodium amytol, I'd say you reduce it somewhat, but not a lot. Not significantly. Still, it's the man's life. Your choice, gentlemen."

There was no hesitation. "Let's get started. Hook him up," Hornbill ordered crisply.

The gaunt physician nodded and began arranging the IV drip. He wrapped a rubber tube around the thick hairless arm and began pounding the inside of the elbow with his fist, getting the veins to swell. He looked closely. Then with one deft, effortless motion, he slipped the needle in.

He released the clamp on the tube. The bottle suspended from the wooden overhead beam showed a rising trail of miniature bubbles. The solution began invading the GRU general's system, spreading into every vessel, breaking down the will to resist at every turning.

Hornbill inched the wooden chair closer to the bed and waited for the physician's nod. He pressed the *record* button on the miniature recorder. The eyes of the general had already lost much of their fire.

Then Hornbill began his questioning.

—————————————————————— 54

The Night of the Long Knives.

It began at 10:43 P.M., Vienna Standard Time.

All power was disrupted within the Soviet Embassy at Reisnerstrasse 45-47. When the backup system kicked in, the lights flared with an unnatural brightness for a moment, then the backup failed too. This was all the more remarkable, as batteries and circuits had been checked earlier that day by security technicians.

The duty officer had received a phone call from General Mescheryakov, who verbally authorized the technicians' inspection visit, but said certain state security matters might detain him personally until tomorrow.

The *residentura* was now entirely isolated from the outside world. Most important, it was isolated from the main GRU communications facility near Moscow, at Vatutinki. By a great stroke of luck, the technicians ordered by General Mescheryakov had not yet left Vienna, so they were quickly summoned to deal with the emergency.

The senior GRU duty officer, Major Pavel Panyushkin, opened the bunker for the technicians to make the necessary repairs.

"Totally fucked up," observed the chief technician, a tall, almost cadaverous looking individual. "But no matter. We'll have everything working in an hour, perhaps less."

Major Panyushkin looked pleased. General Mescheryakov had not yet returned, and might try to contact the *residentura* through the communications bunker. The general would not be pleased if it were inoperable for long. He would seek the first available scapegoat, and it would be Pavel Panyushkin.

As the bunker door closed behind the technicians, the *Spetsnaz* officers and men on duty looked curiously at the array of equipment the experts had lugged in with them. It all seemed rather elaborate to fix a set of batteries, one commented.

"We have a series of fried circuits here, comrades," retorted one of the young technicians. "We have replacement boards, all our testing equipment, and certain security devices of a classified nature." He leaned closer to the GRU officer and confided in a near whisper. "We cannot, after all, overlook the possibility this may have been sabotage."

Panyushkin nodded wisely. The enemies of *Otechestvo* were everywhere, and enemies of the GRU were especially numerous. Sabotage would not, he agreed, be entirely out of the question.

The technicians bent to their task, bringing out meters to check for breaks in the circuits, hygrometers to analyze the electrolyte remaining in the big lead batteries, and other odd-looking pieces of equipment.

The chief technician asked Major Panyushkin if the bunker was secured before they proceeded to their next stage, which was to check for the possibility of sabotage.

Panyushkin responded that all GRU personnel were within the *residentura* on its two floors, with the exception of General Mescheryakov and several of his staff. And, of course, the one armed GRU guard standing just outside the safelike door leading to the embassy itself.

"Excellent," approved the chief technician. "We don't want certain eyes to observe our procedures. GRU, yes. But any of the others—" He let his tone drift upward.

All seemed to be going well. The engineers ran their tests, nodding happily at the swings of the needles on their meters, talking with each other about certain digital readouts. The officers and men in the *residentura* relaxed, joking with each other. Other than the technicians' battery lanterns, flashlights provided the only illumination. The mood was almost festive. They were all sharing a small emergency together, an emergency shortly to be fixed by the fine engineers who happened to be in the right place at the right time.

Then one of the *Spetsnaz* non-coms noticed the repairmen putting on what appeared to be either respirators or some sort of gas masks.

He was reassured that these were only a precaution for the electricians working close to the batteries, for the acid often gave out noxious fumes. Beyond six feet from the batteries, you didn't have to worry.

The *Spetsnaz* man nodded in understanding, Nevertheless he edged back a bit as one of the technicians opened the lid of a battery case. *One couldn't be too careful,* he thought. *I'd hate to spend months in hospital with blistered lungs.*

His fears of a hospital stay would not be realized. Something beyond his worst imaginings would.

The personnel nearest the technicians were surprised to hear a hissing issuing from the small white fire extinguishers the experts had brought with them.

A GRU lieutenant, a former fireman in his home city of Kiev, peered closely at the valve of one of the extinguishers. He was on the verge of asking why the valve was open, but then his central nervous system ceased to function.

The hissing continued. The only other sound in the bunker was now the falling of bodies.

In a few moments the extinguishers were turned off, and there was a five-minute wait as the technicians checked for the fluttering of pulses. There were none.

Then a switch was thrown and the lights went on. The ventilation fans started up. In approximately fifteen minutes, after checking an atmospheric spectrometer, the chief technician gave a signal. His men removed their masks.

The chief opened the door leading to the embassy, and told the GRU guard standing outside that Major Panyushkin wished to see him at once. A problem with one of the men, he said.

On the cement stairs leading to the lower level, the guard was shot cleanly through the back of the head. His executioner was the chief technician, Lev Alekseiyivich Bakunin, Major, KGB. The guard toppled like a puppet suddenly snipped from its strings, his weapon falling with a clatter to the bottom of the stairwell.

Vienna Center existed no more.

With synchronized precision, KGB troops swept through the Soviet Union like an avenging scythe. GRU personnel were slaughtered in the hundreds of thousands. Losses were especially heavy on both sides where bases were manned by *Spetsnaz* forces.

Outside Moscow, the entire village of Vatutinki was razed. Attack bombers, followed by KGB troops and crack tank corps, left a field of blackened smoking rubble. No prisoners were taken. Survivors were shot on sight in accordance with the orders of the KGB chairman.

By dawn, the GRU had been reduced to a tenth of its former self. *Spetsnaz* units were incorporated into the KGB, with the exception of those units known to have given specific support to the *Otechestvo* uprising.

The entire GRU was reorganized into a new and considerably more docile department of military intelligence within the KGB. As the Soviet president said in making the historic announcement, "Few things are more important to the security of the state than the objective and professional collection and analysis of military intelligence. What better place in which to practice that vital function than in the Committee for State Security itself?"

Colonel-general Petrosyants, known also as The Owl, was apprehended at the Finnish border just as he was about to cross. Petrosyants, known to have been a strong supporter of the madman Feliks as well as Chief of Staff for Mescheryakov himself, had been disguised as a common laborer.

Alert KGB border guards arrested Petrosyants when one noticed the so-called laborer's hands bore no calluses, no signs of manual work. A comparison of the man's papers with a KGB State Criminal Alert printout soon ended the charade.

Regrettably, Petrosyants was shot attempting to escape.

55

Through the Looking Glass.

As was often the case at the end of a successful operation, Hornbill was cheerful to a fault. And when Hornbill was cheerful, he talked irrepressibly.

"Can you imagine a world in which everything is precisely as it seems?" said Hornbill, savoring his second brandy and soda. "I for one would find it unendurable. But there are people, good decent God-fearing people, who would vastly prefer it. My brother, Clifford, is such an individual."

Pretorius, on the receiving end of this monologue in Hornbill's room in the Schwarzenberg, had never known of the brother's existence.

Noting the surprised look, Hornbill hastily added, "Oh, yes. Strange as it may seem, even *I* am capable of having a sibling. Clifford is a certified public accountant, and a terribly conscientious one. Clifford would never work out in our trade, Michael. He insists that all should be *precisely* as it seems. Clifford and I," he confided, "don't speak."

At this, Hornbill placed his glass on the bureau, and sat down as if not quite trusting the engineering of the hotel chair. He picked up his long churchwarden pipe and began to light it.

"Speaking of things being seldom what they seem," Hornbill began, "I'm afraid I should clear up one or two bits."

Pretorius looked quizzical, but Hornbill took his time as he completed the elaborate pipe-lighting process. "Now then, Michael," he finally said, pausing to direct a series of puffs at the ceiling, "I must tell you Miranda Mathieson has been very much a part of our machinations. Her plea to you was actually suggested by Dick Coldwell and myself, in fond hopes you would bite. And bite you did. We have it on tape, actually."

Pretorius was thunderstruck. "That telephone tap? That was *yours? You bugged her apartment?*"

Hornbill favored him with a mock-innocent but distinctly

Cheshire-cat-like grin. "Got you right in the spirit of things, didn't it? And wasn't Miranda magnificent? She directed you right to the bug. We knew you'd find it and assume the lady was under siege by the bad guys." Pretorius by now was speechless.

"Oh, yes," said Hornbill, warming to his task, "acting was what Miranda did before she was married. In fact, she'd had quite a budding theatrical career. Even appeared once in a Moss Hart and George S. Kaufman show on Broadway. So you see," he said, taking time to draw a few deep puffs, "Mrs. Mathieson was simply doing what she knew best. And for a very good cause."

Pretorius looked dazed. "So she was playing me along," he said, shaking his head. "As were you."

"Um. Exactly." Hornbill beamed approvingly. "We needed her to get you stoked up just a bit, to remind you of a few debts you owed not only to her, but to her son as well."

By now Pretorius was pouring his own second drink, a small glass of chilled aquavit, thinking back to Lewis Carroll's *Alice in Wonderland,* concluding that nothing in *Alice* was as bizarre as the convolutions of the intelligence trade.

"Well," he said after a moment, "you turned out to be accurate as hell about my reactions. But why didn't you just send one of your regular people over? Just *order* somebody into it." Pretorius finished the aquavit at a single toss. "In short, why me?"

Hornbill looked pained, as if the answer were all too obvious. "Because, my dear boy, we couldn't use anybody official for fear of the GRU dodging back into the woodwork." He got up from his chair, and began pacing again, caught up in the rhythm of his own thinking.

"It was essential to appear as if CIA—and the rest of the U.S. intelligence community—had bought the idea that Mathieson had been both an addict and a suicide. But we wanted somebody experienced and motivated enough to complete what Mathieson had begun, before they terminated him.

"GRU Vienna figured we'd been on to *something,* but they didn't know what. They just knew that any knowledge was potentially dangerous. At the time, we actually knew damn little, but your appearance on the scene made them curious as hell. They had no idea who you worked for, who you were—only that you were American, and that you had some sort of link with Mathieson. Which, of course, was precisely what we wanted.

"We needed to see what—and who—you'd draw out. And draw them out you did. Yes." Hornbill puffed on the long pipe, watching the coils of smoke slowly unwind and drift up into the darkness.

At length he became aware Pretorius was silent. He looked over to discover him staring out the window at the Palais gardens.

Pretorius, after a pause of a few more moments, realized there was a silence in the room, and spoke. "So you're pleased with the outcome?" he asked.

"Mmm." Hornbill made a contented sound. Pretorius continued looking out the window.

After a while Hornbill realized Pretorius was lost in his thoughts. "You'll want to be getting back to Devon soon as possible," Hornbill prodded, hoping to interrupt his brooding.

"What?" Pretorius half turned away from the window.

"I said, you'll be wanting to get back to Devon, I suppose."

"Yes. Yes, I guess I will," returned Pretorius in a toneless voice. Hornbill recognized what Pretorius was now going through, that he was reliving the operation, step by step. He'd seen it time and again, in all kinds of people, after all kinds of assignments. It was a kind of decompression, an adjustment. It was tough any time, but worse, far worse, when deaths were involved.

Finally in the silence, Pretorius turned from the window to stare at Hornbill with a sad, almost haunted expression.

Hornbill spread his hands in a gesture of acknowledging the inevitable. "It's always this way, Michael. It never gets any different, nor any better. People get killed, usually for nothing. People get compromised, also usually for nothing. The only thing that matters is the operation, the objective, what the damn thing was supposed to *do.*"

Pretorius looked at him in a very level way, much as a rifleman might take a sight on an object at a great distance. "And all the people along the way," he said, "all the ones that die, that get killed. Are they just some kind of Agency business expense? Just something to enter in the books?"

Hornbill shook his head sadly. "There's no intelligent answer to that. You know it. You've been in the business a long time now."

Pretorius nodded distractedly, and returned his attention to the gardens of the Palais Schwarzenberg. His eyes looked through the glass to a world in which lovers would walk, and children would laugh, and a life of a different sort might, just possibly, continue a few centuries more.

"Yes," he said. "Of course."

_____ 56

Conversation Between Friends.

Kiharu Ishida's hair was sleek and black, swept up in the centuries-old tradition of the *geisha*. She set the lacquer tray down and carefully positioned the tiny *sake* bottle and the two cups. As she bowed low, her kimono revealed the powdered pale gracefulness of her neck. She was delightful. The two men smiled at each other.

The *shoji* slid shut and the two were quiet for a moment. The *ryotei* (geisha house) was a valued place of refuge, a retreat from the clamor of Tokyo. Indeed, in stressful times such as these, it was considered more necessary than ever. More and more high-powered executives were dying of a new disease: *pokkuri byo,* or overwork.

To the geishas and staff of the *ryotei,* one of the men was Yukio Higashi, financial controller for a large and respected electronics manufacturer. The other was Hiroyuki Fujita, a lobbyist in Washington.

Neither was any of those things. The first was Kenji Nomura, head of the *Renraku Bu,* codenamed Dragonfly. The second, Isamo Jinruki, *Nibetsu's* chief of covert operations.

The men had been friends for nearly forty years. They met

regularly at the *ryotei,* where they shared many of the anecdotes peculiar to their profession, and traded such information as would give advantage or solace to the other.

But on this evening the atmosphere was different. The room was in the tranquil, traditional style. A low table between the two men, a *tokonoma* framing a Chinese scroll on one wall, clean *tatami* beneath them. Still the room felt electric with tension.

As Nomura poured *sake* for them both, Jinruki spoke. "The Second Section has a few problems."

"Oh, yes?" Jinruki placed the cups of *sake* carefully.

"Their material is not being considered in a favorable light, especially compared to yours."

"Too bad. Miho is a good man. I think he does a fine job."

"He's still a bureaucrat," Jinruki said. "With a bureaucrat's petty jealousies."

Nomura inclined his head, as if to indicate, *A great shame, but what is one to do?*

"This is why I wished to speak with you today," continued the other. "Miho has decided to create an unpleasant situation. A situation which, in fact, could be disastrous."

"What are you talking about? Why are you being so—?" Nomura looked up, meeting the other's eyes with curiosity.

The answer was abrupt. "He's decided to initiate a discreet, very high-level investigation. An investigation into your sources."

This was bad. Very bad indeed, thought Nomura. *The one thing you never did in this business.* "What do you think he has in mind?" he inquired, keeping his tone neutral.

"I think he wants to find out if you've got a two-way street," returned the other candidly.

"And why would he think that?"

Jinruki held up the thin porcelain cup of *sake,* examining it minutely. "You don't have to ask that question. You know why."

"The quality? The timeliness?" Nomura asked with a wry smile.

"Quite so. He thinks it's too good to be true. Unless you're giving something in exchange, something which would make it worth the Americans' while."

Nomura sipped in silence for a moment, lost in thought. "And what do *you* think?"

A discreet tap at the *shoji,* and Kiharu came in once more. Holding one sleeve of her kimono out of the way, she removed the empty cups and the porcelain flask, replacing them with another flask, another pair of cups. Bowing, smiling, she left, silently drawing the two screens together.

Jinruki looked at the table, then leaned forward, supporting himself on spread hands. He looked into the other's eyes. "I *know* how good your work is. It is beyond reproach. In fact, irreplaceable. And I know you. You would never betray *Dai Nippon.* But—" He began examining the surface of the table, as if there he would somehow find the right words.

"But what?" Nomura prodded gently.

The other looked up. There was pain within the brown eyes. "But you, like all of us, are capable of compromise. The degree is the only thing open to question. Would you give away anything genuinely detrimental to us? No. Would it look that way to the Prime Minister, to *any* politician? No."

"So what are you saying, old friend?" Nomura leaned forward.

Jinruki drew a deep breath. Then: "I'm saying cut off the tail of the dragon. The people who will look into the matter are good. And they have excellent contacts among the Americans; not as good as yours, but good. If you do have a two-way street, they will not stop until they find it. Unless you terminate it first. Unless you make it impossible for them to speak to your source."

Then, in a soft, almost inaudible voice: *"If they do, they will ruin you. It is inevitable."*

Nomura considered this. "How imminent do you think this—investigation is?"

"From what I've heard, they've already started. Do you know anything about Project Socrates?"

He nodded, keeping surprise from reaching his eyes. *Project Socrates was a DIA program which gathered intelligence on foreign technologies, and compared them to the U.S.'s own technological efforts, as an aid to planning. It had begun in 1988, after he'd started feeding Hornbill and Beeson the material on Japan's Fifth Generation project. He suspected much of the Americans' information on Fifth Generation was based on*

*his own efforts. And probably 30% to 35% of the Americans'
information on Japanese superconductors, exotic structural
materials, high-performance computers, and many other classified subjects could—by applying the right pressure politically—be directly traceable to him.*

"Well," continued Jinruki, "we have someone positioned
with Socrates. There seems to be too much of a correlation
between what Socrates is developing as a database, and what
we are being told in the intelligence community. There's talk
of ending our briefings on such topics."

"That means there's pressure from more than just Miho.
That smells like Cabinet pressure."

"Exactly," agreed Jinruki. "Which is why Miho sees it as
an opportunity to take over your responsibilities—if he can
trace it back to you."

Nomura thought this over in silence.

"There's only one solution," he concluded.

The other nodded. "You must make it impossible for
them to talk with your sources. *Whatever it takes, you must
make it impossible.*"

Nomura poured two more *sakes.* This time, the two men
drained them at a single draft.

Their eyes met. A sadness passed between them, and this
reaffirmed their friendship as much, and perhaps more, than
all the many joys they'd shared as well.

_____ **57**

Terminations.

Luther Beeson loved a mint julep as much as any man ever
loved a wife, gun, or good dog. Being a widower and, since
his retirement from the Agency, having little to do with guns,
the general concentrated on breeding good dogs and making
perfect mint juleps.

For the latter, he'd take a mason jar and place a layer of
mint leaves on the bottom, then a layer of crushed ice, then

a very *thin* layer of powdered sugar, then another layer of mint, another of ice, another of sugar, and so on until he reached the top.

Next he'd fill it with Virginia bourbon to the top, snap on the lid, wrap a towel around the jar, and shake it until it grew so cold the towel started to stick to the glass.

Finally, he'd open the jar, place a Band-Aid on the bridge of his nose to prevent the rough glass from cutting it, and have a good long drink straight from the jar.

At the moment the general was finishing his third mint julep of the evening, thinking what a fine world it was indeed, and how *outstanding* it was to have good friends in such a place.

Two of his buddies, Clayton and Henry, had just left in their pickup truck, veering unsteadily down the driveway (the general's mint juleps were noted for their aftershock). He was left alone on the big porch. It was after eleven, and the crickets and tree frogs were ratcheting out their chorus.

He closed his eyes, thinking of the phone call he'd gotten from Arthur Hornbill, and how their strategy had pulled the Agency's fat out of the fire once again. Their strategy, and a little financing from the Japanese connection.

The paramilitary force that had taken the GRU people up at the mountain hut had been the best: a specially trained elite force of Japanese, selected from the *Tokumu Bu*. A special request to Dragonfly had brought them to Austria within twenty-four hours.

And it had worked. Worked like clockwork. *Damn! There's nothing like outstanding people doing the impossible,* he observed, rising and having a good stretch.

He went through the screen door, and closed and locked the big front door, setting the alarm system. Everything else was secure. He went up the big staircase, turning out the lights of the big chandelier on the upper landing as he passed.

In about five minutes, after brushing his teeth and changing into a sharply pressed pair of pajamas, General Luther Beeson eased between the sheets of his big four-poster bed, and clicked off the bedside light.

He could still hear the crickets outside. He closed his eyes and smiled.

The blade was long, and finely honed as a razor, and was through his throat from ear to ear before he knew enough to stop smiling.

Hornbill received the telephone call in his room at the Schwarzenberg, just as he was packing to leave for the airport. Replacing the receiver, he sat down on the edge of his bed and thought hard.

It could be anybody, he told himself. *Beeson made a lot of enemies in his years with the Agency. It could be some antagonist from years long past, somebody who felt he had a score to settle. It happens. Lord knows it happens.*

But the more he thought, the more he felt it had something to do with the Vienna operation. The hair on the back of his neck told him so. The icy feeling he got down his back told him so. And Hornbill had learned long ago never to ignore signals like these.

He got up and began pacing the room, hands in pockets. *Whoever did it,* he knew, *would also be after him, and would strike fast and professionally.*

Where, if he were planning this, would he terminate someone like himself? He got on the phone again and got hold of Pretorius, who was booked on a later plane the same day and had just come back from the Kärntnerstrasse, shopping for a gift for Susannah.

"Michael? Arthur. Look," he said without preamble, "Luther Beeson's been killed. There's a possibility, a very *slight* possibility, it may have something to do with the operation here. If that's so, I'm next on the list. So, quite frankly, I want your help. Can you do a little light bodyguarding until I'm on the aircraft?"

A pause as he listened. Then: "I'm very grateful. Come over here right away. And have you disposed of your weapon yet? Good, then by all means bring it. We may be dealing with serious people. What?" He looked at his watch. "In about—ten minutes, downstairs."

In the tiny village of Takara, in Mie Prefecture, the tradition of *Ninjitsu* is not taken lightly. At least four centuries of ninja have been born, raised, and trained here.

Ninjitsu more or less died out in the nineteenth century.

And despite the best efforts of Hollywood and Tokyo film-makers to convince us to the contrary, no more than a dozen men still practice *Ninjitsu* to any serious extent. Two of these presently live in Takara, and it is no accident, for the legends are very much alive there.

Some years ago in Takara there lived a youngster named Sato Hiraoka. At the age of six, Sato was begging his grand-father to tell him more of the great *ninja*, men like Hanzo Hattori and Sandayu Momochi. As the boy grew older he seized every opportunity to learn more of the martial arts, and the special weaponry and techniques of *Ninjitsu*.

Sato was bright, an eager student. He excelled in school in every subject. But he was obsessed with the idea of becoming a *ninja*, and one of the two practitioners living in Kura saw possibilities within the youngster. And so Sato entered into his apprenticeship.

Within twelve years, Sato became expert in virtually every aspect of *Ninjitsu*, from the throwing of the tiny *shiraken* to the *kyoketsu-shogi*, a device with a double blade at one end and a metal circle at the other. He practiced hard not only to build up his skills, but to strengthen his endurance.

At the age of eighteen, the master realized he had taught the lean teenager all that he knew, and so released him from apprenticeship.

He was immediately recruited by *Nibetsu*, and placed in the nucleus of what would someday be the covert action force called *Tokumu Bu*. There he found appreciation for his talents. He was also given additional training in firearms, explosives, and other elements of tradecraft.

Within three years, Sato Hiraoka achieved somewhat leg-endary status within his particular circle. Several assassina-tions of Asian political leaders were suspected to have been his work. He was adept in the use of many weapons, but especially skilled with *yoroidoshi*, the Japanese twelve-inch dagger.

The weapon's silence, surprise at close quarters, and con-cealability made it his favorite. Its only disadvantage was that, in having to work in close proximity to the target, escape was more difficult than with longer-range weapons such as rifles, pistols, or explosives.

Still, the very difficulty of the problem attracted Sato,

driving him to formulate highly inventive strategies, which in turn helped build his reputation.

The current problem presented several difficulties. Terminating the first American at the luxurious farm in Virginia had been child's play.

Here he had very little time: the target—a second American of about the same age as the first—was about to leave for New York within two hours of Sato's arrival.

There was little possibility of *sacchi-jitsu* in Vienna, for taking advantage of the features of the area for a perfect kill. Hiraoka had never been in Austria before, let alone Vienna.

The killing ground was an inescapable choice: It had to be the Vienna-Schwechat air terminal. The only place he could study quickly enough to be able to work out a strategy for both the termination and his own escape.

He placed a call to a supposed clerk in the Japanese consulate. Minutes later, the clerk called back with the information that Arthur D. Hornbill was booked on Pan Am flight 28, the direct flight to New York at twelve noon. He glanced up at the big Seiko display: it was now 10:17.

After retrieving his one bag from the carousel, he entered the men's room and changed clothes, removing the *yoroido-shi* and concealing it in the special acrylic scabbard inside his folded raincoat. He spent fifteen minutes in one of the toilet booths applying makeup and a gray wig.

He emptied the canvas bag, and stuffed the extra articles of clothing in the waste bin, each with the labels carefully cut out.

He left the satchel turned inside out and obviously empty. An abandoned bag, possibly with something in it, would immediately attract the attention of the police.

After leaving the men's room, he showed a duplicate passport with the gray wig and makeup, and booked himself on the same flight as Hornbill. He paid with a credit card. To the ticket agent, he was yet another middle-aged Japanese businessman, one among many.

Next he walked the terminal, learning the layout, the exits, the utility rooms, the hallways.

He went to the mezzanine and looked down over the terminal floor. The obvious danger here was the uniformed soldiers carrying Steyr-AUG automatic rifles patrolling the terminal, fingers near triggers, alert for terrorists.

He plotted where Hornbill would likely come in, the direction he'd take to go to the check-in counter, the way he might walk to pick up a book or magazines, and finally where the gate for Flight 28 was.

He then walked the same routes, checking for positions of advantage. He hoped there would be more people in the terminal as it got closer to boarding time. The more people, the better.

Soon he had his plan. He would choose his cross-over point according to where the most people were milling at the time, make his move, then disappear through the crowd into the bookstore. He would emerge through the other door, gray wig gone, makeup off, raincoat on, and walk slowly toward the gate, displaying his passport—the original one with the much-younger photograph—as he entered the security area.

He took up his position on a lounge chair near the path Hornbill might take crossing the terminal to go to the Pan Am ticket counter. He sat slightly slumped the way a tired businessman might, raincoat over one arm, the *yoroidoshi* within easy reach.

Less than one hour until departure.

The drive to the airport, under other circumstances, would have been relaxing. It was a Sunday, and traffic was light. The rented car was a sleek new BMW, with the kind of acceleration that got you out of whatever trouble it had gotten you into seconds before.

Pretorius, driving, kept flicking his eyes to the rearview mirrors, to the cars ahead, to the on-ramps. Everything from which trouble might emerge. Hornbill of course was resting, eyes closed.

Finally the terminal came in sight and the BMW swept up to the front doors. Leaving the car at the curb until he could see Hornbill safely inside to the plane, Pretorius unbuttoned his jacket, checked the position of the automatic in the holster high on his hip, and took Hornbill's bag.

"Well," remarked Hornbill, "let's see just how safe air travel really is." And the two men walked into the terminal.

• • •

The doors opened to the electric eye. Sato Hiraoka saw the target immediately. *But there was another with him. Younger, with careful eyes. Likely a bodyguard supplied by Hornbill's agency.*

Hiraoka rose slowly to his feet and began walking in a direction which would converge with theirs.

Pretorius scanned the terminal floor. He was reassured by the competent-looking men with the automatic Steyrs. *Not exactly the perfect place for a killing,* he thought. *More than likely, it'll be in New York. More likely the assassin—if there is an assassin—will have his own people set up there. He could be in and out of Kennedy like a shot.*

At that moment a middle-aged Japanese businessman almost collided with Hornbill near a group of giggling French schoolgirls.

Pretorius saw the man, probably a drunk, out of the corner of his eye. He snatched Hornbill out of the man's way. There was a blurred movement, a moment of confusion.

And then he saw the blade, shining and lethal and seeming to move in slow motion although Pretorius knew it was moving faster than anything he could imagine, slicing through the air, reaching toward Hornbill's abdomen, not stopping—and my God he's—

Pretorius swung the bag up and knocked the still-arcing blade from the assassin's hand. Hornbill sagged to the ground, red already seeping between the fingers clasping his white-shirted stomach. A questioning look on his face, as if the important thing were *Why?* rather than the prospect of death.

Hiraoka spun on his heel and delivered a staggering crescent kick, the *mikazuki-geri,* to Pretorius' chest.

Falling backward, Pretorius rolled, coming up just as the assassin was upon him and about to smash his throat with the side of his foot. Grasping the toe and ankle of the downward-thrust foot, Pretorius twisted as he rose from the floor, sweeping his own leg around, trying to dislocate the assassin's knee.

The soldiers were running toward them now, snicking off the safeties of the automatic rifles. The French schoolgirls were screaming, their teacher bending over Hornbill trying, impossibly, to staunch the brimming flow of blood.

As Pretorius swept his leg around, Hiraoka did a spiral fall to the floor instead, loosening the grip on his foot, at the same time using a crushing *ne waza yoko geri:* a side kick coming up from the floor.

It connected with Pretorius' jaw and he felt the teeth break. Staggering back, he tried to clear the mist from his head. But the assassin was advancing nearer and nearer, stiffened hands circling, circling, unmindful of anything but the killing of his quarry.

The young Austrian soldiers stood frozen, not willing to shoot in this crowd, thinking this was only some kind of personal fistfight. But Pretorius knew differently—in the next few moments, with the next contact, one would die.

Pretorius edged back. The assassin advanced, closing the distance. His eyes were liquid pools of death, removed a thousand times from any semblance of humanity. The motions of the man's calloused hands were rhythmic, confident. The assassin advanced a few inches more, as Pretorius struggled to clear his head from the force of the kick.

Then something snapped.

In one fluid movement, with the speed of a snake striking its prey, Pretorius stroked out his automatic pistol and hammered three rounds directly into the assassin's chest, throwing the man back as if a rope had yanked him from behind. Hiraoka was dead before he hit the floor.

One of the young soldiers, automatic rifle wavering on Pretorius' midsection, screamed in near hysteria, *"Gefrieren Sie! Nun!"*

Pretorius froze in position, letting the pistol clatter to the marble of the terminal floor.

Six feet from him, the clear blue eyes of Arthur Hornbill stared upward at the crisscross trusswork of the terminal ceiling.

But the eyes saw nothing.

Hornbill's brother was notified and called to say he would be flying to Vienna to accompany the body home on Wednesday. Home, Clifford Hornbill said, was Galesburg, Ohio.

Pretorius spent six hours in the United States Embassy

with his own people and the *Sicherheitsburo,* answering a barrage of questions and completing the paperwork which would allow him to leave the country while the Japanese knife-wielder's death was still under investigation.

The Austrian security people finally left. After the CIA and the embassy's legal people had talked with him, watching with the eyes people have when they know you've killed, whatever the reason, whatever the morality, Pretorius walked out the embassy's front entrance and into a late spring drizzle.

He looked up at the night sky. The city lights reflected a redness on the brooding clouds. Somewhere nearby—from the open window of someone's apartment, perhaps—he heard a radio playing. He listened for a moment to the music, a waltz. *Strauss,* he realized. *Vienna, City of My Dreams.*

He turned up the collar of his jacket. A taxi slowed to a halt, and Pretorius got in.

_____ 58

Devon.

Together the three walked up the hill, along the single-track road that ran near Chipton, Tippity Van, and Bosomzeal.

It was still spring, but the breeze blowing up from the River Dart cut chill and damp. The sailing had been good, and the food and the wine had produced an appropriate feeling of well-being. As the three walked along the road, cows drifted near the fences, great ungainly heads gazing balefully over rails.

David Lloyd George's stubby legs struggled to keep up with Pretorius and Susannah. In Pretorius' absence, The Dreaded DLG had developed consummate skill in cadging extra food, as the dog's barrel-like body bore witness. DLG's grin was wide. Whether it was to gather more oxygen on his way up the hill or to express satisfaction was not known.

Pretorius had never been as content as now, on this early evening in Devon, following the days of Vienna. Days in which he'd been drawn into the circle of the damned, to be finally released to breathe and to *be* once again.

But the wounds were there still, unseen yet sustained. Susannah looped one warming arm around his waist. He turned to her and smiled.

The cottage lay in the distance over the rim of the darkening hill. The coals would be glowing in the grate and on the hearth would be waiting a torn and tattered collection of shreds that once might have been recognized as a rug, but which was now, in any case, the proud and undisputed property of David Lloyd George.

Outside, the wind from the sea would make itself heard long into the night. But inside tonight they would sleep deeply, and dream well.

Pretorius had come home.

─────────────────── Author's Note.

The technologies and their capabilities in this book, including those of the spy satellite codenamed LACROSSE, all exist. The Defense Intelligence Agency program called *Project Socrates* is real. The ring of seventy-five Pentagon-sized bunkers around Moscow also exists. The militant Russian nationalist group, *Otechestvo* (Fatherland), is gaining in influence and has members in several Soviet governing bodies. The Japanese intelligence organizations cited exist as well, and are engaged in military, political, economic, and industrial intelligence gathering operations throughout the world. However, the Japanese organization called the Council and the Japanese grand strategy known as *Dai Sen Ryaku* may or may not exist.